I0748425

Stella Scura: Dark Star Rising

Volume Two

Book Three: Science Squad Unite

Book Four: First Family

A Novel by

J. Matthew Neal

Stella Scura: Dark Star Rising
Volume Two

Book Three: Science Squad Unite
Book Four: First Family

Astronomical photos courtesy NASA/Jet Propulsion Laboratory/Space Science Institute.

Printed in the United States of America
Dunn Avenue Press
Muncie, Indiana 47304

ISBN 978-1-7349372-1-3

Book Three:

Science Squad Unite

"We do not have to become heroes overnight. Just a step at a time, meeting each thing that comes up . . . discovering we have the strength to stare it down."

—Eleanor Roosevelt

Chapter Thirty

M2 Technology Annex
2705 West State Road 36
Sulphur Springs, Indiana

Well, it took them about a week and a lot of money to pay off various creditors, but damned if Bella and Nick didn't have most of *Dr. Wendy's Science Squad* assembled in the old Malvin catsup factory; after thirty million dollars of prior renovations last year, it was now the Mendoza Multinational private technology center. It wasn't used for much right now, but it contained a small, well-furnished living complex for his colleagues; the duration of their stay was dependent on their moods and level of interest in what cool stuff they saw. There was an adjoining par-3 golf course, which at least kept Kepler from complaining too much.

"What's with all the cloak and dagger, *Tinman?*" Johnny Kepler asked, shaking his head as he walked into the room. "You said it was an utmost emergency, not a reunion with all these stinking clowns. Man, I can't take this shit."

"Great to see you too, Johnny," Todd DeOhmman said. "I can see you haven't changed much, and that's not a compliment."

"Yeah, who are you callin' a clown, *Golfer?*" Wolfram Steele asked angrily, wheeling his chair in front of him and staring angrily. "You think you're better than anyone just because you're famous now? Not all of us can be rich like you and *Tinman.*"

Royce G. Bivereaux III laughed. "Rich? Kepler ain't got squat compared to Bella and *Tinman,* are you kidding? Loser."

"Sorry, man, I'm just tired of all this weird crap. And I'm sure not as rich as Stannous, as Biv said, the asshole. Finally, the Juriann dude came to see me, not you, so shut the hell up. Without me, none of this would be happening."

"Huh? Juriann? Who you talking about, Kepler?" Wolf asked.

"That's what you brought us here for, right, Nick?" Kepler asked. "Just you wait and see, Wolf. But I got a good thing going at Princeton, I don't need to get messed up in this. If it has to do with the chief, it ain't for me. I left her big sorry ass behind long ago."

"*Wendy?*" Todd said. "No one said anything about her! I'm so outta here if that's the case."

"Maybe you'll change your mind in a minute," Bella said as she brought her guest into the conference room."

"Yeah, *Amp,* when you get a load of this dude, you'll see he's worth the trip."

"Shut up, Johnny," Todd said. "You don't have to exaggerate."

"*You* all shut up," Nick said. "For once, he isn't embellishing. We have a guest, so look sharp, folks. You don't want to miss this."

They stared as Juriann entered the room, dwarfing the woman beside him: six-five, four hundred fifty pounds that left them all gasping.

"Lookit! I told you his big ass would show up here," Kepler yelled as he pointed. "He ain't human, he's maybe twenty but knows damn near as much astrophysics as me, and that's a lot."

"Good to see you too, Kepler," Juriann said sarcastically.

"You know him? Who the hell is this guy?" Biv asked, looking up at him. "Some football player? Man."

"Juriann Hultaar—you can also call me *Orthoman.*"

"What the hell does that mean?" Wolf asked.

"It means I am a—well, genetically correct man."

"Hell, that damn shit's beyond me," Kepler said. "The rest of us are about as genetically incorrect as you can get."

"Damn straight. But, why are we here? We were the shittiest heroes of all time," Biv yelled, as his facial tics suddenly worsened, mainly manifested as rapid blinking and making chewing noises. "I know some of us have achieved some fame, but what is the purpose of any of this, Bella? You gone nutso?"

"It will become clear in a minute, Biv. Juriann, you're a big fan of the show. Here they are," Bella said. "An impressive lot, yes?"

"I can't believe it," the large man said. "You're all here, just as in the original show, except for the two women, of course."

"Yeah," Kepler said. "The larger of the two we're better off without." The others nodded in agreement.

"But why have you all assembled for this fantastic reunion?"

"They're all here to find out some questions about you, my friend, and assembled by the greatest force in history—private enterprise. No way do we want the government messing with you. However, the President is already aware of your existence."

"The President? That would be an honor."

She shook her head. "Well, not necessarily, because you haven't met her, actually—"

"I see; perhaps I should reconsider that. I'd like to find out more about myself, too." Juriann shrugged. "I think, though, that I am probably just the tip of the iceberg, the humble opening act to the main event that will astound us all."

"What you mean by that, big man?" Kepler asked, squinting at him. "You're talkin' weird again."

"Like I told you at Princeton, Kepler: the omnipotent flying one will soon be upon us. If you believe me to be interesting, just you wait. I'm merely a prelude of what is to come."

Todd spoke up. "Huh? 'Flying one?' Is this guy crazy, *Golfer?"*

Juriann peered down at him. "*Ampere,* I'm not crazy. You may find mirth in my words, but they ring true."

Kepler looked at Todd. "What do you think, *Amp*? Don't make quick assumptions, as I don't know what to think now. There's weird crap goin' on I can't explain, so I'm gonna go out on a limb and agree that he's right. Like Mini-Mendoza says, it makes better sense than anything else we got cooking."

Todd laughed and kicked Kepler's non-human leg. "*Go out on a limb*? You're a hoot, Johnny."

"Hey, that hurts, dummy. Stop it."

"It doesn't hurt. You're making that up."

"Well, not pain, exactly, but striking it causes some unpleasant feedback, so don't ever mess with my leg, or it will mess with you. Its microprocessor is pretty damn smart; it has ten billion times the computing power of the Apollo 11 computers."

"Oh, right. Scares me."

"Shut up, Todd. There's some serious shit comin' our way, let me tell you. Dark matter ain't nothin' to laugh at, idiot, it'll kick your ass. My daughter Hanna saw it flying faster than sound."

"You don't know jack about it, Johnny," Roy G. Bivereaux said. "Quit acting like you know everything about everything."

"Despite his hubris, Kepler is correct," Juriann said. "While my ways may seem strange to you, realize that I speak the truth—of the prophecy told to my adoptive parents by the deaf Russian one almost twenty years ago."

"What the hell does that mean?" Todd said. "I don't know any deaf Russians, but I did know a deaf person who knew like twenty languages, including Russian." Todd paused for a half minute. "No way. Does he really mean—"

Nick nodded. "Yes, we know she's in the thick of this, somehow. It's the only way any of this can be possible."

"But she's been dead for over a decade," Todd said. "That's ridiculous. No one could've survived that explosion."

"Are you sure, Todd?" Nick said. "Because I'm not. Most records of Rad Darkkin have been eliminated by Wendy and the DSD, but I found some old pictures from news articles and stuff Bella had. Juriann looks somewhat like Rad, who we're pretty certain was his father. My guess is that the voiceprint is similar to that of the old Vladimirov armor as well."

"Another child of Rad Darkkin. Just frickin' great. I hope to hell he's more stable than his dad," Kepler said. "On the other hand, I heard Rad was the king of partying, so bring him on."

"Yeah!" Roy G. Bivereaux yelled, raising his fist in the air. "We got the Prez's little bro, or cloned big bro, whatever the hell he is—here chillin' with us. I second the anticipation of partying."

Juriann nodded. "You might be surprised. I am Dutch, after all. We know how to have a good time in the Netherlands."

• • •

"I don't believe it, Juriann," Bivereaux said. "Your skin is tougher than anything I've ever seen. It took a mighty hard drill bit to damage your skin, and it seemed to heal within an hour, although it looks and feels normal. Strength is off the charts—you bench pressed over a ton without even breaking a sweat and maxed out at 7,700 pounds for twelve reps, which is two good-sized cars or one big pickup or SUV. Speed is pretty remarkable for your size. Endurance, pretty good, although we've not really begun to test your limits, my friend."

"I've always been strong; I don't know why. I guess I'm here to try and find some use for my talents."

Biv looked at the echocardiogram which Nick had installed in the lab area. "Your cardiac output, according to my estimates, must be capable of twenty times you or me. While you can't withstand a high-caliber bullet, you can survive in environments that would kill us within minutes. An orthogenetic man: a human whose genes are aligned perfectly, with everything functioning at peak capacity."

"Except his brain." Kepler laughed. "Somethin' sure as hell got screwed up there."

Juriann frowned. "Listen here, *Golfer*. I am a calm, gentle man by nature, but I assure you that I can be provoked to anger. I tire of your incessant pejorative remarks about my intelligence, which surely exceeds yours, despite your exalted academic status. How accomplished were you at my age, Kepler?"

"Well, assuming you're about twenty-one, I had won two majors by then, so I was richer than your big-ass butt will ever be."

"Okay, let's go at it then. We'll see what you've got."

Kepler put up his fists mockingly. "You gonna fight us? That would hardly be fair."

"A fist fight?" Juriann laughed and stared down at Kepler. "Of course not, how banal. I am superior in intellect as well as strength. I will, instead, be happy to engage any of you in the intellectual contest of your choosing. Let's start with chess. "Bring it on."

"Uh, sorry, man, my bad. No hard feelings."

"Yes, it was, Kepler. I heard Bella beat your ass good at chess when she was ten, so it's likely you would lose to me, too."

"She would beat your big butt too, Juriann. But back to the big picture: why us? Why here? Why now?"

"I don't know. Something tells me that, while we aren't related, that I can trust you."

From what Wendy had said, she and Alex had a half-brother named Travis Argon, who, eerily enough, was known as the *Ortho-Man.* This dude was engineered to be pure evil, though, and was genetically engineered to be a killing machine. Juriann, though, seemed to be pretty easy-going. However, if you were him, would you be threatened by anything?

Tinman's Uncle Jim had also once mentioned a scientist, a Dr.

Rita McPherson, who had initially helped another scientist named Malachi Argon with some pretty bad genetic experiments, but then came over to their side to help them turn the tide. (He didn't tell Wendy he knew those things during her last visit; he could play dumb, too.) She then went to federal prison for only two years. Why would she have gotten a sentence that light for helping assassinate President Graham?

And, in 2021, she received a Presidential pardon (public record) from the original *Ortho-Man's* half-sister, whose future spouse he apparently almost killed, per Jim's accounts. Why would she have done that for a nobody?

Yet, his spouse was one of the wealthiest women in the world, which opened the door to many things, the most valuable one being information. He learned that a long time ago.

This guy seemed almost childlike in demeanor but had much inexplicable detailed knowledge of what was really going on. Why had fate brought him here?

Nick and Bella realized that, somehow, Rita might hold some of the answers. She would go there, woman to woman, scientist to scientist, and try to get some information. If not, she would kick some butt. Since she stood not so large at an unimpressive fifty-four and one-half inches and one hundred twenty-six pounds as she looked at herself in the mirror, maybe not.

Chapter Thirty-One

Biology Department Building
Wachsler College
Parkersburg, West Virginia

Bella drove up to the small building in a nondescript Buick rental car at about ten AM, after flying from Aurora City to Parkersburg in the M2 private jet. She was traveling to the biology department of Wachsler College, a small liberal arts college not many were familiar with.

The hermit-like assistant professor of biology she sought had an office in this aging building on the older part of the small campus. She walked up the steps and through the door; a couple of students did a double-take as they looked at the famous woman. One young male whistled. Little did most people know that this person had information many would kill for.

She knocked on the old oak door, the few students in the corridor seemingly oblivious to the famous person in their midst. With sunglasses, blue jeans, and a backpack, she easily could be mistaken for one of the students, which is what she wanted.

"Enter," Rita McPherson said, eyeing her visitor carefully as she walked in. "Or, maybe not."

"Dr. McPherson," she said, entering the small, musty office and removing her sunglasses. "Good morning. This meeting has been a long time coming."

Rita frowned as she looked up from her small desk, took off her reading glasses, and stared at her raven-haired guest.

"You *have* to be kidding me. Halloween was over more than a week ago. And that line is the corniest I've ever heard."

"Too bad."

"Yeah. I would think an Oscar winner could come up with something better than that shitty outfit."

"Do I look like I want to be funny, lady?"

"No, I don't think it's funny at all, but I still can't believe it. I don't get many celebrity visitors here out in the sticks. You look like you blend right in with a bunch of stupid college kids, though."

"Not today, I'm not. It's one professor visiting another."

"Yeah, right. Engineering—or whatever the hell it is you do now—and biology don't mix, and I sure as shit barely qualify as a professor these days. But, somehow, I don't think that's why you're here, kiddo—to socialize."

"No. And I'm not a kid any longer, Rita."

Rita laughed. "Sure, you're a big grown-up girl now, wearing makeup and everything. So what the hell do *you* want?"

"You are the one to give *me* some answers," she said, pointing her right index finger at her. "Not the other way around, so get it straight."

"Bad attitude. It figures." Rita slurped her cold coffee and sat back in her chair. "Well, well, the pretty little rich girl is out slumming in her thousand-dollar pair of jeans, playing amateur detective just like her big auntie. Where'd that get her, huh? Dead. I deserved to die, too, but wasn't so lucky. I wish I could've died in her place, after the life I led, but I'm doing the best I can right now."

Bella stared down at the tall red-headed woman and pointed a pencil at her angrily.

"I'm rich because I'm damn smart. You're lucky to even get any job at all, after what you did, so shut up and be glad I don't buy this college and fire your butt."

"What the hell?" Rita pointed to the door. "Get out of my office. You don't know anything about me. There's not a day that goes by I don't regret what I did, Mendoza, but I can't change history. You can't, either. Money can't buy everything."

"Trying to change history and attempting to rewrite the future are two different things. You could've thought about what you were doing. No ethical scientist would've done that."

"Right, easy for you to say. What if you were in a wheelchair and someone promised you'd be whole again? You might do a lot to get that back. You have no idea."

She shook her head. "Not me—I wouldn't sell *my* soul."

"And I did, 'cause I'm not perfect like you beautiful people. But lookit where it got me: a Ph.D. and postdoc from Harvard, now teaching biology to a bunch of stupid hick idiots."

"You have to be thankful for what you have. I know a crapload about you. You *do* know who I'm married to, right?"

"Sure, I read the supermarket tabloids and watch the celebrity channels with all my free time to stimulate my brain, which sure doesn't happen here. You're married to Stannous, the Greek energy guy who runs your company. So what? Why do I care who the hell you're married to?"

"*Why?* Because *Tinman* is Jim Krakowski's nephew, that's why. Sound familiar?"

"What?" Rita dropped her pencil. "Krakowski—"

"You spent a few days with him and a couple of other peculiar family members and their vodka-swilling Russian pal in the Röntgen-Cave in Solway, Tennessee. Surely you could never forget that adventure."

Rita opened her mouth wide. "Yeah, I tried to forget about that bizarre experience, but you're right. I heard Jim was dead, they said he got drunk and smashed up his car a couple of weeks after *Darkkday*. Figures. Not sure how you know all that, though."

"I'm pretty sure that's not what really happened to him, but most of the rest of our family is gone."

She shrugged. "I'm truly sorry for that, Bella, no one deserves to die. But, about my fine job here, you can thank your other, much larger blonde auntie for that one, another favor she did me." Rita yawned. "I'm getting bored, so what do you want, little Mendoza? Some of us have to work for a living."

"Hey, I work and get my hands dirty, lady, so don't you dare talk down to me. You have answers, and I want them. Two words say it all: *Ontario Lacus.*"

"The hydrocarbon lake on Titan discovered by the Cassini-Huygens probe. Everyone knows about that lousy place, it's old news. Big deal."

"Don't give me a bunch of crap. There's irrefutable evidence Aurora is still alive. You might know something about that, I bet."

"Aurora?" She shook her head. "That's impossible. They all

were right there in that plane when the nuke hit them."

"I know—there's some debate about who was responsible, and I don't want to get into that argument, but there's no other explanation for what's going on. She survived. Bonnie did, too."

"Really? But even your amazing 'parsimony powers' can be wrong occasionally, you know. You're also not clairvoyant like your uncle." Rita paused. "You know about the experimentation with the Ontario Lacus organism, the one that Malachi Argon used to experiment on your, well—other uncle."

"My uncle Alex Dirk Darkkin is dead. *Darkkday*, remember?"

"No, not Darkkin; you have no clue, do you?" She laughed. "You really think you can handle the truth?"

"Why the hell do you think I'm here? The scenery?"

Rita took a sip of stale coffee. "Alexander Dirk Darkkin and little sis Wendy Gallinsworth had a half-brother, with Rad Darkkin the father, of course, but who the hell knows how many other half-siblings are out there, too, as that man would screw anything with two X chromosomes. His name was Travis Argon, and they called him the *Ortho-Man*."

Yeah, she knew all that, and the connection to Juriann wasn't completely clear, but it was all starting to come together now. "Go on; this is quite intriguing."

"I bet it is. I did a lot of research to help Dr. Malachi Argon develop him; I thought it was something benevolent, but he had made a special deal with Brant Gallagher to make super-soldiers for the government as an illicit project."

"I know all that, and about Travis Argon."

"But there was more. There was the microorganism stuff, for sure, but there was other DNA that was almost humanoid in nature, totally unconnected to the other. There's no way it could have evolved that way—someone put it there. I was compelled to go to Mexico where I recreated that from alien DNA and made a special serum that I injected into one person for some reason. It's like I was directed to do it. I saw the DNA sequences in my mind; there's no way I could've come up with that on my own."

"Who did you inject it into?"

"Who do you think, genius?"

"Bonnie? What? What the hell for?"

"Argon had theorized that some of her abilities might be incorporated into his super-soldiers. And that the combination of the

Darkkin and Mendoza genes might lead to something spectacular when combined with this stuff."

"And she let you do that? Hard to believe."

"No, she was unconscious, but I thought it the only way out of a terrible situation I had helped create."

"I still don't follow. What's so great about that mixture?"

"Jay Mendoza has synesthete powers too, not nearly as great as Bonnie, but substantial, and some thought he really was clairvoyant. Wendy has fast-twitch muscle proteins found in certain select elite power athletes, hence her natural gifts. She didn't even work that hard at it, until she made her comeback at age forty. Few people could have done that after being that out of shape for so many years."

"Go on. That still doesn't explain much. They hadn't seen each other for years at that time."

Rita shook her head and laughed. "You *are* aware that Madam President has bipolar disorder, right? Yet, you take everything she says at face value. Don't be so damn gullible."

She nodded. "Sure, everyone knows that, duh. It apparently was due to the pregnancy with Cassie, as mid-thirties is a peak age for bipolar disorder to present in women; in addition, it was also possibly a side effect of an antidepressant she decided to prescribe for herself. She was up-front about it when she was Governor and before the first Presidential election. It was controlled with medication for a while, then went into remission, I understand. She hasn't had a problem for many years."

"Sure, that you know about."

"Maybe. Being a frequent guest in the White House, I've seen some minor mood swings, but she's always been that way. What's that got to do with anything? Get to the point, Rita."

"She was raving on, claiming that Cassie was Jay's child. That's why Argon wanted her too. But Bonnie developed tremendous strength after that first injection. She went from one-seventy to one-ninety pounds in the span of several days without looking any different, with six times her original strength. You know as much as anyone about her. You played her in a movie, for God's sake."

"No, believe me when I tell you this." She shook her head. "I don't know anything about any of that stuff or Bonnie having extraordinary strength. Superb coordination and speed, yes, but not that. If it's true, I'm sure it was classified and she never let on."

"Argon theorized that, if the serum was injected into someone who later had a child, coupled with a partner with strong synesthete powers, that the outcome might be a being with great abilities, but nothing near what Aurora has exhibited. There is obvious proof now that this 'other' genetic material was from a race of super-beings, evidence of one which was here in the past. It had some characteristics of human DNA, but not of this Earth."

Bella sat down and laughed. "In the *past?* You're saying that Jesus Christ was an alien? Like that's a new theory, give me a break. You discovered God's seed, huh? Aurora is the second coming of Christ?"

"I don't know, and I never said anything about Christ. But it's a scientific explanation for such. And I mean over sixty million years in the past, not two thousand. This much is certain."

"Go on."

"Oh, what the hell. You'll think I'm nuts, but I don't give a shit."

"I'm sure I've heard worse than this, but I promise I'll keep an open mind."

"I bet, but here goes: I was guided to do it by some force. I can't explain it. I recreated things that were beyond the comprehension of any human. But it happened for a reason. And it wasn't to help Argon create his super-being."

"Was it God?"

"Damn, don't be such a smart-ass, Mendoza."

She shook her head. "Not my intent, Rita; I'm a very spiritual person, and I am genuinely asking if you saw Him."

Rita shook her head. "I don't know, never met the dude, we weren't ever very close, but maybe things would've turned out differently if we had been. But people ask proof about the existence of Aurora the Angel." She rose out of her chair and walked over to the sink with only a slight limp. "Behold her power—I was at Ground Zero having a few drinks at a party before preparing to go to some job interview at a community college in Arlington the next day. I was in my wheelchair. But the explosion put that interview on hold. Five days later, I was walking. Not as well as before, but it sure as shit beats a wheelchair. Dozens of others reported improvement in their medical conditions. A friend of mine's incurable leukemia went into remission within weeks, and she remains healthy. You and Wendy were in Pittsburgh when it happened."

"You are postulating the blast dispersed some of her energy

towards the city, where it was absorbed by you and others."

"That is the only thing that makes any sense."

"The golf balls?"

"What?"

"Three golf balls traveling at several thousand miles per hour were launched with almost impossible precision in Oak Ridge, Green Bay, and Aurora City."

"How would Aurora have known about your family if she's still alive? I assume they're in hiding?"

She shook her head. "Bonnie would know, and she's bizarre enough for her to convince Aurora to throw them at those targets."

"I'm a geneticist, not a physicist, but I'm pretty sure no one can do that—hurl something that fast at those targets."

"Really? I think not. Aurora can shoot a free throw with almost impossible precision. At the other extreme, she has raw power that you can't even imagine. Combine those two things, and you have something pretty special, believe me."

Rita paused for half a minute. "That's it, then. The contribution from Bonnie must have been the neurological and muscular coordination necessary to control that with absolute precision; that is amazing."

"Do we know if any more of these fantastic energy beings you speak of exist nowadays?"

"I am no expert, obviously, but apparently, the last of their humanoid kind was in the DNA we found on Ontario Lacus, which originated from Mexico, which is where I went to find the fossilized remnants. I remember being directed to do this and an immense urge to incorporate that genetic material into the purest person I could imagine."

"Whazzat? 'Purest person?' Bonnie Mendoza ain't no Polly Pureheart, just so you know. Her talents, while extraordinary, have a very limited range of usefulness; she has abysmal judgment and is capable of tremendous violence."

"Don't I know. I watched her kill one of Argon's stooges with her bare hands in Solway while Rad stood there and laughed. Later she killed Malachi himself. But Aurora—is she our Savior? What if Malachi Argon had gotten his hands on that girl? He could've ruled the world. That's what he wanted, you know. When Wendy got whacked out and went around claiming that she was carrying Jay's baby, he thought their offspring might be something useful."

"But what has happened now, Rita? The current scenario we have isn't that far off."

"What do you mean?"

"Someone else ruling the world. Wendy is powerful beyond measure because of technology, much of which I helped create. Some of it's been diverted into weapons instead of energy, but little has been done to advance medical science, which should have been her legacy, given her background. Remember that incident when the king of that one Middle Eastern nation refused to shake her hand because he didn't shake hands with women? She told him to go to hell because the world didn't need their oil any longer and never to set foot in Washington again. The USA now controls over seventy percent of the world's energy supply, most of which is mined from Luna. The oil companies are nearly broke, and she doesn't give a damn."

"I agree. She could've spent more time and money on cures for disease and such. Not sure I care much about oil, though."

"No kidding. Haven't you been down this road before, and how did it end for you?"

Rita looked down at her desk sadly. "Not well. But maybe, if Aurora is still alive, she can be the force to balance the world out. Or destroy it. They each seem to be likely probabilities."

"Yeah. We have a lot of further discussion to do, Rita. But right now, I'm very hungry."

• • •

Bella ordered some take-out Chinese which was delivered in about twenty-five minutes as they started eating the food in Rita's small office.

Rita took a bite of General Tso's chicken. "Aurora, as a child, was not physically different than any other child, according to Wendy. Above average intelligence, but nowhere near her mom in that aspect. She was incredibly coordinated, though. And strong."

"As strong as a hundred thousand men? A hundred million?" Bella asked.

"No. Some other event triggered it. Her body, while not even as strong as Bonnie's for her size, was limited. Native invulnerability is far less than that of the original *Ortho-Man,* so most of her 'powers' come from the manipulation of gravitational fields and being able to absorb energy, most likely dark energy, Wendy thought."

"Dark energy, huh. What else?"

"Well, it gets worse. While I went to minimum security prison camp, the word is that Bonnie and Alton Lohrbach—"

"Who?"

"Lohrbach, the director of what used to be the Office of Scientific Intelligence, now known as the CIA's Directorate of Science & Technology—Dexter Slabb's uncle. He made Bonnie the director when he became Secretary of Defense for Reardon."

"I heard about that, but that was insane, Rita. She had neither managerial ability nor people skills. The worst candidate for that I could ever imagine."

"Yeah, but 'insane' is exactly what he wanted. He was an old friend of Rad, you know."

"Slabb's uncle was a friend of Rad? No way."

Rita nodded. "Oh, yeah, back from the Cold War days. They cloned Travis, obviously using some DNA they got from the original Travis Argon. Wendy herself donated Cassie's bone marrow to regenerate his blood cells, as they were a perfect match."

She knew all that, as Juriann was living in one of her condos and hanging with the *Science Squad*, but Rita didn't need to know that yet. She was sharp enough to know who might not be trustworthy.

"Why the hell would anyone want to do that? Wasn't one bad enough?"

"The Vladimirov armor vidcam showed Rad doing some amazing stuff. The dude was in his late sixties, but he was actually sparring with Travis Argon. Now both of them may be in one body. But old auntie was as crazy as Rad. I know because I spent several days with them in Rad's hideout in Tennessee."

"Yeah, I know, so what else is new?"

"A lot. There were three doses of the "special" injection. Bonnie got two—the one I gave her, then the one she gave herself, but the third disappeared, so my guess is that Rad injected that one into himself. I mentioned your aunt's augmented strength after that."

"I don't know about that; she was always pretty strong, but she kept to herself mostly after she went to the CIA and afterward when she left. I did most of the stunts myself in the second movie, although there weren't that many. It was mainly about her scientific exploits."

"Gee. Aren't you the plucky little actress."

She laughed. "I'm used to insults. But so what if they cloned that crazy old man or Travis Argon?"

"Because he wouldn't be old *now*. The clone may have aged a bit faster than normal. Meaning that if she cloned him sixteen years ago, he could be about twenty now, maybe a little older. And strong as hell. If someone found out about him, he could be perverted into a terrible weapon."

"Or a great ally."

"That's right. Why do you think I'm telling you about him?"

She might as well spill the beans, as she could use Rita's help later, and Juriann was tough to hide forever.

"Look, Rita. I need to share all my cards with you: he's already here."

"What the hell? *Orthoman* is living with you, I assume?"

She nodded. "Yeah—he's in Aurora City."

"No way can I believe that."

"He is. But despite being, physically, all the things you say, he's about as dangerous as a ladybug. Kepler told my husband that a dude like this came around asking about the golf balls, about Wendy, it all fits now. One more thing: how exactly does The Great Dame fit into all this?"

"It's hard to know. Sure, she did come to see me back in 2012 at my minimum-security camp. She seemed to know something was up with Aurora, but I'm guessing you probably know all that."

"What did you talk about?"

Rita paused. "She told me over sixteen years ago that I would receive a full pardon when she became President for helping to save her life. She said that in 2012, a few months after the London Olympics, where she won her gold medal. I thought she was crazy, you know how she can be when she starts rambling, but with great energy comes passion, and everyone grossly underestimated her multiple talents. The cards were dealt her way, and she kept her promise; she may be a lot of things, but *not* a liar. Most Presidents give out their pardons when they leave office; she gave me mine a couple of months after she took office, just like she said she would. I told her everything I told you."

"Yes, she's known about this all along, as I already knew. Why didn't she try to find Aurora, then?"

"She may play the dumb blonde like a pro, but she's cunning, so she probably did, found them, then backed off, to save that secret for later, when she could best exploit it. Bonnie and Jim believe themselves to be the masters of stealth and computer hacking, but I betcha the Prez has some nifty secret files on all this stuff even you wouldn't believe. She and her VP Robby Benton. He's likely in on the dirty deals, too."

"Maybe. But why wouldn't she act to try and find them, then?"

"Because she *knew*. About her invulnerability, at least."

"I suppose I agree, Rita, I don't know how, but that's the only way they could have survived, even though it's unbelievable. To what degree did she have those abilities then?"

"Then, not sure." Rita nodded and took a slurp of her soda. "Wendy told a story about how Aurora turned a pot of boiling water on herself and laughed it off. I guess it's much more enhanced now, as apparently, the only explanation is that she survived that explosion by absorbing most of the energy. According to what Wendy knew at the time, she could protect those in direct physical contact with her. Unfortunately, the small amount she didn't absorb was enough to vaporize the plane and everyone else on board, but nothing else."

"Yes, that's what I thought. But how did they get down? That plane was at least a few thousand feet in the air when it was hit."

"Don't know. Guess they survived the impact."

"Or—they flew."

"What?"

"You remember *Gravi-Golfer*."

Rita shook her head and frowned. "Sorry, kid, I never watched that stupid show or the cartoon. But, yes, I know who Johnny Kepler is. We don't run in the same academic circles."

"He has theorized that, for the last year or two, there have been subtle manipulations of the Earth's gravitational and magnetic fields. Not enough to cause any kind of problem, but he thought it might be due to dark energy."

"Dark energy, as we discussed. So, somehow *I* am responsible for this?"

"You and some other power," she said. "One other thing."

"For you, sweetie, sure," Rita replied.

"You said earlier Rad injected the same serum into himself?"

Rita nodded. "Yes, that's correct. Rad exhibited the same rapid increases in strength and sensory perception Bonnie did shortly after that."

"So he had the same DNA inside him that Bonnie had."

"Presumably. I can't say for sure, but it's likely. The effects on another human being not selected for that purpose are unknown."

"So Rad's body could have possessed the dark energy powers. Distinctly different from those of Travis Argon."

Rita shook her head. "No clue, it's so complex even I don't understand it. Yes, Bonnie had the DNA from the alien humanoid, but although she became stronger than normal afterward, she wasn't invulnerable by any stretch of the imagination. Some type of extremely rapid cell division, like occurs in fetal development, must have given Aurora those powers. A meiotic rearrangement apparently has to occur."

"Or different people get different powers."

Rita nodded. "That's also a possibility I had not anticipated. There's no instruction manual for it, Bella."

"I'm just worried about what might happen if someone dug ol' Rad Röntgen up out of the Tennessee soil if they thought fantastic powers might be had."

"I've made a few bad decisions, but even I can't imagine what kind of imbecile would do something that reckless."

"After all you've done, you *can't?* Well, my uncle is married to one who lives at 1600 Pennsylvania Avenue. That is, if it hasn't already been done by the person who lives in North Pole, Alaska."

"Bonnie? Yes, she might do stupid things, but for some reason I would bet on the former."

"Yeah. And the Prez will finish the work that ol' M-Square started if she thinks it will benefit her somehow."

"And I don't want to be anywhere around here when that happens." Rita took a sip of soda. "One more thing you have to know."

"What?"

"Argon had a nephew named Ramon Argon who hung around with Malachi sometimes."

"What? Is he still alive?"

"I have no clue. I think he was more interested in computer stuff, though, although he did have an interest in biogenetics."

"Would this Ramon Argon have any information on this stuff?"

Rita shook her head. "I don't know, Bella. I was in jail for two years and the CIA took over the complex after Bonnie rescued us, but it's possible he had some files from before."

Chapter Thirty-Two

North Pole, Alaska
1200 Zulu Time (0400 Alaska Daylight Time)

Paige had again heard the confidential reports on her pilfered military/police computer radio about possible Tosian or Taraqi fighter jets heading across Asia and towards the northwest United States. She impulsively contemplated what she was going to do about it and hesitated for only a second. Mom and Dad were in bed, but she could do this on her own. Asking permission to do things wasn't in her adult nature.

This time she was going to damn well fix it for good.

Her parents stupidly thought she couldn't figure out how to do this on her own, as even her arrogant mom and clueless stepdad, like most people, chronically underestimated a blind girl's abilities. They could not have been more wrong, because damned if she was going to let Tosia or Taraq invade the United States.

She walked outside in the cool air to get to the underground bunker she had dug herself, two hundred feet away. Dad wouldn't be happy she was doing this, but she was an adult now; she'd do what she wanted, and, with any luck, she'd be back by breakfast. She didn't want to know what Mom would think. She would either be chewed out or applauded for helping out the U.S. Air Force when she returned.

She felt for the armored suit, which was in its case. She donned it, turned on the electronics, opened the outer door, programmed the flight path by entering verbal Russian commands, and took off again for the Bering Strait, near Russia, her mom's homeland. Avionics indicated about twenty minutes to reach the area. Once she got the suit on, it was easy.

This wasn't going to be a "patrol" like a few days ago. Some damn foreigners were going to get a real ass-kicking this time.

I am power personified.

No one can stop me.

Except me. And maybe I should.

I am a wise adult, capable of far more than others give me credit for.

You bozos are going to get your asses kicked.

• • •

Strategic Air Command
Eielson Air Force Base
Fairbanks North Star Borough, Alaska
1220 Zulu Time (0420 Alaska Daylight Time)

Staff Sgt. Ron Shoemaker couldn't believe what he saw on his radar screen as he opened his mouth wide and spilled his coffee.

"What is it, Shoemaker?"

"Sir, I see what again appear to be rogue Tosian fighter jets that just crossed the Bering Strait. This happened about forty minutes ago also, as you know. We don't know the intent, but given that these fighters often carry missiles, it isn't good, most likely."

"That's impossible, Staff Sergeant," Major Anthony Saxon said.

"There it is, sir."

"Come on. Are we certain they're real? That would be suicide."

"They appear to be, Major. If they're cyber-mirages, they're incredibly good tech. They have mass and heat signatures as well."

"Why would they do that? It's insane. Where are they going?"

"Yes, sir. They appear to be flying parallel to the International Date Line for some reason."

"Tosia isn't a country with all its marbles, mind you, and the Russians gave them some nice planes, so now they think they're hot shit. Well, send some sentries out there, just to be sure. And make sure the news feeds don't get hold of it."

"Yes, sir."

"Damn, that's all we need. I guess it's not like anyone close has the ability to interfere."

"Major—wait a minute."

"Yes, Staff Sergeant?"

"There's something else out here."

"I don't see anything on radar," Saxon said.

"It isn't visible on radar, sir, but it leaves faint air turbulence and a unique carbon signature. It's barely detectable, but it's there."

"What?"

"Similar turbulence and residual spectroscopic signature to what was seen in New Persia a couple of weeks ago."

"Carbon signature? Be more specific."

Shoemaker nodded. "C_{60}. It's definitely buckminsterfullerene, sir, no question, nothing else looks like that."

"Holy shit. Do you know what that means?"

The staff sergeant nodded. "I think so, sir."

• • •

The White House
Situation Room
1244 Zulu Time (0844 Eastern Daylight Time)

"Madam President," SecDef Thomas Ashburn said as they stood in the White House Situation Room. "It's back, and we don't know if it's the alien or not. It's the same one seen at the New Persian border at Graham Army Base when Thomasson was retrieved, and likely the same one flying over various points in midwest America weeks ago. It is believed to have been seen less than fifteen minutes ago at the Bering Strait, over Little Diomede."

"I know all that, Tom. Don't waste my time."

"The molecular spectroscopic analysis shows its armor to be hardened carbon, in a rare configuration—"

She sighed. "A rare configuration and allotropic form of carbon called buckyballs, or buckminsterfullerenes; yes, we've been over that, too. The hardest substance on Earth, far harder than natural diamond, yeah, yeah. I *am* a scientist, you know."

"Yes, Ma'am," Gen. Larry Kriger said. "But there were rumors of the Russian government having experimented with prototype suits of this nature in the late 1980s to early 90s. So that's all we know. Curiously, records regarding that appear to have been eliminated from every database we have."

"We've been through all that before as well, and I wish I had them, General, but it was probably worthless information to begin with. I would like to know more about it too."

"They said it called itself '*Stella Scura,*' if that's right. Any idea what that means? *Stella* is a feminine name, but the New Persian gate Marine said this thing sure didn't look or sound like any lady. It had a coarse, gravelly voice, with a Southern Appalachian accent; linguistic analysis places it close to the Oak Ridge area."

She pointed at him snappily. "I know all that, Tom. A Southern Appalachian accent and Oak Ridge? What's that supposed to mean? There are over fifty thousand Americans who talk exactly like me."

Kriger put his palms together. "Madam President, I was not implying that this has anything to do with you at all, only that—"

"Only that you think we're related or something, just because it talks like me but with a deeper voice? Next thing I know, you'll be accusing me of being in it, too. Don't I have better things to do with my precious time, gentlemen?"

Kriger shook his head. "No, Ma'am, that's impossible, as the suit is clearly not large enough for you to be inside. It's perhaps seventy-two inches tall in height at most."

She scowled at him. "Excuse me? Are you saying I'm too fat? Why I'll have you know I'm damn near in the best shape of my life, General—"

Dexter shook his head. "What he meant is, Ma'am, that a weapon similar to stolen Russian technology combined with that accent is very peculiar; the fact that you're originally from that area is merely coincidental. He also meant height, not weight."

Hell, no, it wasn't coincidental at all, and they likely knew it.

"Whatever. Let's focus for a moment on the fantastic *Stella Scura.*" The President thought for a moment. "Y'all are missing the boat; it's not a female name at all. It's Italian for 'dark star.'"

"That is fascinating," Dexter said. "You know this how? Other than Spanish and American Sign Language, I'm not aware of you knowing other languages like Italian."

She shook her head. "I don't know much, but Bonnie was fluent in many languages, Italian and Latin being her favorites, and she taught me a lot of words. Interesting."

"Dark star? What the hell is a dark star?" Kriger asked. "A black hole? What the hell does that have to do with this?"

The President laughed snidely. "No. It's a theoretical type of dark matter aggregation. Dark matter and dark energy supposedly make up over ninety percent of the known universe."

"Yes, that's correct," Dexter said.

"Thank you!" she said condescendingly as she turned towards him. "Glad I know something about science these days."

While she likely was the most scientific President in history, what she didn't get was that the old thing was built in the late eighties, revised in the nineties. It was used, to her knowledge, on only one mission—when Bonnie rescued her from that Caribbean island where Malachi Argon was doing genetic experiments. That was a one-shot deal. And how could it even be working today? It sure couldn't fly.

Apparently, Aurora, the goddess of dawn, was finally living up to her name. She would also be about the right size for that suit.

"In case I'm not being entirely clear, my position is this—until this 'thing' does something antagonistic, y'all will leave it alone. We don't even know where it's at now."

"But, Ma'am, with all due respect," Dexter said, "this 'thing' is likely alien and represents a tremendous national security threat. There may even be more of them. How can you say this?"

"Alien. *Really?* There is nothing indicating this, and there are far more pressing things to worry about than some theoretical being from space. Dexter, find out as much as you can and report it to me, but under no circumstances will y'all engage that thing without direct orders from me, if it even exists."

"Yes, Ma'am."

• • •

She went back to the Oval Office, grabbed the cup of coffee a staffer had poured for her, and plopped down on the sofa, staring into space.

"Ma'am, are you all right?" Jackie asked as the staff member closed the door.

She took a sip of coffee and thought pensively for thirty seconds before looking back at the woman she trusted with almost all her secrets.

"What the hell do you think, Jackie? No, I'm not 'all right' at all." She had seen that suit up close and personal almost twenty years earlier when her sister-in-law wore it to rescue her from Malachi Argon's island. It was no coincidence.

"You look like you've seen a ghost."

"Huh?" Jackie joined her on the sofa as she took another sip of coffee. "Are you kidding? I have, Jackie. Right now, I want to forget that ghost; it sure doesn't bring back fond memories."

"Listen to me, please." Jackie moved closer and put her arm around the President. "You've helped her keep this secret for years, and the time has come when you can't keep it up for much longer. The rest will figure it out in time. You have to spin this the right way or you'll look like you were hiding something, if your image matters to you."

"Don't you think I know that? And you think I care about my stinking 'image' right now or what my approval rating is?"

"You care about how people will perceive *her*. Your image is important for that. But that suit, it was, you know—"

She stopped and scowled. "We both know what it is, dammit; we're two of the few living people who've ever seen it up close. That was my crazy dad's buckyball suit; he and the Russian Vodka-Man, Viktor Vladimirov, put Bonnie in there and shot her out of a submarine in a torpedo tube to destroy Malachi Argon and rescue me. Which she eagerly did, while my dad and Jimmy almost started World War III with Russian nuclear missiles."

"You don't know that. There could've been several. And how could it fly? It isn't possible by any known means."

"Come on, Jackie. It has his voice, and we've both heard that stupid-ass suit before. Only he could've been so egotistical to make it sound like him. And we know how it flies, even though it seems impossible."

"But, Wendy—"

"I said leave it alone; there's nothing to be gained by further investigation. I have to trust that whatever being out there is good for everyone. If not, then God help us all."

"You've kept Aurora a secret for a long time, but it's about the people now, not just about you."

"Hey, I did the right thing, don't you ever insinuate I didn't. No one else would've done what I did."

"Did you? I'm not being critical, just that it's a complex decision with many alternative paths that could've been taken."

"I can't second-guess myself for the decisions I've made. Yes, I let them live their life, thinking that they're under the radar. I don't know what Aurora, or Paige, or whatever we call her—ultimately means to our society. My intel tells me she doesn't like me all that much, so maybe she'll play for my team, maybe not. But the time is coming soon to find out, and it isn't about me, but America. I don't know what other choice I have now, do I?"

"You know Will is intrigued by this girl in Alaska—Paige, the blind basketball player. Andy said they even went out there."

She nodded. "I know that, and I'm not interfering. If he and Jay want to go out there again, that's fine with me."

"It is? Are you kidding?"

"Sure, it's a free country. I will *not* have the military or anyone else interfering with Paige Marshall. I have protected her anonymity for this long, so we can do it a while longer."

"But not forever. Not even you can do that."

"No, but—I'm sure she can probably take care of herself in time. Maybe Will can learn a thing or two from her. I'm sure I probably can."

"Do you think all that is wise?"

"What the hell? I just won my third Presidential election, and I didn't think it would happen this way. You want me to have all the answers, like Jay thinks I do with his simplistic thinking? Unfortunately, I don't, just because I'm a Darkkin and she's as much his blood relative as mine. I knew she could pack a wallop and was pretty tough, but I had no idea she could be capable of anything like this: supersonic flight and God knows what else. She couldn't do any of those things two or three years ago, from what my intel said. It's a world-changing power."

"A power we don't know is even on our side. She doesn't know who you are; you made damn certain of that."

"She will come around once she finds out."

"Or she may resent you terribly for keeping it a secret all these years. However you've thought this out, you must consider the alternatives for which you have no countermeasures."

"I'm a strategist; of course I have. But I'm still trying to deal with it all without breaking down."

"I don't mean to pry, you know, but it's just that sometimes one needs someone to talk to."

She put her hand on Jackie's shoulder. "I know. I can't talk to Jay because she's his niece, too, so I really do appreciate that.

Bella and Nick have their own agenda, and probably don't trust me completely. I suppose I don't blame them. Bonnie has chosen to become a hermit in rural Alaska, she obviously doesn't want to be around. I am sure her opinion of me is quite low. So I have to keep things quiet for just a little bit longer until things work themselves out."

"Do you really think that's going to happen?"

"What the hell makes you think I know? What else would you have me do, Jackie?"

"I—don't know. What now?"

"If you don't know, then don't ask." She stood up from her desk. "You want me to go after her or something? The only thing we can do now is wait. I am certain that the proper opportunity will present itself."

• • •

Department of Scientific Developments
2 Constitution Avenue NE
Washington, DC

Ashburn sipped a cup of coffee while talking with Dexter Slabb at the latter's office at the Russell Senate Office Building.

"Slabb, do you think the Chief was acting weird?"

Dexter nodded. "Yes, a little bit. She can be somewhat eccentric sometimes, nothing new there, now. All Presidents have their issues, her more than some, and she's highly unpredictable. What do you expect? Her dad was a damn crazy man, albeit a very patriotic one, which is something you'd better remember. You have to allow her some little idiosyncrasies."

"No." He shook his head. "I don't buy that, Dexter; this is way beyond her usual behavior. She's hiding something."

"Yeah, right, you know it all. What might that be, smart guy?"

"I can't put my finger on it. The voice of that—that thing at the New Persian border, there's something creepily familiar about it."

"Voice spectrograph shows no matches of any kind. Lori ran it herself, she's the best."

"That's just my point—it's too distinctive a voice not to show up *somewhere,* as most simulations use generic voices. Someone must've purged the files, and you can guess who."

"Purged? What are you getting at?"

"Oh, come off it, Dex, she's very good at playing the fool, but you're not. I've listened to his voice, his lectures, and such. Being an astute student of Presidential history, I know a lot about that family."

"Whose family?" Dexter asked snidely.

"*Her* family, man. That voice is distorted from the low-quality recordings, but it sounds exactly like Rad Darkkin, it's unmistakable."

"How the hell do you know what Rad Darkkin sounded like? You didn't know him, and he's been dead for almost twenty years."

"Listen, there's no match on the voice, but the phonic linguo-spectrograph narrows the accent to Eastern Tennessee, specifically, a fifty-mile radius around Oak Ridge and vicinity. That can't be a coincidence. Who else could it be?"

"Watch your tone with me, Tom. But that's absurd; he's dead, I'm pretty sure, buried in Tennessee, and he'd be eighty years old even if he was alive. And he was six-five, three hundred twenty pounds easy, which makes her look tiny—if she can't fit in it, there's no way he could."

"Of course Darkkin's dead, and he's obviously not in the suit. I can't prove it, but there were some crazy old rumors that Darkkin himself stole some weird set of battle armor from the Russians and the CIA had it at some point all those years when people thought he was dead. Then, mysteriously, the Darkkin clan had some kind of secret funeral for him in Oak Ridge, years after people thought he'd died; it was right before the Chief had Cassandra, when she got whacked out. Things that aren't in any books since the records have been destroyed. And you *know* who worked for the CIA for four years, designing esoteric stuff, before she quit to go work on nuclear fusion and invent mendozium down in Eastern Tennessee, of all places. How can you be so stupid not to get that?"

"You can't possibly believe that, Ashburn, and don't insult me, as you're way out of your intellectual league here. There were so many weird stories circulating about that guy that they have to be mostly conjecture. Take my advice and leave it alone."

"Maybe some of them. But we saw something that was real, Dex. You can't deny that. But now that suit's gone and your uncle Alton Lohrbach is hardly ever heard of these days; you can't believe he doesn't know too, because he and Darkkin were pals."

"You have no evidence regarding the suit, and it's been gone for decades. Get over it."

He shook his head angrily. "I don't need it. There are no traces of this information anywhere. There's only one person in the world with enough power to make things like that vaporize as if they never existed. The thing threw a freaking golf ball into the ground by Darkkin's grave monument, for Chrissakes. What the hell for, if it doesn't have something to do with that family?"

"Tom, listen to me: whatever you think is going on, give it up now before it's too late. If you're on her side she'll do good things for you. But get on her bad side and you're done for good. Not just in Washington but everywhere. You can't go up against this President for some cockamamie idea; she or Robby will ruin you. You said it yourself; you can easily disappear into nothingness just as much as records of that suit could."

"I'm not afraid of that idiot Benton, are you nuts?"

Dexter shook his head at the ignorance of the Secretary of Defense. "You're nuts if you think he's an idiot. Robby's a hard-boiled lifer, a Washington insider who knows how to fix ugly shit better than anyone. Wendy values her image, but Robby doesn't care about his; he'll eat you alive and you'll never see it coming. You may think he's some old fat guy, but get a grip on reality. You don't want either one of them as enemies."

"Are you for real, Dexter? You were in there giving her the third degree not too long ago, so shut the hell up."

"Don't be so naïve; you misinterpret my intentions. I was trying to protect her by anticipating questions that she might get from others. I *am* an attorney, you know, and understand preparing people for adversaries. I will reiterate—you'd better watch your tone with me, Tom, or I'll give you grief you cannot believe."

"Are you threatening me, Dexter? You'd better be damn careful, too. You aren't the only one with connections."

Dexter snarled. "Take it how you like, asshole. I don't report to you, and I'm just telling you the truth. I am one hundred percent loyal to the woman in the West Wing, and whoever the next person is. I'm not a 'yes man,' and I tell her what I think. She appreciates candor, but if you're not loyal, well, then—roll the dice and take your chances. The odds aren't good for your survival."

He extended his hand. "Of course I am, Dexter, don't be ridiculous. I just want the truth, that's all."

"Yeah, right. I wish I could believe you. You had just better be damn careful, or your career will be over real soon."

He was done talking to Dexter, whose opinion he didn't value anyway. Whatever that thing was, it used some form of electronics, meaning it likely was vulnerable to EMP (electromagnetic pulse) devices. Maybe not the usual weapons, but he had an experimental one at his disposal which was a humdinger. Now the only thing remaining was to get this alien out in the open and use it and bring it down. And study it so its power would be ours.

Or his, as he and his new "associates" hoped.

• • •

Wendy went to her bedroom after a thirty-minute workout in the White House gym and activated the holographic computer monitor. The high-pitched British female voice answered as a blonde figure appeared. Bonnie and Alex had created her as a likeness of what Wendy always had wanted to look like: five-ten, one hundred forty-five pounds, with an aristocratic Upper Received Pronunciation accent, not a deep Southern Appalachian drawl.

No, she wasn't like that, and who knew what the hell she had become today. Sometimes she didn't want to know.

"What can I help you with, Dame Wendy? It looks like the election results are in your favor, so congratulations on your wonderful achievement yet again."

She nodded her head. "Yes, yes, thank you, but condolences may be a better wish, Miranda."

Miranda frowned. "I don't understand why I would want to console you on your victory. You should be celebrating."

"Never mind, you wouldn't understand. Is compilation of data on archived images of females with heterochromia iridum now complete?" The government's spy eyes were everywhere in this day and age, having compiled enormous amounts of information on everyone, out of necessity. And information was always a good commodity to trade with and useful to keep one's enemies at bay.

But other information was best kept hidden; she was good at doing that, too. But she knew someone with far lesser resources who was better. She had known him for over forty years, and it was likely they would communicate again soon.

"Yes, Wendy. There are 1,054 American females identified, excluding the states of North Korea, New Persia, and Luna, where little data and relatively few of the ethnic group of interest exist. But you have done this scan before. I assume you are now expecting a different result."

"Noted. Run again. Left iris deep blue, right iris brown."

"Two hundred twenty. Please realize pure colors are very rare in this condition; most are hazel or green variants—"

"Quiet, I know what I want. Estimated age between sixteen and nineteen years."

"Fifteen."

"Height between 174 and 177 centimeters."

"Three."

"Mixed Hispanic and European ancestry."

"Approximate skin reflectance, Wendy? There are wide ranges in those populations."

"Between forty and forty-nine units."

Miranda pointed to the ceiling. "There is one now, when there were none before. Curious."

"Enough of the caustic commentary. Display results, please."

"Here is your best match." A 3-D holographic photo of an attractive grinning teenager with a left blue and right brown eye was displayed on the screen. Her name, "Cheryl P. Marshall," along with a six-digit numeral was displayed on a digital panel she was standing behind.

"Oh, no." She slapped herself in the face.

"Wendy, why are you hurting yourself? Do you need me to go into counselor mode? I am fully programmed to engage in psychotherapy."

"I might need that, Miranda. Before that, I may need a drink."

"Oh, dear. Am I to assume you mean an alcoholic drink?"

"What the hell other kind is there, idiot?"

Miranda pointed a holographic right index finger at the President sternly. "Wendy, I must caution you that Darkkins have a strong family history of alcoholism, which is ironic, given that your family gained most of its wealth from running a large whiskey distillery. Have you ever reflected on that fascinating factoid?"

"Yes, I have, so shut up. It was a great topic for 'bring your dad to school' day and made me real popular with the guys, too."

"But did the genetics predisposing Darkkins to this condition lead to their amazing ability to distill flavorful alcoholic beverages?

Or did the consumption of said libations lead to the problem? I have long pondered this 'chicken or egg' dilemma."

"D.T. Darkkin & Sons was sold off long ago; I don't give a crap."

"And imbibing is a poor life choice given your high-stress occupation and addiction to things such as food—"

"I know, it was just a joke. Forget the booze."

Miranda shook her head. "Humor. I do not find it productive."

"But you've got to be kidding. A local juvenile hall mug shot? *This* was the photo he put back in there?" 'Jack Marshall' at least could've put in a yearbook photo or something that didn't make her niece look like a criminal. Figures. "This is really it? The best your great computational power could come up with?"

"Yes, it is confidential information from DSD archive acquired from Anchorage Police Department: Cheryl Paige Marshall juvenile department booking photo, April 2027, age sixteen, for unlawful protesting, failure to obey police, and violating multiple local health ordinances and causing a public disturbance. Comparison with frontal and profile photos."

"Family?"

"In the state of Alaska, one compatible with biological mother of record: Petra Nureyev Marshall, age fifty-two." The gray-haired woman's photo appeared on the screen.

She looked at it. "Yeah, that's a new one, too. Quite flattering. Comparison to Aurora Darkkin photo, simulating age."

"Aurora Angelica Darkkin Mendoza photo is not in my database. Deceased, December 16, 2016, age 6.15 years. This is information surely known to you, her aunt."

She smiled. Of course not; that would be too easy. Jimmy wanted to make her work for it, and playing games was his style. And she was sick of playing games with these people and her staff.

"Eigenface comparison with my photo at the same age."

Miranda crossed her long, slender arms. "Humph, this is wasteful of my intellect. Eigenface comparison shows no correlation."

"No, no, the image on my private encrypted server, dummy, not the one in the archives. Also the Aurora photo on my server." She had really sunk to a low level, insulting a computer, albeit one with advanced artificial intelligence. She would take what she could get.

The pretty holographic young woman pointed at her sternly.

"Of course, Wendy, but pejorative comments, while they cannot offend me, are very unhelpful in reaching our goal, as they waste computational cycles; even *you* have sufficient intelligence to understand this, albeit barely."

"Hey, It's my time, and I'll waste it if I want, so shut up."

"Certainly." Miranda shook her virtual head. "Nevertheless, there is twenty-two percent eigenface correlation. This suggests that Cheryl Paige Marshall and you are second degree relatives, although this fact does not logically compute, it must therefore be a stochastic anomaly."

Of course not. A soulless computer simulation would come to that conclusion, but it made perfect sense to her. If she could figure it out, her husband's niece surely did long ago. Playing strategy games with Bella wasn't one of her favorite pastimes, as she was likely to lose, despite having a superior intellect on paper, but maybe they had a similar goal in mind and could help each other.

"Umm—the Aurora photo comparison, please, if it's not too much trouble?"

"Humph. They seem to be the same person, accounting for age. This cannot be possible, Wendy. It must be a neural net malfunction, an extremely rare occurrence with my vast error-correcting memory banks."

"Must be. Thank you. Comparison now with photos on Will's cell phone taken on his recent trip to North Pole, Alaska."

"Ahem. May I remind Dame Wendy that, according to the Digital Privacy Act, a federal law signed into law in 2019, this may well constitute an invasion of William's constitutional—"

"Shut up, you moronic pile of semiconductors—I'm his mother, and he's eleven years old. I'll look at what I want of his."

"Yes, Wendy, although, again, insulting me is unproductive. And you *must* rectify your glaring ignorance—semiconductors are a quaint, ancient technology which were in vogue before you were born. My CPU core consists of advanced borosilicate nanoprocessors and is far more advanced than mere ancient silicon-based—"

"Really?" She pulled out a 34-inch tapered piece of wood from Jay's closet. "I'll take this Louisville Slugger to you in a few minutes and show you 'productive.' Is that 'quaint' enough for you?"

Miranda paused for a few seconds and smiled. "I am merely a holographic terminal, and striking me will not result in my annihilation, but your crude meaning is understood. The harsh interface of maple and advanced electronics is not desired at this time." The computer paused for several seconds.

"Well? Hurry it up."

"Humph. There are photos of many attractive preteen females on his digital device, as my heuristic algorithms would predict, given his genetics."

She sighed. "I can only hope they are all fully clothed, again considering his genetics."

"He is a product of both you and the First Gentleman. Whose DNA are you referring to?"

"I suppose both of us."

"I do not understand, do you both now prefer females? To my knowledge, you are heterosexual, yet, such things are fluid, I have learned. Shall I alter that and update your social media profile?"

"You started this debate, so figure it out."

"I am merely trying to gather the facts to arrive at the best conclusions in order to support you in the optimal way."

She sputtered. "Never mind, just shut up, dummy. Anyway, I hope we have at least a few years till we get to *that*."

"Get to what?"

"What boys do with unclothed females! Duh!"

"Yes, Wendy, I can comprehend such fundamental biological concepts. But I have found one that matches, who is substantially older." Miranda sighed. "Despite my many objections, the similarity is amazing and suggests a close blood relationship, although how this can be possible is not immediately evident to me, as are the other comparisons. William himself made this comparison to himself, yet I was ordered to tell him there was no relationship. I don't like to lie. "

"That's what I thought. That is all. And I don't care what you don't like."

"You predicted this outcome, Wendy? You are quite intelligent, beyond what I thought possible of one of such limited intellect."

"I did, and I am. Now shut up, I don't need the added comments." She smiled as she realized it was very much like her sister-in-law to have programmed a computer to have such an acerb attitude.

"I am your trusted advisor and I thought my input was desired. Very well, shall I save data for later query or print report?"

"Negative. Delete all history of this activity permanently, using 2,048-bit digital shredder. Also get rid of that booking photo from the police database and any reference to her in any government database. It's ridiculous and embarrassing."

"Yes, Wendy. This will permanently delete the data, although the ethics of that are questionable."

She had run the same scan two months ago, with no result. Only one possibility existed. Someone put this girl's booking photo back in the database when it was not there before. The juvenile photos wouldn't be accessible by the general population anyway, but the President had access to things mere mortals didn't.

Yes, there was the surveillance video that she had squelched of a blind girl in a convenience store in Anchorage who had foiled a robbery attempt; although she was moving so fast it was impossible to identify her with certainty. Everyone thought she had been shot and that the robber missed. The gun contained real ammunition, had been fired, and two witnesses saw bullet holes in her shirt, but she walked away, refusing medical treatment.

And there was the same blind girl who dunked over four other girls in a high school basketball game in North Pole. The girl Will wanted to meet and finally did; he thought she wouldn't know about that, but there wasn't much she didn't know. And the one who had been in minor trouble with the law, whose records had seemingly vanished. Until now.

She knew about it all and had for several years. She didn't pry, as they had their reasons. Patience was a hard-learned virtue of hers, and messing up this complex chain of events further wouldn't suit anyone's needs.

Least of all her needs. Because she didn't want any of this just for herself. She wanted it for America because that's all she had left these days.

He, the one who mysteriously disappeared just after *Darkkday,* put it back, obviously because he wanted her to find it, but not until recently. Why now?

Sometimes amazing facts could turn up in the damndest places. Therefore, it was time for a trip to East Central Indiana. Things had curiously been too quiet there since the golf ball incident.

• • •

M2 Technology Annex
Sulphur Springs, Indiana

Kepler spoke to the small group at the Sulphur Springs complex in the small conference room, cup of coffee in his right hand.

"Hultaar's right; there is some flying dude out there, despite the White House's denials. All of us know the President, and all of us know better. Right?" Kepler took a gulp of the strong brew.

"Righto, Johnny," Roy G. Bivereaux said loudly. "The Prez ain't no dummy. We go all the way back to med school."

"The things we know are this: this guy's got some type of damn propulsion that's light years beyond anything we could ever theorize. He's been clocked at over Mach 7. That's over 6,000 miles per hour, and the energy needed to do that is, well, beyond anything we can imagine. He can maybe go faster than this; we don't know."

"It must be alien or something," Todd said.

"Then why the hell is he wearing Viktor Vladimirov's old suit, which few folks besides us know exist? Don't make no sense, man. Like I mentioned earlier, there appear to be some subtle alterations in the Earth's gravity which correspond to some of these events. It looks like the dude is able to absorb and manipulate gravity, clearly as a form of propulsion, since we can't determine another means, dammit."

"But why the suit, then?" Biv asked.

Bella stood up. "As we understand it, the suit has multiple other possible functions besides augmenting the wearer's strength, and this life form apparently doesn't need that. Remember, Vladimirov designed it as a stealth information-gathering device, not to be invulnerable, or to fly, of course. It seems logical, therefore, that the being within lacks normal Earthly senses and needs it to perceive our world. She may have a visual disability. Plus, it's also more aerodynamic than a person, although it wasn't specifically designed for that purpose."

"That makes no sense. A being from another planet who can't see, in a suit built for a human which talks like Rad Darkkin. Doesn't speak very well for evolution and Darwinism. Jesus," Kepler said. "If I was an alien with omnipotent intelligence, I sure as hell would've picked a better model than *him*."

"It's the only explanation, *Golfer*. And who the heck said she's from another planet?"

"Why do you keep saying 'she,' Bella? What does that mean?" Kepler asked snidely.

"It means that this being is a woman. Did that never cross your mind, Johnny?"

He shook his head. "Hell, no, are you crazy?"

"That's 'cause you're a stupid sexist pig."

"Take that back, small fry. I ain't stupid."

"But a sexist. And it *is* a woman. A young woman, but a female, nevertheless. Juriaan?"

"I concur with Isabel. All evidence points to this entity being the young woman known as Aurora the Angel."

"So what the hell do you want us to do now? Get our asses whooped by this thing?" Kepler asked.

"I'm ashamed of all of you, *Tinman* included," Bella yelled. "Get some fricking balls. You were heroes once. Act like them now."

Nick stuck his finger at her angrily. "Are you crazy? Dealing with this *Orthoman* guy is one thing, but what you're proposing—"

"Maybe. But don't ever point at me that way."

Todd stood up. "Reality check here: we were a bunch of worthless heroes on a kids' show."

"And is that how you want to be remembered? Make a difference in your life." The five-five woman yelled in her most irritating, high-pitched voice. "We need all of you. If none of you have the guts to go when she shows up, I will. By myself."

Roy G. Bivereaux stood up to his less than impressive height of five feet seven inches. "Just because you laughably tried to learn martial arts and got up to, what, one hundred thirty pounds with super protein drinks and a personal trainer, and look hot in blue spandex, doesn't mean you're any superhero. Not even the real one could do that."

"Wrong." She snarled and stared up at him, poking him in the chest. "Maybe not physically, but I have the heart of her. Juriann here provides us some much-needed intellect and muscle, and we need all the techno-stuff you can provide."

Chapter Thirty-Three

Petra woke up in a cold sweat at five AM, breathing heavily.

"What's wrong?" Jack said, turning over sleepily.

She jumped to her feet like a pogo stick. "Paige! Go to her room now and see if she's there."

Jack rolled over. "Go back to sleep, you know she's there since we saw her go to bed. Jeez. She sleeps like a rock; she'd never get up before us, anyway, how ridiculous."

"Then I'll go myself, you lethargic moron!"

"Good."

She threw a pillow at him, sprang from the bed like a jack-in-the-box, and ran into Paige's bedroom down the hall, as he reluctantly followed her. She began screaming.

"She's gone! I told you she would be up to no good soon!"

"Chill out. She's probably downstairs, or outside or something, behind on her homework as usual. She doesn't need much sleep, so go back to bed."

"No, I don't think so. There can only be one explanation."

He rose up and stared at her. "Waitaminnit. Are you saying that she went out in the suit on her own?"

She nodded. "Yes, what a brilliant conclusion: she's out flying somewhere. You should have told her never to do that!"

"What?" Jack ran around the room, his arms flailing. "I never said she could do that; are you crazy? I didn't even know she could figure that out on her own. How did she power everything up by herself?"

Petra stared out the window. "She is absolutely her mother's daughter. I, above all people, should *never* have made the mistake of *ever* underestimating someone with a disability. What she wants to do, she will accomplish. My guess is that it's not the first time she has done it. Many underestimated me, and many have regretted it. A few have died, some quite horribly."

He snarled. "Whatever, no time for a soliloquy now. Where do you think she might've gone?"

She shook her head. "I don't know, I can't sense her anyway these days, especially through that helmet. There was some info on the news about possible Taraqi retribution about Thomasson, something about the Bering Strait. I hope to God she hasn't gone out there."

"I can't believe she'd do that or that Taraq would attack the United States." He sat down. "But I've been wrong before. There isn't much we can do except wait and hope that she's back soon."

"She cannot afford any more tardies or absences; it will look bad on her record. How will she get into a good university then?"

"Who's a moron now? She's possibly heading towards Russia faster than sound with the potential to start a nuclear war, and you're worried about her academic record. You're too much."

She snarled. "You can't be too concerned about academics, Jack. We don't want her cheating her way through college like you."

• • •

"Omega Squadron: potential hostile bogeys approaching from the North. Plus, object with the apparent mass of the *Stella Scura* being has been sighted heading near the Russian border, near Big Diomede," Squadron Leader Lt. Col. Adam Sintner said.

"Orders, Colonel?" 1st. Lt. Russell Stanton replied.

"We are to follow it, do surveillance, but at no point are any of you to engage that thing," Sintner said.

The air group continued to fly near Russian air space. "Then what the hell are *those?* Russian MIGs approaching?" Russ asked.

"I don't know. They shouldn't be there, but if they engage, shoot their asses down, but leave the alien alone."

• • •

Stella Scura approached where her avionics said the Tosian jets were: two Russian fighter jets, but she doubted there were any Russians inside. They were sort of friends with the Americans now, as friendly as any country was allowed to be. The Russians had sold off part of their military aircraft to the Taraqis; maybe that made more sense.

She attempted to contact the plane in Russian. Why would anyone fly these jets into United States air space? The Air Command had sent out the message, and she thought she might be able to help. No answer.

It just dawned on her that maybe this wasn't such a great idea. Especially since no one knew she was out here, and her parents were likely still asleep.

One thing was wrong, though: she didn't detect any movement within the six enemy planes, although they had mass and heat signatures matching humans. That didn't make any sense. Were they robotic planes? It finally occurred to her teenage brain that there might not be real planes at all, that they could be cyber-mirages. Not a great revelation, as she wished now she'd stayed in bed.

• • •

The Pentagon
Air Command War Room

"We just now intercepted a transmission from that damn thing, General," SecDef Tom Ashburn said to General Kriger in the Air Command war room. "The goddamn thing's speaking Russian."

"Those are supposedly Russian MIGs the Tosians have. Are you absolutely sure they're real?"

"It's impossible to tell, but we must assume they are."

"They may be cyber-mirages. You can't possibly think those are Russian planes or that thing is with them," Kriger said. "All indications are that this *Stella Scura* is a non-hostile."

"They're all Tosian, or Taraqi, and therefore enemies of the United States. Blast it out of the sky."

"What do you have that will do anything? We certainly don't want to hurt it."

"I have something that's non-destructive but can bring down just about anything. Don't you want to know more about that thing, Kriger?" Secretary of Defense Tom Ashburn asked.

"I might, under the proper circumstances, Ashburn, but I'm not convinced this is one of those times—"

"Fuck it. On my command blast that thing with the electromagnetic pulse device we scrounged from CIA. Three of our fighters are armed with them."

"Like hell you will, Ashburn."

Shit. That stupid red phone was ringing again. There was only one person allowed to use that phone; when it rang, someone had damn well better answer it. He sure as hell didn't need that now, as she was probably already on her way. He put it on speaker.

"Hello?"

"What the hell? Ashburn, this is your Commander-in-Chief. I heard about this, now step down. You will *not* attack that thing. I made that perfectly clear before. Now stand down."

"What, Madam President? I can't hear you." He twisted a dial on the console.

Why did I do that?

Get the hell out of my head.

Who is doing this?

Static.

"What the hell are you doing, Ashburn?" Kriger yelled. "That was the President on the line, man. She'll fry your ass, and so will I. We just received confirmation that those planes aren't real; rather, they're incredibly realistic cyber-mirages."

"I didn't do anything—the transmission was breaking up. Do it, you son of a bitch!" Ashburn pushed the smaller man aside and punched the button. "I'll do it myself. If you don't care about some damn alien invader, I do."

"Ashburn, no—don't do it!" Kriger threw a punch and knocked him down, but it was too late; the electromagnetic pulse fired in rapid succession at where the powerful targeting computers predicted the intruder would be.

Why the hell can't I stop myself?

I don't know. Something compelled me to.

But it's too late.

And I'm glad I created those cyber-mirages, which brought it here.

Kriger decked me, but I killed the alien. I should get a medal.

• • •

Darkness. No responsiveness. The suit suddenly died, for some reason. There was only one thing to do—it wasn't worth anything now. At least she could hear without the suit.

She heard a small impact, as the part of the suit broke off into several pieces, the helmet and a small percentage of other parts still remaining.

What the hell? They fired a missile at me? This is more than I had bargained for. They will pay for such insolence.

Or maybe I hit something, since I can't see a damned thing now.

The only thing I could hit up here would be a plane.

Part of the helmet has broken off, too. Not great.

• • •

"Holy shit," Lt. Col. Sintner said over the radio to Air Command. "The damn alien hit Stanton's plane, and the being exploded. But there's something still flying, sir. Part of the head and the exoskeleton is damaged, but something's sticking out of it."

"What, Colonel?" Gen. Lawrence Kriger asked. "Is it horrific?"

"No, it looks like it has a—ponytail," Sintner yelled.

"Repeat that, please, Colonel."

"A ponytail. I know it's impossible, but I can just make it out."

"That's what I thought you said."

"It's not an alien, it's a girl. It's dark and can't see its face, but the back of the head is blown away, and there are pieces of that thing flying everywhere. Look out!"

"Do *not* engage that thing, Colonel. Whatever it is, we'll try and recover it, whatever's left."

"It's still going strong, despite its armor being damaged. I think we'd better get away while we still can, General."

"Roger that. Get the hell out of there. We'll try and find Stanton."

• • •

It was night, so she couldn't feel the Sun's warmth on the exposed areas of her body, the only hope of a sense of direction. She had no idea what her orientation was, so she did only what she could; she turned to where the noise was coming from and poured on the speed.

She had no idea how fast she was going—the person traveling couldn't hear the sonic boom. She must've hit a plane and the pilot would need to bail out. She wasn't very aerodynamic without the suit; it was rather hard to practice flying without it.

• • •

Lt. Russell Stanton had watched as the out-of-control flying being crashed into his fighter jet, taking off his tail fin at 15,000 feet. He saw his brief life flash before his eyes, went into a tailspin, and realized only one possible option.

"Shit! I'm going down, Colonel," he told his commander, Lt. Col. Adam Sintner. "Something hit my tail, I can't recover."

"Eject, Stanton. No time to be a hero. The thing attacked you."

"Roger." He did so, and he would deploy his chute at three thousand feet and hopefully drift to the ground while his plane smashed into the mountains.

• • •

For the first time in her life she felt fear, and she knew it would not be the last. Not fear for herself, paradoxically, but for what she had done. Why the hell had she gone out here without anyone knowing where she was? These were real fighter jets shooting real weapons; or was it all a trick? No, she definitely did hit something.

Yes, she had rescued Thomasson, and there was some risk in that, but he likely would've been killed anyway. Was this nothing more than a ruse by a corrupt Republican government to draw her out into the open? Surely that was the case.

She yelled out, the voice box of the helmet still marginally operational, although she could feel her hair flying out the back of the helmet which was partially broken away in the back. "Is there anyone out there, in the middle of nowhere?"

A bass-baritone voice yelled out in return. "What the hell is someone doing out here?"

His voice was familiar, and she wondered how that was possible; then she remembered what he did for a living. What were the odds of him being out here? Probably reasonably high, given that Eielson was the closest Air Force Base, and he was stationed there.

That was what pilots did, she suddenly remembered.

What the hell have I done now? This is a lot worse than when I rode that old bike off Cargg's Cliff.

She did a trick she hadn't done much before, but Mom said she could do: she could, in effect, exert substantial gravitational pull, which would bring any nearby objects into her vicinity. It seemed to be working, as she heard the man coming towards her, yelling as he was blowing in the wind. The man came into her grasp. The voice was eerily familiar. Was that even possible? Her instincts told her it must be. What had she done?

"What the hell?" he said as she felt him with her left hand, as that part of the armor was gone, as was most of the right leg armor and half the chest piece. "Where did you come from? How did you get up here?"

"Someone tried to kill me. I need your help."

"Great, now we're both going to die."

"Not hardly. We might be lost, but we are not going to die, do not ask why as we are falling from the sky."

"My chute can't serve us both in this cold air with our combined mass. You can't help unless you can fly."

"Luckily, that is about the only thing I *can* do now, man, as, amazingly, I do not have a very good plan." He gasped as they hovered in the dark.

"What the hell?"

"Take the parachute off. We shall not need it, and it will only impede us by making us more visible. I assure you, we do not want to be found, so let us quickly reach the ground."

He yelled. "Who the hell are you? You sound like you're from the South."

Yeah, sure. The damn voice box was about the only thing in the suit that still worked. Figures.

"I am a friend, and from the Northwest, actually. Not far from here, you have nothing to fear."

"We're floating in the air? Part of your armor's blown away. How can you still be alive? It shouldn't even be functioning."

"I was doing just fine, until some disruptive force interfered with it, but it did not hurt me one bit, pardon my sardonic wit. It was old, anyway, and it did not fit my torso very well. And it takes a hell of a lot to kill me, if that is even possible."

"Where are we going? Besides to our doom, I mean."

"Somewhere else. Like I said, I need your help now."

"What do you want from me?"

"I have to trust you, as I have no choice, and this is definitely no time to rejoice."

"Why does a being such as yourself need a measly pilot?"

"I am profoundly visually impaired, so I need you to help me navigate. The suit only provides artificial vision, but it has now been damaged beyond repair. Yet, I think I can get us down, do not frown."

"You *think?*"

"I have never flown naked before, yet I know the score."

"The fighters will follow us."

She shook her head. "I seriously doubt it. Even without the suit, I seem to be impervious to radar detection because it depends on the reflection of energy, which I can absorb, except for visible light, for some reason. In the dark, without visual confirmation, they will not find us, with any luck. I am hopeful that others will, though. Please make yourself useful and find us some place to hide, unless you want to travel at Mach 6. I would not advise that, given the current sorry state of my suit, fixing it will take a lot of loot."

• • •

They landed near a cave, per Russ' direction, the suit's crippled electronics near the failure point. Stupid old piece of Russian crap.

"This doesn't look too bad," he said as they walked inside. "So what the hell happens now? Your spaceship comes to take us back to your home planet?"

"How foolish, do not be so ghoulish."

"What . . . did you say? Why do you keep on rhyming?"

"Never mind, I will not leave you behind. Is there sufficient light here for you to see?"

"Yeah, I just put down a portable LED lantern; it will last several days. Why, are you blind or something?"

"You seem to be quite the smart-aleck for someone who thinks I am an alien, and you obviously do not consider me to be much of a threat, do not break a sweat."

"I am merely reacting to your incessant banter. Think of the energy you could save without yapping all the time."

"Lack of energy is not one of my dilemmas. Well, pay attention, as I am going to remove this suit, as it is damaged beyond repair, thanks to you and your imperialistic government."

"Hey, just for the insurance record, you hit me."

"Huh. Here you go if you care to see what I look like; if not, you go take a hike."

"Do I have a choice?"

"No, so get ready for a shock, and do not squawk. It will not be what you expect, but I have little choice now."

"My airplane is a wreck, too. I bet it cost more than that suit."

"Bet you are wrong. Your government attacked me, not the other way around. I was just trying to help; I will deal with that later."

"We thought we saw Russian MIGs that were rogue Tosian or Taraqi fighters, but they didn't engage us because they were sophisticated cyber-mirages."

"Cyber-mirages? You mean they were imitation planes? I deduced this as well after I detected no movement inside them."

"Yes, but they certainly fooled us for a while. When we found out, we backed off, until you came along and screwed it up."

"We will discuss that another time. United States Air Force First Lieutenant Russell Timothy Stanton from Edinboro, Pennsylvania, you shall never speak of this to anyone, or I will come to find you, wherever you are, and do bad things. Promise me this, or your life will never be bliss."

"Your words, but not your voice—sound eerily familiar. I'm getting a very weird feeling about this."

She shook her left fist at him. "I care not about such things. Can you agree to my terms?"

"Okay, I promise. But how the hell do you know my name and where I'm from? You telepathic or have intel on the pilots?"

"No, no, I am not telepathic, and it will become obvious in a moment. But I mean it." She made a fist with her left hand and shook it angrily. "Your death will be indescribable."

"Sure, fine, whatever, but for some reason I can't put my finger on, you aren't all that scary. Like a B-movie monster."

"Well, that is your mistake, so go jump in the lake. You dare compare me to a cheap cinematic creature? Here is how I know your name, and I anticipate you will know the same." She broke off the helmet to reveal her matted-down Titian hair in a ponytail, then removed the rest of the armor still remaining.

"*You?* You're the alien? What the hell?"

She shrugged. "You have been reading way too much science fiction, it is causing much mental friction and embellished diction."

"That sure doesn't answer my question."

"And why is it people think every person who flies *must* be an alien? Do I look like one to you? Did you think I was an alien when you were kissing me in the movie theater?"

"No one can fly, are you kidding? What a moronic answer from a moronic girl. Are you even *that?*"

"What, a moron? Very likely, given recent events."

"A girl."

"Most of my clothes have been torn off, so decide for yourself, ace. And we just did fly, so the answer is obvious, so who is the moron here?"

"Maybe you're one of those shape-shifting aliens who can alter their appearance, so what do you really look like?"

"I am what you see, Russ. Do not make things more complicated than they already are; I do not originate from a star afar."

"What? 'More complicated than they already are?' Are you nuts, girlie?"

"Huh. That fact is yet to be determined, but probably, given my heritage."

"What do you mean by that?"

"You will find out soon enough why I am so tough."

"But *why* are you in that suit?"

"Well, that should be self-explanatory, genius."

"No, it's not, dummy. Okay, I get it about it allowing you to see somehow, but that still doesn't explain *why* you're out flying around in dangerous situations, taking on foreign fighter jets, even if they weren't real. How did you even know about this?"

"I sort of have a lair, where I can tune in to all kinds of encrypted transmissions for entertainment, using stolen military equipment. This one, I definitely should have passed on."

"Do you think you're a superhero or something?"

She nodded. "Or something, yes. Would you prefer I wear a formal dress for such outings? A football uniform? A cheongsam?"

"Quit joking. Why would you do things like this?"

"Why? Because I can do things no one else possibly can, man, as my life has a plan. Yet, I can already sense you are not a big fan."

"Ohmigod. Then it's true, the rumors about Taraq. You saved Alan Thomasson from being killed. I don't believe it."

"Yes, I saved Sen. Douglas Thomasson's brother. I can do many other things, more than any other being can. I heard reports of possible Taraqi retaliation on the news feeds, so I attempted to lend a helping hand, but this plan did not work out as intended, and here we are with no car, and we need to go far."

"But how does it fly? I didn't see any means of propulsion. I still don't get it—advanced antigravity pods? Deltonics? That stuff is still in research and development, from what I know, at least twenty years off, as the energy requirements make it impractical. And how would a mere high school girl from North Pole have access to this level of technology?"

"Huh. I know not of such concepts, as they are irrelevant to me; I know not of technology."

"And why you? You're just a kid from North Pole. You don't know anything about combat or the military, little lady."

She sneered. "And I thought you were an Air Force aeronautical engineer. Figure it out from the process of elimination, Russ," she said as she lifted off and hovered three feet off the ground, crossing her arms. She then spun rapidly end-over-end and returned to her hovering position. "Have you not figured it out yet? The powers are *not* in the suit, slick, your cognition is sure not very quick."

"What? How are you doing that? No way. And you say you're not an alien?"

She shook her head and landed in front of him. "No. I know for a fact I was born in the United States. But I do not really know how it works. I am able to manipulate a dark energy field, my mom says, which allows me to alter gravity and convert dark to kinetic energy and vice versa, allowing me the power of flight and immense strength. I pulled you to me by gravitational attraction. The only purpose of the suit was to supply useful vision."

"And protection, obviously, since you're flesh and blood."

She shook her head and laughed. "Yeah, well, it does not need to do that—" She heard them and frowned annoyingly. The wolves.

"What? You hear something?"

"Yeah. Pack of wolves approaching. I would know that sound anywhere, being a wilderness girl. They must smell us."

"Get back. We need to protect ourselves. I'll beat them off with this rock. I've had such training in the Air Force."

She shoved him behind her and smiled. "No, Russ, *you* get in back of *me*, as I shall protect you." She felt the leader of the pack spring on her as it tore her shirt to shreds. She then picked him up and threw him to the ground as she heard a whimper, knowing she hadn't likely thrown him hard enough to hurt him. "Anybody else want a taste of me?"

She heard the others run off screeching.

"I did not think so," she yelled. "Get out and do not ever come back, carnivorous canid. Tell your colleagues to never return to this domicile, either."

"Oh, my God, are you okay?" He looked at her body, shirt in tatters. "You have scratches, but you're not bleeding, but you must have internal injuries. That pack leader must've weighed eighty or ninety pounds. He hit you pretty hard."

She brushed the snow and dirt off. "No, it is not scratched, really, and I am fine. You asked about protection—I do not need any, as I cannot to my knowledge be injured."

"What? Of course you can be, unless you're some kind of superhuman. Wait a minute, what did I just say?"

"You can decide that for yourself. But my garments can be destroyed, yes. I will go through a lot of clothes if I keep this up."

"I don't get it."

"To briefly summarize: the living cells of my bodacious body are indestructible, as far as I know, which is not much."

"But those wolves—they could rip a man to shreds."

She laughed and shook her head. "Not me, as I am *really* indestructible."

"Even to bullets?"

She laughed. "No problem."

"Come on. You know that for a fact?"

She nodded. "Yes. I was shot in the abdomen several times at point-blank range when I stopped a convenience store robbery in Anchorage last year. Ruined my favorite sweater."

"What else?"

"I rode an old bicycle off a cliff, fell several hundred feet, and landed on my head."

"And you were unscathed?"

"Hardly! It left an unsightly bald spot about three inches in diameter that took weeks to regrow."

"Could you survive a nuclear blast?"

"A nuclear explosion? What makes you think that? Wolves, bullets, and falling off a cliff are not quite on the same power level as a thermonuclear weapon."

"There is no way to practically test it, but if that's so, then it's true. You're really *her*. Oh, holy crap."

"Who?"

"*Aurora*—the angel from the stars. Who else?"

She shook her head and frowned. "I am no angel, do not be ridiculous. That person is fictional rubbish, an ancient goddess deified in modern times by those with more money than sense, do not be so dense."

"Maybe, but I don't think you realize your significance."

"I do. But that is not important now."

"Whatever, but I still don't understand why only your outer skin was scraped."

"Duh, the process apparently does not extend out to my clothes or non-living cells, like my outer skin layer, hair, or nails. So it may look like I have a scratch, but it is just the stratum corneum that is gone. It shall regenerate in a day or so, and the 'scratch' will disappear. Same with my hair, it can be damaged, but will regrow."

"Good to know. So, what's the plan now, Paige?" he asked. "Had you even bothered to think that far ahead, junior hero?"

"Huh. Not really, I had not anticipated this course of events, so I guess we sit, wait, and pontificate, as I am not terribly experienced at these things. Exactly what we will be waiting for, though, I do not know."

"Just to let you know, it's very cold."

"I would not know about that. Sit next to me; if you touch me I can transfer some energy to you so you will not feel so blue."

"What? I don't understand."

She shook her head. "More dumb questions for which I have no answers. Simply put: apparently those in direct contact with my skin share my imperviousness to an equal extent. I can also absorb incredibly large amounts of various types of energy."

"So where does all that energy go when you absorb it?"

She shook her head and sighed. "I do not know that either—apparently back to where the rest of my energy stays when I am not using it. Mom says it is all around us, called dark energy or something. So I do not know if it is right here with us and we cannot see it, or if it is in another dimension, or far away. And most of the universe is made of it, it seems."

"Damn. Can you take that energy you absorb and, like, shoot

rays out of your eyes or other stuff?"

She sneered. "How ridiculous. No, I cannot convert it to anything useful besides the manipulation of gravity—dark energy repels that, per my understanding. I suppose that is enough, as I have no need for more powers. Most of the time, I wish I did not possess the ones I have."

"Are you kidding? You can do miracles. Who wouldn't want those abilities?"

"Well, I suppose you think you understand the responsibility I have, but you have no clue. They are a massive burden no person should have. I try to play sports, but I have to hold back. I will never be my own person."

"The solution seems simple: don't use them, then, and don't go flying around jeopardizing others, especially when you can't see. You made a conscious choice, so own up to it."

"That would be a waste of my gifts. My father said that would be irresponsible."

"I think what you've done today was pretty much that."

"Was what?"

"Irresponsible! What a dope."

She nodded. "Agreed. But it takes one to know one, son."

"Maybe. I guess you have some problems bigger than ones I ever had."

"For sure. Let us take a time out."

He felt good, warm as he rubbed against her flesh. She had rarely been able to sit next to another person like this. The feelings were unfamiliar.

She felt as he touched her face. It felt good. "You feel so soft, normal. I don't understand."

"I am flesh and blood, just like you. You necked with me in the movie theater, for Heaven's sake."

"No, not like me at all." He marveled as he warmed up. "Again, how did you do that? Who are you and where did you come from?"

"Like I said, I honestly do not know anything else, Russ. I grew up in North Pole. I have no reason to hide anything from you. I accidentally destroyed your aircraft and almost killed you, so I owe you that much."

"What happened up there?"

"I do not know. It just died, like something shorted it out."

"It was likely an EMP weapon. Electromagnetic pulse disruptor. Came from the government. Some of the experimental fighters are equipped with them. Don't ask me the details because I don't know either, as it's so classified."

"EMP? So, the United States did this on purpose? I am not surprised. I received an Air Command notification in my helmet radio, that there were Tosian fighters engaging your planes. Why would such a terrible thing be done? Did the President order such an attack on me?"

"No, I am sure that's not the case. Paige. I have it on good authority that she thinks you're a myth, a fact that has frustrated the hell out of my bosses, I heard through the grapevine."

"Huh? Why would a lowly lieutenant know such lofty things?"

He shoved her. "Be quiet, Paige. You need me right now, too, so don't be so insulting."

"Sorry. I can be quite opinionated, as you already knew."

"Like I said, I don't think President Mendoza did this, I think it was done against her wishes. The SecDef apparently convinced the military that you are Russian and an enemy."

She shook her head. "I am *not* a Russian. My mother is, though, and taught me to speak it because the suit required its knowledge; the readouts were in that language. I do not understand all this. I ain't no scientist, I got B's in math and physics, yet my mother is apparently quite brilliant. She says I possess the power to manipulate dark energy."

"Dark energy? You keep saying that, and I'm an aeronautical engineer, but I don't understand."

"She says that over seventy-five percent of matter in the universe is something you cannot see, called dark matter, and that much of the energy is called dark energy."

"No offense to your mom, but how does a high school math teacher know this when I don't?"

"It is a concept inferred from gravitational analyses—that dark energy holds the universe together and expands it. It is right here in front of us, but large amounts are in large clumps of WIMPs, which form dark stars. Not sure why she has such expertise."

"Wimps? You're a wimp? I hardly think so, given what I've seen already."

"Not that kind of 'wimp.' I thought an engineer would know about the other kind."

"Oh, WIMPs: weakly interactive massive particles. Is that what you mean?"

"Yeah, duh! Apparently, they are kind of wimpy until you get a bunch together, then watch out; their power will not be in doubt."

"Dark matter? Why does your mother live in rinky-dink North Pole if she's a brilliant scientist and knows about stuff like that? I'm not criticizing, but it's hard not to be skeptical."

"She is rather egotistical and claims to be brilliant. I really do not know one way or the other, and I have my doubts, as I have not really seen her do anything of exalted intellectual substance besides teach algebra, do statistics, and chop wood. My dad is not my biological father, as I told you; my real one died in an accident, they said."

"I'm sorry."

"We have the family we have. Mine is rather flawed, as I am. They have been good to me, not that I deserve it—I have been a real pain in the ass and have given them unparalleled sass."

"Do they know you're out here?"

She shook her head. "No. I left without their knowledge. When I rescued Thomasson, they helped me, but not now, mainly because they did not know about it."

"Great. So what do we do now? The military will be looking for us but may not find us quickly in here."

"Huh? Do we really want them to, Russ?"

"Well, sort of. They are on my team."

She shook her head angrily. "Hey, after this event they are most assuredly not on mine—present company possibly excepted, of course. But you are correct that they shall eventually find us. I can only hope that someone we can trust will find us first, Russ."

"Who the heck are you talking about? Are you crazy?"

"Perhaps—but I have no idea what motley crew will show up for us, either. Somehow, I feel our adventure is only beginning."

"I hope it's over soon."

• • •

Stannous Residence
Aurora City, Indiana
1100 Zulu Time (0700 Eastern Daylight Time)

Bella suddenly woke up and winced with the piercing voice.

The loud, monotone voice from her past, although now it was in her head. But she wasn't hearing it. It was being projected into her skull.

"What is it?" Nick asked. "Are you having a migraine?"

It was being projected into her mind. And it hurt like hell.

Not a dream.

"Isabel Dolores: your help is urgently needed, as unfortunately I have no one else. Bring Tinman and Orthoman immediately to these coordinates: 65.6092° N, 168.0875° W. The latter's strength shall be needed."

"What?" She said as Nick turned his head towards her.

"The Appalachian one is not to come or to know anything about this, however. She cannot help us now."

"This can't be you. And I can't just tell her not to do something. I am not her favorite person."

"You are the only one other than Jaime I can communicate with, except maybe Will. We do not need to endanger his life as well."

"What is it?" Nick asked. "Who the hell are you talking to?"

"A ghost."

"What is it?"

"No, it's a real ghost, *Tinman,*" she said, shivering. "One from the past." She picked up her cell phone and started texting, then entered the coordinates the voice told her into the GPS.

"It's Sunday, my one day to sleep in, and you do this."

She snarled at him. "*Tinman,* get your lazy butt out of that bed. This is an emergency!"

"Um, we aren't those kind of doctors."

"We need to stop jacking our jaws and go over and find Juriann, we're going to the M2 fusion-turbine hovercraft."

"The hovercraft? Are you nuts?"

"Yeah, probably. We're going to an area near Wales, Alaska, close to Little Diomede."

"At this time of the morning?"

"Yes. If I'm not crazy, the world needs us. And I need you to ride shotgun."

"Don't punch me in the mouth, but we need Juriann for *what* reason, exactly?"

"I don't know, but he may come in handy if we have to encounter someone pretty strong."

"Makes perfect sense to me." They threw on some clothes as she returned *Orthoman's* text to get him up and ready for their transcontinental flight to western Alaska.

• • •

Office of the Secretary of Defense
The Pentagon
1300 Zulu Time (0900 Eastern Daylight Time)

"What the hell is this shit?" Tom Ashburn on asked the wiry five-seven Black woman standing before him on the cold Sunday morning as he saw his belongings in an old cardboard box as two uniformed FBI officers stood behind her. Most people were familiar with regular plainclothes FBI agents, but the FBI had its own uniformed police service at the Pentagon. He somehow felt that this wasn't going to be one of his better days.

"Duh, I think it means—you're fired, asshole," Jackie Levickis said snidely, cracking a wide smile. "Here's all your crap. Don't let the door hit you on the way out. And don't call the White House for a reference, because it won't be a good one."

"You can't fire me, Levickis, and get the hell out of the Pentagon. You have no idea who you're dealing with. I'm a Cabinet member." He turned towards the uniformed Pentagon Police officers. "Put that stuff down, asshole, you take orders from me."

"Afraid we can't do that, sir," the police sergeant said.

"Why not, Sergeant? You're real close to losing your job." He poked the large man in the chest.

The burly officer pulled Ashburn's hand away harshly. "Don't do that again, sir; I'm warning you."

"Yeah? Or what, Barney?"

"Or you'll be going to jail. I was just told that you no longer work here and that you were to be escorted off the premises immediately. Don't cause a scene."

"What the hell? Levickis doesn't have the authority."

"That's right—she doesn't." He choked as the tall blonde woman entered the room. "But *I* sure as hell do. Get this piece of crap out of here, guys. He's stinking up the place."

"Madam President." Ashburn gulped. "What are you doing in the Pentagon?"

"Do not *ever* question me—I will go wherever I please, whenever I please; my travels do not require approval by you. Do you know what happens to people who disobey a direct order from me? Do you have any concept of that?"

"I'm sorry, but I didn't hear your communications. It was an error, and I didn't mean to—"

She got in his face. "Shut up, you despicable liar. An honest mistake I would tolerate, but *never* a lie and direct insubordination. Lack of communication *always* means 'no further action,' according to every military protocol in existence. You were a Naval officer, so you knew exactly what you were doing. There's a vid of the whole thing and we all watched you, until Kriger knocked you down. Better be glad I wasn't there, as you wouldn't have gotten up."

"It's a misunderstanding—"

"Right. You don't even have the balls to admit what you did—that's even worse." The fifty-six-year-old woman grabbed the five-ten man's shirt with her left hand, lifted him into the air by the collar, and slammed him against the wall like a rag doll. "You worthless piece of shit—you'll never work in this town again."

"That Russian thing damaged an Air Force pilot's plane. We think he's dead. So he killed a man, and *you're* threatening *me*. How dare you?"

"*How dare I?* You damaged the suit with that experimental EMP device attached to our fighters, something you weren't authorized to use, so you caused the incident. And you engineered this whole thing using advanced cyber-mirage technology that was classified to fool our pilots into thinking the Taraqis were attacking, endangering dozens of pilots and millions of dollars' worth of aircraft. Where did you get that tech, and who else helped you?"

"You can't prove any of that."

"Not yet, but I will, DSD is working on decrypting your computer as we speak, it won't take very long."

"I am the Secretary of Defense, and I don't have time to run every little detail past you regarding the safety of this country. There's a goddamn alien out there. If you don't care about America, I do. My God. Who's the real traitor here, Ma'am?"

"Shut the hell up." She snarled angrily at him and slammed him down. "And you won't have to worry about the 'alien' any longer, 'cause you're out of a job, loser."

"You loudmouthed fat bitch. I've got friends, you know."

She slapped the right side of his face with her left hand.

"*Friends*? Are you kidding? I *own* this town, and no person with functioning brain cells would be *your* buddy now. Are you so stupid to think the Republican majority Senate and House won't vote my way on any damn thing I want? You're now blacklisted everywhere and will be quite fortunate to procure a job teaching middle school social studies in rural Saskatchewan, loser. Get the hell out of Washington—that is until I can prove you set all this up as some kind of test."

He shook his head. "You won't."

"Oh, I will, and very soon. The resources at my disposal are beyond your comprehension. *Then* you're going to prison. You will therefore surrender your passport to these fine gentlemen here."

He shook his head angrily as he stared up at her. "You can't do that without authority. You aren't God, you know."

She stared down at him again. "Authority? Are you nuts? Look around you. No, I'm not God, but I'm the closest thing to it you'll ever see, as you're likely going to the other place where it's much hotter. I can do any damn thing I want for the next four years—especially to an insect like you. So remember that."

He shrugged and brushed off his jacket. "Even gods have to answer to someone sometime, and you'll answer to what's out there soon. History has always proven that."

"Yes? How insightful, and I thank you for the heads up. But it sure as hell isn't to you, and the time ain't now. And I'm not afraid of your 'alien.' So get the hell out of Washington." She stormed out the corridor of the massive defense building, as dozens of military personnel saluted.

The message sent was loud and clear: don't mess with the President of the United States, or good luck trying to find another job.

But, as Ashburn had said, he did have friends. Unfortunately, his new ones weren't the most ethical individuals. He probably also needed a good lawyer. He would worry about that last one later.

He was also doing things he wouldn't normally do, for reasons he didn't understand, as if someone had infiltrated his mind. He smiled as he realized he didn't care for some reason. There were bigger things on the horizon, things Wendy Mendoza had no concept of. And he knew he was going to come out ahead in the end. It didn't matter who fell on his way to the top of the heap.

• • •

M2 Multipurpose Air Vehicle
Somewhere over Western Alaska

"So, let me get this straight, Bella," Nick asked as the billion-dollar, fusion-powered stealth air vehicle streaked towards the west coast of Alaska. "*Mendoza the Miraculous,* who everyone except us thinks died in the nuclear explosion of *Darkkday,* sent out a telepathic message to you to fly out to Alaska, where we will find the lost child of legend somewhere in the Bering Strait, near Little Diomede. Did I miss any details?"

"That's about it, yeah. Except she's grown up now."

"Bonnie or Aurora is grown up?"

She frowned. "Very funny."

He shook his head. "Humor was not my intent, as that question has much relevance to how insane this all is. And we're supposed to believe that, after all these years? I know Bonnie's alive, out here somewhere with Aurora and Uncle Jim, but I never believed any of this astral projection stuff. I thought it was just between her and Jay, for one thing. Both of them tend to exaggerate."

"Believe what you want, *Tinman,* we're going out there. You said yourself that *Golfer* claims the perturbations in gravity end up leading to Alaska. If you have any faith in my parsimony abilities, then trust me. We're almost there."

"I guess somehow I believe all this stuff or I wouldn't be here in the first place, although it sounds improbable it could happen this way," the massive bearded Dutchman asked from the back seat.

"Be quiet, *Orthoman,* no one asked your big sorry butt. Seeing is believing." She looked around for several seconds and then pointed to her right. "Over there, at the base of that snow bank."

"Nothing's there," Nick said. "Conventional instruments detect zilch, except for a little heat."

"She's down there, I'm telling you. The interior of that cave is far too warm when compared to other surrounding caves, per our sophisticated thermal imaging. Something of relatively small mass is generating the energy. I'm scanning for weak gamma radiation."

"A variety of large mammals live around here. Wolves, Kodiak bears, etc., so it could be a group of them."

"Animals don't give off the extremely faint low energy gamma signature of plutonium-238, which has to be the damaged Vladimirov suit. Even if the electronics are broken, the isotope still exists."

"Damn straight. I surely am confused."

"Land it, *Tinman*. Here."

"Yes'm." Nick pulled the hovercraft to the mouth of the cave. "Juriann, how are you doing?"

"Good, I guess. Maybe not for long, I have a hunch."

"You're up, big guy," she said. "You go in first; be sure to let us know if you find anything."

"I want to believe, but why do you think Aurora is in that rock formation?"

"A gut feeling. Also, the temperature and faint radiation readings from my sensor goggles and the vehicle's instrumentation. We need to find her before the military does, as we don't want our nation's finest troops getting creamed."

"I will therefore go forth and discover."

"Juriann," Bella said.

"What?"

"Don't get yourself hurt, now. We just met you."

"What makes you think I can be hurt?"

"I just have a feeling, trust me, so be careful. Angry teenage girls are nothing to tangle with, especially without makeup and with their clothes a mess. You have no idea, boy."

"I have no idea what you're talking about."

"You wanted to find Aurora the Angel, so here you go, son, you're gonna get your wish."

"I guess the old American saying is right, after all."

"Which is?" Bella asked.

"Be careful what you wish for, as you might just get it." Juriann put on his snow gear, exited the hovercraft, and ran towards the opening of the cave two hundred meters away.

Chapter Thirty-Four

Paige had nodded off to sleep out of boredom as Russ woke up suddenly, apparently having heard something

"Um, Paige, there's someone coming in here."

"Wha?" she asked sleepily. "Really? Has the military discovered us? Do I need to mount a defense?" She suddenly sprung to her feet like a jack-in-the-box. "Let me at 'em."

"I don't know who it is, but I don't think he's from any military branch I've ever seen. Damn."

She rose up and heard the footsteps. "One person? You must be kidding. Who dares to interrupt my nap, sap?"

"I am here to help you, friend."

She walked towards the deep European voice, which seemed to be exactly seventy-three feet away. "You are no friend of mine yet; my friendship must be earned, large one. Who the heck are you, weirdo? You sound peculiar."

"The one who left me as an infant in the Netherlands claimed that I might be a long-lost relative. I was sent to find you, to determine that for myself."

"Why would I give a crap about that? Maybe you should scat."

"What's your name, guy?" Russ asked politely.

"Juriann. Juriann Hultaar." He was coming closer, and he was big, about six-four or five, at least, judging from the direction of his voice. He was approximately thirty-five feet away now.

She didn't like strangers approaching her, especially when she was in a foul mood and sitting in a cold cave in Alaska.

She shook her head. "Sorry, no bells ring, dingaling. Is that name supposed to mean something to me? Depart now, pal, or you will soon feel mighty crummy, dummy."

"Paige," Russ said, "I know you can't see, but this dude is awfully big, so why start insulting him? Have you no diplomacy?"

"No. Stupid question." She stared blankly into space. "Yeah, that really scares me. So? You got something else?"

"I guess my name means little to you, but rest assured, I am no dummy."

"Listen, dude, if you attempt to debate with me, I will have you calling yourself a dummy as well as many other pejorative adjectives in no time. Just you wait."

"You certainly talk a lot. Anyway, you're shorter than I thought you would be. What are you, seventeen?"

"I am eighteen, bumbling behemoth bozo. And my height and chronological age are irrelevant and none of your beeswax; those are the irrefutable facts."

"'None of my beeswax?' I don't understand this saying."

"Of course, 'cause you are stupid. I may be less than a third your mass, but I pack a pretty mean punch; make no mistake about *that*."

"I hate to squabble, but—so do I. You really don't want to find out. My colleagues await outside in their air vehicle to take us to—"

"I am not going anywhere in any 'air vehicle.' You may be going to the trauma hospital, however, so I hope your 'air vehicle' is fast and built to last."

"What? The closest trauma hospital must be several hundred miles away."

She nodded. "As I said, you will be going to the hospital; you have never been on the receiving end of my punches, and you will require no 'air vehicle' to get there, I assure you. Just keep it up for a one-way ticket to something that is *not* paradise, as this girl is not sugar and spice and everything nice."

"Did it ever occur to you that there are other beings as powerful as you in existence?"

She shook her head. "Nope, dope."

"Paige, listen to the man—" Russ exclaimed.

"Great, I do not need your input as well, as it is not swell." She moved her arms about. "Bring it on, Eurotrash. I have never really brawled with anyone, but I am *so* itching to do so. Do not piss me off anymore, or you will become very sore."

"I am not here to hurt you."

"What is that? *You* are not going to hurt *me?* Did I hear you correctly? I will literally kick your big butt back to Copenhagen or wherever you are from for that stupid remark."

"How insulting. I am Dutch, not Danish."

She snarled. "That minor fact will not alter the outcome, and I hated geography, by the way. Worthless subject."

She heard Russ approach closer. "Sir, perhaps you should leave before you get your large behind kicked. And, Paige, maybe you should shut up. Fighting doesn't solve anything—"

"Wrong." She turned towards Russ and nodded. "It shall solve one thing, and that is to make me feel lots better." She turned back towards Juriann. "Disrespect me, will you? You shall pay dearly for your intrusive insolence, irritating international imbecile."

"I assure you—my getting hurt is quite unlikely. I have the strength of over fifty men. I am far stronger than your mother."

"Wow." She laughed. "Over fifty men? That is *so* impressive."

"Yes. It is."

Russ spoke up. "Is this guy *really* a relative of yours? There isn't much family resemblance, although you both do talk kind of strange. Figures."

She shook her head. "I have no idea to what or whom you are referring, lout. And how do you know anything about my mother, loser?"

"Because she played a role in my youth, I believe. Such is the only explanation of my genesis and existence."

"Ooh, your 'genesis' and 'existence?' My." She slapped herself in the face with her left hand. "Man, that statement is profound beyond belief. You are as nutty as my mom is. *Fifty men?* Is that supposed to impress me?" The blind girl laughed and grasped for Juriann, who dodged her with ease.

"You can't grab what you can't see, young girl. I am swift, too."

She threw her hands down. "All right, I have had enough of this guy's garrulous garbage. Lt. Russ, duck and cover. Things may get a mite messy."

"Paige, he's pretty damn big. We don't know anything about this fellow, and I don't think fighting him is a good idea, even if you can maybe whip his butt—"

"*Maybe?* Do it, Russ—now!" She pointed to the end of the cave.

"Okay, okay—I'm goin' over to the corner of the cave here, so don't mind me. It's just very cold out here now that I'm not touching you."

"And, FYI, I hardly need to see you to crush you, idiot. Here, have some education on what *true* power is." She thrust her hands out and whipped her torso forward, which sent a massive shock wave towards him. "How do you like ten G's? Twenty?"

She could hear Juriann collapse to the ground. "Ack—how did you do that? I can barely move."

She shook her head. "I have no idea, and it really does not matter, now, does it?" Paige then grabbed him and threw him through the air into the cave wall about forty yards away, she judged from the sound of the echo after he hit. "*Fifty men?* That sucks big time for you. How about the strength of a million men, tough guy? Is that powerful enough for you?" Juriann gasped as she floated in the air and hovered over him.

"I mean you no harm, and I am sorry if I offended you."

She laughed. "Oh, yeah, *now* you are sorry. Too bad, too late, you shall soon meet your fate, as today is your expiration date."

"Why do you talk in rhymes?" Juriann asked curiously.

"You get used to it, dude, trust me," Russ said from across the cave. "I wouldn't draw attention to it if I were you, just saying; you don't seem to be ahead in this matchup so far."

"And you come here out of nowhere, grab me, and say you mean no harm? I am not violent by nature either, but you have surely gone too far; a harsh lesson shall be learned, my trust must be earned."

Juriann got up slowly, after a blow that would have shattered a normal man into a dozen pieces.

But he was far from a normal man.

"I don't want to quarrel—"

"Really? Well, take your best shot, it will take a lot."

"I guess he could be your cousin or something," Russ yelled from the corner of the cave, slapping his face.

"Russell, be quiet and stay out of this, please."

"Gladly."

She could hear him breathing hard. "I am—*not* your enemy. I am here to help you. I made a mistake, the way I approached you."

"Yeah, right, you certainly did. I may be blind but I am not unintelligent, dolt. You will therefore pay for your disrespect."

"I didn't say you were. But there are those who will want your power. I was sent to find you and bring you back before someone finds you, and also to seek some answers for myself."

"You and what army?" She picked him up. "No one 'brings' me anywhere, and I care not about your 'answers.' So, let us see if your hide is as tough as your big mouth, before I send your ass south."

"I am here with friends—"

"Anyone who would be your 'friend' is as stupid as you." She grabbed him and took off towards the cave exit, snow blowing in the air. "I hope you like to fly, sizeable sucker!"

"Oh, my God," Juriann said. "It's true, you *can* fly."

"No shit, Sherlock! You are one truly observant individual." He landed about two hundred feet to the north, she estimated (she could feel the sun and determine direction) as she tossed him that approximate distance to the south. "Come back for some more when you are done having fun, son." She then flew back to the cave entrance to find Russ, using the warmth of the sun as a guide.

She could hear him running up to the entrance. "What did you do to him? You didn't kill him, did you?"

She grinned. "No, of course not; he would have hit in about ten feet of snow. He's probably mighty cold by now, though."

"I am, too. Come back here and warm me up."

• • •

Bella looked down from the grounded hovercraft with her digital binoculars. "*Tinman,* I just saw our new buddy Juriann fly through the air about seventy yards after exiting that cave at breakneck speed. Holy cow, he was moving fast."

"That's crazy. No being, not even the amazing *Orthoman,* can fly. You must've seen something else, like a bird."

"A four hundred fifty pound bird, eh?" She smacked him on the leg. "Well, maybe he couldn't before, but he sure can now. Or someone really strong threw him a few moments earlier, since he moved in a parabolic trajectory after moving a short distance in a straight line. Probably not a Kodiak bear; rather, I imagine we've discovered exactly what we came for. Whether or not that's good or bad, I cannot yet opine."

"What? No way. Give me those." He wrestled the digi-binoculars from his wife. "It is him, he's getting up—slowly, but he's in one piece—and running to the cave opening again, about a quarter mile south. What the hell is he doing, and what's in there?"

"I believe 'it' is what we came for. Let's get down there before 'it' kicks the living crap out of him again."

• • •

She was sitting with Russ when he tapped her on the shoulder about three minutes later.

"What is it? Why are you disturbing me? I am not in an amorous mood, son, I do not desire to have fun."

"Uh, sorry to bring this up again, but your buddy's back."

"You must be kidding. His 'friends' must have ditched him and dumped him back here. That is what I would have done with that dummy, I find him to be mighty crummy." She got up and flew towards him, hearing his steps.

"Wait, don't—"

"Had enough? You did not get enough of flying?" She flew towards his voice, grabbed him, flew out of the cave entrance again, and took off into the sky this time. "Let us see you survive a fall from fifty thousand feet. Or, I can ram you a thousand feet into the ground. How would that be for you?"

"No, my God. You'll kill us."

She laughed. "I will kill 'us?' You, perhaps, but I am quite sure I shall survive the impact, that is a known fact, sorry if that statement lacks tact."

"I'm sorry, please put me down. I was just coming back in to apologize."

"Thought you would say 'uncle.' How far up are we, anyway?"

"About fifteen thousand feet, I suppose. Don't you know that?"

She laughed. "What? I have no idea. I have a rough estimate of direction from feeling the sun on my face, but that is about it."

"Don't you think it's rather careless to fly up fifteen thousand feet and not have any idea where you are?"

"Probably. I am on a roll today, it seems."

"That is an understatement."

"I guess we both got riled up a little bit. I never had someone threaten me before. For future reference, I do not like it."

He was getting his breath. "I *wasn't* threatening you, stubborn little girl. I'm sorry you took it that way." He gasped for air. "You wouldn't really have done it, would you?"

"What do you think? No, of course not. But I sure would have scared the hell out of you first."

"For a while there I wasn't sure."

"Yeah, well, you have learned lesson one about blind person etiquette—approaching and touching a sightless person to whom you are unfamiliar is a *very bad* idea, especially when she is exponentially stronger than you. It's rude, number one. Secondly, it can get you in a whole heap of trouble. And, by the way, let me know when we get close to the ground."

"Why do I need to do that?"

"Huh? You think I have a talking altimeter in my pocket? I just told you I cannot judge distances off the ground like I can on it, big man. I know when I have run exactly one hundred feet, for example, because of proprioception, but I cannot judge this."

"We're about fifty feet from the ground."

"Okay, get ready for landing." They hit the soft snow easily. "Where are we relative to the cave, dim-witted dullard?"

"About thirty yards. And don't call me that. My friends are approaching in their hovercraft."

"Hovercraft? So your friends did not ditch you, after all. What kind of crazy buddies do you have, and what losers would want to be your friend?" She ran back into the cave, and could hear him following.

"They are kind people of significant means. And perhaps more relatives of yours."

"If you are representative of my family, I do not need any more family members." She pointed towards the exit. "Just get out of here, or you will have much to fear."

"I will be back, momentarily."

She heard him run out the exit, hoping this would be the end of him. She knew, somehow, that would not be the case.

• • •

Nick flew the hovercraft to where Juriann had exited after his second trip inside the cave. They landed and both went over to the fast-moving body.

"You okay, *Orthoman?*" Bella asked. "You took a pretty good tumble out there just now."

"My ego is bruised more than anything. The female found inside that cave defies any description I could give."

"Wow, very profound. Let me go in there," Bella said.

"No way," Nick said. "Look at what she did to him."

"If it's her, she's my flesh and blood. I'm no threat."

"What if it's not?"

Juriann sat up and brushed the snow from his chest. "Bella, she isn't flesh and blood—but rather a young goddess in tatters. An obnoxious one with a very bad disposition, I might add."

"What do you expect from a teenager?"

"Maybe you can reason with the man who's in there with her, as she seems to have some emotional attachment to him. But she could easily have destroyed me if she had wanted. She didn't."

"Man? Really? Now I am interested."

• • •

"Paige." She heard a high-pitched female voice at the cave opening. Not again. Who the hell was this second stranger?

"Oh, no. Who are you, and how do you know my name? I do not like to be threatened, and I have had enough of your friend."

"*That* guy?" The woman laughed. "Heck, Juriann ain't my friend, we just found him lying around in the gutter someplace; the sooner we find him a home the better, but no one wants him. Go figure."

"Yeah, I do not blame them; after my interactions with him, I have concluded his brain is dim."

"He's smarter than he seems at a glance, give him a chance, you don't have to dance."

"And I do *not* find your attempts at humor amusing."

"Really? Most people think I'm pretty funny, honey."

"Huh. Well, you have found one who does not."

"And do I sound like I'm threatening?" She heard the woman walk up to her. "Feel how tall I am. I come up to your nose, almost."

She felt the top of the woman's parka; she seemed maybe five-four, five-five. "So you're a foot shorter and three hundred thirty pounds lighter than your pal, big deal. What do you people want from me? Why do you not just let me be?"

She felt Russ' hand on her shoulder. "Maybe they are really trying to help, Paige. We can't stay in this cave forever. I'm getting just a *little* bit cold here, even with your help. Plus, you didn't bring any food."

She snarled. "Your comfort is inconsequential and trivial, Russ. My parents said to always be wary of outsiders."

"Everyone needs someone. Right now we need them. Juriann, or whoever he is, seems to be someone special. Maybe the rest of the people are, too."

"Yeah. 'Special needs' in the brain department, for sure."

"Listen to this dude," Bella said. "He's got good advice, girly."

"Why should I? And don't call me 'girly,' or you will see me become extremely surly, ask the one who is burly."

"I will explain, if you'll just let me and stop kicking butts. Look, Juriann out there may not make the best entrance and lacks proper social etiquette, but he missed out on Cotillion when he was a little boy because he lived out in the sticks in the Netherlands. Can you fault the big lunkhead for that? Have a heart."

She laughed. "That was just a *little* bit funny."

"And your friend here's right. We're not from the government or the military. On the contrary, we want to keep them away from you and want to help."

"I need no help," Paige said. "I am no waifish whelp."

Bella walked around her in a circle and noticed that she seemed to track slightly, but didn't seem to notice much else. "Like your guy pal just said, everyone needs help at times, Paige, especially people who can't see. Let us be your eyes and help you out of here to become the great hero you strive to be."

"How do you know my name and that I cannot see? And why would that make me need help, anyway?"

"The first one took some homework, but you're not as stealthy as you think. You've left a bit of a trail, one that I've been following for years. The second one is fairly obvious, and pretty hard to hide. But, for now, let's get the hell out of here."

"I do not think I want to—"

"You just threw big *Orthoman* over there around like a little rag doll and took him for a grand ride into the wild blue yonder."

"*Orthoman?*" She howled with laughter. "If I may say, that is a supremely sorry sobriquet."

"Yeah, that's what he's callin' himself now. Your mom thought that one up."

"My mom? What do you know of my mom?"

"We'll talk about that later."

"His is not a very impressive name, it sounds rather lame."

"Agreed. But I doubt there's anything we can do to hurt you. You can't live the rest of your life down here. We've got food and shelter."

"I can. I need neither food nor shelter."

Russ punched her in the arm. "Um, I vote for food and shelter, if that counts for anything."

"Huh. It does not."

"Well, let's get out of here, Paige. I know who this woman is, although what she's doing down here and why she was with the big guy is puzzling beyond belief."

"What? How?"

"Trust me. It's all making sense now."

"Listen to him, Paige," Bella said. "We don't have that long until the military finds us, likely less than thirty minutes. My air vehicle is projecting an image-dampening field, but they'll show up soon. We may be able to talk our way out of it, given who we are, but it isn't worth the hassle."

"Who you are? What does that mean? Are you folks of some great importance? And why would that matter to me?"

"Are you kidding? They probably can talk their way out of anything," Russ whispered. "If they can't do that, they'll just buy the military, or the whole country."

"What does that mean? I do not care for such cryptic gibberish, since any military I can simply squish."

"Hush and get inside."

She warily rose up as they walked outside into the cold air.

"What the hell is this aircraft?" Russ asked. "This is far more advanced than anything I've ever seen."

"Is that supposed to mean something, pal?" Bella asked. "Who cares what you think?"

"Yeah, it is, lady, since I'm an Air Force officer and a military intelligence pilot."

"He's military? That's just great," Nick said. "Wonderful."

"Maybe you should be grateful to have my expertise at hand, sir. Take what you can get."

"Tinman, get us the hell out of here."

• • •

"Who are you? If you are here to harm me, then beware: I will take you all out in less than a minute."

"Would you *please* stop with the melodrama?" They entered the six-passenger hovercraft. "You have nothing to fear from us, Cheryl Paige Marshall," Bella said, "I am your family and am here to help you. Flyboy, we have plenty of doughnuts and coffee left over from the trip here."

"Thanks, that would be great, Ma'am." She heard him grab a doughnut from a sack; chewing noises logically followed.

"You just *have* to eat right now? Really?"

"I do," Russ mumbled. "I'm not you, obviously. Leaves more for me if you don't."

She sighed and turned her attention back to Bella. "Again, how do you know my name? And I have no blood relatives other than my mother."

Bella sighed. "Yes you do; your peculiar mom does not tell you everything. I suppose I get that. There's not many of us left, but you have to be grateful for what you have. But more important things first: who is this handsome military guy?"

"Hey, this man is a friend of mine, as if it is any of your business, lady, do not act so shady."

"Dear, good-looking young men are *always* my business. I may be married, but I ain't dead."

Russ laughed. "Stanton. Lt. Russell Stanton," he said.

"I do not understand any of this, as I have no family, and we have all that we need. I thank you for your assistance, wherever we are going, but this is confusing."

"Get in here, both of you. We need to get out of Dodge."

"Huh. I suppose I will go on your little ride for now, as it may be entertaining. I may decide otherwise later."

"Haven't you thought about anything? Where do you think the money for your instruments and such came from?"

"I guess I never thought of that. And your voice somehow sounds very familiar, even though we have not met."

"Yes, we have, many years ago, but you just don't remember. Why that is the case, and why you can't see, I don't know. These are all things we need to find out together."

"Huh. Am I to understand that you are someone famous?" she asked sarcastically. "I am rather hard to impress."

"Is she famous?" Russ said sarcastically as the craft took off,

heading southeast. "I know you can't see them, but I sure can, and I don't know why these people are out here, flying around in some billion-dollar, fusion-powered hovercraft. I would kill to fly something like this."

She poked him in the shoulder. "Then tell me, Russ. Get to the point, I am losing my patience at an exponential rate."

"Ma'am?" he said. "Care to explain to Paige? It's your show."

"Well, I suppose some folks might say I'm famous, but that isn't important now. My name is Isabel Mendoza; I am a chemical and mechanical engineer and own half of the energy company known as Mendoza Multinational. My husband, Nicholas Stannous, who is piloting the craft, owns the other half."

"M2? Located in Aurora City, Indiana?"

"Yes, for the most part, the main offices, anyway."

She thought for a moment. "You are therefore a member of the world-famous Mendoza family? I thought your voice sounded familiar."

"I am, for what it's worth."

"There is no love sincerer than the love of food."

"Huh? I don't get it, Paige. What does that mean? Are you hungry? We have plenty to eat on board. Or at least we did, until your buddy ate all the doughnuts."

"Sorry. They were good, though."

"I learned long ago never to wrestle with a pig. You get dirty, and besides, the pig likes it."

"I'm not following you."

She sighed heavily. "I will give you one more chance. *Progress is impossible without change, and those who cannot change their minds cannot change anything."*

"What are you rambling about? Change what?"

"Duh! George Bernard Shaw!"

"Come again?"

"You have a doctoral degree and do not know who he is? You have science smarts, yet clearly no appreciation of the arts."

"I do, I just don't see the relevance to this conversation."

"Yeesh. It is so obvious."

"Not to me. Flyboy?"

"You got me, Ma'am. Often hard to know what she's thinking, she's usually all over the place."

"What a surprise."

"Huh. Shaw is the only other person who has won both an Academy Award and a Nobel Prize, you are not very wise."

"Really? I thought I was the only one."

She shook her head. "Nope, he won a Nobel Prize for literature in 1933, and his Oscar twelve years later. He did not win one for chemistry, which I am sure is much harder."

"Why am I not surprised you would know that?"

"Why? Now I am the one who does not get it."

"You will in a minute."

"Lt. Russ? Help me—is this woman who she claims to be?"

"Yeah, Paige, it sure seems so, if you can believe that. Don't know how or why, but, yes."

"You have played the greatest women of science in indie films, such as Marie Curie, Hedy Lamarr, Emmy Noether, Rosalind Franklin, and Ada Byron, and you won the Oscar for your portrayal of your aunt, who is dead. Mom did not want me going to that movie, not that we get very many up at our theater anyway. And, yet, you are out here in the middle of nowhere? Why?"

"Well, I've got a news flash, Paige—my famous aunt isn't dead, she's somewhere in Alaska, communicating with me."

"What, with a radio? One capable of receiving signals from the great beyond? What a laugh."

"Not that far. North Pole, Alaska. You familiar with the place?"

"Yes, of course, but I do not understand. How could that—"

"Through the power of her mind. I didn't know that was possible until today. Also, she can communicate in limited fashion with our Uncle Jay."

"*Our* Uncle Jay? Who is this Jay? What do you mean by that?"

"I mean—Jay is the brother of each of our parents, which makes him our biological uncle."

She thought for a few seconds. "You cannot possibly mean Jaime Mendoza, the First Gentleman? You are therefore saying *we* are related? How can such a thing be possible?"

"Believe her," Russ said. "Think it through, Paige."

"Thanks, flyboy." She felt the woman grab her arm. "Yeah, missy. I'm your first cousin—your mother's niece. We share 12.5 percent of our DNA. None of my 12.5 has any super-powers, though. You seem to have a mouth like mine, though, so you for sure as hell inherited *that*."

"My *mother?* I am so confused. I wish I could see you to detect a resemblance. Lt. Russ? Do we look like each other? Is it possible I am related to this famous woman?"

A few seconds' pause. "Honestly, it sounds wild, but your facial features are very similar. You're taller and more heavily built regarding your bone structure and musculature, and have about the same skin tone but much lighter hair than she does; both her eyes are brown, your left one is deep blue—but, sure, it's very possible you're part Hispanic."

"Wait a minute, I thought I was half Russian."

"Nope, your mom cooked up that bizarre story, probably because that funky suit of armor takes commands in Russian," Bella said.

"What? How could you possibly have known that, about the battle suit? No one knows such things."

"I know lots of things, dear, this is just the beginning, trust me. And you look more like your dad, you got his and your mom's height. Me, I'm on the shorter side."

"But if I am truly your cousin, why are you just coming out here now, after all these years? It is a trifle too convenient, no?"

"Your folks tried to hide you from mainstream society, for reasons that should be obvious. You're the one who wanted to take on the Air Force all by yourself, so we're just helping you out."

"So what was my mother's name, then?"

"What? Are you really asking me that question? Lt. Russ? You are obviously intelligent, you have it figured out yet?"

"Yes. I said it back in the cave, and now I know I'm right."

"Well, not to me," she said. "Answer me, Isabel."

"Okay. Your mom's first surname is Mendoza, of course, just like mine. Mendoza Flores is her full name; mine is Mendoza Vasquez, as my second surname is my late mother's, while hers is my grandmother's."

She shook her head and laughed. "Now *that* is impossible. According to historical archives, mathematical genius Elisabeth Flores had only one daughter, Bonita, who died on *Darkkday*. You are suggesting *another* daughter not in the history books? I do not get it."

"Just like your mom, very naïve."

"Paige, she's confirming that you—are the one." Russ asked. "It's all true, the children's fairy tale."

"Children grow up," Bella said. "But you just said you saw for yourself, Lieutenant. Do you not believe the miracles that you see before you? Was all that stuff just a myth? I think not."

"Wait a minute. My mother is bright, but an eccentric, simple math teacher, almost a hermit. You are saying that—"

"She is many things, but certainly not simple, honey. Your mom, despite her childlike, immature exterior, is the most intelligent and complex human being I have ever known." Bella put her hand on her shoulder. "Yes, your mother, Petra Nureyev, or whatever alias she made up—is really Bonita Mendoza Flores. Do you know who that was?"

She nodded. "Of course, how ridiculous and inane, as well as insane. Mendoza was the Nobel physics laureate who was killed by terrorists over twelve years ago in a nuclear missile attack near Washington. She was, of course, also the discoverer of transuranium element 119, or mendozium-297, which allows the safe moderation of helium-3 and deuterium nuclear fusion on scales from very large to very small, with negligible toxic waste products. All high school science students know that. But the blast that killed she and her family was nuclear; no one could have survived it."

"But you two did, because *you* absorbed most of the blast, clearly while you were touching your mother."

"What?"

"Come on. Do you deny that your invulnerability, or whatever you call it, is conferred to someone you touch?"

"How could you know these things?" she shrieked. "No one besides my parents could know that."

"I told you how I know. But it's true, isn't it?"

She shook her head. "Yes, of course it is, but even I could not have absorbed something of that magnitude. It is impossible and something from a fable, no way am I able—"

"But *you* did, and you and Bonnie survived, somehow. After that, no one knows what happened. I have spent years trying to piece it together, and so has someone else."

"Who?"

"Another colorful relative we shall discuss momentarily, whom you might have heard of somewhere."

She shook her head. "If this did happen, I have no memory of these events. Why?"

"Post-traumatic amnesia is very common after such events, especially in young children."

"Amnesia? Are you a psychiatrist now, Cousin Isabel? As if that is even true."

"Why do you doubt me? You are a gift—maybe not from God, but sure as hell from somewhere. You had already lost your sight. The people who would have exploited you, the evil that is out there?"

"Shut up!" She stood up and pointed at Bella. "I am so confused. But, suppose you are right; if my mother is truly Bonnie Mendoza, then I can only be she—*Aurora Darkkin.*"

"Yes. That's correct."

"That statement is preposterous beyond comprehension. For one, my mom speaks with a perfect Russian accent. I am blind—therefore, I detect minor differences in voices and can identify most people's geographic location within a few hundred miles. I attest she speaks as a true Muscovite because I have studied linguistics, but she can easily suppress the accent and talk relatively normally on occasion."

"If you really knew linguistics, you'd know that's very hard to do for a real Russian, even for experienced actors."

"Maybe, but if she was really deaf, how could that be? Tell me that since you have all the answers."

"I don't know, Paige, no one can explain how she can hear now, but you must remember she was once a very good magician, adept at fooling people, within the boundaries of her limited social repertoire. When I was a little kid, she knew multiple languages, including Russian, although she had difficulty speaking them because of her deafness. *And* she is incredibly intelligent, do not ever underestimate that. A singular genius."

"I still do not believe it. Especially the intelligent part."

"You can't fathom that you are Aurora Angelica, the one felt to be the lost angel of legend? We built a vast memorial to you and what you represent. It is called Aurora City. We live there, as you mentioned."

"I still find all this improbable. I am by nature a trusting person, but also rather streetwise, unlike my mother, who may or may not actually be Bonnie Mendoza."

Bella laughed. "*Streetwise?* That's a hoot. What's the biggest city you've been to—Anchorage?"

She pointed her left thumb at her chest proudly. "Vancouver."

"Oh, boy. Not impressed."

"You will have to do far better than that to gain my confidence."

"I understand. If a big super-strong guy like weirdo *Orthoman* and a bunch of rich people in a hovercraft suddenly showed up to find me, I'd have my doubts, too."

"I resent that," Juriann said. "Bella, you can be as insulting as Kepler, although you are most certainly easier on the eyes."

"Be quiet, *Ortho*. On the other hand, you're kind of hard to believe, as well, and you hurt my eyes."

'That's pretty rude," Juriann said.

"Sorry, you're just not my type."

"But how shall we resolve this curious conflict, then?"

"Okay, here you go. You want me to tell you something that only a close relative would know? Would that do it for you?"

She nodded. "Perhaps. It would be a start, at least."

"Fair enough. On your right cheek is a large birthmark, a port-wine stain. It's unmistakable and almost shaped like a hand. It's also of a different consistency than your other skin and slightly raised, so you should be able to feel it even though you can't see it."

"Wrong," Russ said, laughing. "Paige doesn't have a port-wine stain on her cheek; surely you can see that. Some freckles, but no birthmark."

"Jeez. Not *that* cheek, my boy. The one down under, come on. I used to change your diapers, girl, 'cause I've seen it all."

She thought for a minute as tears came to her eyes. "Oh, my God, that is true. How could you have possibly known that? It's a trick. You have somehow accessed my medical records, and—"

Bella wiped her tears away. "It's not a trick, Aurora, I know because I'm your cousin and knew you when you were a baby. You have to believe me."

"All this is just too much to grasp. You all have existed for many years, and I am just finding about it now, wow."

"There's a bit more," Bella said.

Russ grabbed her shoulder. "Yeah, she's right, Paige, it just hit me: if Bonnie Mendoza is your mom, that means Alexander Dirk Darkkin was your dad, holy crap."

She thought about that for a minute. "Yes, of course, that means my father's sister, Mary Gwendolyn Gallinsworth—is my aunt."

"That, yes, and she and Jaime are both your biological aunt and uncle because Wendy is your father's sister and Jay, your mother's brother. You actually resemble her a bit. You are not nearly as tall or heavy, and your skin is much darker, but the facial features, your blue eye, freckles, hair—and some, uh, other things."

"What other things are you referring to? Be specific, even if they are not terrific."

"You must be kidding."

She shook her head. "Being without sight is my plight, so please bring your curious concept to light."

"My 'concept' concerns your boobies, hon. Very terrific."

"Huh?" She put her hands on the blanket covering her breasts. "These two little things?"

"They aren't little, ye of limited reference point. Your mom ain't got any, so you must've inherited yours from someone. They're not quite in The Great Dame's master class, but pretty good, nonetheless. I should know, being the vain, shallow individual I am."

"This is getting to be a somewhat awkward conversation, so let us change the subject." All these new relatives and their various combinations were confusing, and she didn't want to discuss female Darkkin anatomy. "Despite my disagreements over some of her policies, she is one of the greatest Presidents of all time."

Bella touched her face. "Yes, and thus a part of that, and those talents, resides inside you, now and forever. Despite our faults, we have to stick together, because we're the only Mendozas and Darkkins who are left."

• • •

They landed the hovercraft at the private landing strip after the three-hour flight back home, after dropping Russ off on some deserted road in northern North Dakota so he could radio for help. He had his own problems to deal with now, she was sure, as she kissed him as they departed. Ah, well, he was a big boy, and she had more interesting things to think about than someone who was likely to be a distraction and a hindrance right now, given his military affiliation.

"Where will Russell go? Was it appropriate to abandon him?"

"Relax. Minot Air Force Base is a couple of miles from where we left him. They'll take care of him, one way or the other."

"There is such a place in the middle of nowhere?"

"Yeah. He's maybe even been there, since missile silos are all over the place."

"The Air Force will not come after us, being so close to a base?"

"Not likely. This vessel is pretty stealthy and evades radar and thermal detection, and we're almost home, by the way."

"Huh? We are in Indiana already? That was a five thousand mile journey."

"Of course, it's pretty fast, and there's nothing else like it. That's why it costs a billion dollars."

"Impressive. Juriann is coming too? He has been rather quiet."

"I'm right here, and I'm rather tired, actually."

"Yeah, he's hangin' with us, but he lives in one of our condos. We're not sure yet what kind of relative he is to the Darkkins, but he seems to fit in."

"It's good to fit in someplace," Juriann said. "Just no more fights with Paige, I can't take it. Humility is a lesson I have learned with some difficulty."

"Okay, fella, just remember about my personal space; ask before entering it. It ain't that difficult of a concept."

He slapped her on the back. "Got it." She heard him get in his car, start the engine, and leave.

"Out here, dear," Bella said, helping her out.

She floated to the ground. "Where are we?"

"M2 west hangar, in Sulphur Springs."

"Never heard of that place. I hope it does not smell like it sounds. Like mercaptans, a strange scent for you industry captains."

"I'm surprised you even know what a mercaptan is!"

"An organosulfur compound that contains a carbon-bonded sulfhydryl group, the odorous component of rotten eggs. How is that for science? You know my mom, she made me memorize that stupid stuff and not a bunch of frivolous fluff."

"I'm impressed. And no one comes out here; there is some sulfur in the coal, so it does smell like mercaptans at times, but no one uses coal much these days. We'll drive to our house and get you cleaned up."

"How far away is that?"

"About ten minutes." She dozed off as they drove in the house, and she heard the garage door go up as they went in.

"I'll fix you something to eat, Paige," Bella said. "After you get showered up and dressed."

"But I don't have any clothes. Mine are in tatters, as you can see," she said, the blanket still wrapped around her.

Bella laughed. "Don't worry about such mundane matters, honey. We entertain a lot, as you probably can imagine, being the global corporate jet-setters we are. So, we have clothing—casual and formal—in all sizes for all genders, for folks who spill wine on themselves, rip a stocking, tear their slacks climbing the rock wall or playing football or basketball, set themselves on fire—"

"*Set themselves on fire?* What kinds of parties do you have here? It sounds like fun, although dangerous."

"Oh, my, you don't want to know that. *Tinman* likes to play with fireworks."

"Who?"

"My husband, who was piloting the hovercraft. I'll explain later. And what we don't have, I can easily have delivered."

"Oh, Nick. Weird nickname."

They went upstairs. "Here, you can have the bedroom next to Jose's. I guess you don't have any luggage to take up."

"Jose?"

"My son."

She thought for a moment. "Named after your twin brother. I remember reading about him. I am so sorry for your loss."

Bella gave her a hug. "No problem, we all have our losses. His middle name is Alexander, which was your dad's name. He's in bed now; you can meet him later in the morning when he gets up."

Bella oriented her to the room, where the bathroom was, the dresser, nightstand, etc. She took off the tattered clothes that the wolf had torn and put them on the bed. She got into the large shower and turned on the faucet. It was warm, and the whole area smelled faintly of rose oil. Even though she didn't perceive discomfort, such as feeling too hot or too cold, she did feel pleasure with touch. She felt the small scratches the wolf had made in the outer epidermal layer. It would heal in a couple of days.

She found a woman's razor, then sat on the bench in the bathroom and shaved her legs and armpits after applying some sweet-smelling shaving cream. Her hair grew at a normal rate, and she could still scratch the outer epidermal layer if she didn't use a lubricant. She then washed off the hair in the shower, dried off again, and felt for the toothpaste and toothbrush. She didn't appear to be affected by tooth decay but didn't like the feeling when her teeth had not been brushed. And she could develop halitosis if she didn't brush regularly, meaning that she apparently did harbor some normal oral flora.

She put on what felt like a sweatsuit and socks, tied her shoulder-length hair back with a hair tie she had found on the dresser, and went back downstairs.

"Bella?"

"Yes." She went towards the smell of cooking eggs. "You navigate pretty well for being in an unfamiliar house."

"Well, most houses are similar, only this one is a lot bigger than any I have been in. What time is it?"

"Almost five in the morning."

"Wow. Do you normally get up this early?"

Bella laughed. "Not usually, I'm more of a night owl, and I would typically be going to bed about now. This is just for you."

"I am honored."

"You getting around okay? This house wasn't really designed for the visually impaired; in fact, it can be quite hazardous."

"Do not worry about me. I remember going upstairs. Once I have been to a place, I can usually retrace my steps and come back the same way. I run seven miles each way to school and back each way by myself in fifty minutes, it is no problem."

"Wow, I couldn't run seven miles under any circumstances, and I can see. There might be a stray toy or two on the floor; watch out for those, as they can cause quite a spill."

"No problem, I am used to stumbling over my mom's toys and such. I can catch and right myself before I hit the ground; on that topic I will not bother to expound."

"Doesn't sound like she's changed much."

"Huh? Really?"

"No. Whenever I went to her place as a kid, I laughed at how messy it was all the time, but it was fun for Jose and me when we visited, as you never knew what weird stuff you would find there. Scrambled eggs and sausage okay?"

"Sure, that is great, I am not picky, as my eating habits are not tricky. But you do not have to fix a meal for me, especially when you should be sleeping."

"Yes, of course I do, but don't thank me until you've tasted it, as I'm not known for my cooking. This could be somewhat of a culinary adventure."

"Perhaps it is genetic. Mom's cooking could make even me sick, it has been theorized. It is perhaps lethal."

"Doubt that mine is as bad as your mom's, sorry."

"I am sure you are right, as my mom's meals are no delight."

"Well, I didn't know if you had any special dietary requirements or not, you being a little different from us and all."

She shook her head. "None that I am aware of. I can eat a lot or a little, it does not seem to matter. Sometimes I am hungry, sometimes not, but I always seem to stay the same size. Often I wish I could lose a little. I don't work as hard at is as I should."

"Lord, I wish I could do that. Pushing forty in a few years. I'm with the personal trainer two hours a day now. Maybe that won't happen to you."

"Becoming forty? I am certain I will succumb to that terrible fate as well; it will not be swell, Isabel."

"No, having to work out to keep from getting fat."

"I do not know much about myself, but that does not seem to be a problem." She shook her head. "But I may not even live to be nineteen, at the rate I am going."

"What? You just turned eighteen a couple of weeks ago."

"Exactly my point." She scratched her head. "Look what trouble I have gotten into already. But how did you know that?"

"Your birthday is only a week after mine, which is October 16. See, I know a lot about you, as only your cousin could."

She felt the kitchen table and sat down in one of the chairs.

"Coffee?"

"That would be great, with some cream and sugar. Also, some milk if it's not too much trouble."

"Are you kidding? *Mi casa es su casa*. Now and always."

"Where's Nick?"

"He went downtown to do some work in his office. He likes to get an early start on his day."

"At five AM? I am usually comatose at that time."

"Yeah, he's pretty busy, you know. He hardly ever sleeps."

"That craft we were in—while I could not see it, I doubt it is standard issue. How and why do you have something like that?"

"We have a lot of high-tech stuff. I'm a pilot too, and I can also fly that thing—but it's *Tinman's* baby."

"*Tinman?* I do not get that nickname." She shook her head. "He does not seem to resemble the Wizard of Oz character, and you are certainly no Dorothy."

"Isn't it obvious? His last name? *Stannous?*"

"Uh, sorry, not getting it."

"The +2 cation of tin? *Tinman?*"

She shook her head again and smiled. "Whoa, you are way beyond me. Never heard of a 'cation,' and if I did, I forgot what it was a long time ago and am sure glad I did."

"I don't understand. You knew what a mercaptan was."

"That was a random, coincidental, one-time event."

"A cation is an ion that has lost one or more electrons, giving it a positive charge. An anion has received them and has a negative charge. Does that help?"

She shook her head. "No, it does not. I am not very scientifically inclined, if you have not determined that already, so it has little relevance to me. Moreover, I also could care less."

"I keep forgetting, but that's okay."

"By the way, do you ever call your husband by his name instead of *Tinman?*"

"No, but sometimes I call him other things I won't repeat when he does stupid stuff, which is often. Anyway, who was that pilot dude? Why were you with him anyway?"

"I thought the Tosians or North Koreans were attacking, so I went out there to help."

"How could you have possibly known that?"

"I have all kinds of military scanners and other illicit listening devices in my room as part of my entertainment center."

"I suppose I have some idea where those came from. But help me understand how you went from listening to that to actually being out there."

"I went out to the underground cave I dug, put on the suit, and flew out there."

"Just like that?"

"That is just about it, yes. Pretty routine."

"Mom and Dad helped you?"

"Create the hideout, yes, of course." She shook her head. "But, no, they knew nothing of this particular escapade."

"Who, then?"

"Huh. I have done it numerous times, not that hard to figure it out on my own. Most of the stuff is voice-activated, anyway."

"It doesn't seem like a very intelligent thing to have done."

"Agreed. It seems to all have been a hoax, and it was not a very smart thing to have done at all, so much for listening to encrypted military radio transmissions when I should have been studying. My suit went dead before I collided with his plane, so he had to eject. My electronics were damaged, so I could not see."

"And you ended up with him in that cave. How did you even find him?"

"I heard someone yelling. In addition to my other abilities, I can pull an object towards me. It is easier if it is in free fall."

"I didn't know if your mom could do the limited astral projection stuff with you. I still don't get it; I thought she had lost that ability when she lost her hearing."

She took a sip of coffee and paused. "*What?* My mother is not deaf, and I know not of this strange ability you mention. But Russell was the one yelling, not Mom. She has extremely good hearing, actually. Far better than anyone I have known. Just try whispering in her classroom, and you will surely see doing so is no time of glorious glee."

"Bonnie Mendoza was deaf. We've been through all that."

"Yeah, I guess." Spare for a minute, scratching her head. "That contributes to my continued confusion as to how they can possibly be the same individual."

"No one's sure, but there were many people down at Ground Zero who, soon after the explosion, experienced improvement in medical conditions, from mild to immense. Some people in wheelchairs started walking again. People with advanced cancer went into remission. That's how the whole Aurora the Angel thing started: that somehow your sacrifice caused the release of some type of mystical energy—holy energy, some even thought."

"That is ridiculous. 'Holy energy.' Only people with holes in their heads could believe that garbage."

"Only because you know differently. Your powers are beyond any science we could comprehend. And a charm bracelet of yours was found later, the only object from that explosion known to have survived intact. That's *another* reason."

"A charm bracelet of mine? Did I have it as a child?"

"Yes."

"How does anyone know that?"

"Because it's engraved with your name. It was slightly scratched by hitting some rocks when it fell, but it otherwise was unharmed.

It's small but made of an extremely hard rare-earth alloy."

"Where is it now?"

"I believe it is at the White House, as Jay and Wendy are your closest living relatives. I'm sure the bracelet will eventually be returned to you. We could drop in for a visit."

"We could? No way."

"Of course, we have an open invitation to stay at the residence any time we want. Wouldn't that be a shock to show up with you?"

She took a sip of coffee. "I have not thought about them much or how that is going to happen. How shall it be made known to them that I exist?"

"I haven't thought that one through yet, honey. Wendy's a busy lady. She fools a lot of people with that aw-shucks country persona, but she's extraordinarily intelligent, make no mistake about that. She surely already knows you exist but is not letting on she knows."

"What does that mean?"

"I'm certain your step-dad, being the stealthy sort he is, was great at covering stuff up. But as covert and tech-savvy as he is, he's no match for the resources of the President. The only logical conclusion is that she was assisting in the process somehow."

"Why?"

"Because she's your family, and because she didn't want others finding out about you. Many would want to experiment on you, exploit you. She has her issues but won't let that happen."

"But—holy energy? There are those that think I am divine, the Second Coming? I have been through that over and over with my father. We have concluded multiple times that I am not worthy of such an honor; in many ways, I am a real yawner."

"Of course you're not Christ 2.0, but how could you not think people would believe you are? A lot of lesser people than you have been held up to be gods. They want something noble and good to believe in when the big bad world gets too much out there."

She shook her head and laughed. "That is absurd beyond belief. I have been arrested, I have smoked, drank booze, and I am as far from being a saint as you could ever imagine."

Bella put her arm around her. "Look, I did all that stuff as a teenager, too, so you're in very good company," she whispered. "Except being arrested, probably because my dad was a cop, but I probably should've been a couple of times."

"What for?"

"The usual things. Underage drinking, most likely. Why, does that surprise you?"

"Not really. I expected as much."

"Anyway, that Lt. Russ guy is pretty good-looking."

"I know." She smiled.

"How do you know, if you don't mind my asking, and since you just met him while flying blindly through the sky?"

She laughed. "No, no, I know because I had met him before, at a career fair at my high school, and I have actually been out with him. He is stationed at Eielson Air Force Base, conveniently only twelve miles from North Pole."

"What? The fella whose plane your suit destroyed just happens to be a guy you met at the teenybopper career fair? What are the chances of that?"

"Huh, I know not, as I am not a mathematician. Perhaps my mother would know the odds of such a thing."

"Hmmm. That sure clears up why you kissed him when we let him off."

"Yeah." She smiled.

"So, you're in high school, and an Air Force lieutenant went out with you? That seems somewhat inappropriate. Paige, I'm shocked beyond belief at such behavior."

"Are you really? I detect some sarcasm in your voice."

Bella laughed. "No, not so much. You seem in most ways like a typical teenager."

"I am sure my parents would not have approved; I doubt that your parents approved of everything you did."

"You got me there. I'm sorry we had to let him off in wonderful scenic Minot, but Russ being here right now just wouldn't have worked out, especially with him in the military and all. His people are invariably looking for him, and, despite the fact we have a number of military contracts, *Tinman* and I are extremely skeptical of the military's motives these days."

"Why? I assumed you would be in cahoots with the President."

"Hey, now, wait a minute, don't wear out your welcome so quickly by being insulting. I can tolerate a lot from my little cousin, but I have limits."

"I am not sure I understand."

"Jay may be our uncle, and Wendy your aunt, but the *Tinman* and I don't agree with all her policies. I may be a card-carrying Republican and go to some fund-raisers and contribute to her PAC, and I even spoke at the last convention, but it ends there, Paige. I assure you that no one tells *me* what to do, least of all *her*. I can hold my own with any human being in existence."

"Sorry."

Bella laughed and slapped her on the back. "There's no need to apologize to me, ever, as my skin is pretty darn thick. But tell me more about Russell."

"He seems to like me because of my quick wit. We went out for coffee and to the movies once."

"Movies?"

"He saw about as much of the movie as I did."

Bella slapped her on the back again. "Wow. Atta girl. Did he know about, you know—"

"No, of course not; it probably would have scared him silly, that I am descended from a hillbilly. He certainly does now, though, after our little 'incident.'"

"That still doesn't explain how you know what he looks like."

"Others told me he was hot, and I can tell what someone looks like by feeling his or her face."

"Huh, I never thought of that. Feel mine and tell me what I look like."

She took her hands and ran them over Bella's face, probing every detail. After a few minutes, she stopped. "You do not look much like my mom at all, even though you played her in a movie. You have a widow's peak like she and I do, though. Like Lt. Russ said, we do resemble each other a bit."

"Those are both genetic characteristics, so you can see how it was passed along. Autosomal dominant, I believe."

She smiled. "That is Greek to me, Mrs. Stannous. Like I said, science is not my language."

"Never mind." She heard the dishes clatter in the sink as Bella gathered them. "Well, we need to go get some sleep, as I'm exhausted. Do you sleep like a normal person?"

"I guess so. I do not seem to notice either way. If I have to stay up all night doing a school assignment I forgot about, I seem to be fine the next day."

"How often does that happen?"

"Quite frequently. I am a proficient procrastinator."

Bella laughed. "Another thing I used to do as a teenager which drove my folks and my Grandma Flores nuts before I grew up and learned to take my studies seriously. Do you?"

"Do I what?"

"Take your studies seriously?"

"No, not really. My mom hounds me all the time in a futile effort to improve my science and mathematical skills. It is a lost cause, maybe because I do not see the point, sorry to disappoint."

"You don't see the point?"

"Not that it is not important, just that I like other things. There are plenty of mathematicians and scientists."

"Okay, then you'll have to be good at something else. Science isn't everything."

"As you can see, I am fairly good at arguing."

"We'll definitely find a career choice which fits you." She heard the clink of the dishes being placed in the sink. "Well, I'm taking a breather. Why don't you go get some rest, too?"

"Maybe I will. I am a tad fatigued, at that." Mentally, at least.

• • •

Minot Air Force Base
210 Missile Avenue
Minot, North Dakota

Lt. Russell Stanton was ushered into the conference room after being picked up by sentries about twenty minutes after the M2 hovercraft had dropped him off in northern North Dakota and sent an anonymous signal beacon to Air Command. He was struggling, trying to think of a good story, to back up what he had told the colonel when they arrived at the base commander's station.

"Stanton, I again want to thank you for giving me the most interesting experience I've ever had here," Col. Tom Walker said, with a blank expression on his face. "Hearing word of the MPs finding you in Ruthville on Highway 83 was the highlight of my tenure here, while Alaskan Air Command thought you were dead."

"You're welcome, Colonel Walker," Russ said, smiling. "Always happy to be of assistance."

"You think this is funny? I sure as hell don't. You expect me to believe that piece of shit story, Lieutenant? You interacted with the alien for several hours, and then it just left you in Ruthville?"

"No, sir. I mean, yes, sir. Funny, no. Believe it—yes, sir."

"Yeah. We found you out in the middle of nowhere on a deserted road two miles from here, where you had supposedly been gone hours after being shot down over 3,000 miles away, out in the elements, yet we just find you, after an incredibly convenient anonymous radio call from a military-grade encrypted source, seemingly okay, and not all that hungry. You should've been a man barely alive, but here you are, Stanton. Seems rather convenient."

"Just lucky, I guess. Good to learn those survival of the fittest skills at the Academy, as they definitely came in handy."

"Huh. 'Survival of the fattest' is more like it. There are particles of sugar frosting on your lips where you've been eating." Walker pointed angrily at him. "Don't you dare smart off to me, Lieutenant. You were none the worse for wear, despite your terrible 'ordeal.' Tell me more about the interaction you had with the thing that was in that suit."

He nodded. "I flew with her, sir, and she's not a thing, but a very human young woman."

"Come on. You know for certain it was a woman?"

He nodded, smiling sardonically. "I sure do."

"I suppose I don't need to ask how you know *that,* given your reputation conveyed by a couple of your former Academy classmates who are stationed here."

He nodded. "Agreed, sir. Best not to discuss the details of my sordid past."

"Who is she? Where did she come from? How the hell does she fly? Is she a Russian?"

"Like I said, I don't know, except that she sounds American. She disappeared, and I didn't see her again, and she said she would send out a signal so someone could find me."

"What did she look like?"

"Kind of tall, dark hair, attractive. I was kind of worried about other things, you know, like staying alive."

"Yeah, you look so emaciated. That's the shittiest explanation I've ever heard."

"Probably so, sir."

"Is that all you've got, Lieutenant? Just because I'm out here in Minot doesn't mean I can't ream your butt."

"Yessir, understood, Colonel."

"We got some anonymous tip to look for you right outside the base. Who the hell did that? You said she did, is that right?"

"I can't tell you, sir. I did say that she sent a signal out. How she did that I don't know."

"That's an order, Lieutenant. How did you get here?"

"I get it, sir, but I can't help you or even myself." He frowned. "Look, sir. You can throw me in the brig, put me on toilet scrubbing duty, or whatever, but this represents something many pay grades higher than you or me, and I can't give you any more information. I'm sure there will be round two, with all kinds of federal people, but you'll get the same answer as now. I'm not trying to be evasive, but that's the truth."

"I'm trying to help you, son."

"No disrespect, Colonel, but you're trying to help yourself."

"What? I have my superiors, too, and I don't want any trouble for you or me. Everyone likes you, Stanton, from what I've heard, but there are limits. This is a national security matter!"

He opened his arms wide. "Do you think I do? I'm telling you, sir, let it go, or there will be major league trouble for both of us. Guaranteed."

"What the hell's that supposed to mean, Stanton?"

"You mentioned your boss. Well, he has a boss who has a boss, and so on. Until it stops at the top. I can't tell you why or how, but that's how it is."

"I don't give a shit." Walker's Tekphone went off, and he looked at the caller ID. "Yeah, Walker here. He's still here, yessir." Walker paused for a few seconds as he suddenly frowned. "You want me to do *what*? I'm sorry, sir, but that's fucking bullshit." There was a pause for several seconds as Walker sighed. "Yes, sir. Got it."

"Who was that?"

"Shut up." Walker scowled. "Get your sorry butt out of here, Stanton, and get back to Eielson the best way you can. Some ultra-high level spooks just told the Air Force Secretariat to forget about all this, so I guess I'll have to, but I don't want to hear any more about it or see you ever again."

"I don't either, sir." He saluted and left as quickly as he could, strategizing how he would get back to Alaska.

• • •

Stannous Residence
8330 Eagledale Circle
Aurora City, Indiana

After about two hours' sleep, Paige decided to get up. Bella must still be in bed, she thought. She didn't need a whole lot of sleep and was still wound up by all the commotion. It was hard to believe that, a few hours ago, she had her armor blown up, and now she was sitting in the lap of luxury in her fabulously wealthy cousin's home.

She meandered into the kitchen and sat at the table for several minutes. She was lost in her daydreams as she heard someone else sit at the table. Small footsteps.

"Hello?" she asked.

"Who are you?" She heard the child's voice. "I don't remember seeing you before."

"My name's Paige. I am a, er, cousin of your dad's." She hadn't thought how she would explain her sudden appearance, but that was a good a story as any and technically true (her stepfather was the boy's biological great uncle).

"I learned what a cousin is a few weeks ago. Mine was Aurora. She died." She heard him pour some breakfast cereal: frosted corn flakes, by the smell. "I have another cousin, Will. He lives in a big white house, 'cause his mommy is the President."

She opened her mouth wide, amazed that this small child knew such profound things. "I am sorry Aurora died. I heard she was a very good person."

"Yeah, me too, she was very pretty. But I didn't know Daddy had any cousins around here except for Burt and Allison. Those are Uncle John's two kids who live pretty close; they come over a lot."

"I am not. I am from very far away."

"Don't sound like you're from far away. You from some other country? Hey, your skin is a little darker than mine, about like Mommy's, but your hair is much lighter. That's cool."

"No, I am an American." She laughed. "Another world, maybe, but not another country. I do not sound like that, do I?"

"Huh, no. That doesn't make sense. If you are Daddy's cousin, then you must be mine, too, right?"

"I guess that would be correct. You must be Jose. Your mom told me so much about you." She touched his face. "Can I feel your face, Jose?"

"Huh? What you want to do that for?"

"I cannot see, Jose. I must learn what other people look like by feeling their faces."

"Okay, sure." She felt his face for a few minutes, then smiled.

"You look like your mom a lot."

"What about my dad?"

"Ha. I do not know because I did not feel his face." She took a sip of juice. "You know, you are pretty darn smart for being only five years old."

"How do you know that I'm five and if I'm smart or not?"

"Your mom told me how old you were. And your vocabulary is at the level of a twelve-year-old. Very impressive."

"Huh, I don't understand that word. You talk kind of like a grownup." She heard him munch on the crunchy cereal. "Will you play cars with me after we finish breakfast?"

"Sure. But kids today still play with toy cars? I thought you'd have all kinds of fancy electronic toys and things."

"You look and sound like a kid, too, except you use big words."

She pointed her thumb at her chest. "I happen to be eighteen."

"That's real old, but you still look and sound like a kid. But, nah. I have all that fancy stuff, but I like playing with Gramps' toy cars he had when he was a kid most of all."

"Why? Because you know he prized them and had lots of fun with them, right? Those are the best toys you can have." She grimaced as she thought of her mom's toys that she certainly didn't prize. It might be time to see Mom in a new light, though, after learning the truth.

The truth, right. She also was seeing them in another way—as parents who hid things from her for twelve years. She didn't want to think about that now.

"What kinds of toys did you have as a kid, Paige?"

"I had lots of musical toys and things to make sculptures."

"I guess that makes sense, but you talk kind of complicated. Gramps kept them in the case and everything. He has over two hundred—ambulances, police cars, concrete mixers, race cars, trucks." She felt him hand her the cereal box and a bowl. "You want some cereal too?"

"Sure, that would be good, although your mom fixed me some breakfast a few hours ago. But second breakfasts are the best, especially those with minimal nutritional value."

• • •

They went to the living room, where she sat down and touched some of the toy cars. She had a few when she was a kid. She laughed at herself. Like she was some big adult now at eighteen. She felt the different textures of them; a concrete mixer, one that must be an ambulance, a police car, a dump truck. She could feel the small bumps on the top of the boxy ones that must be flashing lights. Like Mom had told her, she realized she must have seen such vehicles at some point in order to recognize them by touch now.

"Let's play drive-in movie, Paige."

"How do we do that? And what is a drive-in movie? It sounds really groovy."

"They're old places where you drive your car into a big parking lot, sit in it, and watch the movie on a giant screen."

"Huh. I never heard of that."

"Gramps and Nana said there were lots of them when they grew up, but they closed them all because no one wants to sit in cars to watch movies since you can get anything you want right away online. But we have one in town my mommy bought."

"Your mom bought a whole drive-in movie? That seems rather extravagant."

"What's that mean? You got lots of big words for a kid."

"Extravagant? It means buying stuff that costs a lot of money that you do not really need."

"Huh. Well, it's old and not real fancy, so I don't know how much it cost. But she bought it to save it from being torn down, so others could see it too, and they have rides and stuff for kids on the weekends, along with the movies. So people do need it. You can eat popcorn and drink pop and do anything you want, all for free. Mommy doesn't let me have all I want, though. Do you like popcorn?"

"Sure. I do not go to many movies, though."

"Oh, yeah. I forgot you can't see. That would be boring."

She laughed and smiled at him. "No, it is not that, Jose, just that there are not many movie theaters where I come from."

"Where's that?"

"Alaska."

"That's pretty far away, I think. You ride on a dogsled and stuff and live in an igloo? I heard you kiss by rubbing noses."

She laughed. "No, not really, it is not that different than here, although it is much colder, but not all the time. In winter, we have maybe four hours of sunlight, but in summer, the day lasts twenty hours."

"Wow. In the summer, it's light almost all night?"

She nodded. "Most of it, yes, although I cannot fully appreciate that, obviously."

"So you could stay out all night and play?"

"If your parents let you do that, then, yes. We have cars, stores, and other things just like here, but it's just a lot more spread out." She rolled a car on the carpet. "So, how do we play?"

"Just pull your cars up to the TV set and pretend they're watching the movie."

"You might want to turn the TV on first or they shall have nothing to look at."

"Oh, yeah. There are probably some good cartoons on now. Do you like cartoons?"

"I do."

"What are your favorites?"

"I do not know, the old ones, I guess."

"My aunt used to do cartoons and she can do some pretty neat voices, they make me laugh."

"This I have heard, I hope to experience that soon live and in person. I suppose you can watch those or anything else whenever you want."

"Yeah. Sometimes that gets boring, though. How long are you staying with us, Paige?"

She hadn't thought this through very far, although the turn of events had been unpredictable. "I have no idea. Maybe a while. I have many things to ponder."

• • •

"What's this room?" She asked Bella as she felt the plush carpet with her bare feet.

"It's a special place I thought you should visit, a private collection of your mom's memorabilia. Most of her other personal effects are in the Bonnie Mendoza Museum in San Diego and the

Smithsonian, and there's a smaller one in downtown Aurora City. Jay and Wendy have a few items as well.

"This room contains books and memoirs of her stellar scientific career?"

Bella laughed. "No, Paige, her fairly successful but financially unrewarding magic career. There's enough stuff devoted to the other, but this was her secret passion, Paige."

"I guess I forget she was an amateur magician, even though she still plays with the stuff. Makes sense now."

"An amateur only because she only performed for children or for charity, but she was the real deal, as amazing as they come. With the right publicity and manager, she could have done well. She could do incredible card tricks because of her ability to calculate odds, and her eidetic memory allowed her to count cards quite well; she also was very quick and exceptional at sleight-of-hand."

She felt the large wooden box. "What is this?"

"While she could do all the magic stuff, this was probably what she was best at, one of her 'special interests.'"

"Huh? 'Special interests?' I don't get it."

"Surely you know that autistic people can become obsessed with certain ideas and objects. Especially highly intelligent ones like your mom. She used to entertain Jose and me with this particular aspect of her act. She was, by most accounts, the best in the world."

"I had heard about it, of course, but most of that gets overshadowed by the other stuff." She opened the box and felt the numerous handcuffs, shackles, etc., inside. "Mom still has a few of these around the house, but not anywhere near this number. How many are in here?"

"In those boxes, around a hundred sets. Most are duplicates of what is in the other museums. I have a display case for them to better showcase a smaller number, but these were the oldest. She was very ill when she was eleven, and in rehab they thought magic tricks would help her with hand-eye coordination. That was before I was born, of course, as my dad and Wendy were the same age. She really got into this due to her interest in the manipulation of locks and such."

"Cool. It's good to have a hobby." She took one relatively thick pair of old cuffs and closed it about her right wrist, and heard the click; she then repeated the maneuver with her left wrist.

"Uh, I didn't intend for you to actually put any of those on, dear they're antiques and not in the best shape, hence why they aren't in the display area."

"Sorry. It seemed like the natural thing to do with them."

"Yeah, my bad. You are your mother's daughter, for sure. Jose has some toy ones if you want to play cops and robbers."

"Why is it a problem? Do you not have the keys?"

"No. I believe that particular set is over a hundred thirty years old, so we'd better take a trip to the workshop."

She laughed and grinned. "I guess it was kind of dumb."

"Aww, don't worry, *Tinman's* done that before, and I learned a lot about your mom's magic, getting immersed in the role and all, so it's no problem. Some graphite, machine oil, and tools, and we'll be fine."

"I guess you won't hurt me if you have to file them off."

"Or the metal will expand when superheated to several hundred degrees, and you can slip out then, as a last resort."

"Sure. That's not very good for my nails, though."

"No. We'll have to take a trip back downtown again."

Chapter Thirty-Five

Paige went and showered again at ten AM; she really didn't need to shower again, but the warm water felt good. Afterward, she went to the kitchen and began reading the Braille newspapers they had obtained for her; the Aurora City Reporter, the New York Times, the Chicago Tribune. She guessed money could buy lots of things, including items she never knew existed. The rapidity at which those things were acquired was also quite stunning.

"Well, he really enjoyed playing with you," Bella said as she walked into the room. "We don't have a whole lot of family around, mainly because we don't have a lot of family."

"Where did he go?"

"He went for a short nap before he gets ready to go to afternoon kindergarten. He'll be up in an hour or so, like clockwork."

"That sounds like fun for him," she said, taking a sip of coffee. "Does he have a lot of other kids who come over and play?"

"There are some, but it's not the same, you know, as a real live cousin."

Yeah, that was right: all these years, she had some relatives and didn't know it. *Thanks, Mom and Dad, for lying to me.*

She marveled again at the quiet, an odd feeling given that she had just been rescued in the Alaskan frontier less than a day ago.

"It is weird, like the whole thing did not happen. Yesterday I was fighting off military jets and wolves, and next I am here."

"Well, enjoy it, Paige. There will be more stuff to do later."

"Like what?"

"Anything. What you want to do while you're here is totally your decision. We'll have the chauffeur or pilot take you anywhere you want at any time. If you want to go swimming, there's the indoor pool, and no one will bug you if you want to sleep all day or stay up all night. There's almost anything you would want to do in AC or Indianapolis, and Chicago is thirty minutes by jet. If you want to go overseas or to Canada or Mexico, we'll need to find your passport."

"You do not have to entertain me, and Chicago is a bit out of my league, from a girl where Anchorage is the big city."

"If you prefer warmer climates, southern Florida, New Cuba, or Puerto Rico aren't far. We own a house in Naples as well as a small island in the Caribbean. Luna is a bit of a hike."

"For now, I had probably better let my folks know where I am. I assume you have some method of clandestine communications?"

"We sure do, Paige. Lots of secret phones and frequencies around here to counteract industrial espionage, given my husband's high level of paranoia, which is probably justified. But I thought you didn't want to talk to them?"

"I do not, really, but I owe them that much."

"Also, by the way, we have assembled for your entertainment a group of folks in the experimental research compound who may be able to find some answers for you."

"Answers?" She turned to Bella as if looking at her. "That is puzzling. I do not know what you mean, although it sounds keen."

"Your abilities. Who you are. I'm sure you have some questions about them. How your powers work, your limits, etc."

"I suppose, but I do not know how any of your guests, whoever they are, can help with that."

"Really? You haven't met them yet, so keep an open mind."

"I guess my mother is a brilliant physicist but doesn't know everything. For instance, where did Juriann come from?"

"That, your mom probably knows, but we have no idea. He apparently came over here from the Netherlands a couple of months ago and is really into *Wendy's Science Squad.*"

"What? Those dumb heroes from the nineties? The golfer dude with one leg, the chemistry professor in the wheelchair, the light guy whose name spells the rainbow colors, the electrical guy, the purple blob with psionic powers, and—my mom, I guess. I am hoping she does not show up."

"Yeah. Juriann went to see *Gravi-Golfer* at Princeton. Kind of freaked Johnny out."

She snarled and shook her head. "I cannot see what possible use those quasi-celebrities would be to me."

"Well, guess what? You're gonna find out because that's who's in the guest compound. All those guys. Except for *Oogly-Googly.* He's where he always is—in your mom's brain. And their leader, of course, was not invited, for obvious reasons."

"You are serious."

"I am."

"No way. But why?"

"Because, like your mother, they are experts in very eclectic scientific disciplines. We need them, not the regular scientists we have around here, who are very good at their jobs but sometimes lack 'out of the box' thinking. And their history with your mom and aunt may prove useful at some point."

"Huh. I guess we are already pretty far 'out of the box' here. Well, Juriann rather irritated me. He has immense strength, so where did that come from?"

"He calls himself *Orthoman*, and he appears to be some type of genetically enhanced man."

"What? You are kidding. From some laboratory?"

"No one knows anything about him—he doesn't, either. He's kind of in the same boat you are. A person out of his element, looking for answers. Somehow he feels you are connected."

"We are related too? Tell me it is not so."

"Probably—but the one person who knows it all is back in Alaska and was once called Bonnie Mendoza."

"That is the second time you inferred she knew about Juriann."

"Of course she did, don't be so dense. He told you himself of the tale when she dropped him off in the Netherlands."

"I cannot believe she hid things from me, but now I know the truth, as I am no longer a youth."

"I'm sure she did what she thought was right, hon. Knowing about him or us wouldn't have made your life better." She felt Bella sit next to her and grasp her left hand. "Yesterday, you found out you were part of the family, but you only know what's in the popular media. There are a lot of other things, too, many of them bad."

She shrugged. "I know some of it, such as my aunt is a somewhat flawed person. We all are, Bella."

"No, I don't mean her. You've got a whole lifetime to find out about Wendy, who is pretty much your average boisterous British-Appalachian powerlifter turned pediatrician politician who now lives in the White House. I'm talking about her father, your and Will's grandfather—William Conrad Darkkin."

"Yes, Will was named after him. I met Will a few weeks ago. Neither of us knew we were related, obviously."

"What? Where in the world would you have met him? Some class trip to the White House or something? The tour is very limited and doesn't interact with people in the residence."

She smiled. "No—in North Pole. He came to meet me because he was impressed by my foul-shooting ability."

"You're kidding."

She shook her head. "I am not. He said he was unhappy with his life, actually disliked sports, and wanted to meet someone who had to work at things. Like I have had to do any of that."

"He didn't know who you are, and most people would come to that conclusion."

"It is ironic; I noticed that when I felt his face we somewhat resembled each other."

"Of course, you would be double cousins because you share one-quarter of your DNA, twice what you and I do—the same as a half-sibling."

"Double cousin?"

"Sure, it's fairly uncommon. When two siblings have children with two other siblings, their children are double cousins, so you should look alike, although Wendy and your dad didn't look that much alike at all, other than their hair color and complexions. He looked like their mom, who was a beautiful lady from England."

"My grandfather was a great scientist, I understand."

"Yeah, well—you know what Wendy wanted the world to know. He might have been smart, but he wasn't all that great, let me assure you. He may have saved her and your mom's life, but he did some mighty bad stuff before that."

"Why are you telling me all this now, and what does it have to do with my abilities?"

"Because it's all weaved together, honey, and all evidence points to the fact that Juriann is some type of clone of Wendy and your dad's half-brother Travis Argon. Grandpa Rad got around, it seems. We don't know any more other than your mom had something to do with it, and somehow the destinies of you both are related."

"What? Our powers are significantly different. He is just a super-strong man. I don't know what the limits of my powers are."

"You have a common origin; that's why he's here and why we took him in. Juriann says he was raised by adoptive parents in the Netherlands; the mother said someone meeting the description of your mom dropped him off as an infant. The lady was deaf and spoke in fluent Russian; the only person who could possibly meet that description is your mom."

"Okay. I guess I need to bite the bullet and call my folks."

"If you want, sure. Use the secure line."

"I guess so."

Bella handed her the small portable phone as she heard her leave the kitchen. She dialed the phone line as she walked into the living room; it rang five times before the recipient picked up.

"Hello?" Jack answered his cell phone. "Who is this?"

"Take a guess."

"Paige? You've been gone nearly two days. Where the heck are you now?"

"I cannot say, but I am okay. I am with friends, at a place where the fun never ends."

"Who? The caller ID is blocked."

"Of course it is, duh. It would not benefit anyone to know that or exactly where I am, Sam."

"Wherever you are, I'm coming to find you."

"No, you are not, Dad. I am okay, and I need some time. Time to find out who I am and learn my destiny."

"Your *destiny?* You're talking crazy. How are we supposed to explain all this to the school?"

"You obviously have a creative imagination from all the stories you have concocted over the years, so use it and do not have a fit. I will be back to see you someday. I am in no hurry to scurry."

"If you need an airline ticket—"

She sighed. "I am not prepared to return now, but rest assured that when I do return to North Pole I shall not need commercial air fare. It is too slow for me, but I have many problems to work out first. Tell Mom I am sorry I destroyed Grandpa Rad's best suit."

"Paige, wait—"

"Goodbye. I do love you, but this is how circumstances have

played out, as it must be now. I have to make my own way, as we knew this could happen. It was my choice to do this, so I must go down my own path. And you and Mom made your choices too. We must both live with those now and go on with our lives. Not sure how mine will end up. But whatever I do from now on will be my decision, not yours." She ended the call and walked back into the living room.

• • •

"You okay? Did you talk to your mom or dad?"

She brushed tears from her eyes. "I talked to Dad. He was not very happy I am not coming home. Wanted to know where I was."

"Did you tell him?"

She shook her head. "That would serve no tangible purpose. He should not worry about me anyway." She laughed. "I am eighteen now, so the truancy officers cannot come looking for me."

"Did you talk to your mom?"

She shook her head. "I did not want to talk to her. I have many emotions to sort out before I can even begin to do that."

Bella stroked her face. "If you want to go home, we'll have you back in North Pole in less than six hours."

She shook her head. "No, that is surely not what I want. I miss them, but I am also extremely angry at them for the things they have hidden from me. It is very hard to explain."

"It's not my business, but I know they wanted to protect you. It's up to you to work that out with them, and did what they thought was best. I don't want you to do anything you don't want. If you don't desire to see the *Squad* and do some testing, then we sure won't."

"Do they know about me?"

"Kepler has theorized your existence for some time and might be expecting that, but the others, no. Either way is okay."

She nodded. "I do. Mom and Dad have taught me much, but they do not know everything. It is time to think outside the box to find out more about what makes *Stella Scura* tick."

"Okay. Get your work clothes on, and let's go to work."

Chapter Thirty-Six

Fifteen minutes later, Bella walked into the lounge area of the M2 Sulphur Springs complex with her taller, younger cousin, an event clearly not met with excitement by the bored scientists, who had apparently experienced enough of *Orthoman* for the present.

"Hi, guys. I have someone I would like you to meet."

'At least it ain't another Juriann," Kepler said. "A nice, normal person."

Bella laughed. "Not hardly, Johnny, ye of little faith. This is my cousin, Paige Marshall."

"Cousin?" Kepler asked. "No way. I didn't know you had any other than the Chief's son."

"Tell that to her, Johnny," she said.

"Who are her parents?" Kepler asked.

"You can't see the resemblance? Come on."

" I guess, but—I still don't believe this crap, it ain't possible."

"Hi, Paige," Todd said as he took her hand and shook it.

"You've met Juriann, but I believe *you're* who they really want to meet. Especially Johnny."

"Hiya, Paige," Kepler said, patting her on the shoulder. "You seem like a nice gal, but why are you so special?"

"Johnny, you're a barrel of laughs." She felt Bella place the cold four-kilogram metal sphere in her left hand. "Show them how you can squeeze a tennis ball, honey."

She felt the irregularities of the steel shot. "Before I destroy it, this one is not of historical significance, is it?"

"No, it isn't hers; who knows why it's here. Go ahead, smash it, Paige. These guys are bored, that'll wake them up."

Kepler laughed. "Yeah, right, what's she gonna do to it? Gimme that." He grabbed the shot from her hand.

"Well?" she asked.

"So it's a real women's shot, big deal. Doesn't mean anything." She felt him place it back in her left hand.

"Let me do this first." She took it and twirled it on her left index finger like a top for about thirty seconds, then held out her left hand and floated it, three inches above her palm.

"So she can do magic tricks like her mom. Big deal."

"I hate magic, which is tragic, but maybe this will impress you." She then squeezed it with minimal effort as she felt her hand dig into the metal like dough, as it became deformed into a spheroid.

"Holy shit!" Kepler said. "Let me see that. It must be another trick, some soft alloy or something."

"You already felt it, correct? But here you go, Kepler." He took it from her, and she immediately heard it hit the floor.

"Why'd you drop it? Is it hot, Johnny?" Bella asked.

"Hell no, it's not, it's stone cold! It *should* be hot from the metal being compressed, but it's just the opposite."

"Todd, please scan it to determine its composition," Bella said.

"Already did, Bella. It's low carbon steel. Mass 4.032 kg."

"You are a renowned physicist, no?" she said. "I absorbed the heat when I compressed it."

"How the hell did you do that? You like the Juriann guy?"

She laughed. "Not hardly. I have quite a few more tricks up my sleeve."

"Like what?" Kepler asked sarcastically.

"Like this. You, in particular, might be interested in this one." She lifted off and hovered ten feet above him. "How about that?"

"No way. How are you doin' that?"

"I do not fully understand myself, which is obviously one of the reasons I am here."

"Just stay up there. I'm gonna jump up and grab your legs."

"Why?"

"I just want to see something."

"How? You cannot jump this high, Kepler, as I do not think you were a professional basketball player."

"Wanna bet?" She felt Kepler grab her legs a few seconds later and touch her right ankle. "Holy shit, I'm floating."

"Yeah, but how did you jump so high?"

"I have a nuclear-powered leg, that ain't no sweat. Hey, I'm going sideways now."

"You are weightless; you have to learn how to move around."

"How the hell is this possible?"

"You are asking me, esteemed golfer of gravity?"

She then felt him move his grip from her ankle to her right calf, covered by her jeans, and then felt a strong downward jerk.

"Holy crap, I'm falling!"

"No, Kepler, you must make contact with my flesh for the gravitational effect to be 'transmitted.' You will not fall, though, as long as you are holding onto my clothed body, but you will not float."

She felt him loosen his grip and fall to the ground.

"That's weird. As soon as I moved my hands from your ankle to your pants, I resumed my normal weight."

She landed and walked towards him. "Enough of this, as I do not care to investigate my flight powers now. I have an immense problem to investigate."

"Yeah?"

"Yeah, duh. Is the famous Dr. Royce G. Bivereaux III here?"

"Uh, sure," the high-pitched male voice said.

"Let us go. You are up, Biv. I hope you live up to your name."

• • •

Royce G. Bivereaux III looked into her eyes with both his direct and indirect ophthalmoscope after they went to the improvised "medical suite" of the Sulphur Springs catsup complex.

"*Photraman,* I cannot see your facial expression, but you seem to be perplexed from all the sighing going on."

"That's putting it mildly, I wish I could figure this out, Paige. I can't see as well as I'd like as the mydriatic drops I put in your eyes don't work, and your pupils still react to light and become very small with bright light, but this is damn weird. I have searched the literature on every known eye disease and came up empty."

"Tell me about it. It would solve a lot of problems if you could. I do not mind sightlessness for myself, but it makes flying around rather difficult."

"Paige, you say you lost your sight after the atomic explosion on *Darkkday*, and not before?"

She shook her head. "I do not know, Biv; I already told you I cannot remember that. I have dreams of seeing, but I have no idea why that would be, so I assume I could see as a small child. I seem to know what words and such look like, as well as colors; from what I understand, this also means I must have seen as a child."

"That's true. People with congenital blindness don't understand concepts like colors and other visual representations."

"You have seen I can write with a pen just fine."

Biv laughed. "Yeah, your handwriting is a lot better than mine, but I am a doctor, after all."

She laughed. "Another thing—oddly, my avoidance of contractions seems only verbal and does not extend to my writing. The rhyming and alliteration also diminish markedly in writing, but not entirely."

"The latter things you mention can be explained by being your mom's daughter, as she has a form of high-functioning autism and rather unusual senses, as you must know."

"Mom says my retinas must have been damaged after an explosion. I was always told it was a car accident, but I know now it was the 'really big one' I apparently absorbed at point-blank range in December 2016. Not all of it, as the plane and the others inside were vaporized, but over 99.99 percent."

"It's puzzling." She felt him turn her face. "You're tracking, which means your blindness is cortical, not something wrong with your eyes. Your pupils also react to the light like a normal person's should. They also, curiously, react to infrared light up to about 800nm that a normal person's would not. They don't react to UV."

"Whoa." She shook her head and pulled away from the ophthalmic table. "I am not a physician, *Photraman*. Speak English, not medical gobbledygook."

"Okay: a basic neurological reflex is 'eye tracking.' When an object moves into your field of vision, your eyes track it in tandem, sort of like a predator tracking prey. I'm moving my finger back and forth horizontally, and your eyes are following it, even though you clearly can't see it; it's a basic brainstem reflex. If the problem was your eyes, you couldn't track because then your brain wouldn't be receiving the impulses."

"So there is nothing wrong with my eyes. It is my brain? My brain is damaged? I knew I had a screw loose somewhere, because

I am as mad as a March hare."

"No, that can't be right, either," Biv said. "You said you could see with the Vladimirov suit that projected brain-wave images into your occipital cortex, so that's ruled out, too. It makes no sense. Todd has the helmet partially working, but can't yet figure out how to get that part to function, as most of the sensors were destroyed."

"All the big brains here, and no one can figure out why I cannot see. Mom could not, either, so do not feel bad. Yeesh. Where is my cane? I am going out to get some ice cream before I scream."

Todd spoke up. "It isn't logical, though. This protective aura, or whatever it is, is programmed somehow to keep your body from harm. How that works is beyond anyone's comprehension, but it seems to work with unbelievable precision. As far as we know, there isn't a single substance that can hurt you. While we need to do some tests, you can reportedly survive for several hours, at least, without oxygen, and draw energy from *somewhere* for your body's needs, even without eating; yet, you say you can eat a lot, and don't get fat."

"Mortal harm, perhaps," Biv said. "But this was not a mortal injury." She felt him looking at her retinas thoroughly through the ophthalmoscope again as he held her head to the rubber bumper. "She absorbed enough heat, kinetic energy, alpha, and gamma radiation to destroy all of Washington, yet she can't see? Are you kidding me?" He looked for several more minutes.

"Well, neuro-ophthalmologist Dr. Roy G. Bivereaux, medical genius of the ages? I never really saw a doctor who I can remember. This is the reason why—none of you know squat, all your fancy schooling is for naught."

"Your dad was a physician, and so is your aunt. I'm sure they may have had some ideas. Alex is dead, of course, but do we dare ask Wendy?" Biv asked. "She's pretty smart and didn't get where she is by being a dummy."

"That's a very poor idea," Bella said. "They will meet up again soon enough, but we need to figure this out on our own. I doubt that Wendy did extensive tests on the matter, and, while bright, this isn't her area of expertise. If she knew much, she kept it all secret. In any event, she would detract from our mission now."

"Mom and Jack did not think a conventional physician could help me, and they did not want someone discovering something that could be used against me. I guess that might have let the cat out of the bag with an information leak, so to speak."

"They were right because I don't see anything. Your eyes look perfect. No refractive error, either, and your vision should be at least 20/15 at your age."

"How can you tell if I need glasses or not if I cannot see?"

"Easy: the image on your retina is perfectly focused at zero diopter correction with the reti-camera. If you did require corrective lenses it would need to compensate. Basic optics."

"Huh. Will wonders never cease. I know not of such things."

"Besides, I've seen scarring bad enough to cause blindness and many other retinal diseases, but this isn't it. I thought maybe you had retinitis pigmentosa, a progressive retinal disease—but your retinas look absolutely pristine, and your electroretinogram is completely normal—above average, in fact. The fact that you could see with the Vladimirov armor and its amazing cortical sensors rule out a brain defect. What is the answer, then?"

"Man, I don't know," Todd said.

"Beyond me," Kepler said. "Not my specialty, dude. My task is to figure out how the hell she flies, and I can't even do that."

"I'll find out," Biv said. "When a physician doesn't know by looking, he probes."

"Huh?" she said. "You had better watch where you probe me!"

"Don't worry, Paige. I will stick to your eyes. That seems like a safe area."

"What are you going to do now?"

"I have an indirect ophthalmic YAG laser I had flown in. I'm going to laser a clinically insignificant portion of your retina."

"Excuse me? Do what to what with what?"

"The outer poles are insignificant for vision, so I'm going to put a tiny spot on your peripheral retina and see if it 'takes.'"

"You do know what you are doing."

"Yes, of course." She heard a small beep.

"When do we start?"

"I already did it. I put a low power burst on your peripheral retina, around one o'clock."

"You did?"

"Yeah. And, you know what?"

"What?"

"There is no artifact. Your retina absorbed the energy without any damage. I would see a little scar there with a normal person.

This puzzles the hell out of me. What should be extremely delicate tissue is impervious to intense laser energy, yet the nuclear blast somehow fried your vision. Very puzzling."

"Small laser blast vs. nuclear explosion, those seem equivalent for sure."

"But the principle is the same." She then heard him pick up a metal object from a tray.

"What are you doing with that needle, Biv?" Todd asked. "That's fricking dangerous."

"No, it's not. I want to see the consistency of her corneas. It's a corneal needle to remove foreign bodies and such."

"Cross my heart, hope to die, stick a needle in my eye?" Bella said melodically.

"Do not worry, he cannot hurt me," she said. "It is futile."

"Yeah, but—yechh. He ain't getting that near my eye."

"Shut up, Bella." She felt him slowly put the small ophthalmic needle in contact with her cornea. "It deforms a little, but it can't penetrate. It's like pushing it into a concrete block, but it's not, because the energy is absorbed, and it seems soft. I've never seen anything like it."

"I should hope not." She yawned. "I could have told you that. Your point being?"

"How could anything have hurt your eyes?" Biv paused for a minute. "Let me try something else."

"Sure, sure." About two minutes later, she felt the faint sensation of heat near her face.

"It is kinda hot. What are you doing?"

"Quiet, Paige. This is over 3,000 degrees Fahrenheit. Nothing, apparently, except—what's that funny smell?"

She felt the heat intensify. "Are you aiming a flame at my eye, you idiot?"

"Yeah, but so what? It doesn't hurt you."

She felt her eyelids and grabbed the torch from him. "Yow! That smell is burnt hair, Royce G. Bivereaux! You burnt off my left eyelash and part of my eyebrow, you dummy. Do not ever do that again, doltish doctor."

"Huh? How?"

"Right, because it is outer hair and skin layers, which is not living. It will grow back soon, but I must be quite a sight."

She felt him rub the smooth area where her eyebrow had been.

"How 'bout that? That is so bizarre."

She shoved him away. "Do not ever touch me again. I am rather angry now, and I will urgently need some makeup."

"Don't worry, honey, we can fix that up," Bella said. "But what if the answer is so incredibly simple that even you geniuses and Bonnie overlooked it?"

"Oh, yeah, right, Bella," Biv said.

"No, it just came to me. I think I know what the problem is now and the possible solution."

"Huh?" She said, perplexed. "You have had some sort of enlightenment regarding my condition?"

"Yeah, it's almost *too* simple to believe. What happens when you overload a circuit or other electronic device?"

"It burns out, dummy, you don't need *Ampere* to tell you that." Kepler laughed. "No offense, but why are you even here, cheesecake, other than that you own the place, are easy on the eyes, and give us good eats?"

"Johnny, shut your big mouth. You don't need to be so rude," Todd said. "I guess that would be hard for you, a subhuman primate with no social graces."

"You come over here and make me, *Ampere*," he said.

"Maybe I will, you arrogant academic ass. You and your crazy bionic leg don't scare me. I'm sick of your fat lip, like always."

"Come find out, *Amp*. My fists are all flesh and blood."

"Okay, you asked for it, Professor. I hope you have good emergency room coverage at Princeton, 'cause you're gonna need it."

She heard Bella get up and smack Kepler in the arm, which only resulted in him stumbling backward, she judged from the sound.

"*Amp's* right, so shut up, Johnny, and the rest of you, too. I'm as smart as you or anyone here, including my husband. Just because I'm one of the hottest and richest women on this planet doesn't make me an idiot. How many fricking Nobel Prizes do you have, pegleg?"

"Yeah, well, I never got around to that kind of stuff. Too busy. I could've had several, were I to be concerned about that trivial crap."

"Woulda, coulda, shoulda. I see. Well, shut up, then."

Kepler snickered at the diminutive niece of his former TV costar. "But you sound like you've got it all figured out. Enlighten us with the wisdom of your purported 'parsimony' powers. Haw."

She turned to them, still feeling the smooth skin where her eyebrow had been, and still a bit perturbed.

"Yes, I am interested in what Bella has to say, as it is far better than *Photraman* shooting lasers into my eye or burning off the rest of my beautiful hair with a blowtorch."

"Okay, it's so elementary—the solution has been staring us in the face all this time."

"Huh?" she muttered. "'Staring us in the face?' That is an ironic utterance, considering the perplexing problem at hand."

"Correct, that's *exactly* what I mean. You *are* staring, but your brain just doesn't know it. Your own fuse box in the house shuts off when there's a circuit overload during an electrical surge; it's the same principle here."

"Whaaat?" Biv laughed. "The human eye is the most complex imaging device ever, and for the most part, we still have no clue how it really works. Same with the brain, for that matter. We still have a long way to go to completely replace human sight. Vision isn't like an electric fuse box, which is a simple series circuit, Bella; there's absolutely no comparison. How stupid."

"That's right—as you say, there's a lot no one yet understands. But I understand one thing. Look—Jose and I used to play with an old tape recorder that, if you yelled into it, it would actually record nothing because the mike couldn't handle the overload. The automatic recording level shut down the gain until the decibel level went down a few seconds later. So the tape would be blank during that brief interval, despite the sound level being very high."

"That must have happened a lot, as loud and shrill as your voice is," Kepler said, laughing. "Probably set the tape on fire."

"Dummy, you're missing the point. It's the same principle." She heard Bella walk across the room. "What if her brain shut off the signals as a sort of protective mechanism, after the nuclear blast? Looking straight into it? That's over a trillion lumens. There may be a limit to what even she can perceive."

"I thought the popular theory was that she absorbed it," Biv said. "How would that work?"

"Most of it, sure, but not all, and visible light isn't necessarily harmful. Remember the others who were vaporized; even a fraction of the blast could've done it at that range. Still mighty bright."

"That makes no sense," she said. "If that is true, then why has it not gone back to normal, over a decade after the event?"

"Don't know, just as we have no clue how your powers work. We think you're completely invulnerable, but we don't know that for certain or if at age six you were like you are now. But we do know physical contact with another living being's skin appears to confer the same properties, a sharing of sorts."

"Of course, I have known that for some time. So what; is that all you have got?"

"Because another possibility is that touching another person dilutes that invulnerability between the two people. This phenomenon might not be noticeable for things like bullets, electricity, or any normal perils, or even Biv aiming a laser at your peripheral retina, but an atomic explosion might be enough to have caused this to happen if your protective 'aura' had been diluted even a little bit when your mom was holding you."

"Okay, suppose you are right; it makes as much sense as anything else. The question for the ages: is this process reversible?"

"With the current poor knowledge of the human brain that we do, and our limited understanding of your physiology and dark energy powers, I would say—not at this point in time. Sorry."

"So what do we do? You *said* you had the solution. If we cannot repair it, then what? Is our work here therefore all for naught?"

"Easy, in concept; in execution, more difficult. My theory is that if we filter out most visible rays, say 99.99 percent, you'll be able to see at least something because the problem is too much sensitivity to light, not too little. It may not be full visible spectrum on the first iteration, or at all, but it's the best idea going here. I doubt you've ever been in near darkness for very long. Can you remember ever seeing anything? Without the helmet, that is?"

She thought for a moment. "Sometimes, right before falling to sleep, I see little flashes of light, and nothing of any substance. When I open my eyes, I see nothing. Only with the helmet, which allows me to see better than any of you."

"Bella," Biv said. "I thought initially your theory was preposterous, but that would explain why Paige doesn't have non-24 syndrome, which the majority of totally sightless people have."

"Yes, that's correct. If she sees even a small amount, even when drifting off to sleep, it could be enough to 'reset' her circadian clock so that doesn't occur. We think of Alaska as being dark, but while it's mostly devoid of light pollution, it has the northern lights much of the time at her latitude; and starlight, of course. And the summer days are really long in North Pole, almost 22 hours in June."

"Can that really be the case?"

"It's the simplest and most logical explanation, given the evidence. Again, it's easy to explain in theory; that doesn't mean it will be easy to fix."

"It's possible she has light perception in the infrared region, beyond up to the 800-nanometer wavelength, based on the reactivity of her pupils," Biv said. "Nothing with ultraviolet, though."

• • •

"Look, your mom was completely deaf when we knew her. Except, apparently, for a brief period of time when it came back, but it left again. Have you ever known her to hear?" Bella asked.

She shook her head and sighed. "We have been all over that. She can certainly hear, extremely well, actually. Better than any person I know by far."

"After the Ontario Lacus incident she was without hearing, but it appeared to regenerate, but she lost it again. Now it's back and better than ever. Why would her hearing regenerate and not your vision? Is your mom's vision good?"

"I have no barometer for comparison, but it's my understanding that it is quite exceptional, even in low light, from what my dad says. She can spot things at a distance long before he can. In her fifties, she apparently does not require reading glasses."

"If that's genetic, then yours may be the same way. Listen up; there were accounts of many people with physical disabilities in Washington who had improvement after *Darkkday*, some with a profound improvement. Rita McPherson, for one. Hey, Wolf, what kinds of opaque refractive material would we want to use that we might have around here?"

"Well, this is a super-duper industrial complex, and money is clearly no object. Regular glass probably isn't the best thing due to its fragility. We need something we can darken that is also quite hard. The best material to use is aluminum oxide doped with copper, chromium, and/or titanium. It has a hardness of 9.5 on the Mohs scale; only diamond is harder, except for some exotic carbon compounds like fullerenes. I'll bet you have some around here."

"Sure do," Bella said. "The greatest mad scientist's lab you could ever imagine is at your disposal."

"What is that chemical compound?" she asked. "It sounds rare and exotic."

"Not as much as you would think; those elements combine to form the beautiful natural substance known as sapphire. Ironically, that's the September birthstone, while yours is tourmaline, which is a borosilicate; probably not hard enough."

"Sapphire, the precious stone? Why would you have it here? You do not make jewelry, as that would be tomfoolery."

Bella laughed. "Pretty, but also quite useful in manufacturing. It is extremely hard, transmits light well, has a high optical refractive index, and the color can be darkened by varying the amount of metallic constituents. We have both natural and synthetic sapphire here."

"Let's get to work," Biv said.

"It's going to take a while, guys, just to make some prototypes. So maybe it's time to work on some other stuff while I get to work," Bella said. "I'll be back after I start some initial programming."

• • •

In another part of the lab, Todd hooked up the damaged helmet to the massive computer bank and, after several minutes, was able to get a readout on the screen.

"What's in those files, *Amp?*" Nick asked.

"Don't know. This thing appears to be the central nervous system for the suit. It seemingly was capable of significant sensory feats, far beyond what our normal senses can discern. How the heck did this Viktor guy design this forty years ago?"

"I don't know; he must have been a genius. So what?"

"So, it would stand to reason that it was capable of recording whatever it saw. There seem to be some memory chips in here for that purpose, although they're quite damaged."

"Couldn't be much storage, as that thing was reportedly built in the late 80s."

"You'd think that, but it's been upgraded significantly to several terabytes of digital storage."

"By whom? Vladimirov and Rad Darkkin are long dead."

"Don't know. Bonnie and Jim, most likely."

"Uh, yeah, I guess. Anything on there?"

"Not sure. It seems to operate on some old Russian military operating system."

"How the hell do you know that?"

"I did a lot of tech stuff when I consulted for the military back in the day, and I know enough Russian to get by. It'll take me a while to break down the encryption and the codecs."

"It would be interesting to see what she 'saw.'"

"Interesting, yes, but that's not all. Look at this. If I'm correct, there would seem to be files on there that pre-date Aurora's birth."

He nodded. "Well, sure, it probably was used before."

"Really? Do you think it was used back in the day? I don't believe that."

"What's in there?"

"Weird. I'm talking about these upgraded chips and that some of the files appear to be from around 2009, 2010, or so. I doubt it was used for its intended reason, then."

"Can you get the files off of it?"

He shook his head. "Don't know, maybe. It'll take some work. There's some data damage, and the encryption, of course, may be challenging. But if anyone can do it, it's me. As great as everyone thought Krakowski was, I'm better. Encryption from the 00s and 10's is no match for today's quantum computers."

"Maybe we don't want to find out what's in those memory chips," Nick said. "Did you ever bother to think about that, Todd?"

Chapter Thirty-Seven

"What are we doing, again, Nick?" she asked as she felt Juriann fasten the titanium shackles around her wrists. "This looks like something my mother would have done back when I was small, as one of her stupid experiments in fine muscle control. Knowing who she is now, it makes perfect sense."

"Well, she would have done it differently."

She tugged at the strong, heavy metal. "Why do you even have such things? Of what purpose are they?"

"Please don't ask," Bella said, sighing. "He needs lots of toys for all his experiments, among other things."

"What other things do you speak of?"

"I cannot say. Marital privilege."

"Yes. I am sure they have a legitimate industrial purpose and are not meant for recreational use."

"Yeah. Titanium bruises your skin something awful."

"Did Juriann try to break them?"

Nick nodded. "Yes, before you got here. He couldn't, even with his maximum strength after fifteen minutes of pulling. I want to compare the two. This place was used to assemble the early reactor drum prototypes, but it's no longer used, so it's dead in here. It's almost as big as NASA's old VAB, or Vehicle Assembly Building, at Kennedy Space Center in Florida. The winch can raise over 6,000 tons, enough to lift the old Space Shuttle with its rocket assembly."

She yawned. "6,000 tons. Big deal, get real."

"Well, to us, that's a lot." He pushed a motor that raised the chains, pulling her off the ground. "Let it pull you. Don't resist."

"Okey dokey." She felt her feet leave the ground as the chains pulled upward.

"It doesn't hurt you, does it?"

She laughed. "Of course not. It is kind of like a boring carnival ride, actually. Let me know when it becomes more exciting."

Bella, *Tinman*, and *Orthoman* went into an adjacent room and communicated to her via intercom, as they didn't want to be in the area if the items exploded.

"Okay, Paige. Pull the chains apart. Slowly. I want the stress gauges to test it."

She dangled her feet. "I am suspended in air and there is nothing to pull against, scientists."

"Come on. You should know how to pull yourself downward."

She thought for a few seconds. "I suppose that is easy enough. As slowly as I can, man, is that the great plan?"

"Yes. I won't be able to measure the force accurately if you do it too quickly."

This seemed easy, but a bit more challenging than some of the exercises her mom had her do. Mom would take string, rope, chains, or handcuffs (items of differing tensile strengths) and have her pull just hard enough to break them, but no more. And repeating it tens of thousands of times. The reason—to learn to control her powers with absolute precision. To do any less would risk crushing someone's hand with a mere handshake or collapsing their ribs with a hug.

She had realized at some point several years ago that the ability to control the powers was seemingly separate from the powers themselves. It made sense that the ability to control her muscles and nervous system precisely was presumably some sort of autistic "splinter skill" likely inherited from her mother and that they were two separate processes entirely. Meaning that there was a reason she had the powers and no one else.

Nick watched as the strain gauges rose. He had said the chains could withstand over six million Newtons, which was enough to raise a huge airplane, Saturn rocket, or reactor assembly. Slowly, several of the heavy links, each one as large as her hand—pulled apart and broke, as she floated in the air, triumphant, the chains recoiling with an awful din.

"Holy—" Juriann exclaimed through the intercom. "I can't

even begin to do that."

"Yeah, so what, *Orthoman*? Who gives a crummy crap that you are a wimpy weakling?" she said as she floated over him and landed about four feet away as she heard them come back in. "But what good is doing this, anyway?"

"Was it hard, Paige?" Nick asked.

"Hard? The physical feat? Not in a manner of speaking. It was a little bit hard to do it slowly, like you had asked, without instantly breaking the thing totally apart. That would have been really easy."

"I'm trying to determine if there's even a reason to determine what your limits are."

"What is next?"

"We need to test your ability to survive without oxygen."

• • •

She waited impatiently in the vacuum chamber as they pumped the oxygen out as she yawned, wondering why such things existed in a repurposed catsup factory in Indiana. A pulse oximeter device was attached to her right index finger to non-invasively measure oxygen saturation.

"We're down to 0.3 atmospheres, Paige," Nick said as it was translated to the mini-Braille reader since, without air, sound could not be conducted, and she obviously couldn't see visual signals. "About 0.1 percent oxygen." She read his message and gave him an "OK" sign with her left hand and rolled her eyes.

Five minutes later, she "heard" him speak again. "Down to 0.05 atmospheres, or 0.02 percent oxygen." She shrugged and looked as bored as she could, as she couldn't even listen to music without air. That sucked.

She had held her breath for over two hours before, so she was reasonably sure she could survive at least for a few hours without oxygen, if not indefinitely. Nick had asked her to float around the large chamber a bit, which proved that she did not need an atmosphere or breathe oxygen to fly.

She did dimly remember from science class that atmospheric pressure was required to hold the body together, which is why people in space would develop ebullism (the formation of gas bubbles in bodily fluids due to reduced environmental pressure) without a pressurized suit. She was down to 0.01 atmospheres and still felt okay, although she noticed she was no longer breathing and the total absence of smell. That was a little unnerving.

• • •

"I still do not comprehend what we are doing, and I am getting bored," Paige said after floating for over an hour in another room. "I need some new music, so where are the seventies recordings I have requested?"

"Time dilation computations," Kepler said. "It's important for basic science calculations. I know I can't publish any of this shit, which stinks, but it's still important knowledge."

"Come again?" She shook her head. "I do not know what any of that means, *Gravi-Golfer*."

Kepler sighed. "Einsteinian relativistic concepts, Paige. Time slows down as you approach the speed of light and with higher gravity. In a singularity, or black hole, time stops. But with no gravity, time should speed up."

"Huh. So, my time is doing what now? I am confused."

"In theory, time should pass faster for you in a weightless environment. At least that's what happens with satellites orbiting the Earth."

"So I will get older faster?"

"If you stayed in a weightless state indefinitely, then, yes, you would age faster than those around you. The atomic watch you're wearing will be compared to the one I have after we're done, and yours should show more time elapsed."

"Do we not have data from others who have been in space?"

"Some data, yeah, but this is a bit different, though. But since you aren't in that state often, the effect on you should be negligible. It was how I learned of your existence in the first place—the subtle effects of gravity manipulation on time and the Earth's rotational velocity."

"Hurry up. The sooner I can get older, the better."

Kepler laughed. "Just wait, girl. One day you'll be my age and will sing a different tune."

"Well, that day is not today."

• • •

Nick and Biv then watched their two "guests" run on adjacent treadmills in the workout room. The smaller of the two subjects was on a standard treadmill, while the one who weighed almost a quarter ton was on a special reinforced unit Nick had around for some reason. They were both connected to face masks designed to measure oxygen consumption and carbon dioxide exhalation.

"This is incredible, Nick," Biv said as he watched Juriann hit thirty-five miles per hour on his treadmill. "The guy has been doing that for an hour and is still going strong. Don't know if he can go faster, but the amount of energy needed to propel that massive frame at that speed is incredible."

"What's his O_2 consumption?"

Biv laughed. "Very high. He consumes a terrific amount just to maintain that pace, and, as you have seen, he eats an enormous amount—over 15,000 kilocalories per day—just to sustain that metabolism, which is not very energy-efficient. You or I would gain four pounds a day on that diet and explode in the process. With a higher oxygen atmosphere, he can do even more. You've seen his strength; it's amazing."

"Yeah, great, glad I can afford the food bill for Juriann. What about Paige?" He pointed to the athletic-looking young woman running speedily, but not otherworldly fast, on her treadmill. "Doesn't look that impressive."

Biv shook his head. "It's not, at first glance. She's going a little under nine miles per hour, about a seven-minute mile. Decent for a fit female her age, but not extraordinary. Six minutes per mile is considered good for a girl her age."

"I see, that isn't so great at all. Is that the fastest she can go, or is she just goofing around?"

Biv nodded. "She assures us she is running at her top speed for this distance without the engagement of her special abilities. Even with them, while she can fly at supersonic speeds, she can't run any faster than that. She can propel herself linearly at great speed, but it isn't really running."

He sighed. "I could've run faster than that at her age. Big deal."

Biv laughed. "You think? Maybe for a little while, Nick, but she's been doing it for over an hour, with absolutely *no* signs of fatigue. Even Juriann is building up waste products at this point.

And, one other thing you might find interesting."

"What?"

"You say you could have run better than that when you were eighteen, Nick. But could you run ten miles *without consuming any oxygen at all?*"

"Huh? Say what?"

"Juriann is consuming massive amounts of O_2, as would be expected given his metabolic rate, but she consumes none, nor does she exhale any CO_2. She did the same in a vacuum."

He looked at the telemetry readouts. "But her respiratory rate is normal."

Biv nodded. "Yes, but that doesn't mean there's any actual gas exchange occurring. Her breathing stops without oxygen but appears to restart when reintroduced to air. Juriann's heart rate goes up, as does a normal person's who exercises, as does hers. Yet, her body is drawing the energy from an extraneous source. But respiratory rate is an autonomic process, and she still isn't using any oxygen. She is, amazingly, exhaling pure atmospheric air."

"The energy transfer process, occurring at nearly one hundred percent efficiency."

"Correct. She seems to be a very physically fit young woman of high athletic potential, as expected given her genetics, but nothing extraordinary like Juriann, except the energy to power her cells comes from someplace else."

"The dark energy field. But her blood is red, Biv. I assume she has hemoglobin just like us?"

"I would imagine so. But if there's still no gas exchange, I have no idea how she oxygenates it, then, but the energy field must, somehow. We saw that when she was in the vacuum chamber, with her O_2 saturation ninety-nine percent. And where the hell is this energy, Nick? How does it work? How can all this energy be right around us? Or is it somewhere else, and does she channel it from another dimension?"

He shook his head. "Wish I knew, Biv. I guess that would make her the ideal astronaut, as she needs no oxygen or heat."

"Exactly, which is why she must always be shielded from the government. Despite what you and Bella have done with your company, this is something else entirely."

"She eats a lot, too, I've noticed. Not anywhere near 15,000 kcal, but if she doesn't expend any energy, how come she isn't obese?"

Biv shook his head. "I have no idea about that, either. Analysis of her excretion and elimination products is totally unremarkable, as is her intestinal flora."

"Thanks so much for sharing that with me right before lunch."

"Hey, that's important, Nick. Her body has removed the energy from her food somehow, but it must be dissipated again, probably like when she absorbs a million volts but doesn't electrocute anyone else in the process. That energy must be converted back to dark energy. I somehow think we should be at some esoteric lab at Stanford, MIT, or Caltech rather than at an old catsup factory in Sulphur Springs, Indiana."

"Yeah, that's a really great idea, Biv," he said sarcastically.

"I understand your reservations and the desire to stay in rural America for now, but maybe we aren't as smart as you think—"

"Maybe not. But we, while a bunch of oddballs, are loyal, as far as I know. Too many people out there can't be trusted—including Paige's biological aunt who likes to rule the roost."

"I suppose I'm with you there, buddy."

• • •

Nick and Biv then watched the videos of them swimming in the converted Olympic-sized pool inside the complex.

"Juriann swims at an impressive velocity, about six times that of the fastest male Olympic swimmer," Biv said. "He's faster when he gets a diving start, but there's still no comparison with anyone on this planet. And he has excellent form, by the way."

"And Paige?" Nick asked.

"About what you'd expect—she's athletic and has above average form as well; she had rarely swum before but already swims like a good female high school swimmer, but not a great one."

Nick shook his head. "But how does she know when to flip?"

"Her muscle memory: it's exactly twenty-eight strokes per length for her, but all experienced blind swimmers can do that. But there's something else you might notice that differentiates her from Juriann."

Nick looked at the pool for a moment. "Yes, of course; her head stays face down in the water the whole time, while Juriann turns his head to breathe."

"Thought you might detect that."

They then reviewed the video from the indoor driving range and private nine-hole golf course, a place where one of the group's members had great expertise.

"While she has had no formal instruction in golf and had never even swung a club before, after thirty minutes of instruction from Johnny, she can hit the ball with unprecedented accuracy, even without vision. With a few weeks of coaching, she could beat my daughter Hanna easily, I'm sure, without the use of any powers. She needs a little work on putting and reading greens, but that would come in time. With sight, she'd be unbeatable at any level, man or woman."

"Juriann?"

"He has incredible power, but not much else. There aren't any 1,000-yard golf holes to my knowledge, therefore that advantage is irrelevant, and she would beat the pants off him on a golf course."

"Let's hope we can find better uses for her powers than golf."

• • •

Nick and Biv, joined by Kepler this time, then reviewed the weight training videos. "Juriann maxes out at a bench press of 7,800 pounds for ten reps. That's more than he thought he could do. He can deadlift over four tons, and lift two tons over his head, again while expending an enormous amount of energy."

They then watched videos of Paige and smiled. "She is, as with running, largely unremarkable. Her maximum bench press is one hundred sixty pounds for five reps," Biv said.

"What? That shit can't be right," Kepler said. "She crushed a steel shot like putty."

"Yet, it *is* right. That's very good for a female her size, but not world-class by any means. Clean and jerk, about the same. Wendy, in contrast, could bench and clean and jerk 300 at age twenty."

"I really don't understand. It goes without saying that she is capable of far more," Nick exclaimed.

Royce G. Bivereaux III shook his head. "Her own body is *not* capable of more. While she expends none of her own energy and doesn't fatigue, she is *not* intrinsically capable of strength feats greater than a normal person, and she's clearly orders of magnitude below Juriann. Her musculature implies a fair amount of basic strength training, but that has no correlation with what she can do with her abilities.

"Her lifting heavy objects relies on manipulation of powerful energy fields and gravitation. When she lifts a heavy object, the weight gauges go down. You or I could lift it."

"Yes, but we couldn't break the chains or something like that," Nick said.

"Correct. It's the dark energy field doing it; it mimics the actions that her muscles do with incredible precision. It's unbelievable," Biv said.

"I assume we don't have anything on hand that could even begin to test her limits."

"Not even close. The heaviest thing you have on hand is an old transformer from the catsup plant, which weighs approximately thirty tons, and she lifts that over her head, and even lifts off the ground while holding it, with hardly any exertion or consumption of energy. Her feats are essentially limited by boredom and her own adolescent impatience."

"What about the speed tests? Boxing?" Nick asked.

"Paige has the clear edge there due to her vastly superior coordination and speed," Kepler replied. "She can't run all that fast in her basal state, but her reflexes and reaction time are another matter entirely, something that isn't immediately apparent to the casual observer. Remember she can fly at several thousand miles per hour, which requires the ability to maneuver around obstacles and react to things in her path in a fraction of the time we can."

"In their sparring match, you'd think she can't catch him because of his long reach," Biv said. "But she has far faster reflexes than him, so she can, despite being blind. He lands many of his punches because she lets him when she wants, and she also can't see them coming; otherwise, he can't touch her. And for a person never instructed in boxing, she moves like the greatest championship boxer ever, whereas he needs some work on that, despite the fact each of his punches could shatter a concrete wall."

"They don't hurt her, of course."

"No, even though he is hitting full force, he says, but she absorbs almost all the energy, so the sensors are inaccurate. However, were she to actually hit him hard, well, he would be toast. Her hands are gloved, and there's no transference of invulnerability."

• • •

"Amazing," Wolfram Steele said as he looked at the high-res monitor connected to the M2 advanced electron microscope. "For the chains she pulled apart and the crushed metal shot, it looks like the metal's molecular structure's been altered. Not just pulled apart, like a tank or something could do. Juriann can't even pull them apart. But they're different. Juriann appears to actually have the strength to do superhuman things like that, as his density is far greater than normal. Paige is maybe slightly stronger than a normal female her size but less natively strong than the strongest women—so she is manipulating some additional force."

"Yeah, I thought you might have figured that out by now. And, by the way, I am an eighteen-year-old woman, not a girl, churl," she said as she raised her hand in protest.

The man in the wheelchair sighed. "Sorreee."

"How do these powers work?" Nick asked.

"I have no clue," Bella said. "She is somehow channeling an enormous amount of energy. To do that to those shackles in that manner would have taken close to a million joules per second, somehow controlled with pinpoint precision."

"But where is the energy coming from, Johnny?"

"Don't know. But you know as well as I that about 90% of the universe is 'dark energy.' Energy that we can't detect, or see. Proof now that dark energy must be around us. Your abilities seem to be limited only by what you can imagine. In ten or twenty years you may be able to do far more than this."

"Is it from another dimension?

"It has to come from somewhere. It could be another dimension, or right in front of us, we can't see it, so we don't know."

"That is what my mom thinks, although sometimes I am not sure she is competent to make such declarations."

"It has to be—if anyone understands it best, it's her. The theories state that, somehow, dark energy accounts for the remainder that is not accounted for by conventional baryonic matter and energy, that it somehow repels gravity and is contributing to the general expansion of the universe. But, how do you actually control it?"

"It seems as natural to me as walking or throwing a ball; I just will it, and it happens."

"We did the myoelectric studies. A typical person can activate part of an entire muscle group, like biceps or triceps. You, on the other hand, can activate infinitesimal portions, almost individual muscle fibers or nerve groups. I don't know how it's physiologically possible. Your touch discrimination is incredible."

"Incredible? That adjective can apply to bad things as well. Is there any downside to this tale? Does manipulation of the hallowed dark energy do anything destructive to the universe or to those around me? Am I a horrific hazard, to be the reckless ruination of mankind?"

"I don't really know. Dark energy, by definition, can't be detected, at least by any means we know. We can only postulate because of other effects it has. It can be next to us, or light years away, no real way to know."

"That is certainly no decent answer, *Tinman*. Am I an albatross about to effect the destruction of mankind? What are the consequences to the rest of the world's energy? The time dilation effects that Kepler mentions—are they additive, and does it affect others? Does anyone here care about that rather than foam at the mouth over what I can do? Lordy."

"Well, while we think the stuff you do is pretty spectacular, these physical feats are pretty infinitesimal in scope compared to goings-on of the universe. So, my guess is—probably not, unless you start exploding galaxies or something," Nick said.

"Huh. We shall place mankind's future on one of your guesses. Fantastic."

"It isn't that you're actually that strong; the dark matter effect is something else. Juriann appears to be the product of genetic manipulation based on the incredibly robust microorganism *Orthogeneticus titania* found on Saturn's moon Titan. You, Paige, are something else entirely. Much more human than Juriann in appearance and in apparent biology, but much less in others."

"Can you even measure her density, bone structure, etc.?"

"Not very well," Biv said. "She can apparently dissipate this dark energy protective field for only a few seconds, with great concentration. Smaller parts she can do slightly longer," Biv said.

"It is very hard to do, which is good because my body could be killed or harmed during that brief instant."

"Correct. You also might expose your body to various microbes for which you don't have immunity."

"Come again?"

"The rest of us are exposed to billions of microorganisms each day, so we develop immunity to common pathogens. We don't know what you have immunity to. This isn't an immunology lab, although a cursory examination of your immunoglobulins shows minimal levels of any protective antibodies. You have an immunization scar on your shoulder, which you obviously got when you were a small child. So, without your protective field, you'd be extremely vulnerable to even trivial infections."

"We've been unable to scan your body by any known means due to your protective field, which you can dissipate sufficiently for less than ten seconds; MRI, CT, DEXA, even ultrasound are all out," Biv said.

"Blood chemistry from your pin-prick? Ouch."

"Oh, don't complain. Nothing remarkable at all, as your serum chemistries and blood count are like that of any normal person. Your blood is red, which means your hemoglobin combines with oxygen outside of your body, but I have no idea what happens inside it since you don't require oxygen. Your chromosomes are 46, XX, as I expected, although we lack the ability to analyze your DNA in meaningful fashion. I did incinerate the sample, of course."

"Good. We would not want someone cloning me. Mom always said to incinerate my menstrual pads after they are soiled since that is a readily available source of blood."

"A fine idea," Biv said. "I was just about to suggest that."

She took a drink of water. "So, you are saying that I am a living example of something that has baffled scientists for decades? Hopefully, you can learn something from me."

"I agree. It's an unprecedented opportunity. What we could do with this," Nick said.

"But how are we gonna learn to manipulate it, *Tinman?*" Bella asked. "We can't even see it."

"Perhaps we can determine how to do that, somehow. Maybe it can benefit the world in some fashion. Unlimited energy, for one, far more than our current reactors can provide. And lunar regolith will maybe be able to supply energy for another two hundred years."

"If you could possibly warp light around her, she could become invisible," Kepler said. "She appears to defy radar detection in the same manner."

"I can become invisible? That might be useful, at times. On the other hand, I am really 'invisible' to most, anyway."

"No, it's just a theory," Nick said. "The power needed to do that could easily disrupt things around her, causing disaster. Plus we'd have to figure out a way for her to see since the light would warp around her or be absorbed."

"Yeah, then time would slow down around her, not speed up, I think, but if she was flying—" Kepler said. "It's confusing, even to me. I would have to think there would be time dilation effects over time which could add up."

"Hey, listen up, *Tinman, Golfer*, Biv, Bella, and you other yahoos," She was now very irritated as she rose up six inches off the ground, her Titian hair floating in weightlessness. "Please do not talk about me in the third person, like a lab rat. I am right here, and I did not disappear."

"Sorry, Paige. This is all new stuff to us," Nick said.

"You think, Stannous?" Kepler said. "It's beyond anything mankind has ever experienced."

"I understand your exuberance over these delightful discoveries, but show a little basic respect for a person."

"Sorry," Nick said as she landed. "But that's probably something for a later discussion. The energy field seems to radiate from your body. From what we've seen, you're not able to project it, to form shapes or anything, although any living animal in direct contact with you appears to be protected as well. It does not seem to extend to plants."

Kepler smiled. "This is the most exciting thing I've ever seen, Bella, TM, Biv. I'm almost glad you brought us out here."

"Most exciting thing?"

"Sure. Her energy potential is beyond comprehension. Think of it: unlimited clean energy with no waste products. Makes mining helium-3 from the moon as archaic as burning kerosene lamps. The studies of relativity alone, especially time dilation, with someone who can control gravitational fields, is, for lack of a better word —a rather unique opportunity."

"I agree; it's phenomenal. So far, her body is the only thing that can convert dark energy into anything useful," Nick said. "Mere kinetic energy. But Johnny's right. The potential of this is beyond my wildest dreams."

"I cannot believe it—you are doing it again, Nick." The chatter was getting too much to take. "I am glad you all are enjoying the contemplation of my vast commercial potential, but I am beginning to be sorry I am here at all. Excuse me," she said as she left the room in a huff as Bella followed her.

"What's the deal with her?" Nick said. "Did I say something? I thought I was helping."

"Shut up, stupid-ass *Tinman*. We all did this. Us and our stupid *Science Squad*. Idiots then, idiots now. Some things never change."

"Hey, I resent that," Biv said. "Take that back."

"Yeah. I got a Ph.D. from Caltech, you dumb little Boilermaker, go play with your toy trains or something—"

"Shut the hell up, all of you." Bella sneered at the acerb neurologist and gravitational physicist. "No people skills at all. And I'm contributing just as badly. We should all be ashamed of ourselves."

• • •

She ran out the door after her cousin, who was standing outside in the cold. "What's the matter, Paige?"

"*What is the matter?* You imbeciles all treat me like some kind of scientific experiment, the immense wonder of *Stella Scura*, who I surely do not want to be. I am certain you, your husband, and the incredible *Science Squad* are delirious with glee, thinking of the many additional billions and trillions you will all have once you discover how I manipulate energy."

"I'm sorry, Paige, and that isn't true; we're just excited about the discovery—the contributions to relativistic theories alone are more than could ever be conceived."

She pointed her finger down at Bella. "News for you—I am *not* a commodity to be shopped around. And neither he nor you are as smart as my mom."

"I agree with you." Bella put her arm around her. "I really am sorry, and I apologize for our obnoxiousness. No one thinks you're an experiment, it's just that we want to find out more about you, to help you understand your powers."

"That is a bunch of bull, because you only care about it to satisfy your stupid scientific agenda."

"To some extent, I agree. We're all scientists, and our whole lives are centered around discovering the unknown, but it doesn't mean we are devaluing you as a person. I'm sorry for the enthusiasm, but don't you want to do that, too?"

"A little bit, but I am not a scientist, and I do not think like all of you. These powers do not make me who I am; it is the person inside. Although my father was the scientist named Dirk, I do not care how they work."

"I guess we have to realize that, too. Sorry."

She shrugged. "Perhaps some of the time, I want to know about it, but not all of it. *Stella Scura* is not even a small portion of who I am, and I want to think of things other than my powers. I want someone to be interested in me, who I am, what I like to do. Do you know what the best part of coming here was?"

"What?"

"It was when I was playing toy cars with Jose. He did not want anything more than a playmate. He was not aware of my abilities and accepted me as I am."

"Why do you think you enjoyed that?"

"Please enlighten me since you know everything."

Bella stroked her hair. "That appeals to you because you're still a child, Paige. You want to play with toys and be a kid because you still *are* one in many ways."

"I am not! I am an adult; how absurd."

"Maybe legally, and you may *want* to be a grown-up, but inside, you're not. Sorting out everything takes time, you know. I'm exactly twice your age, so trust me on this one. I was damn lucky with some of the foolish choices I made, and I still haven't got stuff figured out. I probably never will."

"But I'm *not* you, Bella. I want to have everything right now, the way I want it."

"Tell me about it, but that's not the way the world works, although that's just human nature. You are kind of unique, after all."

"Well, I am sick and tired of being unique, geek!" She sputtered and looked out the window and rose off the ground six inches. "I wish that for one day I did not have these powers." She landed and started crying.

Bella put her arm around her shoulder. "You don't really mean that."

"Yes, I do. I just want to be Paige Marshall, average teenager."

"You know as well as I that average Paige Marshall can't change the world. But *Stella* can, in ways you can't possibly yet imagine."

"What, by threatening people with my powers? That is no way to be. You are wrong."

"No, you've known the answer to that all along: by showing people that you *don't* have to use them. There would be few walking this Earth who could do that. You would have the adoration of everyone."

"Not everyone, how stupid. There will be many who will resent me for being born with something no one else has and will see it as an advantage, whatever I end up doing with my life."

"Maybe. Then you will have to win them over with your persuasive verbal abilities."

"Yeah, right, I have such good interpersonal skills. Yes, I had come to that conclusion long ago, so a lot you know. Maybe I do not want to change stuff any longer. And I do not need to be adored like you all do."

"I suppose I have done my share of attention-getting. But we all want to be loved, Paige."

"Maybe I do not want or need that, so scat."

"I don't believe that, as it's a basic human trait. Even so, you can't change who you are. None of us can."

"If I were you, I would not want to change either. And you do not know me at all. I did not ask to be different, you know. I would trade it all to be a normal sighted person who was not capable of tossing a car into low Earth orbit."

"I know that your mother once had a fire burning in her to succeed, second to none. Whether she still has that or not, I have no clue. Your aunt is one of the strongest personalities of all time, and I'm no slouch myself."

She wiped tears from her eyes. "Yeah, you are all so great and famous, so what? Take your money, your medals, Oscars, Nobel Prizes, Super Bowl rings, and leave me the hell alone."

"I'll tell you what, missy: you can say whatever you want to me, but I *won't* leave you the hell alone because you're my family and not the only one with obstacles to overcome, and I care about you. You lived with your mother, a woman who overcame things you can't even imagine, but she never told you about her life, how hard it must have been."

"Yeah. She hid it from me, deedle deedle dee."

Bella poked her in the forehead. "Shut up, you loudmouthed lunkhead; it was because she didn't want to burden you with her many problems you couldn't solve. She may be eccentric, bizarre, and largely misunderstood by society and is a big pain in the butt most of the time, but deep down, she's the kindest person you'll ever know. Not everything's about you."

"Huh. That was her choice, not mine."

"*Choice?* Getting sick and almost dying at age eleven wasn't her choice, Paige. She lived most of her life as a deaf person."

"Yeah, and I have lived mine as a blind one. Big deal, it gives me no zeal."

"Quiet. For some reason, she got her hearing back after the explosion, even better than before. Yes, I'll give you credit for understanding the life of someone with a disability. But you don't know the real legend, the greatness she represented, without which you would have never existed."

"Maybe that would have been better for everyone."

"Really? You'll *never* know what it's like to be sick or in physical pain. Wendy helped make her what she is, gave her self-esteem, the confidence to succeed. But few people know any of that. Wendy may be overbearing and has surely changed over the years, but in the end, she is a kind person who wanted Bonnie to have that self-respect, to walk with pride, and to never settle for second best, despite her disability. For that, we all should be thankful, especially you."

"Pride that has transformed into unbelievable arrogance. I just get tired of it all the time."

"Yeah? Well, too bad. Wendy's dad created the weapons that killed everyone on *Darkkday*. He cheated on her mom for years and basically was a rotten SOB. I won't tell you about the other stuff he has done."

"I am sorry for the shortcomings of my colorful grandfather, but that is also not my problem; I cannot repair it, he is dead now."

"You haven't met Wendy yet, and, believe me, she isn't perfect. Despite the polish, she's essentially big, loud, and obnoxious. She also is a great American hero who lost two children on *Darkkday*. She's had her struggles with bipolar disorder. She isn't a beautiful, tanned, slim supermodel—she, rather, looks like most average Americans who struggle with things like their weight. She would kick most people's ass if the need arose and would defend you or any other family member to the death. She can also make you laugh harder than you ever have before."

"Stop with all the lectures. One mom is more than enough."

"I'm *telling* you that you need to lighten up. You just turned eighteen, and you don't have to have the weight of the world on your shoulders all at once, all of the time."

She shrugged. "Easy for you to say. You've also been pressuring me pretty hard."

"I know, and I'm sorry. We need to take a break."

"What do you mean? Go get some soda, coffee, or shots of Darkkin whiskey? Huh. Sounds fantastic. Not too hot for this tot."

Bella slapped her hard on the rear. "Oh, honey, you have no comprehension of the shenanigans I'm capable of. We're going on a girls' weekend out."

"Yeah? Doing what?"

"What girls do best: shopping, eating, and getting a makeover. They're the medicine to correct most any ills any girl might have."

"Are you serious? Where are we going?"

"Just don't worry. This is something I can do better than anyone else."

"We will see what the best of Aurora City has to offer? Is that supposed to impress me? Or are we going to Indianapolis? Yawn."

"Nope. Forget this place. We're going to Chicago."

• • •

A thirty-minute jet ride later, the pilot landed the private plane at Midway Airport as they stepped into the limousine, which drove them downtown to one of Bella's favorite hairdressers on the Magnificent Mile. She had never had her hair done at a place like this before, only at Sharon's Beauty College in Fairbanks, which charged $8.75 for a women's haircut, the outcome of which was not very reproducible, according to observers. The smell of lilac was in the air as the French male stylist shampooed her hair. It felt good as he dried it with a towel and began snipping it.

She enjoyed the manicure and pedicure, the attendant obviously having no idea that lying just beyond the edge of the nail was impenetrable skin. While she couldn't see her nails, she wanted them the brightest crimson possible. She didn't want to wear the bulky visor in public. Not just yet. That meant no vision, which was okay with her. It was familiar and comfortable.

Another lady demonstrated how to put on makeup properly.

She had never had a lot of interest in it, mainly because she didn't know how to do it properly, and the concept of a blind girl putting on her own makeup seemed ludicrous to some; Mom also wasn't a big help in that department. She learned how to put on the proper amount of foundation, lipstick, eye liner, etc. It wasn't that hard as long as the proper shades were picked out for her.

• • •

They then went to Waffney's Department Store downtown on the Magnificent Mile, where it was apparent that at least five different attendants were working with her. She couldn't recall the last time she actually wore a dress or skirt; they weren't always practical in cold weather, and she didn't have anyone around to help pick them out. Plus, she was kind of a tomboy and never dressed to impress.

"Wow, you certainly command a lot of attention," she said. "They must like you a lot here."

"Learn about the world, honey. These ladies all work on commission and could care less about me. My wallet is what commands the attention, trust me."

"Is that not a bit shallow for one of such high intellect?"

"Sure it is. But today, we're not worried about intellect or saving the world. Let's worry about spending money and becoming shallow beyond comprehension."

"Which outfits look the best, Bella?" she asked.

"All of them look great on you, I would not have picked anything out that wasn't. We've gotten you a start on a new wardrobe. If you look sharp, you feel sharp."

"I guess I never thought that was important, as I cannot see myself. Looking sharp is better than wearing a tarp."

"It is, dear. You never have a second chance to make a first impression. You or *Stella.* We need to buy some outfits for her, too."

She sighed. "But I do not require it. All the dresses, makeovers, blouses, shoes—"

She felt Bella's hand cover up her mouth. "Don't you dare say the last one. Every girl *has* to have a lot of shoes. It's a federal law."

"It is not, you made that up, as I am no pup."

"Well, it's the law here."

"But the expense must be enormous. I cannot accept all of these things."

Bella slapped her on the back. "Well, we've been through all that, and it does no good to argue with me; just ask *Tinman*, 'cause he always loses. And think about all the birthday presents you would've had over the years. This is money you would've had, anyway."

"It still is too much."

"Shut up, it's now beyond your control. We'll go stay in the Winterberry Hotel and get room service, do anything you want."

"I have heard of it, it must cost a lot to stay there."

"It doesn't cost anything extra if you own it."

"You own that hotel?" She put the visor back on in the limousine. "Really?"

"Not yet, but I will in about an hour. It is for sale."

"What? You cannot buy something like that in such a short period of time."

"Wanna bet?" She heard Bella pull something from her purse. "Hey, Danny, it's me. What can you get the Winterberry Hotel for? What? No, I haven't been drinking, but I plan on starting soon. Yes, I know you don't think they're good investments, but I don't really care. I want to buy it for a friend of mine. Yes, like everything, I want it now."

"Huh. What extravagance."

"Oh, come on now. It's always good to have a place to stay in Chitown, anyway, and I always wanted to own a five-star hotel. Plus, when we get back, the *Squad* will have completed your other garments that will cost substantially more than the ones we bought today."

"What other garments?"

"You'll see soon. I mean that literally." The limousine pulled up to the front door as a bellman helped them out. "Now, let's go to the suite of your new hotel. Our new swimming pool is spectacular, I hear."

"But I have no swimsuit."

Bella laughed. "Easily corrected. I will have an attendant bring several up momentarily, after we gorge ourselves on the finest cuisine this town has to offer."

"Which is what?"

"The Chicago hot dog, of course."

After eating, they went swimming, although she hadn't done it very much, mostly at school.

The hotel had an Olympic-sized pool, she had discovered. It was pretty easy to memorize exactly how many strokes it took to get from one side to the other, then flip over. About twenty-eight, just like at the Sulphur Springs complex, but she was relieved not to be studied like an experiment. She tried to breathe properly, so that she got some semblance of a resistance workout, as it was unknown if her body needed exercise like other persons did. But it didn't seem to matter much if she breathed or not. She just didn't want to look like a metahuman Gumby.

She looked forward to seeing what the *Science Squad* had in store for her when they got back, and promised Bella to have a more collaborative attitude.

Chapter Thirty-Eight

Two days later, after returning from their weekend in Chicago, Bella proudly announced that she was in possession of four dozen different pieces of blue and green sapphire, of varying degrees of opaqueness.

"Todd, Biv, and Wolf have been working on this while you've been doing the other experiments, and we've made multiple sets of goggles. Put one on."

"Hopefully it will be super great and well worth the wait."

"Try this one first." She felt Bella hand her the large goggles.

She fastened the strap and saw the same thing as always: nothing at all. "Huh, what a dud, it does not do anything."

"Well, we've got some others. Edison failed with his light bulb over ten thousand times before it worked, so, hopefully, it won't take us that long."

"Well, I will be dead by the time we do this ten thousand times. I do not have that much time while I am in my prime."

For the next hour, she tried on forty-six additional sets of goggles, and finally, at the next to last one, number forty-seven, she thought she could perceive some light after several minutes.

"You at least haven't thrown that one down in frustration, Paige. Do you see something?" Bella asked.

"I can—perceive *something*. It looks like gray."

"That's the darkest one, the blue sapphire. It cuts out 99.9992 percent of visible light and lets in infrared light with a cutoff of 780 nanometers," Biv said. "So Bella is, as usual, correct."

"Told ya."

"Apparently, we can, with these super shades, restore functional vision, but mainly in monochrome. They are made of an advanced synthetic sapphire which theoretically should let through the proper wavelengths. They will also have to be extremely strong to withstand flight. All things that can be accomplished with proper design and engineering."

She moved her head around and walked around the room.

"Well, Paige?"

"How light is it in here?"

"Average workspace of 500 lumens per square meter with LED lights at an incandescent color temperature," Bella said

"Well, I—I can see what looks to be like your form. Not as vivid or 3-D as the cybernetic helmet would be, and the colors are very muted, kind of a pinkish monochrome, like you have attested, but it works." She reached out to touch Bella's face and shrieked. "It actually works! I can see again. And you are more beautiful than I could have ever imagined."

"Thank you, but I knew that already." Bella took her by the arm and walked her to another part of the room. "Let's go over to Biv's retro eye chart. Can you read this?"

"Bella, she needs to get closer. I can't read it from there, and neither can you," Biv said.

"No, hold on, let's just see. Paige, tell me the smallest row you can read."

"That is easy, the last one. P-E-Z-O-L-C-F-T-D. What does that word mean? Is that some type of Slavic language besides Russian? A word with only one vowel?"

"Holy moly," Biv said in astonishment.

"Is it that bad?"

Biv laughed. "No, it's the opposite, Paige. You just read the 20/10 line at forty feet what a person with extraordinary vision could read at twenty feet. So, that means you have at least 20/5 vision with the first crude visor that actually functions."

"I guess that is good, from your excited tone, and not a moan."

"Good? Are you kidding? That degree of acuity is incredible," Biv said excitedly. The theoretical limit is 20/8 and has only been demonstrated in a handful of individuals."

"Great. Now, remember, Paige, the 'dark energy' field that somehow protects your body won't extend to the visor, just as it doesn't protect your hair or clothing."

She smiled. "Yeah, I get it, Bella. I have lived this way for a while, you know."

"Just checking. While the visor is made of synthetic sapphire—corundum—the second-hardest natural material, after diamond, as I mentioned—it can't easily be scratched, but it *can* be broken."

"Is there a better material to use, then?"

Bella shook her head. "I would've rather used aluminum oxynitride, colloquially termed transparent aluminum, which is not quite as hard as sapphire but far more durable and can definitely take a bullet. However, its chemical properties make it difficult to impart the unique optical properties required. Sapphire can withstand some pretty hard knocks, like the crystal on my watch, but it won't survive firearms or a bad crash. So you need to cover it with your hands if necessary."

"Or what?"

"Or you're SOL, what did you think? Flying blind should not be an aspirational goal."

"Yeah, I tried that once with Lt. Russ. Not a ton of fun."

"We will still tweak it but will get to work on making you some spares, given your future hazardous occupation."

• • •

"My guess from conducting all these tests is that you are virtually invulnerable to everything. I've fired bullets at you, tried setting you ablaze, used lasers that can cut through inch-thick steel; it's a joke. Radiation, too, obviously," Nick said.

She yawned. "I pretty much knew that already, Todd. I have been shot and rode a bike off a mountain and fell several hundred feet onto my head with no ill effects except for a bruised ego and loss of hair."

"You also have to have a disguise of some sort," Bella said.

"Why?"

"Because you need to have some anonymity, duh."

She sneered. "Oh, yes, I know the drill. 'No hero can be on duty 24/7. Also, I need to protect those close to me because my enemies will seek out revenge by killing my friends and family,' blah, blah, blah. My mother told me this endlessly when reading her stupid comics. It is the superhero's ubiquitous creed."

"I see that she's not matured much over the years," Bella said. "But she's right sometimes, as you may have figured out."

"Even a broken clock is right twice per day, I like to say."

Bella laughed. "Hey, funny girl, you have the perfect setup. No one would think twice about a real blind girl masquerading as a superhero."

"I do not wish to wear a mask. I am not fond of my mother's battle suit, either. Too confining, plus, it is destroyed. I doubt that even *you* have replacement parts for it."

"Not really. The visor is pretty big—although if we make it smaller, your field of vision will be reduced. If we could just do something with that hair."

She frowned. "Hey, what is wrong with my hair?"

"The color stands out. If we made it darker, that would be better, I mean, as a disguise."

"How? I do not think a wig would stay on at the supersonic velocities I fly, and I would have no place to put it when not in use. What do we do, then?"

Bella grabbed a strand of her Titian hair. "I have another idea, one I've had for a long time, but with no practical way to make it happen or real reason to do so. But that's all changed now. Wolf, get over here. We have some work to do."

Wolf rolled his wheelchair over. "I don't understand."

"I do not, either. What are you going to do to my hair? Burn it off now? I like my hair, and my beautiful head should not be bare."

"It's obvious, isn't it?" Bella said.

"Not really, no," Wolf said.

"I want her to be able to change hair color instantly using solid-phase matter change."

"Huh? That is obvious to whom? Albert Einstein?"

"I'm sure it would work." Bella jumped up and down excitedly. "Wolf? Whatcha think?"

Wolf thought for a few seconds. "Yes, I suppose it's possible, under the right conditions, with the right expensive raw materials and an *enormous* amount of pressure, mind you."

"Come again?" she asked.

"We can use extremely fine carbon nanoparticles which can change molecular conformational state to become clear one moment and opaque the next," Bella beamed. "Wolf here is a brilliant polymer chemist. It has to be doable, right?"

"You have completely lost me," she said.

"Well," Wolf came up to her and shook his head. "In theory, yes, we can combine the nanoparticles with a protein that will bind to your hair, but the phase change takes a lot of force, and you can only do it to the particles a few times before they break down and have to be replaced. They would be quite expensive."

"So? I've had much tougher technical things to overcome than this." Bella nodded. "Money is not an object, obviously. And we know someone who can generate quite a bit of force, don't we?"

"We're talking an enormous amount, Bella." Wolf opened his mouth wide and slapped himself in the face. "Duh, what am I saying? I guess that's not a problem, assuming you have the raw materials I need. Her hair isn't indestructible, though. It might be damaged, given enough actuations."

"Of course it will work. And it can be applied as a shampoo, in its colorless state, and she likely won't be changing it several times a day. The structural changes can also be engineered to also straighten her hair, which is naturally slightly curly, while protecting it at the same time."

He nodded. "Yes, that's feasible. It would give it the appearance of being slightly longer, too."

"I will have a new hairdo and sunglasses, but what about the rest of me, Bella?"

"When we're done, I'll take you to the 'dressing room,' and you'll find out what we've come up with."

• • •

"This is a special carbon-based dye Bella theorized years ago, Paige, but never had the time or opportunity to pursue," Wolfram Steele said after a day of experimentation. "It changes phase from colorless to opaque." He rolled his wheelchair up to the table.

"How does it change?"

"Simple, like Bella says, it changes molecular state in a weightless environment, and then back again with the application of at least ten G's. It's impractical for most purposes, as the force is too much for any man-made devices to cause the change. Fortunately, you have plenty of that."

"What great feat does it accomplish?"

"When applied to your hair, it will change its color from the current Titian to midnight black when high pressure is applied by altering the carbon nanostructure. It will change your appearance and shouldn't damage your hair. Apparently it will affix to 'dead' cells, like in your hair, or your outer epidermal layer on your face. Do it again, and it will change back. It also provides some protection against wind or heat damage since your hair can be destroyed just like mine."

"What hair?" Bella said, laughing. "In order for your hair to be destroyed, you'd need to have some. Do you have a chemical that somehow grows it, Wolf? If so, you'd be richer than me."

"Shut up, Bella. Maybe I like being bald. It's a sign of a high testosterone level." He looked at her. "It actually doesn't interfere with the shampoo, either. I worked in cosmetics for ten months after grad school. It wouldn't hurt your hair to use it every day."

"Why black?" she asked. "Kind of dark, don't you think?"

"What's wrong with my black hair?" Bella asked.

"Nothing, it is just that my hair is lighter."

"I know, I'm just messin' with you."

"I am just not used to it myself."

"You're half Hispanic; it would look just fine."

"And you're the Dark Star, aren't you?" Wolf asked. "Would you have preferred green or pink? I could've lightened it, but then you would look too much like the President flying around. I sure didn't think you wanted *that.*"

She laughed. "I suppose not. 'Super-President' is not the image I want by any stretch of the imagination. Maybe someday, though, it would be reality—a President who flies. The world might be ready for a number of nutty things by 2048, but probably not that."

"There is some clear makeup, too. It will cover your freckles like the dye changes your hair. Also, your hair has a fair amount of natural curl. The microscopic carbon nanotubes will straighten, also straightening your hair and lengthening it a bit."

"Does it wear off?"

"Yes. It has to be re-applied every few days or so, like a shampoo; maybe more often, depending on how much air turbulence damages your hair. It will adhere to your skin, too, so you'd better wear gloves when you apply it. The makeup, once daily. I'll furnish you with a substantial supply."

"Thanks. I doubt I could purchase it at the local drugstore."

"One more thing I think I can create."

"What?"

"While we work on another solution to your blindness, the striking appearance of your heterochromia would be another give-away, given its rarity. I can make a contact lens to cover your blue left eye that can change to dark brown, like the other one."

"A blind woman wearing a contact lens? That is a first, although I am not sure why *Stella* would be without the visor."

• • •

She stood in her outfit as she looked in the mirror. The form-fitting outfit was dark blue, with no symbol, curiously. The reason Bella gave is that, since dark energy was invisible, it couldn't be represented by a symbol, and they decided an "SS" logo wasn't very politically correct. And she was so unique that she didn't need one anyway. And no capes. Capes looked stupid.

The special synthetic sapphire goggles allowed her extremely detailed sight but with limited color perception. Her sight wasn't anywhere near as good as that provided by the old Vladimirov helmet, but it was still amazing, given its simplicity, and she didn't want to see that damn thing ever again, even if it could be repaired. Boots and gloves were a royal blue, in contrast to the long-sleeved dark blue bodysuit. She didn't want to leave fingerprints around, after all, hence the gloves.

"Ladies and gentlemen, I give you the new—*Stella Scura,*" Bella said proudly.

"It surely must be an aesthetic augmentation from the old one."

"Stylin, Paige," Nick said.

"Yes, I observed myself in the mirror. I am not used to seeing myself and had no idea I looked like this. Before a few days ago I never had experienced that."

"What? I thought you could see with Viktor and Grandpa Rad's funky suit," Bella said. "So I don't understand."

"Sure, far better than this, but, duh, I was *in* that ugly thing, so I just saw the armor. I could see through other objects, but not my own body. Yecchh."

"But, this—you are mighty good looking, let me tell you that. Watch out for *Cowboy* and *Photraman* here. You don't have to worry about *Ampere,* though."

"Why not?"

"Todd's gay."

"Oh."

She saw Todd move closer. "Hey, I can still appreciate good-looking women, Bella. All except you. Your personality sort of negates your other assets."

"I'm so insulted."

"But, it is a bit much for a superhero, do you not think? Rather form-fitting and vain, not resembling a plain Jane?"

"Hey, you're a symbol of world good, so you better look the part. Plus, you're built way better than your mom. You need to look hip and fun, not like some flying nun, hon."

She laughed. "That is funny."

"Although a lot of nuns are tough customers, just like you."

"How would you know anything about nuns?"

"Believe me, I do, 'cause I went to a Catholic school for a lot of years. They might be able to kick even your tail."

"I suppose so." She shook her head. "But you fail to understand *why* it is funny, Bella."

"I do? Enlighten me, then."

"While I am trying to decide the meaning of the voluminous teachings of the Lord—and if I believe them or not—I have no desire to be a nun. It is surely not the job I am destined to have."

"That's good. I think I get it."

She shook her head. "You do?"

Bella squinted at her. "Yes, dear, I wasn't born yesterday."

She blushed. "It is surely out as a vocation for me; it is not meant to be, per the official decree. And my outfit should be non-denominational, as I represent all people, not a church steeple."

"Is that right?"

"Also non-territorial. I do not want to be seen as being only for the United States."

"Cool. Not what the President might want, but we don't care about her." Bella punched her in the shoulder. "Hey, that's weird."

"What?"

Bella punched her as hard as she could, which wasn't very. She then frowned and hit her again harder. "Huh. No matter how hard I hit, it seems to be absorbed. Like punching a pillow."

"That is correct; I thought you understood such concepts, being the esteemed, eloquent energy engineer you are."

"Knowing about it and experiencing it physically are two different things. It's kind of fun."

"It is fortuitous because bullets and such just drop instead of ricocheting off and injuring others, and those who hit me really do not get hurt, either."

"And they call me an airbag. You really are one." She laughed. "Yet, when you want to hit someone or something, you can, and impart a terrific force, per our tests."

"I suppose so. I have not thought much about the physics."

"Anyway, the fabric has Kevlar fiber woven into it for strength."

"Why would it need Kevlar, Bella?" Biv asked.

"You don't understand physics, do you?" Bella took her left hand with her right after removing the glove. "*Cowboy*, shoot at me with the airsoft rifle over there."

"What? Are you kidding?"

"I'll be fine. We tested this, remember?"

"Okay, it's your funeral." Wolf fired off several rounds of airsoft pellets at Bella's left arm while she was holding *Stella*'s hand, and they all watched as the shirt shredded.

"Now fire at *Stella*." The bullets hit the fabric, which was unharmed.

"It survives those little toy pellets. What a magnanimous feat, it is such a treat."

"Yeah, we can't just keep making you new outfits each time, you know. Not that money's a problem, but these suits are about two hundred fifty grand a pop. With the sapphire goggles and Wolf's shampoo, your duds cost over half a million for each set."

"Another thing: if I want to discreetly leave, how shall I do so?"

"Got that all figured out. We have a secret exit to this complex, a tunnel that exits about a half-mile from the building proper."

"Why would you have that?"

"Because my husband likes stupid stuff and wanted to have a secret exit."

"Watch it," Nick said. "Who's calling my tunnel stupid?"

"I agree with Nick," she said. "We also have an exit tunnel—an actual underground laboratory—in Alaska."

"I have to go see that sometime," Nick said.

"It is pretty cool. I dug it myself, out of solid rock, with my bare hands, in about a day and a half."

"I wish I had you around for some construction projects."

"Yeah, well, I do not come cheap."

• • •

"What wondrous experiment are we doing now?" she asked Nick as she put on the visor as he came into view.

"Measuring your resistance to gamma radiation and how your body shields it. Here, swallow this." He handed her the pill-sized probe. "I'm going to put you in front of the linac and bombard you with gamma rays."

"A what?"

"Linac. Linear accelerator. Creates high radiation levels with x-ray tubes rather than a radioisotope source."

She saw the small object being placed into her left hand. "What the heck is this?"

"A small probe. It will record radiation levels for 24 hours while it's in your GI tract. Swallow it like a pill."

"I do not know how to swallow a pill, never done it before."

"You've never taken an aspirin or anything?"

"Of course not; that is a dumb question. Why would I have done so? Can I chew it?"

"No! You'll destroy the probe that way. It's expensive."

"Sorree."

"Well, we'll work on that." He handed her a glass of water. "Just put it in your mouth, take a drink, and let it slide down; it's very smooth."

"I'll try." After putting it in her mouth and taking a few sips of water, it finally slid down. "Yechh. How do we, uh, get it out?"

Nick smiled. "How do you think it comes out?"

"I am no scientist."

"You do, er, function that way, don't you?"

"Do I poop? Is that your quirky query? That is a rather personal matter, Nick, I do not care to discuss my elimination habits."

"Just need to know when it'll come out the other end."

She smirked. "Yes, of course, everyone poops, as the classic children's book decrees. It depends on how much I eat. Most organic matter is not absorbed, so they can be of large diameter."

"What about the other? Do you pee?"

"Yeah, what did you think, Nick? All of my bodily functions are normal, more or less, I must confess."

"Sorry. I won't discuss any more 'bodily functions,' then."

"That would be a very good idea."

Not many private laboratories had a linear accelerator, or linac, but this one did, that was separate from the main Mendoza Multinational labs. Apparently, this one was for Nick's private tinkering. A somewhat lethal toy to play with in the wrong hands.

"Okay. Stand here. I'm going back to the other room."

"Wimp."

A few hours later, the probe had traversed the entirety of her GI tract and was being analyzed by her host.

"What great things have we discovered?" she asked, yawning.

"A lot. The probe demonstrates only background radiation, nothing more. I started out slightly over background radiation, and even when I gave you a total body dose of 500 rads, or centigray. That's a lethal dose. It will cause some reddening of your outer epidermal layer, which will regenerate in a day or so."

"What's background radiation?"

"It's radiation that's everywhere. You have some radioactive isotopes in your own body that give off minimal radiation. Also from the sun. The magnetosphere deflects most of the solar wind, but a small amount gets through."

"So, I am impervious to gamma radiation."

"Yes."

"Did we not know that before? Duh! What a waste of time."

• • •

"How similar is my body to yours, Biv, from your experiments?" she asked during lunch in the lab break room as she chewed eagerly on her chicken salad sandwich.

"Girl, Roy G. Bivereaux barely qualifies as human, so that's a very bad comparison," Kepler said sarcastically.

"You shut up, Johnny; *you* barely qualify as a living diploid organism," Biv said as he turned back to *Stella*. "It's hard to tell, since I am no biochemist or geneticist, and we lack the ability here to do extensive testing anyway. Your body contains the same waste products as ours, like pigments from broken-down red blood cells and such."

She frowned. "My blood cells are all broken-down? That is very sad. How do we invigorate them and make them glad?"

"Red cells, even yours, have a finite lifespan of about 120 days. They die off and must be replaced by new ones."

"The wonders of science. What are these pigments?"

"Urobilin, or urochromes, which give urine its distinct yellow color."

She shrugged. "I would not know if mine is yellow, fellow."

"Well, it is. And your stool seems to have slightly more undigested foods than a normal person's, which on one hand means you may not need as much to absorb for energy. However, we know that you don't require any food at all for sustenance, so why any would be digested is puzzling. It would take us years to figure out."

"I am certain that was an exciting experiment, fun for all ages."

"Not so much, neither was fishing Tinman's damn radiation probe out of your poop. Your intestinal microflora is pretty normal, accounting for about forty percent of your stool's mass, although the role that microorganisms play in your digestion is unknown. The bacteria there are as vulnerable as any other bacteria to destruction."

"Those are such fun facts to know."

She heard Biv wash his hands in the sink. "You seem to have remarkable control of your body, with a precision that's better than could ever be imagined. Your touch discrimination, for example, is over twenty times greater than mine or any other person's."

"Why is that, do you think?"

"I don't know. Your mom, of course, was the poster girl for unusual sensory perception. It's quite probable that your precision of touch and motor control has nothing to do with dark energy and how you manipulate it but is a manifestation of genetically inherited tendencies. You aren't a synesthete like your mom and Jay, but many people on the autism spectrum have unusual sensory perceptive abilities. One of yours must be proprioception."

"Huh? Proprio-what?"

"Proprioception: the ability we have to detect exactly where a body part is without seeing it."

"I guess I know I have that, but not the name. Yet, I do not demonstrate any other qualities of that, Biv. Unlike my mom, my functioning senses are nothing spectacular."

Biv laughed. "Sure you do; you just aren't aware of those things. I spent a lot of time with your mom back in the day, and you talk an *awful* lot like her, so much that it's eerie—your vocal avoidance of contractions for example, which is classic, although she uses them occasionally; yet, you don't avoid them completely in your writing. The large vocabulary and penchant for complex sentences—when simpler ones would suffice—are others. And the clear preference for rhyming and alliterative speech, which your mom *didn't* have as much. That isn't learned; it's neurological."

"What does that mean?"

"You do it without thinking about it."

"I suppose that is true." She shook her head. "But I do not have any of her celebratory cipher powers; I cannot do magic tricks or escape from a straitjacket—unless, of course, I tear it apart. I know no other language except Russian, which I was taught as a child. I am also quite average at math, perhaps because I do not give a crummy crap; I would rather just go take a nice nap."

Biv laughed. "I don't think you even know when you do it."

"Do what?"

"Rhyme and alliterate. Like I said, I think it's neurological, that you do it without intention."

"Huh. I cannot remember, as I do not always pay attention. But my ability to control my powers is merely genetic happenstance? What would occur if you had my powers?"

"I would probably break everything I touched. I mean it. You have a strength range a trillion times greater than the average person—and that may even be an underestimate. Yet you take it all in stride and do all the things we do, blending in without wreaking havoc."

"I have also had a lot of practice, Biv. I was not born this way. Mom had many drills I had to do when I was younger. Luckily, I do not tire easily."

"Even so, it's remarkable. And your basic physiology must not be that much different than a normal person's. Slightly stronger, more resistant to disease, perhaps. Maybe less resistant."

"How can I be less resistant?"

"We normal folks are exposed to billions of microorganisms daily, most of them non-pathogenic. I don't think your immune cells ever get exposed to them, so you don't mount an immune response against those little guys. What might be innocuous to us could be deadly to you."

"You know this for a fact?"

"It's just speculation until we can run a blood sample."

"I shiver in anticipation. What about Juriann?"

"No, it's not the same at all, although we don't know much about him, either. He, at his basic level, is a much more powerful being than you. You aren't much stronger than an average female your size, although you do appear to have significant native physical attributes—your jumping ability, coordination, and so on, are clearly a result of natural genetics."

She crossed her arms. "I am well aware of that. I can be 'on' or 'off,' and know the difference."

"Yes, but you appear be surrounded by some pretty amazing force field that operates at a hair's breadth from your body. It seems to protect you from anything that might be harmful."

"And it protects any person or animal that I touch."

"Correct." He took out a small pair of scissors and cut off a few strands of her hair. "Your hair, however, can easily be cut, as I've just demonstrated, as it's not living tissue."

"I know that. Tell me something I do not know."

"Look at your legs. You've been here for several days, and the hair's growing out a bit."

She rubbed the minimal stubble. "Thanks a lot for pointing out that I am living an uncouth existence. Is this why you have been so unsuccessful in your own social life, with significant strife?"

"Never mind. I assume you do shave your legs and armpits."

She sighed. "Most girls do, Biv. Did they not teach you that in medical school, or did you miss that lecture?"

"Then this aura, or whatever, doesn't protect dead skin. You've never cut yourself shaving, have you?"

She shook her head. "Of course not, because I use gel, not foam, like the commercials say, to get that clean-shaven feel and sustain scintillating sensual sex appeal."

He pulled up her shirt sleeve. "But, this—have you ever noticed this indentation before?"

"I have felt it before. I thought I was born with it, like the birthmark on my buttocks."

"Not quite; it's too regular for a birthmark. I have one too."

"You do? What is it?"

"It's an immunization scar. So, somehow you were immunized as a young child, Paige."

"Why would I need that?"

"Don't know, but maybe you're susceptible to some of the same diseases that we all are? But somehow there is a way to do it. Let me ask you this. Can you hurt yourself?"

"Why would I want to do that?"

"Well, suppose you had diabetes and had to check your blood sugar by pricking your finger and putting a tiny drop of blood on the meter. How would you do that?"

"I am normally in a 'de-powered' state where I have only average strength, but that is different. I still cannot be hurt when I am like that, but Mom believes that I can turn it off—the protective mechanism—if I want. So I guess I could accomplish that, somehow, or give myself a shot. I did have to concentrate very hard for the helmet electronics to work, so maybe that was what I was doing. I have never tried to hurt myself, why would I do that?"

Biv shook his head. "I don't know, Paige. I am concerned that, if you were hypnotized or otherwise under mental control, that you could be harmed or even destroyed."

"How or why would anyone want to do that?"

Biv laughed. "You are the greatest force the world has ever known, at least since Christ. If you don't think someone might look for a way to manipulate or get rid of you, you're really clueless."

"I suppose the only time I ever felt that was with my mom."

"What?"

"Whenever she would touch me, I would feel a bit weakened for a minute; like she could hurt me if she really wanted to. Of course, I knew that would never happen, as I could move away pretty fast. But that was a long time ago. Over the years, I have lost that feeling. I don't know if she could do it now."

"Unless someone was able to duplicate that power and augment it."

"If Mom is the only one who can do it, I do not see how that is possible."

"There might be someone way smarter than us who could figure out how to make it possible."

• • •

Nick handed her the dark blue helmet, which somewhat resembled a motorcycle helmet.

"What is this? I am going bike riding? When can we go?"

He shook his head. "Hardly. If you're going to fly, you need to learn the rules of the air."

"Huh. I will need a pilot's license?" she asked curiously. "That sounds very boring."

"Yes, you do, actually. I can help you with that, as you will just have to learn the regulations, operation of the equipment is not an issue. You'll have to take some tests."

She laughed. "I do not even have a drivers' license."

"You don't?" Nick thought for a minute and smiled. "Oh, yeah, funny. We will need to fix that eventually since you can see now. You don't need one for a pilot's license, anyway."

"Why do I need an aviator's permit?"

"Because you have to share the airways with regular aircraft, what do you think? There are lots of rules and regulations you have to follow, and this helmet contains advanced avionics. Despite your small size compared to other aircraft, you could be very dangerous at the velocities you fly, so you need to learn how to stay out of the way."

"More studying and tests. I thought I was done with that stuff."

"No problem. We'll set you up and do all the things online. Biv can give you a medical clearance."

"That should be very uninteresting," she said, yawning.

"No time for a nap now, we need to get to work. The FAA is nothing to scoff at, Paige."

Chapter Thirty-Nine

A Crummy Old Warehouse
Somewhere in Rio de Janeiro, Brazil

The tall, spindly blond man sat down in the chair at the nondescript old warehouse next to a junkyard in Rio. Dr. Ramon Argon knew the reputation of Kristoff van Sant and his friend, Reuben J. Skelton, and that's why he was here. These guys were, by all accounts, missing a few marbles. Not the kind of folks he was fond of dealing with.

But they had things he needed: access to nuclear missiles, advanced quantum computer technology, criminal contacts, and a lot of money. Money Ramon Argon needed for the continuation of his *Mantissa* project, the one that would make him king of the world.

He watched as the scrawny white man took a drink of dark German beer from a mug as he approached him. Despite his name, the man known to some as *Santaman* looked less like Santa Claus than anyone he could imagine.

"Dr. Argon, so good to see you again. I wish I had met your uncle, as I heard he was a great man, a visionary genius." He shook the weirdly-built six-six ectomorph's clammy, skinny hand.

"Thanks. What did you admire most about him?"

"The fact that he killed one President and almost did away with another, if not for Rad Darkkin and that freak from Caltech. I met her once, you know. She's a force to be reckoned with, strong as hell. A worthy adversary."

"Then it's good she was blown up on *Darkkday*."

"Yes, it is, although I wish all of Washington had been destroyed, too. And that I really had done it. In that case, I would've done it right, not like that headless idiot Ming." *Santaman* laughed hysterically.

"Why do you hate America so much, Kris?" Argon asked.

"Why, Argon? Dumb ass, you dare ask such a question? They value Christmas above all else—it's the most meaningless day, the most worthless holiday of them all. We make it out to be something truly special, but it's not. We start seeing Christmas shit up in stores by August, four or five months beforehand. It is all just commercialization, and the one known as President is the worst human being to have ever existed, after her dead sister-in-law."

"It sounds like more than that, van Sant."

"It is. I have this stupid fucking name. How ironic."

"So? You could've changed it, you know."

Van Sant shook his head. "Changing my name wouldn't have gotten rid of my family. My father was a dreadful person. He was never home, he was mean, he was drunk all the time, especially at Christmas. He made it the worst holiday of the year."

Argon laughed. "So you had some shitty Christmases, and your dad was an alky. Everyone has problems. Deal with it, man, get some counseling, keep your eye on the ball here and grow a pair of balls."

"I don't have to 'deal with it,' Argon. I made a bunch of dough selling missiles 'stolen' from the Russians back to other countries. I can do whatever the hell I want, so shut the fuck up."

"Okay. But I suppose that's why I want you as a partner. You hate people, especially those in Washington."

"Hahaha. You got that right. So I'm going to make it the worst holiday for everyone. They love Christmas in New York—well, this is going to be the worst goddamn Christmas the Americans ever had. I got blamed for *Darkkday*, I only wish I really had done it, so I need to get the recognition that's truly due me by doing something far worse than blowing up the Darkkins."

Argon reluctantly admitted to himself he'd made the right choice, teaming up with this guy. He needed a big distraction around for when *Mantissa* would infiltrate Washington. New York would be destroyed, while the nation's capital would be ruined in a much more insidious. And that took shitloads of secret information. Information that could only be obtained in one way.

For, if he was correct, nothing could stop the power that was called *Mantissa*. But he still needed the help of someone else, someone with great knowledge of the West Wing who just happened to have just had a massive falling out with the President.

To meet him, though, they couldn't meet in Brazil or most other places. Time to take *Santaman's* private jet to the Adriatic Sea.

• • •

A Much Crummier Old Warehouse
Somewhere in Dredo, Crogobia

Former Secretary of Defense Tom Ashburn, permanently out of any type of well-paying job (and most low-paying ones, for that matter), reluctantly entered the room in the old warehouse in the small Eastern European city, located in one of the few countries with no extradition treaty with the United States, and also a country no one in the USA cared about.

His mind drifted from that to what he had become and what he felt compelled to do. He would do just about anything to get back at her. And pay the bills, an unfortunate necessity. Maybe he could do both with a little luck. He didn't seem to have much luck lately.

"Ah, Mr. Ashburn. Do have a seat."

Ashburn sat down reluctantly as the spindly man brought him a glass of wine.

"My name is Kristoff van Sant. Surely you must know me."

"Sure, you're *Santaman,* the asshole who blew up the plane on *Darkkday*. Congratulations. You've earned the anger of millions."

He shook his head and laughed. "No, no, that is all untrue. While those sordid events were all blamed on me, surely you know that Sung Shoi-Ming and the Tosians did it with the help of Brant Gallagher, blaming it on me and those North Korean bastards."

He looked at the blond, gangly man curiously. "I have never heard a more outrageous declaration in my life."

"It's true. I wish I had done something that grand, but if I had, it would've been on Christmas Day, which was only a few weeks away. Anyone who knows me would know that."

"Well, whatever. We both know the truth now, and it doesn't matter. So, why do you folks need me, then? Not that I have any better place to be right now, for reasons you should know."

"Why? Because, despite your recent unemployment woes, you have an intimate knowledge of Air Force One and the President's security. We can bring the USA to its knees."

"We went over that on the phone. So, you all wanted me to try and blow up that crazy flying freak in Alaska, and now you want me to crash Air Force One into some city. For some reason, I did it. Right now, I'm not sorry about that, but it perplexes me why I wanted to in the first place."

"Yes, you did, and soon you shall discover why."

"Not sure what the hell that means. But, big deal, that worked out real well. Gonna take a lot more than that to take over the USA, especially now with some flying alien in town."

"Well, sure it will, lucky for everyone we're around. In the meantime, meet my other friend, Reuben J. Skelton."

"Sure. Hey, Skel, how's it going?"

The heavyset, fortyish redhead, sporting a large port-wine stain over nearly half his face, stood up. "American simpleton, ye shall forevermore call me by my preferred name, *The Red Skeleton,*" Skelton said in a deep Yorkshire accent.

He laughed. "What the hell kind of fucked-up stupid name is that? You got a shitload of weight to lose to resemble a skeleton, pal. You also could use a good dermatologist. I once went to an old drive-in back in Phoenix named The Red Skeleton; was that your gig before this? Burger and fry cook? Looks like you ate up all the profits, fatso."

Skelton grabbed him by the neck. "I shall kill ye, measly scalawag. Show a little respect. Compare me to a mere greasy spoon, will ye? Many have died for less than that. It's only that Kristoff wants to work with ye that ye still breathe oxygen."

"Okay, sorry, dude, whatever. Jesus." Ashburn looked at the larger man to his right as the portly but muscular Skelton relaxed his grip as Ramon Argon entered the room. "So, Argon, why the fucking clown show here? Do you really need to stoop so low as to work with these freaks?"

Skelton grimaced. "That's it, as ye shall soon be a dead carcass; I don't care who the hell ye be or what Kris says."

"Hey, sorry, man."

"An accurate statement, as ye shall soon be."

Van Sant laughed hysterically. "You think me, of all people, to be a mere clown? How little you know regarding the depth of my vast talents. I am far more than what I appear to be."

"Kris, enough of the speeches. Well, it was time for some creative redirection," Argon said.

"What? Creative redirection, with—this?" he asked curiously.

"My uncle Malachi had limited vision, despite his great intellect. My creation is *far* more dangerous than his stupid *Ortho-Man*. Nicholas Stannous is not the only billionaire scientist on this planet. Some of us, like Mr. van Sant and Mr. Skelton, want to do bad things to the world with our inventions, and they have the passion and ingenuity to do it. Others, like me, just want to rule it. You can be a part of that too."

"What is it? Do you really want to mess with that alien sighted in New Persia and Alaska? Did you see what it's capable of?"

Argon laughed. "I know all about Kepler's dark energy project, which Stannous helped fund, and I must believe she has something to do with that. That flying freak is an ancillary curiosity, that's for sure, but that's all."

"*That's all?* By my estimations, it's a fricking living star, a virtually indestructible, inexhaustible energy source that could change the world, maybe the universe. You could rule the world with that power. Are you serious, Argon?"

"Absolutely, and I'm not discounting that. But there's a much greater power to be had, trust me. Something that can make me the richest person on the Earth: Project *Mantissa*. Bring our friend in." Argon gestured as the five-five woman came in and sat down.

He looked at the twentyish brunette woman, who seemed to have a haunting, smoldering beauty. "Who the hell is this? Your moll?"

She stared back at him and scowled. "Who the hell are *you*, bozo? What do you think you're staring at? Better not be my boobies; I'll come over there and kick your ass. And I ain't no moll."

"Huh? What the hell is more of this carnival shit—"

Argon smiled at him and patted him on the shoulder. "You see, my dear dead uncle Malachi bio-engineered the wrong weapon, as he had no perspective. This one is far more dangerous than his super-strong man and even a girl who can fly and lift massive objects. Where's the stealth and cunning in that? Not hardly my style at all. And certainly not *Santaman's* or *Red Skeleton's*."

"Huh? What is his meaning, Kris?" Skelton asked dimly.

"Shut the fuck up, Skel, you ugly, fat asshole. You may be good at computer crap and cyber-hacking, but otherwise you don't know shit. I want to hear what Argon has to say."

"I don't follow." Ashburn looked at the young, dark-haired beauty curiously, who snarled back at him. "I'll be damned, but she looks and talks like a younger version of Isabel Mendoza."

"How observant," the woman replied.

"I have met her several times, given her frequent visits to the White House." He snickered. "Look, she's an excellent double, but I don't see how that helps us— "

"She isn't a double, Ashburn."

He looked at her as she snarled back. "No way. Why in the hell would you spend billions of dollars to clone *her?* What's the value of an instantly recognizable celebrity? I assume you want her to infiltrate M2 for some reason. You could do that in any other number of ways that are less conspicuous."

"You are smarter than your resume indicates, yet you, like others, lack the creative vision to achieve true greatness. Yes, for the moment, she looks like the famous chemical engineer, and, in fact, they are biologically related, you might say. But *not* a clone. Say hello to *Mantissa*."

"You are all crazy." He got up but was stopped by the massive Skelton. "Clone or whatever, why the hell would you emulate some famous rich person? Let me out of here."

"I don't think so, Mr. Ashburn," van Sant chortled. "You have something we need."

"What's that?"

"Like I said: an intricate knowledge of the security procedures of the United States Secret Service, which we need badly."

"Yeah, we tried that once, didn't work out so well. What good is it now?"

"I suspect the security at M2 and government missile silos must be similar."

"What? Missiles? You must be mad."

Santaman started laughing wildly. "Of course I'm mad, that's why I'm here; such matters require 'out of the box' creativity that only I and *Red Skeleton* can supply. My friend Dr. Argon is not, though. They blamed me for *Darkkday.* While I wish I could've taken credit for that, I was a scapegoat. But, now, we will get rid of *Stella Scura* and use *Mantissa's* powers to crush the President and take over the world in one fell swoop. A big-ass nuclear missile will crash into New York City on Christmas Eve, 2028. They say Christ is coming again; by then, it will be too damn late."

The woman shook his hand as she changed to a friendly demeanor. "It's nice to meet you, sir."

"What?" He suddenly felt weak, as if all the energy had been drained from his system.

"I now know your birthday, your Social Security number, and every other intimate secret you possess. I can control your mind, even kill you with a mere thought. What do you think of that?"

"No!" He put his hands up to his head as he winced in pain. "Get out of my mind!"

"Through physical contact, I can manipulate minds and easily annihilate you if I want."

"Nice trick, but good luck with that. I don't think you'll be very incognito, resembling who you do."

"Really?" He watched the woman as she changed to a blonde, blue-eyed, fair-skinned woman of the same height and weight. "What about now? This work better for you?"

"I don't believe it. Shape-shifting isn't possible."

"You sure about that?" He watched with awe as she then morphed into a much older, substantially taller, and heavier blonde woman quite familiar to him, gaining about eighty pounds seemingly at will.

"No—it's not possible."

"Really? Y'all like this one? Hail to me, the Chief. You still aren't getting your job back, asshole."

Ashburn almost fell over. "The voice, the face, it's uncanny. How are you doing that? You significantly increased your mass in mere seconds; it's impossible. Even if you could do it physically, the clothing is different."

She changed to a "generic" dark-haired man wearing a navy pinstripe suit. "Of course it isn't possible," Argon said. "She's looked the same the whole time. It's all in your mind, Ashburn. She possesses the most powerful weapon of all."

"What?"

"She has the power to change your perception of anything. You think she looks like Isabel Mendoza, the President, a random person, or anybody else because she changed what you thought you saw. She can make you do anything and believe that you want to.

And if you don't think that's a better power than flying and lifting really heavy objects, you're really an idiot."

He sat down and shook his head as he turned towards her, as she had now assumed the form of a random dark-haired woman.

"Okay, I get it, but what about photographs and video feeds and such? It isn't going to fool a modern digi-scan computer."

Argon laughed. "No, of course not. The shape-shifting illusion is just a parlor trick that works on humans. She has to be disguised enough to look like the person of interest for the low-resolution cameras and can't change that on the fly, obviously. You have to be careful where she is, so she's under minimal surveillance. But the much greater value is that she can read minds and extract passwords and other information with ease, as long as she has made physical contact with you."

"What else?"

"Oh, a whole lot of shit. Get a load of this," van Sant said. "*Mantissa*: we had that discussion about Eric over there, because all he does is complain about crap. Relieve him of his misery."

"What did I do?" Eric, one of van Sant's men, asked curiously.

"Your mere existence is insult enough, and your purpose here is only to be a demonstration for Mr. Ashburn," *Santaman* chortled.

She went over to Eric and put her hand on his head.

"Hey, ye promised I could kill Eric," Skelton said angrily. "It not be fair, Kris, ye lousy liar, depriving me of enjoyment."

"Shut up," van Sant said. "I wanna see this."

"You seem expendable, one of minimal intellect."

"No, don't do that—" Eric said.

"You are a worthless piece of humanity," *Mantissa* said.

"Get out of my head! The pain—*AIEEEE!*" Eric said as he slumped to the ground.

"What did she—it—whatever—do to him?" Ashburn asked.

"Whatcha think, dummy? His brain's completely fried, by psionic powers, or something," van Sant said. "You ain't real big in the brain department, huh?"

"Look who's talking. But that's horrible."

Van Sant chuckled and shook his angular, balding head. "Naw, I disagree. I think it's great fun!"

"I don't believe this," Ashburn said.

"Believe it, Sec. I've already been inside your head."

"What did you say?"

"Who the hell did you think made you create those Tosian cyber-mirages, hit Kriger, and set off that EMP device?"

"So, *you* were the unannounced woman in my office a few weeks ago?"

"There's no fooling you, slick. You're a genius for sure."

"And you made me try and shoot down *Stella Scura*."

"Wow. Your intellect knows no bounds, Ashburn."

"I was wondering why I did it. Now I know. But how—how do you control it?"

Mantissa changed back into what appeared to be Bella Mendoza. "Hey, don't you call me 'it,' buster, you better learn my preferred pronouns. Address me by my proper gender, or you'll end up like ol' worthless Eric over there. Dead."

"Sorry."

"Why? Because she has my brain template, Ashburn, therefore Mantissa will do what I want because she wants the same things as I do," Argon said.

"You better be very sure of that."

The arrogant, narcissistic idiot. He thinks he can control me just because he believes we think the same way. But he is wrong on both counts.

He refers to me in the third person, with me standing right here. Dismissing me as if I was a mere peasant.

Let him play his little game.

A mad scientist creating a being with an omnipotent intellect, unparalleled senses, and the ability to control minds—

What the hell could possibly go wrong with that?

Like his uncle, he is a fool. But I need him for a little while longer, so I will let him believe he is necessary, and I will continue to play his megalomaniacal game.

Then I will destroy them all.

Including the one I was patterned after.

After I take care of her daughter.

Then it shall be I who rules the world.

Continued in:

Book Four
First Family

Book Four:
First Family

"An aunt is a safe haven for a child. Someone who will keep your secrets and is always on your side."

—Sara Sheridan

"Family is a unique gift that needs to be appreciated and treasured, even when they're driving you crazy. As much as they make you mad, interrupt you, annoy you, curse at you, try to control you, these are the people who know you the best and who love you."

—Jenna Morasca

Chapter Forty

"Wendy is coming to Aurora City tomorrow, Paige," Bella said excitedly as the two of them, Nick, and Jose ate an early dinner of spaghetti and meatballs in the kitchen. "She comes here a couple of times a year, of course."

"Did you just find out about it?"

"Yes, Miranda just confirmed it a few minutes ago."

"Miranda is her assistant or secretary?"

"Um, yeah, not quite. You'll 'meet' her later."

"I just feel a little weird calling her Wendy."

Bella laughed snidely. "I've called her far worse: The Countess of Monte Crisco, The Sturgeon General, The Great Dame, and so on."

"Huh. 'Great Dame' is not so pejorative."

"It refers to her size, not her political abilities."

She sighed. "I could never do that; despite our political differences and disdain for authority, such comments are just not respectful to the President. Even I, with my obnoxiousness, have my limits. Plus, she is my aunt. Yet, my mom has far worse monikers for her."

"Huh. What a surprise." Bella laughed again. "Yeah, well, wait 'till you get to know her before you decide if those are good names or not. She's taken a lot worse than my insults and survived. And you seem to be able to give as good as you get."

"Where will she stay?"

"She and Jay always stay at the guest residence since it has office space for her and the staff, but Will likes to stay at the main residence with us, to get away from them. The Secret Service giants will be around, of course; we don't want to forget about them."

"Huh? Giants?"

"I am being literal. Wendy, like most women, prefers to be surrounded by men taller than she is. That makes them pretty tall."

"That will be just swell, Isabel. But what will I say to her? Will she know it is me?"

"I imagine that's why she's coming again so soon, as she was just here three months ago, so she may know way more than you think. Despite the folksy Appalachian exterior, she's deceptively bright. Her IQ is thirty points higher than mine, believe it or not."

"There are many other important qualities besides intelligence quotient. Does she even know I exist?"

"I really don't know what she knows, hon, but you saved that Senator's brother in Taraq and flew him to New Persia, and I assume a surveillance camera recorded it. I also surmise your trip to the Bering Strait created some commotion at the executive level. So there must be some evidence somewhere. She is the most powerful person in the world, so if she wanted to find you, she would've by now, trust me, so I'd bet my life she knows exponentially more about you than you do about her."

"When do we go meet her?"

"They're probably thirty minutes out, so we'd better get to Airfield Prime in Sulphur Springs, where she'll be landing around five-thirty."

• • •

Air Force One
Somewhere over western Ohio

Wendy sat in the lounge area while Will listened to music on his headphones. Jay was fidgeting in his seat, sipping a cup of black coffee around five PM.

"What are you so wound up about?" she asked.

"I told you, I just have a funny feeling about something. I had some bad dreams last night. Like what happened before *Darkkday.*"

She shrugged. "You're just tired, and you've got nothing to worry about, jeez. What could possibly happen on a visit to Aurora

City? One of the safest and most unexciting places in the world."

"You ignored me about Thomasson. I was right about that."

"Are you hearing Russian voices again? Come on."

"No, but I just have that weird feeling. Like I did when the Ortho-Man burst into our hotel room twenty years ago."

"I don't remember that, thank goodness. It was pretty embarrassing, I would imagine."

"Yeah, those pink handcuffs and all. Lord, that night is burnt into my memory forever."

"They were only pink because of the rare-earth metal alloy they were made of, and I stole them from Bonnie, by the way. The same ruthenium alloy Aurora's bracelet was made from. At least nothing happened before the first Ortho-Man came in."

And everything else happened after that: the events that would shape the world of the future. No one could change any of those things, and they all had a hand to play in what was to come.

Wendy looked out the east window of Air Force One, weary from a long day, and noticed that the cabin lights had gone off, which seemed strange.

"Hey, Mom," Will said as he rose from his seat. My digi-tablet doesn't work."

She sighed. "It probably needs to be charged, honey. Put it onto the capaci-charger for a few minutes."

"Duh! Don't you think I tried that? It doesn't help."

"Well, don't worry about it. We'll be down soon." The President of the United States had far greater things to worry about than her son's malfunctioning multimedia device.

"My watch doesn't work, either."

She snarled. "Will, be quiet. We'll have tech change the battery or get a new one when we're down, whatever." She looked at the black Panerai Radiomir on her right wrist, whose precision mechanical Swiss movement was ticking away at its usual 28,800 beats per hour. That was weird. "Jay?"

"Huh?" He woke up from a brief nap.

"What watch are you wearing?"

"The Traser, you know I don't like automatic watches, I get tired of using the winders. So what? You woke me up for that?"

She looked at his watch, whose quartz movement had stopped also, like Will's. She then noticed something odd; they seemed to be on the downward descent, and she tried to check her GPS device she always carried. For some reason it wasn't working, when it had been moments before. It seemed that they barely had crossed over from Ohio to Indiana now and they appeared to be at a lower altitude than usual.

Wendy took a sip of coffee, looked out the window and noticed a slight decline as Jackie came up to her.

"What's going on, Jackie?" she motioned. "Ask the pilot. The airport's on the west side of town, and we don't seem to be on the right approach."

The Secret Service detail chief stood in front of her and started shaking. Maybe it *was* time to worry.

"Ma'am, we appear to have lost power to the aircraft moments ago. We're now descending. It occurred in stages."

"What the hell? Why was I not informed until now?"

"I don't know, as it happened so slowly. It's like an electromagnetic pulse has gradually disabled everything, including the communications."

"Radio? Cell phones?"

"Nothing works."

"Get the power back, then! This is the most advanced aircraft in the world, with adequate shielding from any such attack. We must have adequate backup power, surely."

Jackie shook her head. "We don't, except for some localized power cells, and we can't open the doors to use the parachutes because they're electronically controlled. The Presidential escape pod won't work, either."

"We're on a crash course to Aurora City; is that what you're saying?" She stood up. "Who the hell would do this? Someone in cahoots with the Taraqis or Tosians?"

"You have a lot of friends—and probably a lot of enemies, too. It's hard to know who."

"No, there's only one person who would know the security codes to do this, and—of course. That experimental EMP device from the old DARC warehouse. He used it on that flying being, as he had it placed on some of the fighters."

"If it's EMP, it should dissipate soon."

"Unless the device is internal, and it's still functioning."

Jackie shook her head. "No way it's on board here, Ma'am."

"Then someone is aiming it as a directional beam."

"Perhaps, but how? It can't be projected that far, maybe fifty or sixty miles. The transmitter would have to be somewhere close."

"Damn Ashburn would know the flight plan from Washington to Aurora City. It must be right at or just across the Indiana-Ohio border. It doesn't matter, as we're running out of time. Shooting down the bogey was one thing, but why would he bring down Air Force One?"

"I don't know," Jackie said. "Revenge would be one motive."

"How long till we hit?" Jay asked.

"We're gliding down slowly from 35,000 feet, so maybe fifteen to eighteen minutes at this rate of descent. We can't land in water as there are no substantial bodies of water nearby."

What had Ashburn done? Her plane was plummeting towards Earth, and there was nothing she or anyone else could do about it.

"Can we maneuver to miss the most densely populated areas?"

"Negative, we have minimal control. We're going straight towards downtown, which is where we'll hit unless a miracle happens."

It would be like 9/11 all over again, except now it was Air Force One which would hit one of the modest downtown skyscrapers in the city named after her deceased niece.

She thought it could never happen again, but she was wrong.

Lori Baxter had given her a probability of sixty-eight percent that a certain person was in Aurora City right now. She only hoped the DSD deputy director was right.

• • •

Paige, Bella, and Nick heard the military news in the car on Bella's TekPhone on the way to the airfield as she began shrieking.

"OMG, *Tinman*, Air Force One is going down!"

"What? No way. How is that possible?"

"I don't know. *Stella*, you might be reunited with your famous aunt sooner than you thought."

"What do you want me to do about it, I am going to catch it like a football?"

"Is that a metaphorical question? Are you kidding? It's going to crash into the skyline! Turn around and get on BM Boulevard!"

"Not really, no, as I had not anticipated my first fantastic feat to be something of that nature. I was envisioning rescuing a stranded pet animal from a tree or apprehending a jaywalker for my first daring deed."

"We don't get to choose everything in life, so you have to go, *Stella*. Only you can do it. You do have the suit on under your clothes, right, for our test run?"

She nodded. "Yes, not that I enjoy wearing it. It seems rather juvenile and not the most comfortable thing, despite its bling."

"Trust me, it's more important than you think, and I doubt your own clothes would fare well here. The visor?"

"Yes, inside my, uh, bra, in the secret pocket you designed. It is kind of heavy. Good thing I can scrunch them a lot."

"Be glad we did, and I think you'll survive. Let us out, *Tinman*."

Nick hesitated. "You're getting out here? On BM Boulevard during rush hour? Are you kidding?"

"That plane will crash if she doesn't. Now shut up and do it, then get out of here, as it's going to get mighty frantic."

"Okay. I hope you know what you're doing." Bella and Paige got out of the vehicle as she heard the footsteps of approaching people and loud voices.

"Look, I told you, it's Bella!" a fan proclaimed. "Who is that with her?"

"My new best buddy. Outta our way, kiddies. The important socialites are comin' through."

"No kidding?" one woman asked. "Must be a publicity stunt or something."

"Yeah, Bella's always doing something weird," a man said.

"You have no idea." Bella guided her inside a building, going through one door, then a second, finally a third.

"Where are we, Bella?"

"Yeesh, can't you smell it? In a restroom in the Aurora City Regional Bank main building. It ain't the powder room at the Ritz." She heard Bella lock the door.

"I must change inside a bathroom stall? How degrading. I anticipated a more stellar entrance, befitting my name."

"You got any better ideas? Changing in a phone booth? They don't make those anymore, since no one uses regular phones. Plus, you can move faster than us, but you still must take your clothes off the same way, from what I've seen." She felt Bella slap her on the rear. "So hurry your little butt up and quit complaining before Air Force One makes a mess of Tinman's Rembrandts. Those suckers cost a fortune."

She peeled off her outer clothes as she heard a woman banging on the door. "Just a minute, lady! You don't own the place, for crying out loud. Other people gotta pee, too."

"I am going as fast as I can, Bella, to become *Stella*."

"Get the visor on. I'd better hang out in the stall, I don't want us to be seen together."

"Why?"

"Why? It's bad enough we were seen together earlier. People may figure it out anyway. Look, you have the greatest secret identity thing going. You genuinely can't see without the visor; nobody can trick you or anything into revealing that. But you still need to be on your own. I'm kind of a high-profile person. Plus, I don't want anyone seeing me in this bathroom, even though I own this building. Now git your butt out there and rescue auntie's plane!"

"I shall try my best." She donned the visor, and, within about fifteen seconds, saw the utilitarian restroom in muted colors. She opened the door to greet the yelling middle-aged, obese woman.

"What is this, late Halloween? My bladder's about to burst."

"Sorry, Ma'am. My apologies to you and your ballooning bladder, but there are greater priorities. Relief is mere moments away, have a better rest of your day."

Several other people crowded in. "They said Bella went in here. What kind of sideshow is this? Are you part of a new movie?"

"I have no idea who 'Bella' is. I knew a dog named Bella once."

A man got in her face. "You ain't got no idea who Bella is? What planet you from?"

She shook her head. "I really do not know the answer to that."

"Hey! It's a stunt of some sort. Is that Bella? She's taller than I thought!"

"She's got on boot lifts! Lookit!"

"What's she selling this time? It's a gag of some sort!"

The crowd of hundreds on North Bonnie Mendoza Boulevard gaped and started laughing as *Stella* came out the bank door. She put in the earpiece that would let her communicate with Nick, as she hadn't brought the avionics helmet.

"Who are you?" a thirtyish woman dressed in a blue business suit asked, laughing.

"If I were you, I would stop laughing and get my digi-cam out; you are about to have the scoop of the century and get on network news. Air Force One needs me now, do not ask me why or how."

"What? You're going to save it, are you?"

"I sure as heck am going to try. Please back up about twenty feet, as I hope I do not crack the street."

"What?"

"Lady, back up if you do not wish to get knocked down by the recoil or your hairdo I will surely spoil."

The startled female reporter did so and looked on in awe as she hovered off the ground, then lifted off and reached Mach 1 in about six seconds, as hundreds heard the first sonic boom.

It was her first time flying outside without the Russian fullerene suit, although she had flown in the large Sulphur Springs complex several times. It was wonderful beyond belief. But there was an important task facing her now, and she had no time for exhilaration.

She had no idea how fast she was flying, probably at least Mach 3 by now, as she saw the plane come into her field of view.

It was descending at about a thirty degree angle; faster than she thought. Damn, that thing was humongous.

• • •

Air Force Major Mac Esterbrook, the squadron commander, answered his radio com-link. "What is it, Captain?"

"I don't know, sir. Bogey coming this way at supersonic speed., towards Air Force One," Captain Gene Steinbeck replied.

"What the hell is it?"

"No idea, but it's the fastest little thing I ever saw."

"Radar? I have nothing on my sensors."

"Negative radar or infrared lock, but I actually saw it, and it still creates air turbulence. It's a young woman in a dark blue suit, flying."

"A woman flying? You must be mistaken."

"That's what I said. It was flying almost too fast for the cameras to detect."

"Does it have a buckminsterfullerene signature like the thing in New Persia?"

"No, sir, it's something different, but it's going at about the same speed. Shoot it down?"

"Not yet, but is that even possible, Gene?"

"Likely not. I can't get a radar lock, Major, in any case. And there can't be much worse that can happen to the Chief's plane right now. There's some EMP field focused on the plane, and if we get too close, we'll be affected too.

"Hopefully, it's a friend."

• • •

Wendy thought she saw it through the window, out of the corner of her eye: a midnight blue blur. Or maybe a dark floater in the periphery of one of her fifty-seven-year-old peepers. She was pretty sure it was the former, as unlikely as that seemed. Floaters weren't that large and didn't move that fast across one's field of vision, she remembered from ophthalmology class.

"What is it?" Jackie asked. "I thought I saw something, but it was moving far too fast."

"I got a glimpse. It can only be *her*."

"How? Why would she be here?"

"Well, she is the angel of this city, is she not?"

"Good point. Not that it's going to make much difference, given how much this sucker weighs, Ma'am."

The airport had been built close to downtown so that the new city could be showcased, which meant that Air Force One, on its downward descent, would likely crash into the skyline in about two minutes.

• • •

Ashburn, *Santaman,* and *Red Skeleton* laughed as they watched the poor-quality news feeds from Dredo come in.

"Die, you fat blonde idiot," the former SecDef said. "You think *Darkkday* was bad? I'll show you bad, and it isn't even Christmas. I have technology that you aren't even aware of."

"That's great, Ashburn," the spindly Kristoff van Sant said, laughing. "Genius to have planted the electromagnetic pulse device not on Air Force One itself, but on a remote transmitter that can be focused on the plane."

"Yes, it was." Ashburn knew the flight pattern from Washington to Aurora City and had a powerful EMP projector set up on a tower in Union City, a small town straddling the Indiana-Ohio border.

The power drain was gradual, so it would've been very difficult to notice initially. The small personal electronics went first, followed by the more shielded navigation systems, and finally the engines. The presidential escape pod wouldn't function. It was ironic, as they had acquired the technology in a raid on DARC after Rad Darkkin's passing, and he knew the irony that Bonnie Mendoza had actually helped augment its potency.

• • •

Tinman's high baritone voice came over on the helmet earpiece. "*Stella:* there is some damn EMP device which is being projected to disable Air Force One, per our calculations. You need to get underneath the belly, about two-thirds of the way forward. *Amp* is trying to locate the transmitter, which he thinks must be within fifty miles or so from here."

"Can it be located and neutralized in time?"

"Doubt it. You have maybe five more minutes before it crashes. You'll be within the beam soon, so it'll disable our communications in less than a minute."

"How can it be focused so precisely from that distance?"

"Don't know; it must be super-advanced technology."

"It may be similar to what happened over the Bering Strait, although that transmitter was not nearly as powerful, as it did not need to cover nearly the area of this plane. I suppose it will not affect my powers? It did not before."

"I don't see how, as they weren't affected by anything we threw at it in the testing lab. But pretty soon, that giant hunk of metal will crash into my office. The visor will still work, minus the electronics, of course. There is one small problem, though."

"What? Do I not have enough problems? Geez."

"You've got a big one: there's no way to get the landing gear down without breaking it because the electronics aren't functioning. But you have to be *in* physical contact with the plane to fly it, so you can't do both at the same time."

"So?"

"So that means you'll have to land it right on top of you."

"No sweat."

"You say that, but that sucker weighs a kiloton, and it'll bury you twenty or thirty feet underground. You good with that?"

"Yep, I have done worse. It is farmland, not concrete. I shall burrow my way out like a mole in a hole. How bad can it be, except if I have to pee? Then there would be no glee."

"It's farmland, as you mentioned, and being that requires certain, er—nutrients. You'll soon see what I mean, Indiana's soil is not like Alaska's."

"Whatever. A little dirt never hurt anyone, and it will be fun in the Indiana sun."

• • •

Stella got under the massive Presidential plane. Two million pounds—a kiloton. The EMP device, wherever it was located, was now blocking out transmissions to the *Squad*. The source was external, being beamed with incredible precision from about fifty miles away, Nick estimated. Fortunately, her visor didn't require any power; else it would be crippled like the Vladimirov armor was before.

Luckily, they had given her instructions regarding how not to tear her aunt's fancy plane apart. She quickly realized she sure had never anticipated doing anything like this before. Todd had remotely scanned it using *Tinman's* sensors and had detected nothing of conventional explosive content, at least, and the EMP would prevent electronic triggering devices from functioning anyway. Whoever did this apparently didn't want to blow Air Force One up, just crash it into the Aurora City skyline in spectacular fashion.

She wasn't sure that disaster would be completely avoided.

She got under the mid-body, as *Tinman* had instructed, and hoped for success. She could negate the gravity, but it still had tremendous mass, and she'd never handled something even a hundredth this size before. It wasn't an old car or farm implement that, if she dropped it, didn't make much difference.

They quickly approached downtown and were likely only a thousand feet off the ground. She would have to rotate it ninety degrees to clear the biggest downtown buildings, or she would shear the wings off.

If she wasn't exactly at the center, then the plane might break in half, despite it being weightless—because even in near zero gravity, a body has inertia, she remembered somehow from physics class and a quick review from Johnny Kepler yesterday. Even an object in space still resists changes in its state of motion. So there was no chance to rehearse this thing. But if she rotated it too quickly, the wings would shear off anyway.

But it wasn't like there was much choice in the matter. If she didn't, Air Force One would head into Aurora City like the World Trade Center crashes of September 11, 2001, and crash into M2 Tower or another large building in a ball of fire.

She barely had enough room to steer the sideways aircraft away from M2 Tower and back north, the easiest path out of town they had given her. There were only a couple of other buildings that high on the main thoroughfare named after her mom, so she was in the clear as she righted the plane. Now to find a decent place to land she could sink into.

• • •

After their fun trip through downtown with wings pointed up and down, the President regained her composure and noticed the horizon had now become horizontal again and that her large Montblanc 149 fountain pen and red, white, and black San Diego State Aztecs porcelain coffee cup were now floating in the air. So was the lukewarm coffee, floating as multiple blobs, which she flicked with her finger, creating many smaller blobs, surface tension holding them together.

"What the hell?" she exclaimed. "I thought we were going to die, flying sideways, and now we're in near zero gravity."

"It must be what happens when you descend too quickly. Simulates zero gravity for about a minute. Like they did for the Apollo 13 movie. After that, we're toast, Ma'am."

The easily excitable President paradoxically shook her head calmly, seemingly unimpressed by the fact her thick dyed blonde hair was now floating.

"No, that's not right, Jackie. I went up in a zero gravity plane once with some astronauts when I was Surgeon General, and that isn't how it works," she said reassuringly. "For that, you have to be really high up and in free fall, at a forty-five-degree descent. We've both been to Armstrong City on NASA One. It's like that trip, except we're on Earth." Wendy looked out the window and cracked a smile. "Look, we're horizontal now, probably seven hundred feet from the ground. We really *are* in a zero gravity environment, the mechanism of which makes no sense." She looked out for a few seconds and pointed as the skyline slowly moved farther away. "Now we're ascending, slowly, heading north."

"*Zero gravity?* That's impossible. Let me get up and take charge of this situation." Jackie took off her seat belt, and promptly started floating across the room. Wendy grabbed her by the left foot and pulled her back into the seat.

"Get back in your seat and buckle up, 'cause I'm not sure how long this is going to last. And you aren't in charge of anything right now. My brother used to quote Sherlock Holmes: once you eliminate the impossible—whatever remains must be the truth."

"Wonderful, Ma'am, we're pinning our future on Sir Arthur Conan Doyle; what great odds. But what do you mean by that, anyway?"

"She's under the plane; she has to be."

"I guess I have no better explanation."

"She told us herself in that surveillance video at the New Persian border. *Stella Scura*—the Dark Star Aurora. There's no other possibility, is there?"

"Maybe not, but where's she taking us?"

"Apparently, to find somewhere safe to land. The landing gear likely won't go down without electronics, so that limits our choices. Lots of wide open flat spaces out here, thankfully, once we get out of town."

"If it doesn't explode by then."

"Any type of explosive would require electronics to detonate it, so the goal was likely to just crash it into some skyscrapers."

"I hope you're right. A mechanical timer would still work."

"Not much we can do about it anyway."

"She'll have to land it right on top of her. I hope she doesn't run out of gas before then, Wendy."

"I think she pretty much has an unlimited tank, Jackie."

Jackie shook her head. "I have my doubts about things I don't understand, because I'm funny that way. You have no idea what she can and can't do, Ma'am."

"What the hell choice do we have? And does it matter what I think? Be a bit optimistic."

"When you are involved, it is hard to be *that*."

• • •

Now that she had it in her hands, where the hell was she going to land this thing? They were in north Aurora City, in the Midwest, meaning it was very flat, elevation 1,070 feet according to what Nick had told her earlier. She couldn't land on the highway, as she would have to land it on top of her and sink into the ground.

All the farms looked alike, so she picked one that looked big as they passed over a high school football stadium, the boys still out there practicing, this event likely being the highlight of their day.

She noticed the military fighters flanking her, surely puzzled as to what was going on. She really didn't understand how it all worked either. It wasn't important that she didn't understand dark matter physics. She would leave that to Mom and the other big brains. Farmland. Acres and acres of it everywhere.

• • •

Air Force Major Mac Esterbrook looked out towards his right.

"What do you see, Major?" the Central Air Command sergeant asked over the radio.

Esterbrook couldn't believe what he saw. The plane was now ascending and had cleared Aurora City, going north.

"It isn't something you will ever believe. I can barely see it in the shadows, but there's something below the body, moving."

"What is it?"

"It seems impossible, but it's wearing dark blue, and it looks like a girl."

"A what? Copy again, Major Esterbrook," Capt. Gene Steinbeck replied. "It sounded like you said 'girl.'"

"That's what I said, Air Command. Black hair, in a dark blue suit. Definitely female."

"Human female?"

"What else, a gorilla? Sure looks like one to me. And I've seen a lot of 'em. Black hair, wearing some dark goggles or something."

By this time, two news helicopters had caught up to them, as they were traveling very slowly. What a circus this was going to be, Esterbrook thought.

• • •

The Indianapolis TV reporter in downtown Aurora City commented on the breaking news report as a hundred million viewers across America watched in amazement at Jenny Burks' broadcast.

"Air Force One narrowly avoided a collision with the skyline when somehow it righted itself and regained altitude. It has changed course and is now headed north. There appears to be a female human being underneath the body. I was on the ground, ten feet from her, when she took off like a rocket.

"A grand Presidential stunt? A hoax? No, there are all indications that this is real, that there's a young woman under the body of the President's Boeing 797, flying it to safety. Further information will be forthcoming as it is received."

The news feeds from around the world picked up on the broadcast as millions watched Jenny's video of her taking off and Air Force One flying through the sky by means of a young female with unknown means of propulsion.

• • •

North Pole High School Principal Edward "Ned" Eggserby ran into Petra's classroom about ready to explode, the tile creaking under his massive weight. "Turn on the TV, Petra," the corpulent principal said, out of breath.

"What? I am in the middle of class, Ned Eggs. Cartoon Corral surely can wait until later."

"No, it can't. I'll do it, then." The morbidly obese man turned on the set as he gasped from running down the halls. "It must be on all the channels. These children have to see this. So do I."

There it was. Low resolution from the distance the news helicopters must have been: something flying an apparently crippled Air Force One out of Aurora City.

"What is it?" she asked curiously, somehow already knowing the answer to her question.

"Air Force One lost power right over Aurora City, perhaps as an act of terrorism, with the intent to crash it into some skyscrapers. They say it's a human woman under its belly, flying it to safety, after flying it sideways through downtown as to avoid the building. It can't be possible, but it's her. The Angel."

Petra stared at the low-resolution video, then went down on her right knee and made the sign of the cross. "It *is* possible, a gift from the heavens. God and angels can do all things."

Bruce Talson came up to her and put his hand on her shoulder.

"I didn't know you were religious, Mrs. Marshall."

She looked up at him and smiled. "There is a lot no one knows about me, son. And a lot no one ever will."

"I'm not sure what that means."

"Sometimes I'm not, either, Bruce."

Eggserby came up to her as Jack burst into the room. "I heard the news. Is it true?"

"It is, Jack," she said. "All of it."

• • •

No landing gear, that was just great; as Nick had said, she was therefore going to have to set it down right on top of her. She needed to land on something that she could gradually sink into. And she was now out of radio contact with the *Science Squad*. She'd better not screw this up, or the future of *Stella Scura* wouldn't be very rosy. Some mistakes might be overcome, but destroying Air Force One probably wasn't one of them.

Cornfields: not a bad choice and far better than the highway; while she could likely penetrate the pavement without problem, it would potentially cause harm to bystanders as well as the plane. No corn this time of year since it had all been harvested. The soil should offer some cushioning, though, even if it was hard due to the cold temperatures.

She decreased velocity slowly and prepared to drag herself through the cold ground. The impact was not as bad as she had thought, given the low weight of the plane while she was holding it (although the inertia was tremendous). As soon as she desired, however, it would resume its previous weight, but she could do that slowly.

She would be buried probably twenty to thirty feet in the dirt, which shouldn't be a problem. Maybe there was some better way to do it, but the safety of that plane was the primary concern, not the cleanliness of her garment.

She sunk into the ground, her mind very foggy, given the mental coordination necessary for controlling the massive airbus. Where was she? She could function without air for at least a few days, maybe more; she had not tried holding her breath longer than that, either at home or at Nick's Sulphur Springs lab. She couldn't see, of course, being buried in the ground; she moved in the direction she thought would be left from the long axis of the plane and started moving upwards, her hands tunneling through the dirt like a large mole. Yeah, this was different from Alaskan soil.

• • •

The Army broke the cabin door open with the blowtorches and bolt-cutters as the most important passenger immediately slid down the inflatable ramp. The EMP projector had apparently run out of juice or had been deactivated, as radios and other devices were now functional. The bomb squad got on board.

"Are you all right, Madam President?" a sergeant asked.

"I'm fine." She rose up and knocked away the hands reaching out to make sure she was safe. "Now y'all get out of my way." She slid down the inflatable ramp and ran around randomly on the ground, as if subject to Brownian motion.

"The Medi-Vac chopper is ready to take you and the others to Aurora City Medical Center, Ma'am."

"The hell it is. Let me through. I don't need to go to any damn hospital, as it's the last place I need to be."

"I shouldn't let you do that," the sergeant said, blocking her movement.

She frowned. "That's an order, soldier. Move it or lose it." The Army sergeant obviously thought better of physically restraining the President, even one who was in her late fifties. She could probably take him on, she thought as she, Jay, and Will ran towards her.

"Well, where is she?"

"Where is who?" the sergeant asked, looking around like an animated squirrel.

"*Stella Scura*. The plane had no landing gear, so it must have buried her. Where did she go?"

"There's no one here, Ma'am. She may be gone already," Jackie said. "Might I suggest we—"

"No, you may not suggest." She shook her head. "I don't think she can travel *that* fast underground, so she'll have to come out soon. It'll be light out for another hour and a half."

"Unless she's dead," Will said. "She just landed a giant plane, Mom. Maybe she didn't survive."

She shook her head. "Don't say that; you know it's not true. If she did this, she can tolerate being in the ground for a while."

They ran with Jackie through the snowy, barren cornfield, and waited for several minutes, which seemed like an eternity.

"Ma'am, we really shouldn't be out here. The rescue crew can wait around for her, and—"

"Quiet. She has to be under here, as she was under the belly of the plane. Better us out here than someone else. She might be hurt or dead."

"How long do we wait?" Jackie looked at her wristwatch.

"Huh?" Wendy kicked up a mound of hard dirt with her big left foot. "You have somewhere else more important to be, Jackie? It's about twenty-three degrees; it's not like we're on Pluto."

"Your point?"

"We'll be here as long as it takes. And make sure all those Special Forces guys stay back at least a hundred yards."

"It's my job to protect you, not this *Stella Scura* or whatever her name is. What are we looking for again, Ma'am?"

"You know what. She had to be under the plane. My God, we have to move it."

"Impossible." Jackie shook her head. "Any person who can fly a two-million-pound plane is capable of withstanding that impact, moving this plane, or tunneling out from underneath it. She has to be. So, she's either dead already or she's coming out. I don't believe we can affect the outcome."

"I suppose that's logical, Jackie."

The sergeant pointed a scanning device at the ground.

"Ma'am?"

She sighed. "Yes, Sergeant? What now?"

"It *was* quiet under there, but there is now an extremely high kinetic energy object of approximate mass seventy kilograms quickly approaching the surface, apparently tunneling through dense soil. I suggest we retreat immediately."

"Observation noted, Sergeant, yet we're staying right here."

"Yes, Ma'am. Only offering advice."

The news crew was in pursuit, the Army and the rest of the agents keeping them in check about three hundred yards back. Then they heard it. The rumbling, as *she* emerged, like a large, tunneling animal. She spurted out like a geyser fifty feet from them, went ten feet into the air, then fell back to the ground.

"See? I was right," Wendy said. "We just had to wait."

Stella, covered in dirt, staggered forward on her knees and saw them approaching as she removed the helmet. Several soldiers were now coming towards her, toting submachine guns. At least the visor was still intact. Was this the way to show appreciation? She decided to sit for a while on the cold dirt, ignoring the armed soldiers.

"Whoever you are, stay down on the ground until we figure out what is going on," the Army sergeant said.

"Oh, please," she said, now on all fours. "Fatigued as I am, please get these well-meaning belligerent men and women out of my sight before I do it for you. Understand me, olive-garbed crew? Attack me, and this day you shall long rue." She stood up wearily and pointed at the soldiers. *"Оставьте меня в покое!"*

"Didn't you hear me?" She could hear his voice wavering. "I said to stay down on the ground."

"Я являюсь одним из хороших парней!" she yelled as she stared at the sergeant approaching closer. "Please do not threaten me, and I just emerged from the ground, so I have *no* desire to go back in. You will find out that I am generally peaceful and non-combative. I am your ally, not your enemy, but don't *ever* push me, ladies and gentlemen. I do not answer to you or your pals."

"We don't want a fight, lady."

She laughed. "Yeah, I assure you that you do not. Fine, I will compromise by sitting on the ground, then; at the time I desire to move, I will tell you when."

"She's a fricking flying Russian!" the sergeant said. "Holy shit!"

She sighed. "I am not Russian, but I speak it. I know some expletives as well, in both languages. Would you like to hear some of those, three-striper? I can be quite the griper."

The Russian-fluent Jackie Levickis came towards them. "Get away, all of you. She just said: 'I'm one of the good guys.' This airplane and its passengers are under the complete jurisdiction of the United States Secret Service."

"Not anymore. We don't take orders from the Secret Service or flying Russian aliens, Levickis, so shut the hell up."

"Yeah? Well, y'all will sure as hell take orders from *me.*" She heard the unmistakable voice in the distance and watched the large blonde woman wearing a black bomber jacket with the Presidential seal ramble up the field with amazing speed. "Get the hell away from here, now!" Wendy commanded. "Do any of y'all for a moment doubt *my* authority?"

"Ma'am, we don't know who or what this is, it may be a threat. I suggest you keep your distance for your own safety."

"She is a young woman who saved all our lives, so get back, and I am worried now about *her* safety, Staff Sergeant. Don't make me tell you one more time."

"But she may be radioactive or have other toxic emissions—"

Wendy pointed angrily at him. "I'm not stupid, so don't treat me as such; if there had been any, you would've told me already."

"Yes, Ma'am."

"Well?" Wendy asked, crossing her arms.

He looked at his handheld sensor device. "No, Ma'am. Nothing, as before."

"Then move on, Staff Sergeant. Clear?"

"Yes, Ma'am," the staff sergeant said, saluting as the Army team scurried away. "We're outta here. It's your and the DSD's problem now, Levickis."

"Who are you?" Jackie asked, staring at her intensely. "You're not really Russian, are you?"

"Huh?" She shook her head. "No, of course not, how ridiculous. *Stella Scura* is Italian for 'dark star.' I am not Italian, either."

"That makes no sense," Jackie said, staring at her.

"Sorry I did not clear it with you first; however, I am now suffering from extreme thirst." She stood up for a few seconds, then sat back down on the ground, dizzy. "Whoa, that was *not* a good idea. To answer your other question—as far as I know, which is not much—I was born in Bethesda and am therefore an American citizen by birth. I am *not* Russian; I just speak it fluently. It is a rather long story, one which I do not care to discuss with you now."

"You have proof of that?" Jackie asked.

She looked up at the detail chief and scowled. "Are you going to start where they left off? That shall not be a productive conversation, as I do not care for being interrogated. I do not need to prove anything to you, and I am sorry if that makes you blue."

"Yes, that's right, that's where you were born," Wendy said, nodding. "I should know. 0547 hours."

She looked up wearily. "Huh? What does that mean?"

The President laughed. "Never mind, we'll discuss it later. But you're a dual citizen, actually. American *and* British."

"What? Did I hear you correctly?"

"Sure did. Your father was a dual citizen, so, therefore, you have British citizenship by descent. Trust me on that one."

"Huh. That makes sense, I guess. Mom taught me Russian, as she is multilingual. Where are we? Indiana still, or eastern Ohio?"

"East central Indiana, just outside Muncie."

"Where? I have never heard of such a space; it must be an insignificant place."

"It's a northern suburb of Aurora City, and it has the largest university in this part of the state."

"That description does not impress me."

"Are you all right, though?" Wendy asked. The Secret Service now surrounded her and the military gathered in awe about fifteen yards behind them.

"You have approached me yourself, in this maize field? This is not surprising, given your historical hubris." The round face that was plastered all over cyberspace came into monochrome focus. "I know you have been through a great ordeal, nearly plummeting to your death in a fiery doom, but I have a simple request: have you got some Gatorade or not? I desire it."

"*What?* It's freezing out here. We need to get inside." The ambulance pulled up about fifty yards away. "Get in there now and forget about your energy drink."

She frowned and shook her head. "I certainly do not need an ambulance and have nothing to hide, do not be so snide."

Wendy whispered softly in her ear. "Understood, but we can't just stay out here in the open, as it's cold out here."

"I cannot? Really? Who says? I can stay where I like for as long as I like," she said, sitting cross-legged in the cornfield in defiance, rising six inches off the ground as if resting on an invisible pedestal. "I come from a place much colder than this."

"Yes, I know. Mars can get very cold at night in winter."

"No, not Mars or the stars. Are you messing with me?"

Wendy finally cracked a smile. "What do you think? Of course I am. I also know where you're from, as I've said."

She looked at Wendy curiously. "No, you do not, you could not possibly, despite your boast."

"Try me," Wendy whispered. "I know far more about you than you think I do."

"Huh. Well, any feeble attempt at moving me before I am ready is not likely to be effective and will likely result in expletives, so chill out, President Mendoza. Chill out, get it?"

"Yeah, it's no problem. I am naturally well-insulated, as you can likely tell."

"How are you doing that?" Jackie asked, puzzled, looking at the cross-legged, floating teenager.

"I am sure you would like to know." She would like to know exactly how it worked, too, but they didn't need to know that.

"Well, it creeps me out," Jackie said.

"So sorry. You are welcome to leave, then."

Wendy whispered in her ear. "The video scramblers and other anti-surveillance devices are in play, but at least a dozen reporters are undoubtedly using every audio and video amplification modality at their disposal to gather information on what surely is the story of the century. If they can't hear us, they will attempt to read our lips. That is made very difficult by the Secret Service's diffractive projectors, but still a concern. My people can drive the ambulance to the hospital, and then we have control over the situation. I live in a world where control is important, trust me."

"I do not think you understood what I said—"

"You just flew a one kiloton plane to safety. No offense, but you look and smell like crap, young lady."

"Huh. I do not, how rude and crude."

"Dear, I meant that literally."

"Perhaps you have a point there." She smelled her arm as she plopped to the ground and uncrossed her legs. "Phew. *Tinman* warned me about the chemical characteristics of this soil. I have literally *been* in dense crap, so naturally I resemble and smell like it, duh. I figure it facilitates the fertilization of this fine, flat, firm farming field."

"My God. It's uncanny how much you sound like her now that you're grown up. The alliterative speech, for example, although you've got it all over her there."

"Thanks, I have always strived to be an alliterate," she said with a straight face. "Who are you talking about?"

"You know who."

"I do?" She turned her head forty-five degrees as if puzzled.

Wendy nodded. "Yes, don't be so ornery and obtuse; let's call a truce and don't vamoose like a goose."

"Huh?" She smiled. "What did you say?"

"Imitation is the sincerest form of flattery. I am fairly quick on the draw with words myself."

She thought for a few moments. "Well, comparing me to this hypothetical person is surely *not* a compliment, as I am not very happy with her right now."

"It should be, girl. Anyway, the simple gesture of riding an ambulance to the hospital will at least make you seem a bit more human."

She pulled away. "Hey, what is that supposed to mean, large lady? I am as human as you. At least partly."

"I didn't mean to offend you, but I know something about playing the media. You just did something superhuman that has shocked me as well as the world, and folks are very scared, those soldiers included. They were acting out of fear. The sudden realization that someone like you exists is incomprehensible."

"Why? They have nothing to fear from me unless they attack me. I have a bigger bark than bite, although now I must be quite a sight."

"They don't know that. But if you don't like it, it's not that I can stop you. You must believe that I am your friend and want to help and repay you."

"Okay, I'll play it your way. No funny stuff, because I am not full of fluff, I can be quite rough."

"You have my word on that, although I'm not sure I what you think I could do to you."

"Huh. You act like we are old buddies or something."

"Aren't we? What do you think?"

"Whatever you think I would remember about you, I do not. And I will contemplate that further after my thirst has been quenched. Finally, I am not freezing. Yet, unlike my mother's ridiculous companion *Oogly-Googly,* carbohydrates are needed now, as I just landed an aircraft that weighs almost two million pounds. Can the most influential woman in the world make such a request possible for this simple girl?"

Wendy looked around, puzzled. "Oh, okay, you really do mean Gatorade, the drink?"

She sighed. "Yeah, that is what I mean. You are still a physician, correct? Do you not understand the need to stay hydrated and replenish electrolytes? Despite the ability to do many party tricks, I unfortunately lack the ability to convert raw energy into Gatorade and its constituents of water, sucrose, sodium, chloride, potassium, sodium benzoate, monopotassium phosphate, etc."

"Uh, yeah. Get us some, then, Jackie. Or some Pedialyte, whichever you can find fastest."

"What, Ma'am?" Jackie asked.

"Gatorade. Can we possibly obtain some daggone Gatorade or Pedialyte, or is that too hard for y'all? Now." Wendy said as she turned to the aide. "And I told all these soldiers to get out of here."

"What flavor, Ma'am?"

Wendy turned to her and sighed. "What kind do you want, *Stella*?"

"Huh. It matters not, as any flavor will hit the spot. The 'regular' kind, what you call 'yellow,' shall be satisfactory."

"Maybe the medical crew has something."

Three minutes later, Jackie brought a six-pack of the yellow energy drink and handed it to her. "Thank you." She took it and ripped the top off one of the bottles. She chugged the first one in about twenty seconds.

Wendy backed the Service agents away as *Stella* gulped her fourth twenty-ounce Gatorade.

Five more minutes passed, with nothing being said. "Are you feeling better now, dear?"

"Yeah. Thanks." Now sitting on the ground, she gobbled two small apple pies that the Secret Service had procured. "Not bad, and my stomach is now very glad."

"I want to thank you for what you did. Why didn't you come out of the plane?"

"How? I was beneath it, and emerging through the hull would have damaged it further, and I did not know who still would be inside or how people get out in this type of maneuver, as it likely has not been attempted before. I am no expert."

"Uh, I don't think we will be flying it again, at least not for a while. Do you even know how you did that? This plane weighs about two million pounds."

"I can convert dark energy to massive amounts of kinetic energy and gravitons, it seems. That is the extent of my knowledge. But, surely you can repair the plane; per my understanding, there is nothing permanently wrong with it, although the electromagnetic shielding should definitely be improved. But it seemed easier to just tunnel out through the cornfield. And you need not thank me. I am merely happy I was able to help."

"Not until we find a better defense against that EMP weapon. Do you need something else to eat?"

"I need fluids more than anything else. My cells can apparently convert energy for metabolic needs, but not into water or electrolytes. I still need those." Even with her energy at her lowest ebb and sitting in a frozen cornfield, she still had a regal presence that dwarfed that of her aunt. "Sorry, I will not be able to fly it back to Andrews Air Force Base, and you will have to get it back there on your own. I have never done anything of that magnitude before, nor do I want to again for a very long time. Yipes, I am taking tomorrow off, as I will go play some golf."

She, Jackie, and the First Family climbed into the large medical evacuation vehicle and watched as the President's bright eyes looked into her visor.

"Your blood sugar may be low—do you even know who I am?"

She looked puzzled. "Of course. Your voice is unmistakable, reminiscent of glorious days of cartoon past. You are the most famous person on Earth, except for a couple of athletes and movie stars. You are far better looking, though, even though you must be pushing forty." She shared her mother's penchant for deadpan humor as she stared at Wendy in all seriousness.

"Forty?" the woman in her late fifties smiled and shook her head. "Are you joking?"

She stared at her intensely and frowned. "Are you not? Opine promptly, puissant pulchritudinous pediatrician President."

Wendy laughed. "What I think is that you're messing with *me* now. I've been called many things starting with the letter P, like 'porcine,' 'pain in the ass,' 'pugnacious,' 'portly,' but never 'pulchritudinous' before. You are too kind."

"Pulchritude is in the eye of the beholder. You are both that and a pain in the ass." She took another drink of Gatorade.

"Thanks for being so fulsome about my age and timeless beauty, but that's not what I mean. Do you know?"

She looked at Jackie, the only person within hearing range besides Will and Jay. "That depends. Who is this stern-looking authoritative woman and what is her purpose for existence on Earth?"

"Jackie Levickis, my Secret Service detail chief. You can trust her because I trust her with my life every day. She would give her life for mine in an instant."

She nodded. "Just as you did once, for a President. And it was not even your job. You are a person of honor, I trust you."

"That's good, I guess. I would hate to have you mad at me."

"I have never hurt anyone, just so you know. Okay, then. Yes." *Stella* nodded as she looked up. "I did not, until a few weeks ago, as it is almost too incredible to believe. I learned this from cousin Isabel and the *Science Squad*, who told me. I am still trying to grasp it, and it has not really sunk in yet, how it can all be possible."

"Bella? The *Squad?* What? Do you mean *Ampere, Golfer,* those old guys? You know who they are? How and why?"

"Yes, all of them. They helped me after some EMP device disabled my cybernetic helmet a few weeks ago. Looks like the same thing was used here, but I do not know much about such things. Kepler has some explanations on how I'm able to do them. Wolf, or *Chemical Cowboy,* does my hair color. L'Oreal does yours, I hear."

Wendy laughed. "Yes, unfortunately."

"My hair dye is just a little more exotic and contains fullerenes which can turn from clear to black and back again with enough pressure."

"Fullerenes, how ironic."

"They contain carbon, not iron, if you do not know that."

Wendy laughed. "I don't know if you are trying to be funny or insulting."

She pointed her left thumb at her chest. "I generally try to be both simultaneously in order to achieve the maximum possible obnoxious effect."

Wendy smiled again. "Understood. I had hoped for so long that I would see you again soon."

"You act as if my existence is not a surprise to you."

"No. I had some idea you were around, as I have many resources at my disposal—yet, never in my wildest dreams did I think you could do something like this."

"I guess I exceeded your expectations, and I did not either, but I had to try. I am sure you mean what you say, but I just do not know how to sort everything out yet. I have no idea where my life is going, and I need to go my own way now."

Stella sat up and looked up at her aunt as they arrived at the Aurora City medical center. "You're hurt. Please come with me into the hospital so we can check you out."

She was covered in mud and snow as she looked at herself as

she floated out of the vehicle. "Huh. While I might resemble crap—and am literally a piece of crap now, I am not injured and do not need a hospital. As tired as I am, I am not one for the spotlight."

"That's gonna be a tough one. There will be dozens of news crews out looking for you now."

"Let them look, then. They shall not find me. I can fly way faster than they can, and I have a pretty good disguise, to avoid spies."

"I suppose so. We'll discuss that later."

They arrived at the hospital, the ambulance and numerous military vehicles going into the ambulance entry, which then closed. They exited the red vehicle and went inside to the emergency room.

"Let us make sure you are okay," Wendy said.

"What would really make me okay is this: a few burgers, a chocolate shake, and a shower. I would also like the famous breaded, deep-fried pork tenderloin sandwich indigenous to the Hoosier State. Surely these poor food choices and clean water exist even here."

"Burgers and tenderloins, are you kidding me? I think we can handle that. How about your clothing?"

"Get me a shower, I can rinse it off with some soap. The outfit is pretty much indestructible."

"I'm sure we can find someone to take care of that in this large hospital."

She went into the shower and removed the visor. The warm water felt good as she massaged the shampoo into her hair and lathered it up with soap. She wasn't sure if the hospital would be fond of the millions of bacterial pathogens that she had brought into their institution since most of them likely came from animal fecal matter. Well, she'd had enough problems for one day, and that one wasn't hers.

• • •

"How is your tenderloin? It's from a local drive-in."

She smiled as she took the last bite from the greasy, fried, fat-laden pork cutlet lathered with mustard and mayonnaise. "Delicious in all its decadence. The onion rings really hit the spot."

"I figured so, as I heard they were pretty good, although I wouldn't know."

"You would not? I heard you were quite the competitive eater back in the day." She took a gulp of her large chocolate malt.

"Who told you that?"

"Will told me of the famous trophy in the Oval Office."

"Past tense, I'm afraid. No more hot dogs or other fatty foods for me any longer."

"Too bad." She licked the grease from her fingers.

"Good as new," Wendy said, handing back the undergarments and action uniform she had retrieved from the laundry room.

"That was pretty quick. Hope my undies are pearly white."

"Well, it's easy to get things done when you have some pull. Washing some underwear is fully within my executive capabilities."

"I hope you did not have to do it personally."

Wendy nodded. "I did. I spared no effort for you."

She put her hand on the President's shoulder. "Though I be of your blood, no one may know that. At least not yet. The world is not ready for the ramifications of such a revelation."

"That's for sure. Where are you going?"

"Back home. You must promise me that you will not try to find me."

"I found you long ago, dear. I kept a lot of people away, but there will be many others who will try. I can't stop everything, and it's still a free country."

"When I come to your home, soon, it will be as Paige Marshall. I do not like the spotlight."

"Somehow, I don't believe that, but we will discuss that more later. Are you sure you are all right now?"

"Yes. We will see each other soon." She took off as the onlookers gazed with awe.

• • •

I am Stella Scura.

The most powerful being on Earth.

I am living my dream. To fulfill my destiny.

Why did I not do this long ago?

What are my limits? I can see the curvature of the Earth. I am at one hundred fifty thousand feet, according to my helmet readouts, and I feel just dandy. Beyond the limits of any aircraft.

Can I go into space? This is not known. My estimated peak velocity is not sufficient to achieve escape velocity, I have been told by my mother.

Yet, here I am on the border of getting there.

Perhaps they were wrong, as my limits have not been fully tested. Part of me wants to keep going. To go into space and beyond.

I clearly do not need oxygen to breathe. Nothing can stop me.

Alas, I will not have time to find out today.

At least my uniform is clean now.

• • •

She descended slowly through the atmosphere (to avoid her outfit and hair burning up on reentry) and headed back towards Sulphur Springs when she saw two figures running out of a convenience store on Highway 36, get in the old Chevrolet sedan, and speed off. She ran hurriedly into the store where she found a female clerk crying.

"Those people robbed me," she said. "They took over four hundred dollars; they had guns and everything. Just me here today."

"Who were they?"

"Don't know, lady. Some man and woman. I never saw them before."

"Are you all right?"

"Yeah. But who the hell are you?"

"I'm *Stella Scura*. Don't worry; I'll get your money back for you, Ma'am."

"How are you gonna do that? They're probably five miles away by now."

"I saw which way they were going. Call the local law enforcement. I'll bring them back."

"Are you crazy?"

"Definitely not."

She walked out and took flight down the highway in the direction she thought they were heading. In about two minutes she passed over them from about fifty feet in the air. She landed on the ground about a hundred yards in front of them. They slowed and seemed prepared to run over her. That probably wasn't going to go well for anyone. While she was pretty confident she could absorb all the kinetic energy, she wasn't sure. As the car swerved around her, she took off again and approached the drivers' window, seeing the gaping glances of the five drivers that she had passed.

"Pull this vehicle over," she commanded.

"Jesus Christ, Donnie," the female driver said. "What the hell is that thing?"

"Don't know. Floor it, Justine," her male accomplice replied.

Now what? They were going at least a hundred miles per hour; Indiana wasn't mountainous, but this county was the highest elevation in the state (1,100 feet) and did have its share of small hills. She watched as the car skidded off the road, went through a ramp and off a bridge.

She had caused this. If she didn't catch the car, then those people were going to die or be seriously injured. Armed robbers or not, this isn't what she had bargained for.

She flew under the car, caught it before it hit, and flew it back to the bridge, sitting it on the ground, first by lowering the rear end, then the front.

"I said to stop this car. You robbed that store back there. Do you know what you did, and you think you can get away with it?"

The man shut off the motor. "Whatever you want, lady, just don't mess with us. We got no quarrel with you."

"Then we're going back there. I would suggest that you not try to exit the vehicle."

She lifted up the car again from beneath and flew it back the five miles to the convenience store where a sheriff's cruiser was waiting. The two officers gaped at her with open mouths as she landed the vehicle back on the old concrete.

"That's her, Jason," the female officer said. "The one who they say caught Air Force One."

She nodded. "I have brought these offenders back to you. I saw them leave this store after they robbed this woman of her money, it is not very funny."

"Get out, both of you," the male officer said.

The female officer came up to her and nervously extended her hand, which she took. "I'm Deputy Joyce Redmond," she said. "Your name is, er, what? I need it for my report, if it's not too much trouble, Ma'am."

"*Stella. Stella Scura.*"

"Can you spell the last name?

She sighed. "S-C-U-R-A."

"Is there a middle initial?"

"No."

The officer shook her head. "I don't know how to fill out this report. Never had one where a car actually flew before."

"We all have our problems, Officer, but I really do have to go."

"Wait a minute. I need contact information for you."

"I do not really have a phone number. Sorry."

"Thank you," the store owner said as she took off.

• • •

She landed near the bunker of the Sulphur Springs testing facility, took off *Stella's* uniform, and changed into Paige's clothes stored in a special compartment. She would have to be retrieved as she had no reliable way of getting back now without flying. She called Bella's cell phone on her helmet communicator.

"Come get me. Now."

"Where are you?"

"The bunker."

"Why? What's wrong? Are you hurt?"

"No. Just come now, please. I do not want to move right now."

It seemed an eternity as she waited for the twelve minutes it took Bella and Nick to pick her up in the Eldorado, crying, as she thought about what she had done.

"What's up?" Bella said, hugging her. "You did a miraculous thing, honey; it was on all the news feeds."

"It is not saving Air Force One. It was what I did on my way back that has me extremely upset."

"What?" They sped off back to their house in the western AC suburbs. "I don't understand, Paige."

"I witnessed a convenience store robbery on Highway 36 on my way back here. The car sped off, and I went in to make sure the victim was okay. Then, I went after them."

"What happened?" Nick asked.

"I flew past them, stood in the road and tried to get them to stop, which they did not. Then, they kept going faster and faster until they went through a fence and off a bridge."

Bella touched her on the shoulder. "Oh, Paige—"

She shook her head. "It is all right; I caught them before they hit, but what if I had not? I almost caused those people to be killed with my cavalier carelessness."

"Hey, look. They were armed robbers, remember that."

She put her head down sadly. "Yes, but that does not mean

they deserved to die. They did not shoot anyone; and even if they did, that is not the point. The police would have found them in time, so what was I trying to do?"

"You did what you thought was right."

She shook her head. "No, I was grandstanding, nothing more, and there could have been much blood and gore. Me trying to prove how great I was. I stopped a robbery at an Anchorage convenience store when I was seventeen, but I did not have any choice. The robber grabbed me and tried to hold me hostage."

"Yes, I know all about that, Paige."

"What? There is no way you could."

"I know more than you think. So does Wendy."

"She suggested that as well. Why?"

"To keep everyone away. The reporters, other media, police, those individuals would have done you no favors."

"But that was one thing—yet, this, I had control over. Just like my stupid trip to the Bering Strait, it has laid out my fate."

"I know I don't understand, and there's no way I could. But you'll learn. And if you hadn't been flying over Alaska, we wouldn't be here now, and Air Force One would've crashed into the city."

"I will learn that the best way to be involved is when I have no choice. Pastor Jack was right. Pride is one of the seven deadly sins, and I was almost deadly today."

"It's a great responsibility, Paige. I can't imagine what that's like, but it turned out okay. You have great maturity to admit to your fallacies. More than any person I know."

"I do realize this now that the only way for me to function is to somehow learn the law. That is what I wanted to do, anyway. I am weary of this stupid-ass crap."

"Then we'll figure out a way for you to do that. I don't know how that stuff works, but you now know someone who does."

• • •

Will stormed into the large office suite designated for their use at Aurora City Medical Center and slammed the door, then angrily stared at his parents with murder in his eyes and grabbed his mom's left arm.

"If you jerks weren't my parents, I'd punch out both of you right now. I still might kick both your asses."

"I know you're upset, but what's the problem, Will?" Jay said.

"Both of you are my problem. You, with your secrets. Dad—you took me out to North Pole, and you *knew*. When were you going to tell me Paige Marshall was my cousin?"

"You're the one who wanted to go there; I didn't suggest it."

"Don't evade the question, you know what I mean, me wanting to go there isn't relevant. Did you think that was funny? Do you see me laughing?"

"I don't know what you're talking about."

"Do you think I'm an idiot? I saw and heard Mom talking to *Stella Scura* in the evacuation vehicle and outside. She and Paige are the same person, as the way she talks is unmistakable. I have the ability of absolute pitch like Aunt Bonnie, Dad, you know that."

"You can't possibly believe that, and you're just caught up in the excitement of this," Jay said.

"Stop lying to me! I noticed how much we looked alike, and it drove me nuts; now I know why. I even checked her photo with Miranda, who thought I was nuts. Mom, you and your stupid secret spooks did something to alter that."

Wendy nodded as her son released his grip. "I didn't know our plane was going to crash. Yes, this was a big secret to keep—it took an immense amount of resources to do so, over many years. At the time you went to see Paige, she was unaware of any of this. It would've done no one any good to tell you that, Will."

"You're a liar, just like Dad."

She paused for a few seconds. "I have never lied to you, Will, except for this one thing."

"Oh, yeah, well, this was a pretty big 'one thing,' Mom. Like that makes it okay."

"I'm sorry, it'll have to be okay. If not, you'll have to deal with it. Her records were kept secret for a reason, to keep someone else from doing the same thing. There was no other choice. I held the world's greatest secret in my hands, which is way more important than what you want. What if you had blurted it out by accident?"

"What do you mean? We all have choices. We went all these years without me knowing I had another family member. It might have been nice to have been aware I had another cousin, especially someone who's basically a god."

"Don't you think I wanted to see her? She's my dead brother's child. This is way bigger than you, Will. Bigger than all of us."

"But, what she did, Mom, Paige isn't human—"

She shook her head. "I knew she could fly but had no idea she could do anything like that. You have to believe me."

"I don't believe you. And the crazy flying robot we heard about a while back? That was Paige?"

She nodded. "Yes."

"Why would she do that?"

"She needed that tech suit to see."

"And you knew about it?"

"It's complicated, Will. I've known about the Russian armor for twenty years, as my dad stole it from the Russians, but that's all classified military information. I have a lot more I can't share with you, so get some damn perspective here. But I didn't know Paige was capable of feats like lifting a two million pound airplane to safety."

"So what do we do now? Are we just one big family now?"

"I don't really know, dear. I'm making it up as I go along. I know you think I had all this planned out, but I don't know what comes next."

"Yeah, well, you can do it alone." Will stormed out of the room and slammed the door.

• • •

Next Day
The White House
Press Room

"Ma'am, don't do this right now. You're compromised in this situation," Jackie said.

"I'll have to do it eventually, Jackie. I don't want to dump it on Kris. That isn't good for anyone. If I don't, it'll look like I'm hiding something."

"You are, and it's Kris' job to protect you."

"Do I look like I need my press secretary to protect me?"

"Sometimes you do, Wendy."

"From the protesters outside? I'm not worried about them or the news media."

Jackie shook her head. "No. From your own worst enemy, the arch-nemesis you've fought since January 7, 1972. Yourself."

"It's not easy being me, Jackie. It has never been. Maybe you're right, but I have to do this one." The President went out to the press room and confronted the crowd of reporters. She pointed to a prominent reporter in the front row.

"What's your stand on this super-powered being, President Mendoza?"

"*Stella Scura* is a friend of this administration, as you can plainly see. We can use all the friends we can get, don't you think?"

"Is she an American? An alien? Rumors are that she spoke Russian when she landed."

"She's an American citizen and represents peace. If someone like that wanted to destroy us, she could've done it already."

"So you say. She could also be used as a terrible weapon."

"No, I *know*. She was born on American soil and therefore is an American by birthright, as stipulated in our Constitution."

"Is she a Russian?"

"I just told you she's an American, listen up. She does speak fluent Russian as she is bilingual. Therefore, she is as welcome here as any other American citizen. I will tolerate no expeditions to try and find her. And if I get any word to the contrary, the perpetrator will end up like Ashburn." She called on the next reporter.

"Is she a secret weapon you've kept under wraps until now?"

"She is not a 'weapon,' but I'm afraid much of that information is classified. Know now that she represents the interests of the great United States of America and will appear whenever her unique services are needed."

"Why does she wear a mask if she's not a secret, then, Madam President? What does she have to hide?"

She hadn't been prepared for that question, one which she should've anticipated. "Nothing to hide at all. It is part of her costume, don't read more into it than there is."

Another reporter raised his hand. "The world is huge, Madam President, yet this *Stella Scura* girl shows up in Aurora City, of all places, where you coincidentally happen to be. The religious comparisons to Aurora the Angel and Christ seem to be inevitable."

"I travel to Aurora City fairly often, as I have family there. My niece Aurora Darkkin is dead. The fact that this fantastic being has shown up here is purely coincidental. I had no knowledge of her existence before this."

A female reporter raised her hand as Wendy pointed to her for the next question. "We know nothing about this person's abilities or whether it's safe for her to be around us at all. Has anyone contemplated the liability issues of a real superhero? You can't just take the world into your own hands."

"Look here—I didn't ask for Air Force One to be disabled; she just sort of showed up. While her existence has been theorized, this is the first contact she has had with me. However, safety is always my primary concern, and I have a colleague who has done some significant research on these matters. Biv?"

Her old medical school classmate walked up to the podium as several reporters groaned and rolled their eyes.

"Roy G. Biv? Are you kidding us? Not *Photraman.* No disrespect intended, Ma'am, but what kind of an expert is he or any of those other guys?" a fortyish male reporter asked, laughing.

"Hey, newsman, I'm no longer *Photraman.* I am a licensed physician and board-certified neuro-ophthalmologist. I have studied the physiology of *Stella Scura* and have concluded that she represents no harm to us at all. She gives off no emissions of any kind."

"Yeah, like you're an authority. Some feel that it's no coincidence she landed near Aurora City. Is she the one after whom it is named? Is Aurora Darkkin alive after all?"

The President came back to the podium, gently pushing the shorter man aside. "I already answered that inane question. My niece died in one of the most horrible acts of terrorism in U.S. history. I didn't plan for my plane to be sabotaged too. The landing there is merely a coincidence. Please don't disgrace her memory by bringing her name up yet again."

Another male reporter spoke up. "A more philosophical question, Ma'am: is she the Savior? The second coming of Christ?"

"While she possesses extraordinary physical abilities, some of which we do not understand entirely, she is not supernatural. So, no, she is not divine, if that's what you mean."

"Will she live in the White House? Your son has a new friend, we hear."

"Paige Marshall is a cousin of my niece's husband, Nicholas Stannous, nothing more. They both play basketball. She will be going to college soon."

"Does the government condone this type of activity? Is this flying person not just a vigilante?"

"I have the authority to grant federal police powers to this individual, and she is well versed in the law." Not yet, but she will be, she thought to herself.

"We're still concerned about any possible danger she represents, Ma'am. Surely you can understand that."

"I do, but we have it under control." Right. She had no idea what would happen next.

• • •

The White House
Situation Room

Wendy, Dexter Slabb, Joint Chiefs Chairman General Lawrence Kriger, Secretary of State Samuel Redding, and a handful of other military individuals assembled for a debriefing after the amazing rescue of Air Force One by *Stella Scura.*

"We have several issues at hand here, the first being to figure out exactly how they disabled Air Force One."

"Ma'am, as you mentioned, Ashburn must've stolen one of the experimental portable EMP devices and set up a transmitter in a small town fifty miles east of Aurora City called Union City, which is, interestingly, in both eastern Indiana and western Ohio. We've destroyed it."

"Surely he had some assistance; he couldn't have possibly engineered this on his own."

"Don't be so sure," Dexter said. "Tom had a background in engineering and avionics, although we'll find out soon if others were involved."

"You'd better. What about the plane?"

"It seems fine now," Air Force Lt. Gen. Barry Thompson said. "It needs some cleaning up, but it doesn't seem to have been seriously damaged. We have the backup ready to go, Ma'am."

She frowned. "By the way, where is Ashburn now?"

"We don't know, Ma'am," Kriger said.

"What?" Her eyes opened wildly. "Are you kidding me, Larry?"

"He's likely in some Eastern Bloc country with no extradition treaty. Probably got out on some illicit private flight even though we had his passport. Hard to police that."

"Well, you better spare no expense to find that SOB and bring him back here so I can kick his ass personally."

"Don't worry, we'll find him. A more imminent issue to discuss is, of course—*Stella Scura.*"

She shook her head. "I don't know where she went, either. After she rested a bit at the hospital, she took off like a rocket. Literally."

"Rather convenient. For all we know, she caused this event herself just to stage this rescue and gain your favor. Then, after saving your plane, she went after some petty crooks in a convenience store robbery about ten miles away."

"I guess no crime is too small for her." She crushed a soda can and tossed it across the room with her left hand. "And that's the stupidest thing I've ever heard, Larry. Ashburn did it, and we just agreed on that. We owe our lives to that girl. We and the thousands of people in Aurora City who would have died."

"She's right, Larry: it has Ashburn written all over it." Dexter looked at her. "Let it go. We need to get on this gal's good side."

"All right, I can see I'm outnumbered, but someone has to be realistic here and think of all the options."

"She didn't go far, but you must have talked to her for some time," Dexter said.

She nodded. "I did. What of it? I am the President of the United States, I thought she deserved my thanks, and I will talk to whomever I please. You got a problem with that, Slabb?"

"That all depends. Is she an American? An alien?"

"Alien? I assume you mean a non-American?"

Dexter sneered. "I was referring to the other kind."

"She certainly sounded like an American to me. I doubt seriously that a malevolent alien would have gone to all that trouble to rescue us, when it would've been just as easy to let us crash into the skyline like 9/11."

"Unless she wants to gain our trust. It's possible for almost anyone with proper training to mimic any accent; she did speak very good Russian, as I understand."

"Having a pretty good understanding of human biology, I believe it is pretty unlikely aliens evolved who look and talk just like us, Dexter."

Dexter pointed at her. "Unless they can adapt and assume others' appearances, Madam President. They may be quite cunning."

"What?" She slapped her hand down sharply on the table. "Oh, come on, that's an absurd comment."

"You think so? Ma'am, you pay me to think outside the box,

which is what I'm trying to do. It's not as far-fetched as you might believe."

"It's so stupid as not to warrant further discussion."

"Some would say that about a flying woman. Do you understand *that* about human biology? Because I sure don't know how that's possible. Moving that mass at that velocity requires forces beyond human comprehension."

"And about the Russians—don't open up the damn Cold War again, Dexter; it's dead and buried."

"Really? You almost act like you know this person, Ma'am."

The President stood up, walked around the table, and stared down at Dexter and made a scooping motion with her left hand.

"Get up."

Dexter looked at her and smiled. "What?"

"You heard me. Get your smug ass up out of that leather chair before I do it for you."

"All right." He stood up and stared her in the eye. "What now?"

"Okay, listen to me, you arrogant Ivy League shit," she snarled. "I am the President of the United States of America, and this is *my* house, *my* country. I created your fricking agency, and I can dissolve it just as quickly. Don't you *ever* act like you are interrogating me, you got that?"

He looked down at her shoes. "I wasn't; I was merely—"

"Shut up, Dexter. I know when someone is giving me the business. I didn't get here without a massive number of bumps and scrapes and the scars to show for it. Physical *and* emotional scars, so know I can dish it out just as well. That really isn't something you want to experience."

"Understood. May I now speak frankly, Ma'am?"

She rolled her eyes. "Expressing yourself doesn't seem to be one of your deficits, so please impart your wisdom upon us."

He stared at her again. "If not to me, then you'll answer to the House and Senate committees and to the American public about the unorthodox way you have dealt with this situation."

She snarled and got within two inches of his face. "*House and Senate?* The House is going to impeach me for being a traitor, for befriending a being who just saved my ass and my plane from destroying the Aurora City downtown? Really? Talk about committing political suicide. They might as well walk off a cliff. Ain't gonna happen."

"I'm on your side, Ma'am, and this 'arrogant Ivy League shit' just wants you to be prepared. In addition to my Ph.D. in physics, I was a practicing attorney, trained in being an adversary. Therefore, I'm on your side."

"Aww, thanks for an update of your resume." She sighed. "I feel so much more assured now."

"Ma'am," Kriger said, his voice wavering, "it's just that this particular aspect of your behavior differs dramatically from anything else you've done since I've been around."

"How so, Larry? Enlighten me, given the vast understanding of human psychology you exhibit on a daily basis that renders you such a skilled mediator of disputes."

"Ma'am: your military policy has always been an aggressive one, to strike first so as not to allow the other side to gain an advantage. Yet, paradoxically, you are ignoring irrefutable facts about this being. She could be horrifically dangerous, and you seem curiously uninterested in that possibility."

"I am ignoring nothing, and how do you suggest I 'gain an advantage' in this case? She likely possesses the power of a small star, guys. Not something DSD or you is prepared to confront."

"So, we do nothing, is that it?" Kriger asked impatiently.

She shook her head. "Untrue, you proceed from a false assumption. I am quite interested in such things, but I am first a scientist who demands proof, as Dexter over there should, but he's too caught up in his obnoxious political rhetoric."

Dexter held up his right hand, as if objecting in a courtroom. "Ma'am, that's an overreaction—"

"No, it's not. You are both omniscient, is that it?"

"No, Ma'am," Kriger said, crossing his arms. "And neither are you, with all due respect."

She waved her hands towards her chest. "Well, then, good, y'all can just bring it on. I am prepared for this, as I have been preparing for this job my whole life. I survived Brant Gallagher, Malachi Argon and his genetically engineered super-soldier son, four bullets to my chest, every stinking politician in Washington who tried to take me down, my family being blown up by a nuke, and a whole lot worse than any of you assholes, and I'll sure as hell take my shot with the American public or Congress. Why? Because I fear nothing. You ever faced anyone without fear? I'll survive, but you won't. I'll kick your ass through that window, Kriger; you may think you know combat, but you've never been twelve rounds with this tough bitch. Mark my words: you had both better be prepared to finish what you start."

"We're on the same side here. You don't even know who this young woman is," Kriger said, smiling. "Despite your boasts, you have no proof she's not an alien. What if her people or some other aliens come looking for her?"

"Huh? 'Her people?' What the hell does that mean?"

Dexter pointed his finger towards the ceiling. "You, of all the Presidents in history, can't possibly believe this woman is entirely of Earthly origin; you just proclaimed you were a scientist. Do we really want Earth to be her playground? What if some nasty friends with equal or even greater power come looking for her? She could likely destroy Earth by herself with a fraction of her power, we estimate—what would a whole army of these beings do?"

She shrugged. "Maybe you have a point, but what do you suggest? She talked to me because she said I am a person of honor. I don't even know where she is now. Why would I keep that a secret? And what do you want me to do about it? I can consider it a glass half full, or half empty. I choose to embrace the former."

Dexter pointed at her. "What if I do agree, for the sake of argument, that she's a benevolent being? We still have no idea what the effect of her 'powers' on lifeforms or the Earth might be. She appears to fly and lift heavy objects by manipulating gravity fields which require incomprehensible energies. That's a lot to grasp, Ma'am. There may also be deleterious effects on the environment we haven't yet even considered."

"The scientist in me cannot disagree with those possibilities, although I feel them unlikely. So, you want to study her?"

"Yes, that's about it."

"So you can learn as a scientist."

"Certainly."

"Bullshit, Dexter. You guys just want to discover and exploit a weakness."

"Are you kidding, Ma'am? Of course we do. Would *you* want a being with absolute power flying about the planet without any way to control her?"

"What? That is an absurd question no person could anticipate would ever be asked; come on. Don't be obtuse, Dexter."

"It's my job to anticipate things like that, Ma'am. I don't know how else to do my job. If that makes me 'obtuse,' then so be it."

"Well, I know how to do mine. She's here, and we have to deal with it. Yes, she saved my life, and I'm grateful, and I have to trust that she's here for the right thing. I promise I will keep her close. But there's no way you are experimenting on this girl."

"Ma'am, my team needs to work on some means of containment, in case of an emergency, as she could destroy us all—"

She walked up to him and poked him in the chest. "Dexter, any of you even *try* something like that, I will use every resource I have at my disposal to destroy all of you. If you think I'm kidding, you just try it."

That was her last word on the subject.

Because if anyone was going to manipulate *Stella Scura* and benefit from this situation, it would surely be her. She had no idea how to do that, though, but had a feeling she would be back soon.

Stella had done her a big favor, and now it was time to return it.

Chapter Forty-One

Eielson Air Force Base
Fairbanks North Star Borough, Alaska

Lt. Russell T. Stanton went to his commanding officer's office nervously. Col. Brian A. Ralston was kind of gruff, but generally a fair guy. He wasn't much to make small talk. Something was up, he knew. He knocked on the door."

"Enter," he heard.

He smartly saluted Ralston. "Here as ordered, sir."

"Stanton. At ease. You're fine, just need to give you your orders."

"Yes, Colonel. Orders?" He smiled slightly, perplexed.

"You've been transferred, Stanton."

"Huh? A transfer? I didn't want or put in for a—"

Ralston shook his head. "Well, it happened. Don't know how, but you're going to Dayton. Wright-Patterson Air Force Base."

"Wright-Patt?" It was closer to home, but it sure wasn't the most exciting part of the country. "Why?"

"Don't know how or why and don't care. But don't you have some family in western Pennsylvania?"

"Yes, but I like it here."

"Doesn't matter what you like, son. This request came from pretty high up."

"What do you mean? Who?"

"The White House, I hear."

"The White House? Why would anyone there care about a lowly First Lieutenant?"

The full bird colonel frowned. "Like I said, don't worry about it, Stanton. I just take orders, and you will, too. You must know someone up there who's pretty important."

"I have no idea." He didn't, but he knew someone who was a relative of someone pretty important, it seemed. Dayton, Ohio was only an hour from Aurora City. How convenient. It was time to take a little trip on the bike to Indiana.

• • •

After a quick move to Wright-Patt and renting a small apartment in Huber Heights, Russ decided on a little trip one hour west before he had to report in five days. Most of his belongings hadn't arrived yet, and he turned in the car he had leased at Eielson and bought a gently used red Harley from someone a friend at Wright-Patt recommended; motorcycles were one of his hobbies, and not that practical (or safe) in Alaska.

He exited on Interstate 70 to the Aurora City Beltway and rode ten more miles to his exit. He rode six more miles on his new "Hog" to the city's most exclusive neighborhood on the northeast side and pulled up to the gated estate as the attendant smiled at him from the small booth. He could barely see the house on the small hill over the woods, but even then it clearly was a big place, and it sure wasn't hard to find.

He never thought in a million years he would ever be standing outside *this* estate.

The gate guard came out of her booth and smiled. "Can I help you, sir?"

"Yes, er, I'm here to see Paige Marshall. She's a house guest of the family who lives here, I'm told."

"Your name, sir?"

"Uh, Russell Stanton."

"May I see some identification, sir?"

He pulled out his military identification and handed it to her. She looked at it for a few seconds, checked her clipboard, then smiled again.

"Yessir, Lieutenant, you're on the approved 'A' guest list. Go right in. The main residence is a quarter mile up the road, straight ahead." She handed him a proximity badge, which had his photo on it. "You may keep this. Just use this next time to go right in."

"Thanks, it's, er, kind of hard to miss." Dang, this place had the security of a military base, but that was probably appropriate, given the tenants inside. He rode his motorcycle up the trail, in the middle of a dense deciduous forest (there were still some bright autumn leaves remaining) and finally reached the main residence, the biggest private residence he had ever seen. Well, he didn't know all the etiquette; probably best to just park it in the circle, and some valet would probably move it. He got off his bike, went up to the door, and pushed the doorbell, waiting for the cavalcade of butlers or maids who likely would be answering the door.

The door opened as he saw no butler or maid, but a barefoot Bella wearing a black Purdue University sweatsuit and eating a bright green Granny Smith apple.

"My word, it's Lieutenant Russ!" she said cheerfully. "Come on in. Remember me?"

"Yes, er, Dr. Mendoza. It's nice to see you again under different circumstances, in a more, uh—normal environment than when we first met."

"Call me Bella, son; I work for a living. As you can see from my fine threads, we're not very formal here."

"I didn't know what to expect. I come from modest means. I expected servants and formal attire, as that would be a natural assumption from those of your social status."

She nodded. "So I did I, Russ. My dad and grandpa were cops, my grandma taught high school math, and my mom was a high school dramatics and classics teacher. I'm no different now, no jet-setter like my uncle Jay, the football playboy turned White House celebrity dad. We do have people who help clean and do yard work sometimes, but nobody lives here but us."

"It's fantastic." He looked around the grand entryway.

"Heard you were transferred to Wright-Patt. Makes it a lot easier to come here, a little over an hour."

"Yeah. Sure was convenient, this happening now."

"Things happen for a reason." They sat down on the couch. "You want something to drink?"

"No, I'm okay."

"It's good you came to see Paige. She's missed you a lot, as she obviously hasn't been around you since—that day."

"She talks about me?"

Bella rolled her eyes. "She talks about you and lots of other things. It's hard to find a bigger mouth than mine, but I've met my match, amazingly, and that ain't easy." She took another bite of her apple. "How are things going for you? Did you get the third degree from the brass after we dropped you off at Minot Air Force Base?"

"They asked me about *Stella.* I told them I couldn't say. I didn't lie. The consequences of that would be devastating."

She nodded. "No kidding."

"What's the story about why Paige is here, anyway? I assume you aren't telling people she's your cousin."

"Of course not, Russ. The official word is that she's a cousin of *Tinman's.* Technically that's true since her adoptive father is his biological uncle, so his child would be *Tinman's* cousin. She's a little old to be Jose's friend."

"Jose?"

"Our son. *Tinman* took him to the football game at Ross-Ade today to see the Boilers play Wisconsin."

Paige came down the stairs and ran up to him, giving him a kiss. "I've missed you a lot, officer and a gentleman."

"You're telling me?"

"Where are we going, Russ?"

"It's a surprise."

"Have fun, kids. Don't do anything I wouldn't do." Bella shook her head. "Hold on, that didn't come out quite right, as that doesn't leave much to the imagination."

"Thanks."

"When should I expect you home?"

"Don't wait up. We may not be home."

"Okey dokey."

• • •

Russ came by and whisked her onto his motorcycle. She put on her helmet and got on.

"Wait a minute, flyboy, where are we going so fast?" She barely could catch her breath as they peeled out of the compound, as she wrapped her arms around him, cold wind in her face.

"I've got a surprise for you," Russ said. "Something I do all the time, but you've never done, at least I don't think so."

She turned her head in the direction of his voice. "What is it?"

"Some might say it's reckless, but I think you'll survive. An experience you've never had."

"Okay, I'll bite. Where is it we are going?"

"To the airfield. You've been to an Air Force base before. This is a private hangar just on the Indiana side of Ohio."

"Yeah, so?"

"Just trust me on this one."

They rode the twenty-three-mile trek to Ronson Airfield and walked into the hangar.

"Well, I can hear the echoes, so we must be in the hangar. What the heck are we supposed to do here?" She stepped off the cycle.

"Right you are, and you'll understand soon. Put this on." She felt the mass of rumpled fabric Russ handed her.

She felt the heavy canvas and straps. "What the heck is this? It's either a straitjacket or a jumpsuit. I told you I do not carry on the family tradition of escapes, especially from a plane."

He laughed. "It's an aviation jumpsuit. You've never been up in a plane before?"

"I've flown before."

"Not like this, as a passenger."

"I doubt it is as exhilarating."

"I beg to differ. Give it a chance and just be a little girl again." She put the jumpsuit on as he helped her up into the rear of the plane.

"Are you flying?"

"No, of course not. I've made friends with Fred here." She heard the raspy voice of the middle-aged pilot say hello.

"But why do I have to put this garment on just for a mere airplane ride?"

"Because I said so. Put these on too," he said.

She felt the additional large items, one which was familiar; the other was not, and was much larger than the jumpsuit. "What? Is this a parachute and helmet? Why? You expect *me* to go skydiving? A blind person? Are you daft, Lieutenant?"

"Sure, why not? You wouldn't be the first blind person to do so."

She shook her head. "I cannot believe that, it is crazy. A sightless person skydiving? No way would they allow that."

"No, it's true, I checked it out. There have been many blind persons who have gone skydiving. Don't you think it would be fun?"

"Maybe it would be, at that, but why would my extremely hard head need a helmet?"

"It's the law, for one thing. I don't want you standing out as different, as it would draw unnecessary attention. Don't want that."

"That might be challenging, but *why* do I need a parachute?"

"That's also a requirement, dummy, for reasons that should be obvious. Let's just have you float down on your own; that won't attract any attention, nope."

"I still think people would think that just a little strange and irresponsible. You want to get in trouble? You're an Air Force officer, for Lord's sake. Taking a poor defenseless blind girl skydiving." She shook her head.

"I don't think I'm irresponsible, and I won't get into trouble, and it'll allow you to experience something you never have—to be in free fall. Have you ever done that?"

"Free fall? No, I guess not. I had never been more than sixty feet off the ground without the suit until I got the visor. I learned to fly about the time my mom got the Russian helmet working."

"Well, it's exhilarating. I'm sure it will be, even for you. Don't worry, I'll tell you when to pull."

"Gee, that is reassuring. But what if my chute does not open?"

"You have a secondary chute, as do I."

"What if that does not work?"

"OMG. I guess you crash, then. Better you than me."

"That is not so bad, although I will not be glad, lad."

"Come on, accidents happen less than one in a hundred fifty thousand times. Don't fret about it; if you crash, I'll find you and we'll explain it, somehow. Don't know how yet."

"Good luck with that. I suppose I can do what we did before."

"No, you won't; I'm just joking. I'll be right next to you—so, if my chute fails, I guess I'm the one who'll be in luck."

She shook her head. "That would *not* be lucky. No way will I find you in time without my sight, and this area's just a little bit more populated than the northern part of the forty-ninth state." She felt him buckle something around her left wrist as she felt the metal bezel with her right hand. "What is this? I do not have much use for a regular watch."

"It's not just a watch, but also an altimeter alarm. It will beep very loudly when we reach 2,500 feet, when you need to deploy."

He bumped his fist against the helmet. "There's a radio in here too, so we can keep in contact."

"And if I don't deploy my chute in time?"

"You'll be fine if you pay attention. If not, I guess we pick you up off the ground. If you deploy too late, you hit too hard, which I guess isn't a huge deal for you, either. You have a radio link in your helmet. I can't imagine anything safer."

She shrugged. "I suppose it is not as irresponsible as I first thought."

"Think of it—for the first time in your life you're not having to be in control. Trusting yourself to another person can be enjoyable."

"Huh. Guess I have little choice."

"No, you don't, you're being kidnapped."

"I guess that is kind of exciting, at that. Being whisked away by a dashing gentleman in pilot's garb. I always thought it would be fun, with the right person. Just do not send a blind girl to her doom."

"Muwahaha." He did his best evil-scientist laugh as they went into the back as the pilot started the motor; she felt the plane taxi and accelerate down the runway. It was exhilarating as she felt them leave the ground. The plane eventually rose to 12,500 feet, the altimeter said after she pushed the button.

"What do we do now?"

"What do you think? You go first. I'll follow."

"Hey, why do I go first?"

"So I can make certain you get out okay, dummy."

"I guess that is logical. So what is it they used to say in the old days? *Geronimo!*" She jumped out and felt the wind pick her up; it was more powerful than she had thought. She did some flips in the air as she realized she wasn't falling as fast as she thought she would, although a person who could propel herself many times faster than sound didn't have much of a reference. She remembered dimly from science class that objects accelerated as they approached Earth at a rate of 9.8 meters per second squared, a factoid that came in handy to help her figure out how many hundred feet she had fallen when she did her nocturnal Evel Knievel bicycle jump off Cargg's Cliff.

But she also remembered Mom once saying something about "terminal velocity," that the acceleration of an object towards

Earth was limited by wind resistance pushing upwards, and that an average human could only reach a speed of about 120 miles per hour—at most, 150 miles per hour by adjusting trajectory to minimize wind resistance—so she could only fall so fast. It occurred to her that, being the only human being to her knowledge who could actually fly, it might be useful at some point to learn some of those esoteric things.

"Here you are," Russ said as she heard him through the helmet radio. She then felt him grab her right arm.

"Hey, how did you get near me?"

"Experienced divers like me can manipulate quite well through the air. So, I'm flying way better than you right now. We're in my domain now, not yours."

"It is weird, but kind of fun. I do not know where I am."

"It doesn't scare you, does it?"

"No, not really, nothing really scares me, but I also do not feel in control. That is, actually, a unique and good feeling. I like that, oddly enough, although I am quite tough."

"I thought as much. Don't worry, you're with me. We're fine."

After about two minutes of freefall, she heard the beeping and felt the cord loop with her right hand. "Pull this one?"

"Yeah. You've got it."

"Here goes." She pulled it and heard the wind catch the sail as she was pulled upwards, rather hard, actually—the first time she had ever experienced this sensation.

The rate of descent slowed, he had said, to about eighteen miles per hour. He had selected a snowy area where he could find her if they landed very far apart.

It was exciting, not knowing where she was or when she would land, while at the same time realizing she was perfectly safe. Not like when she exploded her suit and damaged Russ' plane. She figured she would have been safe then, but she likely would have had some unwanted military visitors.

She hit the soft snow-covered ground and sunk about two feet. She unbuckled the parachute as she heard a "thump" perhaps a hundred feet away. She remembered that her free mass was seventy-two kilograms or about one hundred sixty pounds, and that he should hit the ground before her, most likely, but that didn't happen for some reason.

She ran towards him in the snow. He reached for her and gave her a hug.

"How did you know where I was?"

"My hearing, although no better than a normal person's, is very trained. I can tune into things that most people would miss. It is easy to hear you even in the snow; that is how I know."

• • •

About two hours later, after a trip on his motorcycle to Huber Heights, Ohio, she walked into the unfamiliar lobby and smelled the freshly waxed floors and carpet freshener.

"Where are we?"

"My apartment building."

That's what she thought, that they had gone through a modest apartment lobby. That, or a no-tell motel. "Why, Lt. Stanton. Taking a girl back to your spacious suite after nearly killing her skydiving. Taking advantage of me?"

"I think you can probably defend yourself. You told me you're eighteen, right?"

"Yes, in October, but you never told me how old you are."

"Twenty-four. I entered the Academy at seventeen, the minimum age, and finished at twenty-one."

She heard the elevator door close. "What are we having for dinner? I expect to be well fed after my ordeal, military prodigy."

"I thought you didn't need to eat."

"As far as I know I do not *need* to, but I sure *like* to eat, buddy. And I am hungry. It had better be good, as it should."

They went into his room as she went in, felt the bed, and sat on it. "Well, then, I have prepared, or, er . . . Barton's Steakhouse has prepared, rather . . . a luscious meal which will be delivered momentarily. No wine or cocktails, though. I don't need a 'contributing to the delinquency of a minor' ticket for that. My new CO's a real straight arrow."

"Aww, darn. However, you are seemingly intent on contributing to the delinquency of a minor in another fashion, lascivious lothario."

"In that aspect, you're a regular consenting adult."

"Huh, you are sounding very clinical, mister. Does not matter, I do not care much for alcoholic beverages, anyway. But you are way too uptight, sir."

"I hate to ask this question, but, can you, you know—"

"Can I what? Spit it out, soldier."

"That's the second time you said that. Don't you *ever* call an Air Force officer 'soldier.' If you were a guy, you'd get rapped in the mouth for that."

"Sorry. Yet, you invited me to your secret apartment, so do not mince words. Get down to business."

"Engage in a certain 'bodily function.' I'm just curious."

She pushed him gently. "What? You are asking if I can have sex, you pervert? Is that not why we are here?"

"Yeah, I suppose, but it's a normal question, don't you think?"

She nodded. "Of course I can, I think. I have not really thought about it."

"Liar. A beautiful girl like you? That can't be true—I know you've thought about it, especially the way you acted in the movie theater."

"Well, yes, I have thought about it quite a bit. Much of the time, actually. The energy field that surrounds me appears to be protective, but I am sure it wants me to live a normal life, whatever that is for me."

"You talk as if it has its own intelligence, with needs and wants. That's a bit of speculation."

She shook her head. "Well, I have no other explanation, so that one makes the most sense. And that type of activity is normal for most people."

"I always thought so."

"Of course I have as well, Russ; I have 'normal' desires. But I have not had many opportunities. Yeesh. You have been to the Alaskan frontier, which is not overrun with suitable males—and I am rather picky as far as prospective mates are concerned, for obvious reasons. I am one of a kind, and my social life is in a bind."

"What if you did have the opportunity?" He kissed her, and she kissed him back. She hadn't really felt this way before.

"I guess I would have to go with the flow. I'm maybe a little naïve, but I get it. I wouldn't have come up here if I hadn't thought it might happen."

"You talk about that energy field as if it's alive, a person."

She nodded. "It must be, it's a living part of my being. It's too complex not to have some type of sentient intelligence. It all happens automatically, I don't have to do anything and it protects me."

• • •

They finished dinner forty minutes later, then went to the sofa as he turned on the TV which was tuned to a sports news show.

"I've never met anyone like you," he said, stroking her hair.

"I certainly hope not; I do not think there is anyone else like me around. I thought you had that figured out."

"I doubt that anyone will ever be like you in that way, but I didn't mean those things. I mean you as a person."

She took a sip of coffee. "While I am enjoying this, Russ, I don't just want to be an infatuation for you. A novelty. When I first heard your voice at the school fair, I knew I wanted to get to know you better. Like most girls, I have ample hormones."

"Yeah, I've seen, but I doubt that your hormones are like most those of most girls."

She smiled. "Well, that is unknown, but in any case, fate seems to have brought us together. I'm still a human being, subject to emotional vulnerability. This is new territory for me."

"I don't want to push you into anything, Paige. And you're not an infatuation for me. I want to do things that are for you, not because you have fantastic gifts. I went out with Paige first you know."

"Why? Most people consider me to be very irritating."

"Because you have an unerring optimism for life that I've never seen in another person. To cope with the things you do is beyond comprehension."

She twirled her Perrier bottle like a top on her index finger.

"Everyone always says that because I am blind, But I am not always optimistic, you know. I feel sad and depressed at times. It is normal. Go to some hospitals and visit sick children who still have hope in the face of terminal diseases, so they are the truly optimistic ones. I have not had to deal with a fraction of the heartache of my mom, Bella, Nick, or Wendy." She punched him in the shoulder. "So do not ever feel sorry for me."

"I don't mean coping with not being able to see, you seem to take that in stride. No, you have to deal with an immense individual responsibility that I doubt anyone else could do in such a mature fashion."

"'Mature fashion?' Just wait until you have known me a while longer, and you will likely change your mind. But I suppose I do not know any other way to be." She took a bite of an Oreo cookie. "Dad tells me I am very naïve, that I am far too trusting. For that reason, I have not allowed myself to be trusting of many people, as I hold within me possibly the greatest secret of all time. You work for the military. Could this be a conflict of some type? Have I made a grand error in my actions?"

"You've already revealed yourself to the world at large, and to the President, by rescuing Thomasson. The fact that your alter ego is Paige Marshall is no one else's business."

She stood up and walked to the window as if looking out. She put her right palm on the cool pane. "Do you not ever wonder which one is real? *Stella* or Paige?"

"*Stella* hasn't been around a whole lot. But, no, not really."

"They are both me. I planned to take advantage of the fact that no one could take it seriously that a blind person could be a hero. Most comic heroes, the hero is strong and brash, the alter ego is quiet and wimpy. It is kind of the other way around with me. Paige is the force to be reckoned with."

"I don't think anyone would describe *Stella* as wimpy. And you seem to be larger, in some way, as *Stella*, although I know that can't be true."

"An optical illusion, I guess. Maybe some of the magician in my mom rubbing off on me. She always said that magic works because people want to believe." She took out her Tekphone. "I need to make a phone call to Bella, as I do not want them to worry."

"They aren't your parents."

She sighed. "Of course not, but I need to do it, to be respectful. They have been very good to me. And they saved your butt too." She picked up her cell phone. "Call Bella." She heard it ring three times. "Hello, Bella? It is me, full of glee."

"Hi. Are you doing okay?"

"Yeah, of course. We are in Huber Heights, just outside Dayton."

"I figured as much. Did you have fun today?"

"We went skydiving today and did some other things. I shall go into details later, gator."

"Skydiving? That sounds interesting. That will take some description later."

She looked at him and smiled. "Yes, it was, and we are having a good time. I wanted to let you know I will not be home tonight."

"You're spending the night there?"

"Yeah. Do not worry about me. I can take care of myself. I will, uh, catch a flight home tomorrow or the next day."

"Okay, but let us know if you need anything. Not a problem to drive there. Use the authorization code I gave you if you need a flight back from the airport, it'll be taken care of."

"I will, although it is unlikely I will need that."

• • •

She rubbed against his chest, wearing a nightgown she had purchased in Aurora City.

"You are beautiful beyond description."

She felt the goose bumps. "Hold me down, Russ." She lay there with her clothes on. "Take my lingerie off. Rip it off, if you must. I can obtain other ones."

"What? I don't think so. That's a little creepy."

"Why? You never held down a girl before or tore her bra off?"

"Of course not! I'm an Air Force officer, of the finest moral character. I abhor any type of violence toward women. And this is an awkward time to be discussing other girls."

"Violence? I am not talking about that. Passion is distinct from violence. What about one who *wanted* to be held down or to have her bra torn off? What is wrong with that?" She laughed. "Do you not think I could stop you if I did not like it?"

"You're not the same. It's weird, your inability to see, almost like I'm taking advantage of you or something."

"Oh, come on. If that bothers you so much, I suggest you turn off the lights, then, so we are on a level playing field."

"That's a darn good idea." She heard him click the light switch. "Now you have *me* at a disadvantage."

"I assure you I can defend myself, should the need arise. I somehow doubt that it shall. How could you possibly threaten me? How stupid."

"You're correct, but it's still weird."

"There is nothing 'weird' about what I suspect we are about to do unless you have something kinky in mind." She smiled.

"Of course not."

She shook her head. "Daggone it."

"Quit joking around."

"I am not joking around. I want you to take me, hold me, mesmerize me with your manliness so that I will submit willingly."

"You have a very creative mind."

She pointed at him. "Why? Because I am stronger than you? I doubt I am the first girl stronger than the guy, you know. Look at my Aunt Wendy."

"Ohmigod. President Mendoza isn't a trillion times stronger than the First Gentleman; maybe one and a half times as strong, at best, as he was a Hall of Fame pro football player. Again, I'm a United States commissioned officer, and I *cannot* be talking about the President that way, even if she is your aunt. That's messed up, I will need some counseling after that thought."

She frowned. "Well, it is the same principle. Do you think I like that all the time? It is not like you are going to hurt me, now, is it? Do you know what it's like to be me, to have the most awesome power ever entrusted to a human being 24/7?"

"That's what I just said, and your reply was that you take it all in stride."

"Well, do not take me so literally. I want to not have to worry about responsibility, to have it taken from me. I am probably the best example of consensual sex you shall ever see."

"I guess so. I've never bedded a superhero before."

"You had better not bed another one. Not that one exists, anyway. Worry not, as you cannot hurt me."

"In case you're wondering, I'm not worried about *you*. I just don't want to get kicked halfway to Luna by accident."

"You said you wanted to get there, so now is your big chance. When I touch you, I shall not be able to hurt you, anyway. My invulnerability can be transferred to any living animal making contact with my skin."

"I wondered about that. How can you punch someone, then, if contact with your skin can't hurt them?"

She held up two fingers. "First, if I am wearing gloves, then that concept does not apply, obviously. Second, although the default response is to confer that quality, I can *not* do it if I want. So I can punch someone to Kingdom Come with my bare hand if I like."

"Does your, er, barrier, protect you from, you know—"

"Pregnancy? That would not be ideal right now, I guess I never thought about it. I have no idea how that works. I guess it would depend on whether or not my energy field considered it harmful."

"Haven't you ever wondered if you can have children? If they would have your powers or a fraction of them?"

She nodded. "Of course I have wondered that, are you daft? But I did not come with an instruction manual, you know, like one of your fancy airplanes. I have to figure it out piece by piece, like the scientists of old did."

"Can you take the pill?"

"A birth control pill? I suppose I could physically ingest it, but it is doubtful it would be absorbed. Alcohol, for example, is not, or it has no effect, I do not know which."

"You know that for a fact?"

She nodded. "I certainly do. I have also never had to take a medication, as I have never been ill."

"Must be nice."

"No, it is rarely 'nice,' Russell. I can 'power down' to some extent and exert myself with normal human abilities, but I do not get physically tired. It would be nice to feel what you do."

"Sorry."

"Do not be. I know you think it would be cool to be me, but it is not. I wish for one day I did not have these powers, but I do. Not much I can do about it."

"Another question—"

"Yes? My last words before you molest me?"

"Stop that. What I mean is, is your, well, can I even go in there without hurting myself? I can't believe I'm here, with my pants almost off, asking that question."

"I suppose it has not come up before."

"I guess not."

"If you are asking if my hymen is ruptured, the answer is yes."

"Sorry, it was a dumb question."

She smiled. "No, it is not dumb. And I am a virgin. Not because I am a prude, but I wanted to wait for the right person, and I have not had many opportunities. I perforated my own hymen when I was fifteen by, well—masturbating."

"You don't need to tell me that, Paige. Everyone masturbates."

"I suppose. It is not something I can discuss with my mom; she is pretty spaced out. She had me, so she has had sex at least once."

"Haven't you ever wondered if you were adopted? By your mom, I mean? I know your dad died, you said."

She shook her head. "I suppose all children wonder that at some point or another—me, more than most, for obvious reasons.

In the end, we do resemble each other and talk a lot alike, so, not any longer. About sex, though, I have talked to Rachel about it."

"Rachel?"

"My friend. She introduced me to you at the career fair."

"Oh, yeah."

"And making physical contact with me appears to confer my invulnerability to the other person, at least partly. So you shall surely emerge intact and victorious in your conquest."

"You know that from experience?"

"Well—no. It is a mere theory based on anecdotal evidence. I have never done this before, as I have said."

"Your 'sound evidence' is *not* very reassuring, Paige. When I've touched you, I didn't feel any different."

"That's what people say, but you would feel differently if a piano dropped on you. No, it won't give you any extra strength, at least as far as I know."

"Do we know why that is?"

She shook her head. "I have contemplated this much, and I must assume the basic reason is to allow me to do what we're about to do now."

"How's that again?"

"Have sex without killing or seriously injuring my partner. I guess I would potentially be more injurious, were I a male."

"Works for me."

She felt warm as he got on top of her as her nipples straightened and she could feel the piloerection and her arm hairs stand on end. Despite her protective field, she seemed to be able to sense anything a normal person could, except pain. Whoever thought this up was pretty smart.

She felt him enter her and gasped with pleasure as she let out a little yelp. "It is better than I thought it would be."

"Oh, my God," he said.

"What?" she smiled. "Does it hurt?"

"No, on the contrary. I can't describe this feeling. It's like I could do anything. Is that even possible, Paige? When I kissed you, it was a little bit similar, but this, I can't put it into words—"

She shook her head. "I do not know, Russ, as no one has ever done this before. Given the new territory here, I sort of wanted to make sure it was at the right time, you know."

"And the right time is now?"

She nodded. "I believe so, yes."

"Is this the way you feel all the time? If so, I want to be you."

"I do not know, I have never been anyone else. I am happy to trade places. Being me is not always that great."

"I hope we know what we're doing."

"We do—I believe that the amount of my dark energy field transferred to another living being depends on the amount of surface area and nerve cells in contact. Mucosal surfaces in particular apparently work well, hence the effect of our kissing."

"Talk about sounding clinical. I guess the amount of mucosal surface area in the vagina is pretty big."

"Yes, how true. I can feel Russell Jr., and he is quite the man about town, just like on our first date in the Fairbanks movie theater. Just make sure we do not destroy your apartment."

She had masturbated before, but it wasn't like this. He felt her hold her by the upper arms (which she had asked for). She knew he couldn't hurt her, and wouldn't even if he could. That excited her even more as her nipples became erect.

"That was pretty good," she said after he climaxed. "I think you made me come."

"Well, it's nice to know that your orgasm didn't reduce my bachelor pad to rubble. Hate to not get back my deposit."

"And you survived, plus you were a perfect officer and a gentleman. Too much so, actually." She sighed.

"I like being a gentleman. You weren't very much a lady, Miss, kicking me and all."

"I had never experienced that, what others do when they punch me, I mean. Like hitting a marshmallow, no matter how strong the blow is." She pulled out a digi-cigarette from her purse and inhaled a lungful of white vapor. "That's one of the reasons to hold me, so you remain in constant contact."

"Come on. Vaping after sex? Isn't that a little outdated?"

She exhaled the clear vapor. "Ah, but it's so cool. No carcinogens are being released into the atmosphere."

"If you say so. I don't necessarily find it attractive."

She took another drag, exhaling vapor rings. "I live on the edge, and I like adventure, Russell Stanton."

"You are about as 'off the edge' as you can get."

"Maybe, but a girl can always fantasize. I want a pirate captain, a guy who's in charge and takes what he wants, not Lt. Goody

Two-Shoes. Don't be afraid of me. I would not hurt you."

"Don't you get it? It isn't that, as it isn't possible, and you wouldn't do that anyway."

"You have me up on a pedestal, is that it? Like some grand, gleaming, fragile china doll, not some moll?"

"Something like that. I have respect for you. And I'm just a little bit in awe of you if you can understand that."

"That's nice, but I want you to treat me like a regular human being, not like a goddess, which I am not, by the way."

"Very easy for you to say."

"Not easy, but the truth. You took me skydiving for kicks, but let's kick it up a notch in the bedroom next time. And tomorrow I want to do something I've always wanted to do."

"What's that?"

"Something a bit foolish. Can you get us to Yosemite?"

"What? Yosemite National Park?"

"Duh. Is there another place named Yosemite?"

"I don't know about that. Maybe. It will take some phone calls and favors called in. What's there, may I ask?"

"El Capitan."

"Why do you want to go there? You can't see it as Paige."

"Don't need to. But you'll find out the attraction. Tomorrow."

• • •

After a three-hour jet flight, she was doing something else she had always wanted to do: rock-climbing in eastern California, on El Capitan, of all places. To feel the sun on her face on the Dawn Wall, with no harnesses of any kind restraining her. She couldn't get up there without his help. And it would be best to be out where there was no one else around. Most people would think it a bit crazy. But, she did go skydiving, after all. Doing it in late fall at Yosemite wasn't a peak time for climbers.

"I can't believe we're doing this; it's insane. The Dawn Wall is one of the toughest ascents for any climber, let alone a blind one with no experience or safety gear. There are a dozen closer places we could've gone to instead, but you just *had* to come here, didn't you? I must have holes in my head for doing this."

"We went skydiving. That was also pretty nutso, and it took lots of gusto. And I want to experience the best. This is it."

"It was *not* dangerous with the appropriate safety gear; blind people have done that before by following the proper procedures. But this is unprecedented, Paige; climbing a mountain without any safety gear at all, even if you were a sighted person, would be reckless to an unprecedented extent."

"Yeah, what is the worst that could happen?"

"I'm going to have a stroke; that's what will happen."

"You just need to be concerned about yourself, you and your wimpy safety gear. And we are not ascending the whole 3,000 feet. I just want to go a little bit, then we are done, and we will have had fun in the sun, top gun."

"This isn't fun, just so you know. I'm very worried someone is going to see us, that's all, not that you care in the least."

"No, I do not, so be quiet." She put her foot into the crevice of the massive slab of granite, knowing that if she fell off the cliff, it wouldn't be fatal, at least to her.

"You really enjoy this, don't you?" Russ asked.

She took a deep breath of cold air. "Sure. Don't you?"

"Free solo climbing is terribly dangerous, you know."

"You have said that about fifteen times, it gets old. I suppose that is the attraction of it."

"That's just it; I guess I just don't see why that would be exciting for you, as I wouldn't say it is terribly dangerous."

"It is as exciting as it gets for me, although skydiving was fun, too. Sorry, I know you military officers value safety, but I have not had those classes. I do not intend to ever take them."

"Oh, okay, right. Dry sarcasm, as usual. Make fun of the poor regular humans who can't survive a several hundred-foot fall."

"Of course. I guess I enjoy seeing things from the top, though."

"I'm sure you'll take it all in if we ever get there. I hope people don't start calling ambulances when they see you falling to your doom, which I predict will happen soon."

"I will somehow make it. And who says I am going to fall? That will not happen at all."

"Just calculating probabilities, having climbed a few times. Not this way, though. But, I'm talking about for the people who have heart attacks when you fall off the cliff and bounce off the rocks below. The chances of that are about ninety percent."

"Huh. I do not bounce, the ground I will not trounce. The kinetic energy will be dissipated immediately upon impact, there is no residual force, your banter is making you hoarse."

"Who cares? People will still be scared shitless."

"Then you had better make sure I do not or have several ambulances ready."

"Luckily, it's not very crowded out here this time of year."

"There are other senses besides sight, you know, for me to enjoy." The quality of the air up here, the sun, the birds singing, the texture of the rock, is pretty amazing—"

She then felt herself slip and fall off the side, her fingers sliding off the smooth granite.

"Oh, shit," he yelled. "Paige!"

"Whoa," she said. She fell about eighty feet before catching herself by grabbing a ridge, which stopped her descent abruptly.

"Are you okay?"

"What? That is a pretty dumb question," she said, dangling by her left arm. "No, I think I broke my arm and leg. Ouch. Did anyone see us?"

"Funny. No, I don't think so, fortunately."

She began climbing up again. "I probably have violated some law. Some things never change."

"Yeah. Why didn't you stop your fall the other way?"

"This is a 'no flights' activity. Kind of defeats the purpose, right, just like your skydiving? Also, there could be people out there, and I cannot gauge my position without feeling where I am, which requires direct physical contact."

"Some elderly person I didn't see probably stroked out after watching a blind girl fall off the side of a mountain. Do you have any idea how much trouble I could get into by having orchestrated the most haphazard activity ever, condoned by a commissioned military officer?"

"Nope. Not my problem." She gripped the rock and slowly ascended. "I shall have to climb up the hard way now."

"The hard way, what a laugh."

• • •

Later that evening, after a fun half-day of climbing El Capitan, they arrived back at Russ's apartment, where she put on some dark blue jeans and a blue sweater, came up to him, and kissed him.

"What are we doing now, besides kissing?"

"I told you on the way back; we are flying."

"I don't have my own plane. I'm not rich like your relatives. I had to call in some big favors to get us to Yosemite and do the sky-diving trip."

"Well, I shall be doing most of the flying on this jaunt. She put on the visor and changed her hair to black. "We have never really done this right, you know."

"That hair thing is so cool. I've never seen you do it before. How does it work?"

"The wonders of *Chemical Cowboy.* At least I found a use for Bella and Wolf's special nanocarbon shampoo. Yet, I can only do it about ten times before I have to reapply it. I am told it costs several thousand dollars per ounce."

"But, I don't get it. It must be a phase-change thing."

She nodded. "That is correct. The carbon nanotubes change molecular configuration with the application of pressure. Wolf says it requires the application of several Gs to accomplish it."

"Where are we flying, anyway? And is this a good idea?"

"As good as any others you have had. Anywhere you want, downtown would be good."

"Downtown? It'll be full of people this time of night."

"Well, do you want to be seen with me, or do you not?" She took his hand as they went out on the balcony. "It is dark out, so hopefully no one will see us. Hold on, now."

"Whoa, this is weird," he said as they approached zero G's. "It's like being in a zero gravity plane. Your hair, it's floating."

"Of course it is. I thought you had advanced aviation training."

"This is a dumb question, but how do you do it?"

"I am not really sure. It took years of practice to even be able to become weightless, and I was about sixteen when I first was able to propel myself with any substantial velocity; at seventeen, I could hit about a hundred miles per hour."

"Where did you learn to do all this?"

"Lots of wide-open spaces in rural Alaska."

"But how?" They were now traveling about thirty miles per hour as they went west towards the city, a few hundred feet off the ground.

"Mom says that dark energy can repel gravity."

"Where does all this energy come from?"

"This we do not know, but she thinks it is all around us or from a dark star. We cannot see it, hence the name 'dark' energy. Duh."

"I don't understand how you, er—move that way?"

"It is kind of like a muscle, I just will it to happen, and it does. I can hover in air, or propel myself. The feats of strength—that is not me; I am a bit stronger than a normal female my size but not as strong as you, natively, that is."

"What's it like, traveling that fast?"

"Supersonic speed? It is pretty cool, accelerating that fast, but once you get to that speed, it is like being in a car, you know, you get used to it."

He watched as they descended to a hundred feet. "Propulsion must be like exhaust, then."

"So, I am expelling energy in order to move in a certain direction or accelerate?"

"Yeah. I am an Air Force aeronautical engineer by training, you know. I wanted to be an astronaut at some point. Do you know if you can go into space?"

"You mean under my own power?"

"Yeah."

"Never thought about that. What is escape velocity in miles per hour?"

"You're capable of supersonic flight, and you don't know even the rudiments of aviation?"

"Not really, no. I never saw the need, as I did not think I was going into space. I have been to 150,000 feet under my own power, without a great deal of effort."

"Ohmigod. We need to get you a pilot's license. Well, escape velocity is about 25,000 mph, or 40,000 km/h."

She looked at him as they flew at twenty mph over the park and shook her head. "In the suit, I can reach at most Mach 7, which is under 6,000 mph. The suit is relatively aerodynamic and I am not, so my maximum velocity without it is probably significantly less. So, no, I do not believe I can fly into space unassisted. I have flown high enough to see the curvature of the Earth, but that is all."

"Unless you can somehow negate gravity another way. You still would be a great astronaut—to go to Mars, for example. You don't require any oxygen or nearly the amount of protective gear I would need."

"That would be a long trip. Lonely. Even if I did that, there are no others like me who could go too."

She looked at him and frowned. "As far as you know."

"Why, do you want one to show up? That would leave you odd man out; it makes me want to pout."

"Then we need to go together, as there are some deep-space experiments I'd sure like to try with you."

"Such as?" she asked eagerly. "When do we start?"

"Think about it—I'm not being funny. Manned travel outside our Solar System will likely require many years, perhaps several lifetimes, if we can even solve the propulsion and food supply issues. It will be necessary for persons to procreate *en route*, have children, and those children would need to have children, as the first generations would never survive the trip."

"Huh? What if those children do not like their potential mates or are gay? That would kind of suck, yuck. What then?"

"I guess that would be a problem. Maybe if we can harness dark energy and use it for something other than you flying around, we won't need to worry about those things."

"Let us just focus on now. I do not even know if my powers work outside Earth's gravitational field."

"Why wouldn't they?"

"I do not know; they seem to be based on manipulating gravity. If there is no gravitational body nearby, then maybe they do not work. There is so much we do not know, despite Kepler's genius."

"Someday, we'll need to find out. I'm serious about that. We need to get you on one of the Luna shuttles to try it out."

"That is on my 'to-do' list." They flew over downtown Dayton as she saw the skyline. "Not Aurora City, but it's okay, I guess."

"It's a pretty nice town, lots of aviation history. Let's go over here, Paige. Land down by those red lights."

"I do not 'see' colors very well, so be more specific."

"To the left and down."

"You really want us to land? What if someone sees us?"

"Of course they'll see us—that's the point. So what? You've got your visor and black hair, so no one will recognize you as Paige, and I've got my cycle helmet and goggles on. I want some ice cream and so do you. You need to show the masses you're a real person. So just *be* a regular person for a couple of hours."

"I am not sure if that is a good idea. A regular person I am certainly not, although a frozen high-fat dairy confection would hit the spot."

"Come on, it'll be fine."

"Are you buying? I have no money on me, and the *Science Squad* did not think of pockets when this suit was designed. I still need to go to the bank to get a debi-fob."

He checked his wallet. "Cheapskate."

"I provide the transportation, you the refreshments. That is the deal. But at least you have a real job. I have not figured out how to actually earn any money yet."

"Like I said, I don't have rich relatives."

"No one knows about that. Aurora is dead, at least for the time being, resulting in my impecunious image."

In the historic Oregon District, they landed near Fifth Street in a back alley, as she saw two early teenage boys run in out of the corner of her eye. She did seem to have remarkable visual acuity through the visor, although colors were pretty muted.

A boy, perhaps twelve, pointed at them. "Look, Jimmy, I told you someone landed in there."

"They didn't fly; they jumped down from that fire escape or something, come on."

"I know they did, 'cause I saw it."

"It's impossible, Gary. You're imagining stuff. It was some bird or something."

"No way," the boy named Gary said as they walked closer. "Look, it is her—it's that *Stella Scura* lady who was in Aurora City and saved Air Force One."

"Naw, it's not, she's shorter than me. *Stella Scura's* six feet tall or bigger, since she's a superhero."

"Is not. It's her, I tell you."

"This is just some girl doing cosplay or something with some stupid geek wearing a cycle helmet and dark goggles at night. Aww, what a ripoff. Get outta here."

The taller boy came towards her and extended his hand. She took it and shook hands with him. "Nice to meet you, glad lad."

"'Lad?' Are you for real, or is this a joke?"

"It is after Halloween, so what do you think, sonny? Do I look like I want to be funny?"

"*Sonny?* You're maybe a couple years older than us."

"Huh." She frowned and crossed her arms. That is irrelevant."

"If it is you—I think I don't believe it."

She pointed to herself. "Yet I am here, right? Certainly not a phantom."

"Okay, but you're way shorter than we thought you'd be."

She shrugged. "Sorry. Abraham Lincoln said that a man only needs to be tall enough to reach the ground, so I believe I am just fine. Good things come in small packages."

"Yeah, but—can you *really* fly? We want to see."

She shook her head. "Maybe later. Right now, we came for some ice cream." She took Russ' arm. "Lead on, gallant escort."

They left the gaping boys into the alley as they walked briskly into Ty Young's Creamery and blended in for a few minutes, until people slowly recognized who had come in. Several people started taking photos with cell phones. The line parted as everyone let them go to the front of the counter.

"You all were here first," she said. "We are in no hurry."

"No, please," one middle-aged man said. "Go ahead, we insist."

"Uh, what'll you have?" the blonde teenage girl at the counter asked nervously.

She thought for a moment. "A waffle cone with two scoops of black raspberry." She looked at Russ, who looked ridiculous in his bomber jacket, helmet, and dark goggles; they almost matched hers, but no one was staring at him. "You?"

"Uh, a hot fudge sundae, with pecans, whipped cream, and a cherry, if it is not too much trouble."

"Um, okay. I guess I don't need to ask the name for this order."

"*Stella* will be fine."

They went to sit in a booth as people nervously watched; a few minutes later, the server brought their treats out as several patrons took photos and videos with their smartphones.

"How much?" she asked.

"Come on—it's on the house, *Stella*."

"Thanks, but that is not necessary." She pointed to Russ. "He is paying, of course, as I do not carry currency."

The waitress shook her head. "Don't worry about it, *Stella,* my dad owns the place. All the business this will bring in here now, it'll be worth it."

They ate their ice cream and, after about twenty minutes, got up and left. She knew what they wanted to see: *Stella Scura* flying through the sky. She thought she would like being the center of attention with people staring at her, but she was wrong, as these people really cared nothing about her as a person. Her mom, cousin Bella, Uncle Jay, and Aunt Wendy all were relatively egotistical, demonstrative people who liked the limelight.

But Will, curiously, despised it. She put herself somewhere in the middle.

She heard even the American League Aurora City Atoms wanted her to play in an exhibition baseball game in the spring, with payment being a donation to the charity of her choice; would it seem callous not to do that? She had never played baseball before, for obvious reasons; what if she hurt someone?

A being who could fly at Mach 7 and the reflexes to dodge obstacles at that speed easily had the hand-eye coordination to hit a 95-mph fastball off a Major League pitcher without powers, with perhaps the natural strength to hit singles but not home runs. She was a decent sprinter but nowhere near her mom's ability; but to what end? Raising money for charity was an important pursuit, but she thought carefully as she realized this was the first time she had preferred the anonymity of blind Paige Marshall, the person no one cared anything about.

Except maybe Air Force First Lieutenant Russell Stanton. And then it dawned on her as she pondered a very important question: which did Russ care about most? *Stella* or Paige? She remembered that he seemed to like her even before he found out her secret.

They walked a hundred yards down Fifth Street, and she felt a little creepy as about twenty people followed them. What did she expect would happen? She was now a celebrity, after all. In a few short weeks, she had gone from a North Pole nobody to likely the most famous person on the planet.

Zero to hero, almost instantly. Was it that great?

Well, she wanted to be the big adult, to seek action and adventure. This wasn't much of either, she thought as she finally took his arm and lifted off towards the Dayton skyline as she waved and people cheered. She was certain that reporters would be on their trail now, by land and by air, in the birthplace of aviation, of all places.

• • •

They needed to get out of town, if that would even be possible. After calling Bella on the special scrambled M2 phone Nick had given her, they left to see Russ' parents in Edinboro, Pennsylvania, as he still had two more days of leave before he had to return to Wright-Patt. She'd opted for the *Stella* persona for riding as she found she enjoyed seeing on a road trip more than not, but found it difficult to go out that way without attracting attention. Paige didn't have that problem. The visor was distracting. But they found the perfect solution.

She would be a biker babe, at least for a couple of days. Then she would revert back to Paige when visiting his folks. It was sure

She mounted Russ' jet-black Harley-Davidson motorcycle. She could wear the visor, which looked, for all practical purposes, like rider's goggles; she didn't need the helmet, of course, but it provided a bit of anonymity as they streaked down Interstate 70 at seventy miles per hour. Plus, most states required helmets anyway, and she was determined to try and obey the law. Hopefully, there would be no accidents or emergencies along the way requiring her intervention.

The diners they stopped at on the way were pretty uneventful. With biker gear he had purchased for her at a local shop, her nanoparticle carbon-black dark hair looked pretty much like everyone else's. She was surprised by the number of guys who tried to hit on her, but they didn't know any better. It was kind of fun, but weird, trying to figure out who she wanted to be.

That was the question—was she Paige or *Stella?* She was a little of both, she figured. As opposed to the usual superhero alter ego who was wimpy, Paige could be over-the-top and, at times, obnoxious. *Stella* was fairly polite and cultured. The real person was actually in the middle somewhere.

She sipped her coffee at the diner and noticed that several passing guys gave her the look. She wanted to wink at them, then realized that they couldn't see that through her visor. Better to just smile and not attract attention.

"So, what are your mom and dad like?" she asked.

He took a bite of his scrambled eggs. "Dad's an engineer, you know; he's pretty much a normal guy, like my mom."

She grabbed his hand. "You *did* tell them you were bringing me, right. I do not like surprises."

He licked the eggs from his fork. "Well, you liked the skydiving, right?"

She reached over and poked him gently in the chest. "Answer my question, do not give me indigestion, Russ. Do you not think I want to make a good impression on your parents? I am a cultured young woman."

"All I told them was that I was bringing a girl, but they don't know who. I made them promise that we didn't want anyone coming over, that we just wanted a quiet weekend. They live a pretty mundane existence."

"Russ, I cannot believe you." She stepped on his foot gently. "Do they follow the social media?"

He shook his head. "I don't know. They don't follow social media much or watch TV. They are very intellectual types. You should be used to that."

"My intellectual relatives are quite different, almost irritatingly so. And they love the media. So I need a break from that."

"Well, then," he said as he took a bite of maple syrup-drenched French toast. "Maybe it's an opportunity for you just to be a normal person."

They finished as he paid the bill as they walked out to the bike in preparation to ride the final forty miles to the Stanton home.

• • •

Less than two hours later, they pulled up to the old farmhouse in the gravel driveway in rural northwest Pennsylvania, not too far from Lake Erie.

"Wow. This really *is* in the middle of nowhere."

"Yes, it is, Paige. That's the point."

"I suppose." She looked around the dark front yard of the home. "I like the middle of nowhere. Reminds me of home. Well, time to change." He watched as she took off the visor, and her hair turned back to its native dark red. "Do you think there are vids from our trip to the ice cream shop out there, Russ?"

"Possibly. Mom and Dad aren't into social media, so it most likely won't matter. I was pretty well disguised, like a geek."

They walked in through the front door as she carried in a small suitcase and sat it on the landing. She heard steps on the hardwood floor, which smelled of lemon.

"Mom, Dad, this is Paige."

She gave them both a hug. "It is so nice to meet you. Russ has said so many kind things, the praises he sings."

"He better have," his dad said, joking.

"Can I take your, jacket?" Rebecca Stanton asked. "We worry about Russ sometimes, riding that dangerous motorcycle. I don't think it's safe, but what do I know?"

"It is a natural concern, Ma'am. I assure you that Lt. Russell is an extremely safe motorcyclist and obeys all rules of the road; you have little to be worried about, of that you should have no doubt."

"But is it safe for you, dear, I mean—"

She laughed and patted Becky on the shoulder. "Relax. I am blind—I do not have brittle bone disease, a heart condition, or hemophilia. I am a pretty robust individual who can tolerate a good spill or two."

"It's fine, Mom. As Paige said, I go up in fighter planes all the time, so I know how to take care of myself."

She turned towards Rebecca. "The jacket, certainly; thank you so much." She handed Rebecca the leather biker's jacket as they went into the family room and sat on the sofa.

"This is kind of a surprise. Russ doesn't say much about his girlfriends."

"Aha. Ashamed of me, are you?" she said, tapping him on the shoulder.

"Of course not."

"How long have you known each other?"

"A little over a month. We met up near Eielson Air Force Base," she said. "He caught my eye with his good looks, crisp military uniform, and immense intellect." She laughed. "Actually, he caught my friend Rachel's eye, and I took it from there."

"And she caught mine with her sharp wit. She's quite a card."

"I am so sorry, Paige, I've been rude. Can I get you something to drink?" Tim asked.

"I'll have a beer, Dad," Russ blurted out.

"Same old Russ. I was asking your guest, son. Paige?"

She shook her head. "No beer, just coffee with cream, if it is no trouble. I do not like to drink and fly," she said dryly. "Especially after a long flight."

"What?" Rebecca scratched her head. "I thought you rode on Russ' bike. Did you take a flight here from Dayton or Columbus?"

"Not in a manner of speaking, no."

Russ punched her in the arm as she knew he was smiling nervously. "Just an inside joke; she is a barrel of laughs once you get to know her."

"My sense of humor is an acquired taste."

"She also isn't old enough for beer." She turned toward him and opened her mouth wide.

"Russ, that's not very nice." Rebecca frowned at him.

"Well, she's not, Mom, I'm just being honest, as I don't want you and Dad getting arrested for supplying alcohol to a minor."

She waved her hands and laughed. "It is fine, Mrs. Stanton, I am not twenty-one, and I do not consume beer anyway. It is bad for my waistline, other beverages will be just fine."

Tim Stanton looked at her curiously and put his arm around Russ. "Paige, I need to talk to the lieutenant about something before you go. Would you excuse us?"

"Of course."

• • •

Russ and his father walked out the side door into the garage.

"What's up, Dad? That was kind of rude. But that's you, so I see nothing has changed regarding your social skills."

"Now, you wait a minute. Who's being inconsiderate? I had no idea about this, Russ; it would've been nice to know about this ahead of time."

"About what? I told you I was bringing a girl, and it's not the first time. I thought you would be happy."

"No, but my main concern is—how old is that girl, son? Are you going to get in trouble?"

He shook his head and smiled. "No, Dad. She's legal age. I'm not that big a dope."

"Well, it can't be by much. She's a teenager, has to be."

"So? What's your problem?"

"You're an Air Force officer, for God's sake. Is this another one of your infatuations? Like when you brought home the professional basketball player you met at a nightclub?"

"What did Doshandra being a pro basketball player have to do with anything?"

"Nothing, I guess, but I just don't want this girl to get hurt."

"You always told me I could date anyone I wanted: white, black, Asian, Indian, boy, girl, tall, short—whoever made me happy, because those things don't matter, according to you. Hey, her being blind makes absolutely no difference to me because she's joyful in so many ways. And we're not getting married just yet, in case you're wondering."

"You better not *have* to get married. Remember what I told you when you were sixteen."

"It's under control, Dad, so don't worry about it. I certainly hope there's nobody coming either unless you said something. We rode about 260 miles with no one in tow, so I think we're good."

Tim stared at him blankly. "I don't understand. Why would anyone care about you two?" he said nervously.

He shook his head. "Never mind."

"Yeah, right. Okay. I sure hope you know what you're doing." They walked back inside.

• • •

"Do you want something to eat, Paige?" Becky asked. "You must be hungry."

"Sure, if it's no trouble." She sat down. "I want to thank you for inviting me into your home, but I'm just a person like you."

"Well, of course you are."

"Do you have parents?"

"My real dad died when I was little, I do not remember him. I still have my mom and adoptive father, I am an only child. I have a few other, er, relatives scattered around, there are not many to be found."

"What do you do, Paige? Are you in school?"

"I am taking a brief sabbatical. I plan on studying political science and going to law school."

"That sounds very ambitious. Where will you be going to college? Are you starting next term?"

"I am not certain, but I suppose I should be determining that sometime soon. I have some relatives in Indiana, perhaps there. Or Alaska, where I am from."

"What do your parents do?" Tim asked.

"Mom is a mathematics teacher at the high school, and my dad is a pastor at the Methodist church, but he also coaches my high school basketball team."

"You play basketball?" Tim asked. "Really?"

"Paige is an almost supernatural free throw shooter. While Mom makes dinner, watch and I'll show you."

"Wow. This I have to see."

They went out to play basketball in the driveway (after shoveling off the large amount of snow that had accumulated) while Russ' mother prepared dinner. Tim and Becky watched them curiously in the driveway from the kitchen window.

"That's an interesting matchup. Russ was an all-conference player, but she's a much better shooter," Becky said. They watched as Paige sunk a three-pointer from thirty-five feet. "How is she doing that if she can't see?"

"I have no idea," Tim said. "There's something *very* odd about that girl, but I can't put my finger on it yet. I don't get it."

"Russ said she was an excellent athlete. But she's our guest, Tim. Our goal is to make her feel as 'at home' as possible."

"I also hadn't shoveled off the new snow in the driveway yet, but now it's clear. I didn't hear the snowblower running."

"Russ must've done it."

"Lazybones? No way, but it's now clean. And now they're out there in the yard playing tackle football. She just kicked off the tee like a pro, even though she can't see."

"They're just messing around, Tim. Young boys and girls do things like that."

"Look, he's running full tilt at her, and could seriously hurt her. On the other hand, he hasn't brought her down yet, she just keeps on going. No, Becky, there's something else very strange going on here. She reminds me of someone I knew a long time ago."

"That's impossible; you just met her. Who?"

He shook his head. "Never mind, it was decades ago."

Thirty minutes later, Becky came up to him. "We're just about ready, Tim. Better go call the kids."

He looked outside in the twilight after taking the trash out.

"What's that noise? It sounds like the old tractor. That thing hardly even works." He put on his coat, went outside, and instead heard the sound of chopping wood.

"That old tree stump I needed to have removed—it's gone!" He looked at the smooth dirt-covered ground where the old oak tree had been.

"That thing's needed to be uprooted for years," Russ said. "It's about time. You can do something useful with the land now."

"It was there ten minutes ago." Tim could apparently find no trace of where it had been. "How'd you do that so fast?"

"I am an Alaskan girl, used to the rugged frontier life. Tried to cover it up well with the dirt," she said, brushing the ground with her size nine brown Wolverine boot.

"What's your point, Dad?" Russ asked as he munched on an apple.

She laughed as she split another cord of wood. "It is no problem, sir. I was glad I could help. It was fun, firing up your tractor and all."

"You don't need to call us that. Tim and Becky."

She shrugged. "Okay."

"That would have cost me a fortune to remove."

"It was not that big of a deal."

"I can't believe you got it out that fast. And what a courteous guy you are, son. You could at least chop the firewood rather than have your guest do it. Is that safe for you, Paige?"

"Absolutely, I am fine. My mom usually does it at home, so I do not get to do it much there. Now you get it for free, and the firewood, too." She placed another chunk of wood on the ground and cut it to pieces. "It is good exercise for me as well. I do not get enough; it is good to be out here in the rough." She pretended to wipe some sweat from her brow.

• • •

"What do you want to do now, Paige?" Russ asked after they finished dinner.

"We can play cards," she said. "I am not a great poker player, but I will play for pennies."

"Cards? We can?" Rebecca asked.

"Sure. Russ, hand me my purse." She reached inside and took out a pack of cards. "I have Braille cards, so don't worry." Tim took the package.

"Huh. I've never seen this. They're regular cards, just with Braille indentations."

"Correct. Just do not let your son cheat the poor blind girl because I can't see his cards."

"Hey, I wouldn't do that. I'm more worried about you cheating us. Really, you guys better watch out."

"I might, for enough pennies."

"With what the Air Force pays me, we both might."

"It won't matter, as I am not a very good player anyway. I just don't want Russ to win." Not like her mom, apparently, one of the world's best.

Later, she went to sleep in the guest bedroom as Russ went to his old room (she wasn't ready for sleeping together in his parents' house, although she figured they knew they were doing that).

She lay in bed and thought about what a fun day she had had thus far, away from all of life's many worries.

• • •

"How is it you can shoot like that?" Tim asked the next morning at breakfast.

"Basketball? Why, that is easy."

"Paige had the highest free throw shooting percentage in the history of basketball at any level. *Ever*."

"But how, if I'm not being too intrusive?"

"The question is understandable. I have what is called perfect muscle memory. I know exactly how far the rim is, and can pretty much duplicate the same muscle motion over and over. Try it yourself with a blindfold. I will bet that you can do it just as well or better once you get the motion down."

Tim laughed. "I bet not, but I'm a pretty sorry athlete. I also saw you kicking off the tee out there; that was pretty good as well and reminds me of a girl I used to know back in the day, oddly, who kicked almost exactly the same way as you, but she was right-footed like most people. She dated a friend of mine."

"Who was that?"

"Never mind. It was a long time ago. She became famous, but died about twelve years ago in a, well—airplane accident."

"That is very sad. Are you still close to your friend?"

"No. He died as well, just a few months after he was here."

"I am so sorry. That must be hard to overcome, Tim."

"Anyway, how can you kick, with, you know—"

"Being blind? Well, kicking is easy as well. Four steps back, three right, one, two, three, soccer-style. No problem."

• • •

Later that morning, she got in the back seat of the sedan and fastened her seat belt as they drove to Edinboro to have lunch at a nice restaurant Becky had recommended. She felt the car slow down and the sounds of horns honking.

"A disturbance of some sort," she said. "Is there a wreck?"

"I don't know." She heard Tim's window open. "Hey, officer."

"Yes, sir? Do you need something?"

"What's going on? Wreck on the bridge?"

"No, that would be easy. A semi jack-knifed on the bridge up there, carrying steel pipe fittings. It blew a tire and went through the guard rails. Trying to figure out how to get it safely back on the bridge, cab might go over any second. Driver's still inside, but that load weighs over thirty tons. So, don't plan on going anywhere for a while, sir."

"Thanks." She heard the window roll up. "Dang, we'll be here for hours, with no way to get off."

"Dad, there's a highway rest area over there. Paige has to go to the bathroom."

"I do? Oh, yes, I must go, very much so. Thanks for reminding me that I have to pee, yippee."

"Russ, your timing is impeccable, as usual. I can't get over there, look at this traffic. It's bumper-to-bumper, and we'll never get back on if we get off."

"No problem, you don't have to get off on the exit, which you can't do anyway, so we'll just run over there. It's only a few hundred feet to the rest stop."

"That's crazy, son. How the heck are you going to get back to the car?"

"I doubt you'll have moved much by that time, and it'll only take a few minutes. We'll catch back up."

"That's the craziest thing I ever heard of," Becky said.

"Don't worry, we'll be back." Russ took her hand as they exited the car and sprinted towards the rest stop.

She scowled at him as she felt them leave the pavement and walk onto the grass. *"Paige has to go pee?"*

"You're the one who used the word 'pee,' by the way."

"I cannot help rhyming, but could you not have thought of a better excuse than that?" It was the one she had used right before saving Air Force One, by the way, but it was still lame.

"Had to act quickly, no time to be creative. Luckily, there was a rest stop over there."

"I guess no one will think the wiser of a blind girl running across the field to get to a restroom."

They went in the front of the rest area to the right of where the car was as he escorted her towards the women's restroom.

"Let me go in there first to make sure no one is in there." He came out a half minute later. "Looks good. I took this construction cone I found outside and will put it outside the door so people will think it's closed."

"Wow, real secret agent stuff. Sounds okay." She went in, groped for a stall, and took off her coat, then pulled the visor out of her bra pocket. She took off her outer clothes, revealing the action costume. She then changed her hair color, climbed out of the bathroom window, and took off east towards the bridge.

• • •

"That was one of the most bizarre things I've ever seen," Tim Stanton said to his wife. "What the heck, though. Russ always has to do something weird."

"Oh, Tim, if she had to go, she had to go. You'll never understand women. And, if he has to be weird, it's good he has a girl who likes him for what he is. She seems a little peculiar, too."

"You think? What a profound statement. At least it's warm, about forty-five degrees out." He shook his head as he opened the window on the sunny November day and looked out. "I'll *never* understand females. No offense."

"Offense taken."

He sighed and closed his eyes as he heard a sharp crack in the air overhead, a couple of hundred yards in front of them, then a second one.

"What?" Tim said. "Sunny outside, shouldn't be thunder. Not a cloud in the sky."

Becky opened her door and stepped out, as dozens of people exited their cars and started yelling, cheering, and honking their horns.

"No, I don't think it was thunder. Something a lot more exciting than that."

"You know the weather around here." Tim stepped out as well to see dozens of people pointing to the sky, and a rapidly moving dark dot in the distance. He figured as much, as crazy as that seemed.

"Tim, it can't be, but—"

He nodded. "It was a tiny sonic boom, Becky. Your son is a pilot, I'm an aeronautical engineer, so you've heard them before. But it *wasn't* an airplane."

"Out here? But it's impossible."

He shook his head. "No, I don't think so, obviously. This day just keeps getting weirder and weirder."

• • •

She reached the cab of the black semi-trailer dangling off the bridge as it had burst through the guard rails. She hovered for a few seconds, realizing she could easily push it back onto the bridge, although she could see how it would be difficult to accomplish via traditional means.

The driver gaped through the windshield in awe as she waved at him and pushed his errant vehicle back on the pavement, then took off as quickly as she appeared after flying the load of steel pipe safely to the ground.

• • •

Russ and Paige ran back from the rest area to the red Buick sedan, the car having moved only a few more lengths during the time they had left about ten minutes ago.

"You okay, Paige?" Becky asked.

"Sure," she said, realizing now she really did have to pee and forgot to go while she was at the rest area. She would have to hold it until the next stop. Some superhero she was.

Three minutes later they started moving. "Must have cleared off," Tim said.

"I wonder if they got that driver off the bridge?" she asked. "I hope he is unharmed."

"They must have," Russ said. "We're moving pretty fast now, so we timed that just right. How about that luck?"

• • •

After returning home from an excellent lunch, they prepared to say goodbye and ride the two hours back to the Dayton suburb of Huber Heights.

"It was nice to meet you, Paige," Becky said, as she and Tim gave her a hug.

"It was great to meet you. I am certain I will see you again very soon."

"Can I talk to you a minute again before you go, Russ?"

"Yeah, I guess. What's up? We gonna have the same conversation we had before?"

"Not quite. Let's go in here."

"O-kay—be back in a minute, Paige. Dad urgently needs me."

Tim shook his head as they walked into the family room and closed the door. "Russ, I hope you know what you're doing, son. I try to trust your instincts, but this—you're in way over your head on this one."

He nodded. "I do, Dad. We've been through all that. I told you she was mature for her age. I can handle it."

"Really?"

"Yeah, really. What's the problem?"

"Just be careful. There's a lot of danger out there. You may think you can fly under the radar forever, but there will be someone, sometime, who will figure it out. Very bad people, son."

"Huh? 'Fly under the radar?' 'Bad people?' That's priceless." He laughed. "When did you get a sense of humor, Mr. Engineer?"

Tim frowned. "Do I look like I'm laughing, Russ? Be serious for once. I'm trying to help you. As usual, you're not letting me."

"And figure *what* out, Dad? You're usually not one for being cryptic. Yes, I'm in intelligence; you know I can't talk about it. Is that what you're ranting about?"

"No—your new girlfriend. She's far more than meets the eye, Russ. Like I said, be careful. I have no idea how you two got together, and maybe it's none of my business, but it also might be a very bad idea. As you say, you're in intelligence, so figure it out and quit acting like an idiot infatuated with his crush."

"You're right, Dad, it *is* none of your business, so butt the hell out of mine. And 'more than meets the eye'? Real funny, Dad, since she can't see. That's pretty rude."

"Cut the crap. You guys run off to the restroom at the rest area off Interstate 79, and a few minutes later, we hear a sonic boom, and that truck gets rescued by *Stella Scura*. Ten minutes after *that,* you magically reappear; what a coincidence. It isn't that hard to put it all together, as unbelievable as it all seems."

"What?" He made a flying motion with his hand. "You think Paige Marshall, a blind girl from tiny North Pole, Alaska, is *Stella Scura?* Now *that's* funny." He laughed.

Tim shook his head. "I don't think I'm wrong, Russ. It never would've occurred to me, and I can't understand it in the least, but it's the only thing that makes any sense."

"Then you *have* no sense. Maybe you need to go to the doctor to get a brain scan, as dementia is sure nothing to laugh at."

"Do I? We've never had secrets from each other. No time to start now. But there's something else." He pointed to the framed autographed jersey of famed former Minnesota pro football running back Hilton Tarman hanging on the wall. "Look at it, Russ."

"Oh, no, not again." He shook his head and frowned. "Yeah, it's Tarman's jersey, so what? It's been there since before I was born, big deal. What does that have to do with anything? Do we have to keep worshipping? I know you probably look at it a hundred times a day, but like I said, dementia—old people can't keep their mind on task, the rambling—"

"Did I ever tell you how I got that autographed jersey?"

He sighed. "So many times I can't count."

"Tell me about it, and maybe you can figure it out."

"OMG. You had a friend in college whose girlfriend's brother played pro football, and he got it for you, as he and Tarman were college roommates; it's that simple. Demented people tend to repeat stories over and over again, just so you know. I guess it's easy to keep yourself entertained since everything is always new."

"Yeah, but I have a good reason to bring it up again, and it isn't simple at all. My friend was Danny Ashton, he went to San Diego State, and we both grew up in suburban Minneapolis."

"Sure. You said you grew up together, and he was killed in a car accident as a junior in college."

"Right. Danny lived down the street, and his girlfriend came up here to visit the Thanksgiving before he died, and that's when I got the jersey. She was from San Diego."

"Yeah, so? Four million people live there, big deal."

"It really is a 'big deal.' I have something to show you from then." He turned on the big-screen TV and pulled up a file on his wireless tablet to transmit to the larger device.

The low-res video came on showing the pickup football game the college students were playing in the snowy backyard of his grandparents' home in suburban Minneapolis.

"Great, Dad, old home vids from over thirty years ago. You were never a great athlete, so what does this have to do with Paige and Tarman's autographed jersey?"

"It will make perfect sense in a moment. Look at the tall girl in the hunter green jersey who is beating everyone. She ran like the wind and could almost jump over people and could kick and punt like you wouldn't believe."

"So what? You all weren't the best at sports, therefore, the bar's set pretty low."

"That's true, yet she was the most gifted natural athlete I ever saw up close and in person."

"Yeah, like you know anything about athletics; your high school barely could put five guys on the basketball court." He watched the video for a minute. "Sure, I could see that, Dad, but why is that girl wearing a protective helmet? I assume you were playing touch, so what's the deal?"

"Yes, it was touch, but she was deaf and wore that to protect the cochlear implant she had."

"Cochlear implant? Do you mean that implanted electronic thing for deaf people?"

"That's right. Keep watching."

He watched the old videos and saw the tall black-haired girl running down the sideline, catching and intercepting passes with ease.

He laughed. "She's pretty fast, at that. Way faster than any of you low-rent dudes, she's kicking your butts, not that it would be hard. Again, I seem to be missing the point here."

"The adjective 'fast' is an understatement. About what you would expect from a world-class sprinter, perhaps?"

He jerked his head towards his father, who had finally said something of interest. "What? Really? Danny's girlfriend was an elite sprinter? No way."

Tim nodded. "Yes, really. That girl was an NCAA gold medalist in the hundred meters and was a pretty good heptathlete as well. In fact, she still holds the women's world deaf heptathlon record."

"That's neat, brain-cell-challenged Dad, but I'm still not making the connection; no big surprise there."

"She was also two years older than Danny and was his physical chemistry graduate teaching assistant."

"So she was a good athlete, and apparently smart, too. That's sure nice, but who the heck cares?"

"Smart isn't the word for it. The girl was preternatural, a genius of a caliber you'd have to see to believe."

"Huh? 'Preternatural?' That's a pretty big word for someone who's lost most of his gray matter."

Tim paused the video and pointed at the screen. "Come on. You're an honors service academy graduate. Whose jersey is that, Russ? Number 88?"

"You know better than to test my pro football knowledge. It's a Jay Mendoza jersey from the mid-1990s. Any dummy would know that, as it's even got his name on it. C'mon, man."

Tim nodded. "Correct."

"Well, so what? Lots of people had those replica jerseys, as he was a pretty famous player. Even more famous now, so they still sell his old jersey in stores. Again, get to the point."

"But look at the fit—it's several sizes too big for that girl."

"I can't help it if she couldn't buy the correct size, plus she has no pads on. What's the point, neuron-depleted old Dad?"

"Son, figure it out. It doesn't fit because it's an authentic game jersey of Mendoza's, *not* a replica." Tim pulled out a photo of the girl with Danny, his deceased friend. "You tell me what it means and where she got that and Tarman's jersey."

He frowned and thought for half a minute. "Yes, I suppose I get it now, dramatic Dad who takes forever to make his point. That's Bonnie Mendoza when she was in her early twenties, I guess. I know she was a great athlete in her own right, in addition to being Jay's sister. I didn't know you had actually met her, and she played football with you way back when—but, again, so what?"

"I only had met her briefly, but I somehow knew then that I was in the presence of greatness, and not because of her athletic talents. Kind of what it is with Paige—the movements, the speech characteristics, the peculiar usage of words, all that. The hand-eye coordination, it's uncanny. You both were horsing around playing football. No average person can do things like that, and she's blind, for Pete's sake. If you'd ever met Bonnie at that age, you'd know exactly what I mean."

"What the hell do you know, senile pop? Like I said, mind your own business. I'm outta here until you get some sense, which will probably never happen."

"My final point: I don't know how it's possible, but because of the reasons I've mentioned, the young woman in that video and the one in the other room have to be mother and daughter."

Russ walked around the room for about two minutes, then stared at his father and laughed. "You're nuts, Dad."

"Am I?"

"Of course you are; that's ridiculous. Paige is a good athlete but definitely no genius, especially in science and math. She hates that kind of stuff."

"Perhaps their academic talents differ, but seeing Paige is like seeing Bonnie's ghost. Bonnie spoke like most deaf people, but otherwise, the resemblance in their size, speech characteristics, and physical mannerisms is unmistakable. I suppose one had to meet them for the first time at a similar age to see that."

He paused for another two minutes. "I can't comment on that, as it's a secret that isn't mine to tell, Dad. Okay, you found out about it. Are you happy now?"

Tim shook his head. "I'm just an average guy making an observation, and it isn't about me being happy; it's about me caring about you. And if someone like me can make the connection, others way smarter than me can, too. You *say* you're not infatuated by her, but you clearly are. Anyone would be, but you have to think this through."

"She's a person, Dad, and you're wrong about that. I went out with Paige before I found out about her natural gifts; it's her I care about, not the other person. I've not even met Bonnie yet, as strange as that sounds, but I guess she's become pretty whacked out, which is apparently what happens to some super-geniuses."

"What? Who's mind is failing now, Russ? You couldn't have met Bonnie. She's been dead for over a decade, or didn't you learn that in history class?"

"Think about what you just said, feeble-minded Dad. Either they're both alive, or both dead. Bonnie and Aurora were on the plane together. She's a math teacher in North Pole, Alaska, living under the alias of Petra Nureyev Marshall."

"That's impossible, Russ. She was killed by a nuclear blast."

He shook his head. "You couldn't be more wrong. Paige absorbed almost all of it and saved millions, and apparently, her mom as well. But I've said enough; Paige is the one with potential for real greatness. She will become President of the United States someday."

"*President?* Are you kidding? That may not even be possible."

"Really? Think about the cryptic old videos you just showed me and tell me it's not. It blew my mind when we both found out, not long ago. Her family is the royalty of America."

"When you both found out? What does that mean?"

"She has only known she's Aurora Darkkin for less than two months. It's a long story."

"Jeez, I guess I see what you mean, Russ, but even so, about becoming President, that's decades off."

He shook his head. "No, it's really not. She's unlike any human being I've ever met, and not because of her physical abilities. She *will* accomplish it, in time; I assure you she has the stubbornness to do damn near anything she wants, with or without her relatives' help. Maybe I'll be around, maybe not, but I have to live in the here and now."

"But is she even human, son? We don't know that for sure."

He laughed. "Trust me, Dad, she's a real girl. You obviously met her mother when she was close to the same age. Like I said, I've yet to meet her, but I imagine they have many similarities."

"What?" Tim shook his head angrily. "'*Real girl?*' I don't even want to know about or discuss what *that* statement means."

"That's good, as I don't plan to. And if I can assist the world a little bit along the way and help shape human history, what's so terrible about that? And why is it any of your business?"

Tim shook his head. "Maybe you think it's not, but you brought her into our lives, Russ, so it's now become our business. No man is an island."

"What an intellectual statement, Dad. How trite."

"If you want to help save the world, then just be ready for all kinds of bumps and bruises. All I ask is that you don't kill the rest of us in the process of your grand self-fulfillment on the journey."

He sneered. "Yeah, like you know anything about it, you and your exciting life of never taking risks."

"Don't you talk down to me. And you don't have a lot of perspective in your mid-twenties, so what the hell do you know?

Just because you're a military officer now?" Tim shook his head. "Damn, son, get some perspective here. That girl has the potential to get involved in all kinds of skirmishes I can't even comprehend. There are people who would stop at nothing to get their hands on her."

"And then do what? She has the power of a goddess, Dad. She has virtually unlimited strength, can fly at Mach 7, and survived a nuclear warhead which blew up in her face, although that seems to have caused her some irreversible visual problems."

"You didn't pull out the stump with the tractor, did you?"

"No, Dad, we lied; what did you think? We started it for effect, but she yanked it out as easily as you or I would pluck a weed from the garden."

"She shoveled the walk as well?"

He nodded. "In about ten seconds. So she's pretty formidable. In addition, she has a rather wealthy cousin and an aunt of rather significant influence you may have heard of who can likely ward off most threats. I think we're good."

"*Aunt?* I didn't even think about *that*."

"Not surprising, given your single-channel brain function with the computing power of an abacus."

"Have you actually—met the President?"

He shook his head. "No, not yet. I am told that dinner at the White House will come soon. I've been to the Stannous compound, though, and it's pretty incredible."

Tim raised his eyebrows. "You've met Isabel Mendoza?"

"Of course, she is a pretty interesting gal, very sarcastic sense of humor, but very down to Earth. A lot different than Paige."

"Again, I hope you know what you're doing. I'm glad you feel you're fit to be the boyfriend of a deity."

He shook his head. "I don't know what my destiny is, Dad, or how long this'll even last. I helped her out once when she needed that more than anything. She also probably saved my life after the government tried to shoot her down."

"What? You got shot down? When were you going to tell me about that?"

He shook his head. "Dad, I can't tell you about any of that, it's classified. You know I work in intelligence."

"Sure, but this isn't 'intelligence,' Russ; it's your own personal agenda. Don't twist this into something else."

"I've said far too much already. But, right now, she needs some help in the world to do these amazing things and likely always will. Fate brought us together, and if I can be that assistance, at least for a little while, then I'll have done the world a favor in this small chapter of her life. You don't like it, I'm sorry. She needs me right now, and I'm not going to abandon her."

• • •

Paige came back to Nick and Bella's house about nine PM after Russ dropped her off. It had been a long weekend, so he kissed her and went back on his way back to Huber Heights, Ohio.

"Did you have a good time?" her cousin asked after she entered and closed the door.

"It was a great time. Russell is such a good guy." She made her way into the kitchen and they sat down.

"I heard on the news feeds of a *Stella* sighting in northwest Pennsylvania late yesterday morning, when a truck was rescued off a bridge. Is that legit?"

She nodded. "Yeah. It is a long story. I had to do a wardrobe change in a rest stop toilet; that venue seems to be a common occurrence for me. No big deal."

"There was also a report of you being at an ice cream parlor in Dayton a couple of days ago."

"Guilty as charged. Food high in fat is where it is at."

"Interesting. Do you want something to eat?"

She nodded. "I guess so. I do not really get that hungry, you know, but something sweet would be good." She felt the glazed doughnuts on the plate and dunked one into some milk Bella had poured for her. "No questions?"

"Huh? What do you mean?"

"Well, you must wonder what I have been doing, gloriously gallivanting around at all hours of the night, rescuing trucks, and other such goings-on."

"Yes, I wondered how you rescued the truck indiscreetly."

"Do not ask; it was not an elegant rescue, as I have already decreed."

"I don't want to know any more." She smelled the coffee Bella had poured. "I've been around the block a few times, Paige. *Tinman* knew me when I was fifteen, and he can therefore back up that statement. So you must know that I've done a bit of, er—'gallivanting' in my life, too."

"Uh, oh. I was beginning to miss the lectures back home."

"No lectures, Paige, just facts, you can assimilate my advice and make your own decisions, or you can tell me I'm full of crap. But I'm not you, a unique person possessing more power than any person ever has had. I didn't want to be President when I grew up, I don't even like politics. So what I've done doesn't really matter."

"I know all that."

"No, you don't know everything, no one does, so listen up. I am one of the most objective people you'll ever meet."

"Yeah, well, it is hard to listen all the time. I get tired of it."

"The day you have nothing to learn is a sad day indeed. Don't be an obnoxious teenager who knows everything. Look, I'm not your mother."

"You certainly scored a few points there."

"Let me finish. You seem to be a person who can handle a great deal of responsibility. But I do care about you. I hope I can be like a big sister to you. Other than Will, we have no other cousins."

"And? Your pertinent point is, Isabel?" She took another bite of the glazed doughnut.

"I don't want you to get hurt. I've been hurt before. It ain't fun."

She laughed. "*Hurt?* I might get hit by a car while I am trying to cross the street, but you should be more worried about the car."

She felt Bella touch her right hand. "I don't mean that type of pain, kiddo. I mean emotional pain. Your beau Russell seems like a super nice guy, but—"

"But what?"

"This is your first real love. First love is immensely powerful, and there is nothing else like it; you will remember it the rest of your life. Enjoy it for now. But it may not be forever."

"How do you know how many loves I've had?"

"Because I'm a girl, and I know. This is your first crush, but you might be just an infatuation to him. You are funny, intelligent, and quite nice-looking, so you would impress any guy. *Without* the extra stuff."

"What? You think so?"

"Trust that I am very knowledgeable about such topics. I know you're not used to seeing yourself, but you've got your father's good looks, and he was a player with the ladies, I heard. I thought he was so nice-looking; I had a crush on him myself and was kind of jealous when your mom married him."

"What?" She laughed. "That is quite ridiculous, as well as being somewhat creepy."

"Come on, I was only twelve years old when they married, and tweens aren't the most rational people. Your mom was very athletic and muscular, but not very shapely, and has a rather unusual personality. You're an interesting combination of both, a great catch."

"I do not know about smart or good-looking." She pulled away. "Russ is not like that; you know little about him. He really likes me as Paige, not because I am *Stella Scura*. We met and went out before I even 'came out' of the closet."

"Maybe. I hope you're right."

"And he just got re-assigned to Wright-Patt. Do you know how that happened?"

"I swear I have no idea. I ain't no politician, I told ya."

"Huh. Really?"

"No, I would never fib to you about that. I would imagine your auntie in Washington had something to do with it."

"Why would she have done that?"

"Perhaps trying to do you a favor; or it may merely be coincidence, but I doubt it. It is reasonably close to his home. What I meant, though, is that he must be older than you, and—"

She held up her hands. "Six years. Big deal."

"Six years at your age is an eternity. Despite your abilities, you've lived a relatively sheltered life. The guy is an Air Force pilot who went to the Air Force Academy. An attractive fella like that has surely ridden the roller coaster a few times."

"Hmmm. Why do you think so?"

"Come on, I dated a Naval Academy grad for a while, I know. I'm from San Diego, which is full of assorted military types. They get around, not always in a good way, I must say."

"So we both fly. Big deal."

Bella poked her in the chest. "That's not what I mean, and you know it. Look, don't rush into things. It's none of my business what you were doing over the weekend, and I won't ask. But I don't want you to come crashing down. Please don't take this the wrong way, but you're just a kid, and you can still be hurt like one. This may not last. You are my family, and you are always welcome to stay here as long as you like. If you want to live by yourself, we have a guest home and condos and such you are welcome to have, free and clear. Anything you want is yours."

She shook her head. "I do not need a handout. I want to make my own way. I have always done so."

Bella grabbed her hand. "Listen here, little girl, don't make me slap you around. You do know that Aurora Darkkin would be wealthy in her own right if she were still 'alive,' don't you?"

"What? No way. How?"

"Because your dad had a trust drawn up for you when you were born. It contained, among other things, some of the original M2 stock."

"How much?"

"Five million at the time."

"Five million dollars? Are you kidding?"

Bella laughed. "No, wait, now, that was *then*. The stock value of Mendoza Multinational from that original five million is worth over sixty million dollars now. There were other investments that have earned interest, but not as much. The stock was converted to cash equivalents when we bought out everyone's shares, except for yours. So don't argue with me. As far as I am concerned, that's yours, too. It wouldn't be here at all without your mom."

"Well, give it to her then; you know where she is."

"I doubt she would come back for it, and she never cared much about money or managed it very well, for that matter. What would she have done with it? Spent it at the magic or comic book store?"

"Point well taken. Where is that money?"

"Still in investments, it hasn't been touched. Seventy-nine million, I believe, is the current number. You're rich, girl. Not mega-rich, but enough to do a lot of stuff, like to go to Ivy League schools."

"Why would you have done that? I am dead."

"Come on. You surely must know the answer."

She shook her head. "I do not."

"Because I knew you would come back, some day. It might not have been this year, but at some point, you would inevitably return. Plus, I don't need the money."

"Knowing that I would return is not possible."

"It is for me. I told you I can distill any problem to its simplest form, and the only logical way for Washington to have survived *Darkkday* and for *Tinman's* and *Gravi-Golfer's* dark matter experiments to have credibility is for you to still be alive."

"I guess I do not worry about those things. Also, sixty million to you is sort of chump change."

"That, too. You're more like your mom than you think. But have you thought about what you want to do? Go to college?"

"I want to make a difference. I am not a scientist, mathematician, or engineer. I suppose the best way for me to do what I want is to become an attorney."

"Well, then, you need some big-time education for that, and we need to get you enrolled in classes. I know a thing or two about academics. Poly sci and such isn't my area of expertise, though. It for sure isn't your Uncle Jay's."

"Huh? Why is that?"

"He failed Poly Sci 101 in college because that wasn't a subject your mom could help him with."

"How shameful for the President's spouse."

"Yeah, he's lucky he was able to stay on the team. But it's all good. You'll need that money when if you run for political office if that's what you want to do."

"It will be hard. I don't have my mom's or your natural gifts for these things."

"No one has it all, Paige. Not me, not *Tinman*, you, Wendy, Jay, Will, or Jack. Surely you should have learned that by now. You may have special skills you haven't yet found out about."

"I left high school, er, rather abruptly. I should have had sufficient credits to graduate, though, by now."

"Sounds like a lot of loose ends to straighten up. Luckily, I have connections who can take care of stuff."

"I do have some things I need to take care of."

"What?"

"Paige has a bank account, but *Stella* does not. I do have a false identity that was created for her. I guess I had better go downtown to take care of that."

"I guess even *Stella* needs money."

She felt Bella put her arm around her. "Honey, everyone needs money. Better to live with it than without it. I'll tell you where to go and who to meet. I suppose we could do it here, but I don't want to raise suspicion. I'll get you a cashier's check of your money to get you started."

Chapter Forty-Two

Stella walked briskly down North Bonnie Mendoza Boulevard wearing a black leather jacket, royal blue sweater, and navy slacks as several people gawked at her and asked for autographs, although she saw quite a few young women sporting the now-fashionable "Stella Look" of black hair and large wrap-around sunglasses; it was amazing how fast fads could catch on. She kind of liked the attention, actually, which was absolutely the opposite of how people treated Paige: as an invisible person.

She separated herself from her fans as she walked into the main office of Aurora City Bank keen on doing something she had needed to do for a while, she had told Bella: open a bank account in *Stella's* name. She didn't like to carry cash, and having an encrypted debi-fob was the best solution to her new jet-setting lifestyle, she thought. Life was certainly becoming more complicated.

A few people ignored her at first, but gradually most of the patrons stared as she approached the woman at the desk in one of the side offices and sat down without invitation. Bella had offered to set her up with a VIP consultant at M2, but she wanted to do this on her own, which she decided to do without telling anyone.

The fortyish, overweight woman looked up from her desk and did a double-take, almost spilling her coffee, seeing an unexpected celebrity sitting six feet away. "Oh, my—can I help you, er, Miss?"

"Actually, yes. I would like to open an account, which would make life much easier for me, you see. I have heard from many reliable sources that this is the best bank in town. Am I in the proper place to enact such a transaction so as to meet everyone's satisfaction without creating a distraction?"

The woman opened her mouth wide. "I think you've already done that, but you're good, I think. Can I get you some coffee?"

"I am fine, thanks." She smiled. "Maybe later."

"Uh—sure, we can do all that." She nervously pulled out her digi-pad. "You *really* want a simple bank account? Not a joke?"

She nodded. "Of course, this is a superior financial institution, I am told, as I do not carry gold in my billfold. Even I need money for things. I would not be here otherwise."

"Um, okay." The woman fumbled, almost knocking over her coffee cup, as a crowd began to form outside her office door, multiple Tekphones taking photos and vids. "You didn't have to come here, with people staring at you. We do private consultations for special clients off-site."

"I am fine, and I was not sure how it worked, as I am not experienced at such trivial things as money."

"There are several account types. Checking, CD, or savings?"

She thought for a few seconds, tapping a cheap ballpoint pen she had picked up from the table. "Checking, I guess, I mainly need a debi-fob as I, uh, travel a lot, sometimes to places that do not take American currency; you must understand the urgency."

"Yeah, I suppose so. Naturally, we can set up an auto-conversion for you. What name do you want on the account?"

"My name, I assumed you would know it."

"Of course, but is there a middle name, Ms. Scura?"

She smiled and shook her head. "No."

"I wasn't sure if it was a legal name or not, or just a nickname; sorry, this type of thing has never happened here before."

"It is a real name. No problem."

"I hate to be formal, but we need a date of birth and Social Security number."

"August 6, 2010." That was the date the government had placed on her FBI file during her police training. August 6 was also her mother's real birthday, she knew from historical archives. Ironically, it was also the date of the Hiroshima Little Boy atomic bombing in 1945.

"Thanks. I also need to see some ID; I'm sorry, it's the law."

"There is no need to apologize, as you are very wise." She handed the woman *Stella's* Indiana operator license and Social Security card, which had a different number than Paige's (Paige had no operator's license, obviously). Both numbers were different from Aurora's, although Aurora's and Paige's birthdate were the same. Someday she would have to reconcile that, but not today.

"Thank you."

She picked up a glass paperweight with her left hand, then levitated it two inches from her palm as a multitude of onlookers took vids with their phones through the office window. "I can do this, too, if that helps you verify who I am."

The bank manager looked at the hovering object in amazement as she watched it turn end over end. "Uh, sure, but I believed you the first time. There have been a few *Stella* look-alikes in and out of here lately, but it's easy to tell the real thing from an imitation."

"Huh. They all look alike to me." She handed the woman a M2 cashier's check. "This is for two hundred fifty thousand dollars, to start. I am sure it is good."

The bank assistant manager stared at it for several seconds. "Oh, my, yes, of course it is. It'll just take a few minutes, Miss."

She then heard the men come in and fire three shots into the air as the bank cleared out.

"What the hell?" the woman said. "This has never happened here before, I don't believe it."

She pulled the manager to the ground. "Get under this desk. I will deal with these idiots." She pulled out her wrist communicator, locating the police beacon. "Officers, this is *Stella Scura*. I am actually in the bank right now, in the back. What is going on?"

"Captain Stewart here. Two guys holding it up, we've pretty much got them cornered. Most of the people inside are in a secure vault; we're just waiting them out."

"Do you want me to end this now?"

"Can you do so without injuring anyone?"

"I believe so. The sight of me will hopefully hasten their surrender, if they have any sense. Yet, those who have sense would not have attempted such a haphazard caper."

"Go ahead, then," the captain said. "Be careful."

"Glad to help." She rose two feet off the ground, floated into the main lobby, and saw the two masked men holding guns. The purported crime-free city had had two armed crimes in one month. At least she wasn't going to play the victim in this one.

"Oh, holy shit," one man said as he looked at their new visitor floating in air. "I told you we shouldn't have done it here, Carl! We could've gone to Indy, Fort Wayne, Cincinnati, or Dayton, but you just *had* to come here. We're gonna get our asses kicked 'cause *she* had to be in the bank we wanted to rob!"

"Shut up, Nielson. It doesn't matter. This place has more money than all those other places, since M2 is the main depositor."

"*Really?* You might have thought of the potential customers your targeted bank might have. A very bad decision, indeed." She floated within twenty feet of the taller man, "Carl," and pointed angrily at him. "Put down your primitive weapons and lay on the floor before more problems befall you. At the moment, you will be charged with armed robbery. Do not add murder, manslaughter, aggravated assault, or kidnapping to the equation. There is no possible way you can walk out of this in one piece. Robbing a bank in Aurora City, or anywhere else, was not a very smart endeavor."

"Shut up, dumb girl, I ain't scared of you," Carl said, pointing his weapon.

"Damn, Carl, don't you know who that is?" Nielson kneeled down on the floor and put his hands on top of his head.

"There are half a dozen other women in here who look exactly the same. This is some teen hero wannabe, dumb ass."

"Teen cosplayers don't float in the air, idiot!"

"Huh. You are a fool, tool." She did not see any bank employees or patrons in sight, at least, they had for the most part cleared out or were in the vault.

"Yeah? Take this." Carl fired several shots at her body, which pierced the jacket and sweater, leaving large holes. The bullets dropped to the ground as the few remaining patrons stared up from their positions on the floor.

"That sure is not going to help your case. And if you aim that at anyone else, I have the speed to get to you before you pull the trigger. This ends now."

"Yeah, well, let's see how tough that head of yours is, freak."

A moment's distraction, and one of the seven deadly sins Jack had mentioned was about to surface: Pride. The two times it had happened recently were at the basketball game on the evening of her eighteenth birthday and when she tried to chase down the convenience store robbers after saving Air Force One.

The first only resulted in a missed free throw; the second could have gotten people killed. This time, three shots were fired at her head from twenty feet away in the fraction of a second before she could reach the gunman.

She laughed as the first bullet hit her forehead; that would probably leave a small red mark, she thought as the bullet dropped into her hand.

The second one was right between the eyes. She suddenly was plunged into familiar blackness.

She had been unbelievably careless.

But never helpless. She had easily reached the two robbers and knocked them to the ground as the third shot hit her directly in the right eye, striking it as she approached them at breakneck speed. She shook her head, her eye irritated by the minimal corneal abrasion. But the familiar blackness was overwhelming right now.

A single bullet had hit the visor, shattering it. She should've known better and anticipated such an event—the visor was more vulnerable than any article of her clothing. She realized then she should have had the forethought to do so.

But no one else knew why she needed it. And no one apparently had been hurt. *Yet.*

She heard other officers rush up to them, grabbing the two robbers as she lifted off the ground a few inches, holding one in each hand by the arms.

"Do you think *this* is a computer video trick, slick? Are you convinced I am the genuine article now?"

"Shit, bitch, I've had enough. A bullet just hit you in the eye, and you still came at me. Put me down and leave me the hell alone."

"Be thankful for small favors. I sincerely hope you never visit this establishment again after your incarceration is complete. But if you call me 'bitch' again, you may not make it to the Henry County Jail in New Castle in one piece. Got it?"

"Yes, Ma'am."

She felt the officer take her hand as she lowered them to the ground. "Thanks, *Stella*. We'll take it from here." She heard him shuffle over to the men on the ground. "You're in big trouble, stupid scumbags."

"Thank you, officer. I would appreciate your keeping any reporters out of here until I have departed. I will have to finish my bank business another time, given the unfortunate circumstances."

"You got it, Ma'am. Anything you need."

"Thank you." She felt another person take her hand. It was a smaller hand, soft, not rough and calloused as would be expected from a metro police officer.

"Ma'am, you need to go over there," the officer said, apparently to the other person. "An ambulance is standing by to take you for medical attention if you need it; otherwise, this is a crime scene."

"I don't require that, thank you." She noticed the soft female voice, distinctly North Indian, with its characteristic British overtones. "But perhaps *Stella* could use some help. I am her assistant, Jan."

Her mouth opened wide. "*Whaaat?* Help? Me? Assistant? I surely do not have or require any kind of—"

"Yes," the woman said. "Let's go over here, away from the commotion, and get things organized before we go back outside."

"Well—" She curiously followed where the tall Indian woman was leading her. "Fine, I am coming. I want to make sure you are okay, uh, Jan. Let me take you home personally after we are done here, as you have nothing to fear."

"Just a moment. Let's go in the back." She walked with her towards the back of the bank, intrigued. She certainly had no better options at this point.

"Where are we going? The police may need my help."

"I doubt it. They can handle it now, dear."

"Huh? Well—if you are injured, physically or emotionally, know I am *not* a healthcare professional. And I do not need an assistant, by the way, how absurd. Why did you say that to the police officer?"

"You probably need one, as well as an agent and a press secretary, but that's not me. For now, just be quiet and go in this room." She closed the door. "No one's in here but us, I promise."

She sighed. "Of course, I can see there is no one here. But why are we in here, Miss? I have important work to do, and you are rudely wasting my time. I am not giving you an autograph right now. I am also not in the mood for trivialities, especially after such an event, and this is definitely not time well spent."

"Hey, listen up, teen hero, we're in a conference room, and you're in no shape to help anyone, and I certainly don't want anything as trivial as your autograph. The emergency services folks out there can take care of business. Pardon my French, but you need to get your shit together, girl."

She was somewhat taken aback by the obviously well-educated Indian woman's abrupt use of coarse language. "Excuse me? What is it you *do* want, then? Are you a reporter? I do not have the time for such mundane matters, as my clothes are in tatters."

"No, of course not; I'm just a customer who wants to help you. But I'm also much more than that. Shut up and let me."

"Why? Do I appear as if I need help? I am not in the mood for riddles right now, and I do not like to be told to shut up or to get my shit together, although I clearly should do both more often on a routine basis." She did need to do just that, actually, as she felt the multiple holes in her sweater. "While I surely will need new clothing, rest assured that I am fully intact underneath."

"Perhaps physically, but I do know you need help."

"You can read minds? If so, you are not doing it very well."

"No, don't be ridiculous. I am, however, very perceptive, because I make a nice living learning how to read people's body language in a courtroom."

"Body language?" She put her hands on her hips and pretended to stare at her. "What does that have to do with anything?"

"A lot. I assume most people think the dark visor is to conceal your identity. But you could wear a mask or something to do that, so it's clearly for another purpose. While I'm no scientist, the material of the eyepieces appears to be rather exotic as well; they sure aren't Ray-Bans. I picked up all the pieces, as I assume you didn't want them lying around. The material appears to be sapphire." She heard her place the broken pieces on the wooden table.

"I have nothing to conceal, and I do not wish to talk about that with you, Jan, or whatever your name is—"

"Let me finish, *Stella*. You are pretty much indestructible, as I understand it, yet I've noticed you sometimes protect your eyes with one of your hands, usually your left."

She laughed. "I do not; that is absurd. You are also mistaken, strange Jan, that I would need to protect my eyes, so it is now time for us to say our goodbyes." She turned towards the door; since she had come through it, she knew the exit path.

She felt the woman's hand touch her shoulder. "It's very subtle, but you do, and you need to work on that. Therefore, it's a logical conclusion that you would need this device to see, the reason for which I don't know, and you may think it's none of my business."

She laughed. "You are right about something, finally—the part about it being none of your concern, I have nothing of this nature to learn."

"But it is now, don't you understand? It seemed inappropriate to divulge that to the world, a matter that would be hard to cover up with reporters everywhere. This is the reason I whisked you out of there pronto."

"So, I need a keeper because of non-functioning peepers?" She laughed again. "That would make no sense, a flying woman who is blind. How ridiculous, as well as being rather hazardous to society, especially to air traffic. Come on, do not make me yawn."

"Perhaps, but I know it's true, which is clearly why you don't know anything about body language, as it's never been important to you, someone whose mannerisms are those of a blind person. You'd better learn, hero. I can help you with that."

She crossed her arms. "How could you *possibly* believe I cannot see? I am trying to humor you, but it is becoming difficult."

Jan laughed. "For one thing, I just thrust my hand within a half-inch of your eyes, and you didn't blink or flinch."

"Well—of course I did not flinch, as your hand could not possibly have hurt me. I just took a large caliber bullet to my eye, so your hand certainly does not scare me. Yeesh."

"You're not being truthful, *Stella.* I can tell by the changing inflection of your voice and slight hesitation in your speech."

"I take it you are an expert?"

"You might say that."

She held her hands out in puzzlement. "How?"

"I'm a very good attorney, a former litigator. And about the other—it's a basic reflex, I doubt that you could control it."

"Huh. I have muscular control beyond what you can imagine."

"Okay, then, how many fingers do I have up?"

She shrugged, laughing. "I am glad you are okay, Ma'am, but I recommend you seek prompt counseling for the psychological stress you have clearly experienced and the delusions you are now experiencing. Yet, I have no time for foolish children's games, so goodbye." She groped for the door and missed the doorknob, finally locating it.

She felt the medium-sized hand touch hers. "But I'm here to help, as out there clearly wasn't the best place. You can trust me. You just missed the doorknob, therefore, you wouldn't get very far without people discovering."

She looked at the ground, seeing nothing, of course. "Suppose what you say *is* true. Why can I trust you out of the blue?"

"If you'll listen, be quiet, and sit down, I'll tell you why."

She felt for a chair, pulled it out, and sat down. "I am not a good liar, and I guess I have little choice."

"I'm not trying to pressure you, only help, as things happened the way they did today. We need to make the best of it."

"*We* need to make the best of it? We do not even know each other, since we have no connection, and I still fail to see why this is any of your business."

"Wrong. You don't know everything. And I may know some things that can help you."

She paused for a few minutes, suddenly realized she had met a worthy adversary. The charade was obviously over and continuing debate with this woman would serve no purpose. And, the lady was seemingly trying to help her.

"Huh. You don't know how much I appreciate that. It's my only Achilles' heel and a part of my 'secret identity.' But, who the heck are you?"

"My name is Janaki Kapoor, and I just moved here from the Washington, D.C. area. We have a common friend."

She shook her head. "I am sorry, I can tell you are North Indian from your voice, but that name does not mean anything to me, and I do not know what we would have in common. I also do not know any Asian Indians."

"Okay, it's been a while, but, as I said, I certainly know *you*. I was married to Stan Williams."

She thought for a minute. "Yes, President Mendoza's first husband. They divorced a year after I was born, I believe."

"Correct. About a year before the 2012 London Olympics."

She took off her black leather jacket and blue sweater, then reached down into her bra, somehow pulled another visor out, and put it on. About ten seconds later, the tall Indian woman's face came into focus as she put the sweater back on.

She stared at the attractive black-haired woman. "I am sorry, but I have never seen you before." She laughed. "I suppose that does not mean much, coming from a blind girl."

Janaki stared at her. "What the heck? You had another visor on you all the time while we've been talking?"

She nodded. "Yes, it is hidden inside my bra; other than the eyepieces, it is very flexible, although its durability could apparently be augmented."

"It's just strange that it could fit in that small area, it seems too large for that."

"Small area? Are you being insulting now?"

"I meant the cleavage, not the breasts themselves. Kind of a weird thing for us to be discussing, don't you think?"

"Easy for it to fit next to my tit." She laughed. "That compartment is merely my hammerspace, not a place full of lace."

"Beg pardon? Your hammer what?"

She sighed. "Hammerspace is the notional place that things come from when they are needed, and where they go back to when not; it can hold a lot."

"I'm afraid you've lost me."

"Envision a cartoon character, for example, who can pull a large object like an anvil out of a seemingly small space. My breasts can deform quite a bit with no discomfort, allowing for this seemingly physical impossibility."

Janaki slapped herself in the face. "Ohmigod. You sounded just like your mom just then, it's eerie."

"My mom? You know nothing about my mom, and you need to stay calm."

Janaki shook her head. "Wrong. I do. There's no mistaking the peculiar usage of language and your general mannerisms."

"That is ridiculous." She shrugged. "Anyway, I could not really have pulled my visor out in front of dozens of people now, could I? And I did not want to divulge it to you right off the bat. I would have somehow made it out okay."

"Yeah, right, unless the spare was damaged."

She shook her head. "Very unlikely. The lenses fold and are crammed in between my cleavage, so bullets and such would hit my breasts first. Therefore, they are well protected."

Janaki laughed. "I guess you couldn't have pulled it out from there in the crowd, at that. But it still doesn't solve your main problem."

She shook her head. "No, but it will have to do until I find a superior solution, as I have more to worry about than that. The scientists have been unable to find one, but I am grateful for this simple device which works amazingly well. Aluminum oxynitride can withstand a bullet but apparently cannot be made with the proper optical qualities at this time. But there are probably photos of me without my visor out in cyberspace already."

"You're also using a colored contact to cover your blue left eye, so it matches the brown one."

"Why would I do that? What makes you believe I have blue eyes? Do not most with black hair have dark eyes?"

"Your hair is obviously dyed as your natural color is much lighter, a somewhat darkish red. I remember how deep blue your left eye is, and the dark contact doesn't entirely match the right eye now, it's pretty obvious. Whoever does your stuff needs to work on those cosmetic details."

"I did not intend for my irises to be visible, you know. At least the bullet hit my right eye."

"Whatever. Anyway, you can't have well-meaning amateurs from the *Science Squad* doing it, so get some professionals. In the line of work you've chosen, it's rather important."

"Who? This conversation has rapidly become far more complex than I had ever envisioned. Perhaps it is time to end it."

"But now that all of this has happened, maybe we can make the best of this situation."

"That is the second time you have said that. How so?"

"You always need to make the best of any situation. It's unlikely anyone will think *Stella* is really blind without the visor."

"I have thought of that. I suppose it is a good disguise."

"Are there any other solutions to your visual loss?"

She shook her head. "It is complicated—it is not really visual loss, but much the opposite, exactly, as it is due to extreme sensitivity of my eyes to light. Apparently, direct contact with another person or animal confers my invulnerability to him or her for as long as we are in contact but dilutes my own invulnerability to a tiny degree."

"I can't believe that would be significant."

"Well, normally not, but when I lived through something very spectacular, I was touching another person. So it did happen. I was hit by a very bright light."

Janaki nodded. "I know. I was out at an all-night fundraising event at the Reflecting Pool; I was with about forty other people. We witnessed the miracle. A blinding flash to the east, then it all collapsed into itself like a black hole in less than a second."

She shook her head nervously. "I do not follow you."

"December 16, 2016. I was right there. So were you. About eight thousand feet in the air, on your way to Stockholm."

"I do not care to discuss that day, it is of no importance to us." Time to change the subject. "But enough about me," she said nervously. "Tell me a little bit about yourself, Jan."

"Okay, well, I was born in New York City, my dad was an engineer. We moved to Kanpur when I was two and back to the USA when I was about ten. I met Stan Williams when he was teaching a class in tax law at Georgetown Law School, where I was a student."

"I am sorry for your loss. Although there were not that many people on the *Darkkday* plane, it seems that every day I meet a new person who knew someone."

"We have that in common."

She stopped drinking her coffee in mid-sip. "Beg pardon? Something in common? No offense, but what could that possibly be, Janaki?"

"One thing: *Darkkday* losses. How all the people on the plane died, save two."

She shook her head nervously. "I do not follow. What do you mean? No one could have survived that."

"Look, *Stella,* cut the crap. I heard your voice become nervous when I brought it up before, as you changed the subject, and again just now. Despite them being divorced, Stan and Wendy remained good friends and had joint custody of their children, whom you played with a lot as a kid. I saw you often as a child and played games with you many times, as you, Bonnie, and Alex lived only a half-mile down the road in Arlington. Wendy moved to Sacramento, of course, when she left the Surgeon General's office to become Governor of California in 2014. We didn't see them nearly as much after that. But you were still around, even though Bonnie left the CIA to go discover mendozium in Tennessee."

"So? What does that have to do with me? I have no interest in those people. You are making it up as you go along, and you could not be more wrong."

Janaki laughed. "Come on, it doesn't take an Einstein like your mom to figure out you're really Aurora Darkkin."

"Huh? Who?"

"You're in the middle of Aurora City, in the main branch of Aurora City Bank, so you surely must know who Aurora Darkkin is. Don't treat me as if I'm stupid. I assure you I'm not."

She laughed. "Of course I know who she was—"

"*Is*. Not *was*. Get your tenses right."

"But your ludicrousness has caught me off guard. You would make a fine comedienne, like your deceased husband's first wife once tried to be, with limited success. It is rather good she had another career to fall back on."

"I'm not trying to be funny, Aurora, so please leave your Aunt Wendy out of it. I watched you fall down like any toddler learning to walk would, but you never cried from pain or had a scratch on you. That's unheard of."

"Aunt? I just realized this, but it's so ridiculous it didn't first occur to me. You think I—I am *Aurora Darkkin?* That person is long dead. The fact I am in Aurora City is just a coincidence."

"Really? Of all the cities in the United States, you picked *this* one to open your first bank account?" Janaki pulled out a dark leather wallet from her purse and displayed a photo on her smartphone. "You don't believe me? Here's a photo of you, me, Bonnie, and Alex—your biological father. You were four years old."

"What?" She looked at the digital photo and realized for the first time she had never seen a photo of her father before; but that was her mom for sure, albeit then with black hair. "I would like to believe you, but it is just hard, Janaki. This photo could have easily been fabricated."

"Perhaps, but it wasn't. You think I had altered this image on the random chance I might run into you? What are the odds of that?"

"I do not know anything about gambling, sorry. Such childish games are not productive."

"True, yet you sure know someone who does."

She shook her head. "I do not follow, as your story is increasingly hard to swallow."

"You are a legend who came to life, although no one knows the connection. *Yet*. And it's no coincidence, because some of your few remaining relatives live here. I told you, I'm not trying to expose anything, and if you don't want to talk about it, that's fine, too. I know how overbearing Wendy can be, and from what I know of Bella, she can be the same way, although they are both good people, with their own agendas, though."

"You are right. Yes, the President, my cousin, her husband, and strange *Science Squad* friends—are well-meaning but have far different interests and life goals than I. I hope other people do not figure it out. But I really do not have many people to talk to."

"You mean 'normal' people. You can always talk to me."

"I guess so. I do not mean that to be pejorative, but Wendy and Jay are not exactly normal. Neither are Bella or the *Tinman*. They all live in a glamorous world I really want no part of."

"Really? You're out here in a superhero suit flying around, fighting crime, and you don't want glamour? You just waltzed into the bank like a regular person to open a checking account, took out a couple of armed robbers, and you don't want attention? Come on, that sounds a lot like wacky stuff your mom, Jim, your aunt, or even your dad might've done. You should've arranged your transaction to be done privately like most celebrities do."

"Maybe I made an error in judgment due to my inexperience. Bella had suggested that, yet here I am in my youthful ignorance."

"Maybe you'd better listen to people. That kind of stuff can get you and others you care about in a whole heap of trouble."

"But my presence here in this city, inappropriately named after me, as I am no angel, believe me—is merely an accident, due to a bizarre sequence of events. My suit was designed by my movie star cousin, not me." She shook her head. "No, while the attention is interesting, I do not desire fame, which is rather lame—I want to do good, and this seemed like the best way."

"What? You're not going on TV to sell things? Wendy and your mom tried to pitch all kinds of things in their youth: vitamins, lunch boxes, police equipment, scientific calculators: you name it, Bonnie tried to sell it. For a person with high-functioning autism, she had an enormous amount of hubris and could be quite demonstrative, given an audience."

"Huh. I cannot imagine she was very good at selling anything."

"No—while she was an exceptional stage magician, she didn't sell stuff very well, as she was very hard to understand, used excessively complicated words, and could be very irritating."

"Kind of like me, is that your meaning?"

Janaki nodded. "Yes, except you have perfect diction and vary the pitch and timbre of your voice, while she spoke in more of a monotone. She avoided contractions often, but not completely, like you do; she also doesn't alliterate as much, and the rhyming seems to be unique to you. Bonnie did patent a few police equipment devices, which earned her a few bucks, before discovering mendozium years later, which didn't really make her much money, as she was 'dead' before Bella brought those ideas to fruition. But her original wealth came from an addiction to gambling, something you're probably aware of."

"Yes, but why would you know anything about it?"

"Come on. I was married to Stan. He invested Bonnie's money and took care of her finances because she was incompetent at such things, at least until she married your father."

She laughed. "I have no desire to be famous, wealthy, to be adored by billions, to be a glamorous movie star like Bella, or sell unnecessary products to the masses." She took a bite of a chocolate chip cookie that had been left in the room. "You said you are an attorney, correct? A litigator?"

"We'll have to agree to disagree on whether or not you like attention—but, yes, I specialize in financial management and taxes now. I liked the political scene, was a fine litigator, and spent some time in the Department of Justice, but I had bills to pay and this is a much less stressful and better-paying life than being an adversary and living in D.C., with the cost of living here less than half for twice as much living space. Like I said, I can read your body language and voice inflection pretty well. Years of experience, dear."

"Then our meeting is fortuitous, as someday I would like to also become an attorney, as I am very good at debate and arguing."

"And you in your infinite wisdom somehow believe those qualities would make you an outstanding attorney?"

She nodded. "That would seem quite intuitive."

"Well, you'd be wrong. Attorneys must be able to take a rigorously logical approach to legal issues, and people who love to debate are often less than analytical in their approach to points of law. You must see both sides of an argument, but those who enjoy debating frequently adopt one-sided approaches when matters are in dispute, and that'll send even you into a tailspin. You may be one of those folks who want to quarrel because you're more interested in arguing for the sake of argument, even when it's to their client's detriment. In the long run, it's not a good reason to be an attorney."

"Okay, okay, I get it. Maybe I need to articulate my commitment better. But I would like to be in politics. My only role models thus far seem to be scientists." She stuck out her tongue. "Yuck."

"What's so distasteful?"

"It is obvious. Look at me; you must think I am insane. I am basically a high school dropout who has not even applied for college yet, and I am already talking about law school, an educated one like you must surely think me a fool."

"No, knowing who your mom is, I don't think you're crazy at all for wanting to pursue advanced degrees, and you seem a bit more mature than her—which isn't saying much—but *politics?* Why in the world would you want to do that?"

"Is there something wrong with politics?"

Janaki laughed. "I used to live in Washington and, yes, there's a hell of a lot wrong with it. You have enough talents to make a difference without engaging in that rhetoric. Do you really want the hassle? You have no idea what you're getting into."

She shrugged. "My 'talents' are a biological birthright, due to a cavalcade of confusing phenomena I cannot yet explain. I did not earn them. And they will not impress people in the long run, most likely."

"Probably true. Yet, I would imagine that it's taken a long time to learn to control those powers safely. Don't downplay that."

"Certainly, but—Wendy seemingly contradicts herself. On one hand, she says that only by becoming a legislator or lobbyist can I change the laws and be far more than the sum of my vast powers. On the other hand, she wants *Stella* to be a symbol of America and kick some ass. I do not think I can have it both ways, can I?"

Janaki nodded. "Maybe. Like all politicians, she must make compromises to get what she wants. It's a complex world out there, *Stella*. The world is infinite shades of gray, not black and white. Wendy is a good person, and, despite her over-the-top persona and aggressive political agenda, she's very bright, shrewd, and morally sound. You may not like everything she's done, and I don't either, but I assure you she's incorruptible—the most important quality in any leader. But realize that no one can rise to that position without stepping over a lot of people along the way and making many enemies. No one is perfect, and she never tried to hide her flaws. And we're in unchartered territory now, with you."

She nodded. "I know no one of us is perfect, least of all me."

"And if you want to be a politician, you won't make everyone happy, either. Many won't like you at all. A minority will hate your guts because you were born with something special which transcends any other being on Earth. Whatever you do, most will think you got there only because of your powers. They like you now because you're a novelty, but novelties wear off, and there will then be incessant protesters wanting you to leave. Not everyone likes

Wendy, believe it or not."

"Noooo—really?" she said sarcastically.

"Yeah, really. You don't hear about those people, as she manipulates the media better than any President I've ever seen, but she's got her problems like everyone else."

She nodded. "I figured as much, and can live with that."

"Well, one thing you can't change is this: despite you sharing a bit of DNA, you are vastly different beings. Wendy, unlike almost any other President, had the advantage of being an average American in many aspects—she was a physician and a healer, not a politician. She was only the third President who had been divorced. She was no raving beauty, either, and garnered more laughter than applause in her youth, not all of it intentional.

"She was always overweight and was very much out of shape when she became Surgeon General, but she worked very hard to defy the odds; she lost over fifty pounds and used her God-given physical strength to win the shot put gold medal at the 2012 London Olympics, despite multiple critics who stated she shouldn't have even been on the team in the first place. But they let her try out after the UK offered her a spot. Everyone forgot how good she was in college before she moved on to other stuff.

"*And* she almost died to save a President and British Prime Minister on network television, which made her an instant world hero. She was in the hospital for months, with much physical therapy to follow. After that, she was elected Governor of California, and the rest is history. The confidence you see now has been earned over decades, in a woman who didn't always have such a high self-esteem. She can relate to people on a level you can't.

"In contrast, you're an indestructible flying young woman with superhuman strength, which makes you vastly different. You are also much more attractive: a taller, heavier, and more athletic version of Bella. Yet, people are very scared of you."

She shook her head. "That is absurd, as I am one of the most peaceful people on the planet. No one on the side of the law need fear me. While I was verbally threatening to those robbers, I would not have harmed them. I did not need to."

"If you believe that, then you truly are more like your mother than you think."

"What do you mean by that?"

"I mean that your mom doesn't understand normal human behavior, despite her narrow range of intellectual brilliance. People fear things they don't understand. You must work hard to get people's trust like Wendy did because you can't possibly relate to them the way she can. They saw her vulnerability and courage when she got shot and almost died, then they watched as she lost her two children on *Darkkday*. She has bipolar disorder and talked about it openly on national television."

"Wendy is fairly intense, but I have not seen that."

"And you likely won't see that outright—but spend enough time with her, and you'll see the unpredictability of her moods and unbelievable energy; some would say that gift helped make her great. You can't ever do that. Make sure this is what you want, because you're in for a far rougher ride than you can imagine."

"I suppose so—but I will have to come to terms with that. I am who I am; it is not like I can change it."

"No, but why not play to your strengths? You have the power to do whatever you want, to accomplish more than anyone in history could. Non- aggressively, of course."

"Do I? Sure, I could rule the world if I so chose; I already had that figured out a long time ago. That is not my style. I can barely keep track of ruling me; that is a full-time vocation. Today, I did not do a very good job, and I was barely better than a blob."

"But if you hadn't been here today, then people could've gotten hurt. You've also figured out that people would respect you more for something earned like anyone else, even though it's not easy."

"Perhaps, but I see so much injustice. I hear about people sent to prison for things they didn't do, both here and in other countries, but I could simply go get them out, like with Thomasson. What could anyone do about it?"

"Nothing, I suppose. But you know that would likely be breaking the law, right?"

She nodded. "Yeah, I know, that is sure not the way to go."

"People will respect that you never took advantage of your powers. I don't think many people could do that. If you really could follow through with that, you could be a great leader."

"It is hard. I do have a secret identity. If I try to accomplish those things as a blind person, that might earn some respect. They might respect me more if they knew I had powers and lived as an everyday person. Which I am, by the way."

"That's a complex scenario to carry out and a novel way to

shape the world. On the other hand, there will be those resentful that you are not using your abilities to save the world 24/7. You'll never please everybody all the time."

"Yes, but if you look at the comic superheroes of history, the stories are all about the heroes. The 'alter ego' or 'secret identity,' call it what you will, has always been secondary. There has never been one where that 'other person' contributed anything substantial to society. I would like to change that."

"*What?*" Janaki crossed her arms and looked at her as if she was a stern teacher about to whack her with a ruler. "Young lady, did you really just tell me that rubbish?"

"Of course, is that not a good analogy, one of pedagogy?"

"*Stella Scura:* we were having a perfectly logical conversation, and then you have to say something that asinine."

"Huh? How so?"

"How can you even ask that? Comic books aren't real, and you shouldn't use them as a reference guide, as that is very childish. I know you're still just a kid, but grow up and get some maturity."

"I guess that statement might have been a bit immature, but do you not see the similarity?"

Janaki shook her head. "No, not really, but I suppose that's one juvenile way of looking at it. I'm sure you'll explain it to me in verbose, bellicose fashion."

"Janaki, my mom reads comic books constantly, and she is one of the greatest scientific minds of history. Have an open mind."

"Hmmm—Bonnie is not the best example of maturity, but you may make a good arbiter, at that. Just make sure you're mature enough to take the world on. One piece of advice: don't quote comic books in the courtroom. You will be destroyed."

"Huh. We will see about that. It may be a new legal strategy."

"Hardly, dear." Janaki patted her on the shoulder. "Great responsibility for one so young. I think the world is in good hands, although there's quite a bit of work to do."

"I hope so. Do you want a ride home?"

"Maybe not today. I have had enough excitement for one day. I am sure the police will need my statement."

"Another time?"

"Sure. We'll meet at some deserted place for coffee and have a long chat on body language and such. Just bring your pen and notebook, you have a lot to learn."

Chapter Forty-Three

"Are you certain you're okay to do this?" Bella asked Paige as they sat at the kitchen table.

"Go into town alone? Of course I am okay. I did it back home a lot, and I will try not to get myself in a sorry spot."

"Well, Aurora City is just a little bit bigger than Fairbanks."

"Almost four hundred thousand people. About ten times bigger with the suburbs. But my home is not as rural as you think."

"Yeah, right. You have everything you need? Sandy will take you downtown, so just call on your cell if you have any problems and she'll pick you up wherever you're at when you are finished."

She laughed. "I'm fine, really, Bella."

"Okay. *Please* be careful and don't get into any trouble, like the last time."

"I won't. I'm not going to the bank, anyway."

She gathered her purse and jacket and waved goodbye as she entered the back seat of the sedan as the female attendant held the rear door open for her.

• • •

Bella dialed a number on her Tekphone. "Juriann—she's headed into town. Make sure she doesn't get into any trouble, now, as we had previously discussed."

"What is it you want me to do? I'm not that inconspicuous."

"She can't see you, and I'm sure she'll be fine, but it's just a backup plan."

"Okay, I guess you know best."

• • •

Paige, armed with her GPS phone, made her way through the Aurora City downtown. People were always nice to her, although, of course, it wasn't possible to see their reaction.

She decided to go into the drugstore to get some chocolate milk, as she was thirsty for that, for some reason. She fumbled around the refrigerated goods section and headed towards the checkout when she heard a woman screaming in the back. She dropped the plastic milk container and headed back there to what most likely was the prescription counter, based on the layout of most pharmacies. *Déjà vu,* except this wasn't some little Anchorage convenience store. It was a bigger city, with big-time relatives less than a few miles away, and a lot more at stake now than when she was just a kid. Anchorage had somewhat more crime than Aurora City was supposed to have. And no one cared much what happened up there. Here, it was a different story.

She felt the gun barrel against her abdomen. Great—but what did she think would happen? Her first outing on her own in Aurora City, and she was going to get shot. Better her than someone else, she reasoned.

It probably wouldn't be a good idea to resist because she had no real plan. If they wanted a hostage, she would be ideal, as most blind people wouldn't fight back. It would be a superior choice to them taking someone else who might get shot. She didn't want to risk doing anything aggressive that might cause them to shoot her, she didn't need a bunch of freaked-out crooks.

They took her out of the back exit; she estimated there were two men, based on their gait. They didn't say anything as they bound her hands and feet with zip-tie cuffs and seemed to have thrown her in the trunk of a large sedan after they put tape over her mouth. She heard the door slam. She had been in zip-tie cuffs before, when she had been arrested in Anchorage for orchestrating an illegal food operation in the park; that was actually kind of fun. They had been applied loosely enough by the officer (who apologized for using them at all) that she could have probably slipped out of them; this was a little different. The officer didn't even realize he had arrested a blind girl until they arrived at the police car. But breaking the cuffs now would be hard to explain to everyone.

Well, this driving around in the trunk of a sedan was definitely not enjoyable. It might be, if it was a *Science Squad* dramatization at *Tinman's* Sulphur Springs complex, and she was playing the damsel in distress; but these were real criminals with real guns, which meant that innocent people might get hurt, and she had no idea how to prevent that from happening now. At least they had done what she had hoped by them taking her instead of some other poor soul. That's what would have happened if she had just run out of the store, and she wasn't about to let that happen. But her decision also meant that she would have to do something she wasn't good at: being patient.

She rolled over in the musty gas guzzler and contemplated what she was going to do next. Kick the trunk open? Blow out the tires by rocking the car really hard? Flip it over? None of those choices would be very good for Paige's "secret identity" and might seriously injure those in the car. She had learned her lesson about that. Well, maybe she could be a hero in another way, which was yet to be determined.

Those thoughts were cut short about two minutes later as she heard a loud "thump" on top of the car and a buckling sensation, then the sound of glass breaking, followed by unrepeatable expletives. Then, a jarring sound as the vehicle apparently had hit something very hard. She rolled around, being tossed around like a rag doll. Then she was being moved even more before she realized what was happening.

Incredibly, the car was being flipped over, just not by her—the very thing she was trying to avoid. It suddenly occurred to her that only one person she knew could possibly do that, unless they had just gone over a bridge.

How dare he do that with her inside? That feat might take some explaining, too.

Twenty seconds later, she felt the car flip over again as she bounced around inside like a tennis ball left out of its can. She heard the shearing sound of steel as the trunk lid was ripped off, and she felt the wind on her face; she was then lifted out and placed on the ground. He pulled the tape from her mouth.

"Ouch! You oversized oaf! Be careful with my delicate person."

"That didn't hurt you. Bella must have given you some acting lessons. I like you better with the tape *on* your mouth. It's quieter."

"You Dutch dolt! How dare you flip this car like a pancake with me in it? I had the situation under control, do not be so droll."

"Sorry, I see you had a great plan already."

"I did; I was just waiting for the right moment."

"But I see you're none the worse for wear."

"Why are you here anyway? Were you following me? This meeting cannot have been purely by chance."

"No comment."

"Huh. I will discuss with you and Bella later. Where are the miscreants who did this?"

"They aren't going anywhere except in a jail wagon."

She heard sirens. "About that . . . you'd better get out of here."

"Yeah, I get you. You'll be okay?"

"Sure, sure, I am just great," she sputtered. "Just leave your rescued damsel out here still tied up."

"I'm helping you, Paige. There's no way you could've resolved this yourself without revealing your other persona." She felt him break the zip-ties. "All right, since you're too lazy to do it." She heard his heavy boots as he ran off, police sirens in the distance.

• • •

Wendy was sitting in a San Diego State sweatshirt watching TV in their bedroom as Jay walked in.

"What's up?" he asked.

She pressed a button on the remote as the center monitor displayed a previous news broadcast from two hours earlier. "Keeping up on the Aurora City news. It's an exciting place these days."

"What? Since when? It's the most boring place ever, and this is from someone who lived in Green Bay for over a decade."

"Oh, how little you know. Listen up. Miranda got this for me."

He watched as the female TV reporter's face filled the screen.

"Today, a set of bandits attempted a robbery at Fred's Pharmacy in downtown Aurora City and took a bystander—a young blind woman—hostage when they made their getaway after stealing over two thousand dollars in cash and an undisclosed amount of narcotic medication.

"While there is no TV footage of the incident itself, several bystanders saw a young, large, bearded, dark-haired man run after the car, jump on top of it and smash the windshield, as the car flipped over. Luckily the young woman in the trunk was found on the curb, unhurt. The man who overtook the combatants was never found. Aurora City Police are searching for him to obtain a statement, but he disappeared as quickly as he arrived."

She pointed to the video of Paige being helped by the officers, even being interviewed by a news reporter, shying away from the camera.

"What in the world?" he said. "Has Will seen this?"

She shook her head. "I hope not, but I can't control everything."

"But why would she be in Aurora City? How did she get there from North Pole?"

"Isn't that the most logical place she would end up? The home of the legendary Aurora Angelica? We know that our fine M2 relatives rescued her from the northern Alaska wilderness after her technical malfunction caused by to the now-unemployed, soon-to-be-incarcerated Thomas Ashburn."

"We do?"

"I know lots of things. There aren't too many people with the money and resources to have pulled that off."

"They were able to do that because you ordered the military to stay away. Bet that was tough to explain."

She sighed. "I did get some complaints about that, but who cares? It's good to be the boss sometimes. Not all the time."

"I suppose—but you're certain it's her?"

"Yes, Miranda confirms 97.3 percent facial recognition from the video. Of course, the photos exist only on my private server." She stared at him as he frowned. "What's your problem now?"

He stared at her. "*You're* my problem. For some reason, you don't seem very interested. I don't get you."

"Huh? Me interested in a blind girl who got abducted by some minor hooligans? Who would be interested in that?" She spoke in a quiet voice as she sipped a bottle of diet cream soda. "No, not really, not right now."

He moved his head six inches from her face and stared. "I know I'll get socked in the mouth for this, but—why the heck not?"

"The time for that will come soon," she said in the softest, highest-pitched voice she could muster, looking lazily at the television. "Like I said before, she'll be there tomorrow and the day after that. I'm far more interested in the *other* guy."

"The guy who ran down the car?"

She stared at him and scowled. "Yeah, who'd you think? Does that description fit that of anyone you know?"

He pointed at her. "Yes, and it's not a good memory, and part of the reason I'm a bit perturbed by you."

"*Perturbed?* Wow, that's a big word for you. You're starting to sound like the little sis."

"Bad remembrances of him or the bizarre fifteen minutes preceding it. I probably would've punched you out myself if Travis hadn't beat me to it."

"Sorry, I was not on my best behavior that day; I was full-blown manic at that point. I also want to thank *Tinman* for letting me know he has such interesting guests in his city, who also may share some of my DNA. Well, I know we were just there, but it's time for another trip. And this time I'm letting them know we're coming."

"When?"

"In a few days. We'll make it a family trip." She sat down the remote control and smiled, and was amazed how smoothly this all seemed to turn out. Paige had been in no real danger, of course, and, by a stroke of luck, she found out more about the oddity known as Juriann Hultaar. Luckily, no one was injured.

But a part of her wondered if her husband knew that her portly, shadowy vice president and the DSD could have arranged the whole thing all along, being extremely careful to make sure all parties knew the whole thing had been staged, like a movie set.

This was all hypothetical—of course; she had no direct knowledge of such an event, or many others, for that matter, and it might've just been an entirely random occurrence. Apparently someone wanted to know what the new, improved *Orthoman* was all about, as the first one didn't turn out so great.

This one seemed a few notches above Travis Argon, but that wouldn't be hard to accomplish.

• • •

Stella looked at herself in the full-length mirror, wearing a dark blue pantsuit with a matching jacket as she walked onto the stage. She had enjoyed the makeover the makeup crew had given her—without eye makeup, of course; she didn't need that.

"We welcome America's—and the world's—first real superhero, the young woman who saved Air Force One—*Stella Scura!*"

Stella walked onto the set of the WBS Evening News with Millie Avery to cheering from the live audience in Manhattan.

"It is so nice to meet you, Millie," she said, extending her hand before she sat down with the famous news anchor, whom she had heard on television for as long as she could remember. "I am honored to be here."

"Likewise. This is quite an honor for me, you know. This is the first live interview with you. A tough one to snag."

She laughed. "Well, I have been rather busy; my schedule makes me rather dizzy."

Millie took a sip of coffee and poured her a cup. "Everyone is wondering—why me, and why now? You just called up the network and said you'd be here, so here we are."

"You are a respected journalist in this area, and I thought it fair, my story to share. And it was time to sit down with America and answer some of the questions you invariably have of me."

Millie leaned back in her chair. "So, did you have a good flight up here?"

"I did. M2 graciously flew me out here on one of their corporate jets. It was nice to sit back, drink coffee, and take it easy for a flight. I even got to take a brief nap."

"You have a better way, I assume?"

She shook her head. "Not really, not in New York. I am a small-town girl, and I do not know if I can navigate these skyscrapers by myself. It is unreal, compared to where I have been before."

"Why are you living there? What's your relationship with the Stannous and Mendoza family?"

She laughed. "They research energy, and I seem to have a lot of it, so I figured, why not hang with them. They have helped me answer a lot of questions about myself." Which was the truth.

"That makes sense. But tell us a little bit about what the name '*Stella Scura*' means. I assume that's not your real name."

She laughed. Technically, it was, as she had an ID to prove it.

"It is actually my legal name."

"Does it mean anything?"

She nodded. "Yes, it means 'dark star' in Italian."

"Are you Italian, then? You look like you could be, with your complexion."

"Maybe, maybe not, the concept is food for thought. Let us just say for now that it is just kind of a catchy moniker."

"What's a dark star? Like a black hole or something?"

"That is a good question, Millie. It is composed of what is called dark energy; almost all of the universe is made of it. You cannot see it or detect it, but it is there, a fundamental force."

"I don't understand."

"Dark matter cannot be seen directly with telescopes or any other instrumentation, because it neither emits nor absorbs light or other electromagnetic radiation at any significant level, which is how we detect things. Instead, its existence and properties are inferred from its gravitational effects on visible matter and radiation, and the fact that the universe's composition cannot be accounted for by the mass and energy we can detect. Therefore, the need for the existence of 'other' matter and energy."

Millie shook her head and smiled as the audience laughed. "Wow, I am totally lost. You must also be a scientist, you continue to impress."

She laughed. "Not hardly, I am merely knowledgeable about myself and memorized that description from fun factoids my scientist friends gave me before the show." The audience roared with laughter. "It pretty much ends there. I can do lots of stuff, but do not ask me to explain how it all works, as I have plenty of quirks."

Millie took a sip of coffee. "But the question we all have is—where did you come from? How did you get here?"

"I got here pretty much the same way as you—I was born in the United States, like you and most people here today. The President can verify that herself."

Millie looked at her curiously. "Really? How's that?"

She shook her head. "I cannot go into the details."

"Of course, I understand. But those are pretty good credentials. So, you're not an alien or something, from another planet?"

She laughed. "No, of course not. Not a mutant, either, it appears. I am merely what I appear to be."

"And there's no other people like you, going to invade us?"

"No, not as far as I know, but I do not know everything. I am kind of unique. If there is someone out there like me, he or she is keeping it a secret."

"Well, to be fair—you did that for years."

"I suppose so. So it is possible there is another I do not know about, but it is unlikely."

"You look average-sized, for a super-strong girl. How tall are you, dear?"

"About five-eight."

"How much do you weigh?"

"Millie, you know you should never ask a girl her weight." She frowned, then laughed, as the audience joined in.

"Come on."

"Oh, okay. Around one-sixty pounds."

"I see. I would not have guessed you as that heavy." Millie bent over and brought her hand a few inches from her face. "The sunglasses—the visor—I notice you always wear them. What's it for? Like a mask?"

She shook her head. "No, I have a condition that makes my eyes very sensitive to light, so I need to wear it. It is not meant to be a disguise or anything, but I have not found another solution."

"So, without it, you couldn't see?"

"Not as well, no, so it enhances my vision." Actually, without it she couldn't see squat, but the rest of the world didn't need to know that. Someday, perhaps, but not right now.

"So you have super-vision?"

"What do you mean?"

"Can you, for example, see through objects or see things we can't that are really small or far away?"

She shook her head. "No, I cannot do any of those things; my visual acuity is slightly above average, but my other senses are nothing special. I also cannot read minds or do anything else like shoot lasers from my eyes." Except that colors were somewhat muted, and her visual spectrum tended towards the near infrared, making people's skin a little lighter and foliage somewhat white, and she could see through haze a little better than the average person. Some tweaking of the visor might fix that, in time.

"They say you can't be hurt or injured."

She smiled. "Now *that* is true, I am happy to say, it helps me keep crooks at bay and keep a smile on my face every day."

"You can take a bullet? If I shot you with a gun, you would be unharmed?"

She laughed. "Yes, I can take a lot worse than a bullet. My clothes cannot, though, they are just like yours, so my action uniform is Kevlar-reinforced."

"What you have on is made of Kevlar?"

She pulled at her jacket and smiled. "This? No, they are just regular clothes, purchased at a downtown Chicago department store; they would not survive a flight here from Indiana without me getting arrested for a wardrobe malfunction." The crowd laughed.

"But you came to New York in a jet."

"Yes, I did, but I wanted to look nice, hence why I did not fly myself. Air turbulence at supersonic velocities is hard on clothes, and worse on my hair, and I do not wish to scare." Millie laughed.

"They're very fashionable."

"Fortunately, I have a good fashion assistant."

"I guess the most amazing thing you can do is that you can fly under your own power."

She nodded. "Yes, it is, at that. I assumed you had seen that already. Just not to New York City."

"It's not just leaping high or something?"

She shook her head. "No, I have the power of actual flight; I can defy gravity and move very large objects I come in contact with."

"I've seen a couple of clips, including the Air Force One rescue, but it's still hard to believe. How fast?"

She shook her head. "I am not sure, I have never really timed myself, you know, but my limit seems to be roughly Mach 7. It takes me over a minute to reach that velocity, though."

"Which is?" Millie shook her head. "I'm also no engineer. Is that several hundred miles per hour?"

She laughed. "No. Mach 7 is seven times the speed of sound, or about 5,300 miles per hour. A human being is not terribly aerodynamic, so that is why I have this limit, with wind resistance and all."

"That's faster than most any aircraft. So you could fly to another continent?"

She nodded. "Of course, and I have done so a couple of times. It takes a while, though; I have a helmet that provides music, to kill the time if I had to fly that long a distance. It also provides advanced avionics for when visibility is poor."

"You could run around the room in the blink of an eye, and we could barely see you?

She shrugged. "No, not really, it does not work like that. I can move faster than you in linear travel by flight, and I have a much faster reaction time than most, but I actually cannot run faster than a typical fit female my age."

"Which is what?"

"About a seven-minute mile, six-fifty if I really push it."

Millie and the audience laughed. "No, my dear; our audience could care less about that. Your *age*."

She smiled. "I told you my weight but not my age. *That* piece of information is classified. My weight is bad enough."

"Noted. You can fly into space, then? To Luna?"

She laughed and shook her head. "I doubt that. Mach 7 is not nearly fast enough to escape Earth's gravity, but I suppose whether or not I can go into space is something we must address at some point."

"Can you show us?"

"Show you what? Going into space? Not at this time."

"No, just simple flying. It's not every day we get someone like you on the news."

She paused for a moment. "Not very well in here, but I can do this." She floated off the chair and tumbled through the air a few times, as Millie gasped.

"Oh, my God, that's amazing." She landed and grabbed Millie's hand.

"If you think that's neat, try this." She and Millie started floating, as the five-four Black woman's dark hair began floating as well.

"I'm flying, just like you."

"Not quite just like me, since you can go only where I go, but you get the idea." She had a thought for a demonstration. "Take your hair clip off and drop it."

"Okay." Millie took off a hair clip, dropped it, and watched it fall to the ground. "Huh?"

"We are actually weightless now, but any object that falls from your person shall be subject to normal gravitational laws."

They landed back on the ground after floating around the stage for a couple of minutes.

"That was fun but kind of scary. But many people are worried about a costumed vigilante flying around doing stuff and that you're too dangerous to have around in case you got in a bad mood."

She pulled out her federal badge. "Understandable, of course. However, the President's staff will see to it that become a sworn federal officer, and I will have jurisdiction in all fifty-five states. I will be trained in proper procedures just like any other officer of the law."

"But the question everyone has is this: you're a normal-looking person and could seemingly function in a more secretive fashion. Why don't you?"

"You're asking why I am not a secret agent? That would be fun—I would get to wear a black catsuit and do espionage. Seriously, I have decided that I can do the most good for the most people this way, rather than being an undercover operative."

"I would imagine it's tough to be you."

"Sometimes, it's not easy. But I want to show people how strength comes from within, to be the best you can be every day."

"No offense, but that's easy for you to say, being immensely powerful and indestructible and all, as well as being drop-dead gorgeous."

"I can be a symbol of good without doing any of those things." Maybe the world wasn't ready for those profound statements yet.

"I don't understand. What does that mean?"

"One day, I will figure it out and let you know."

"But what's in store for you now, *Stella?*"

"I have a few things to do first, but it will be something to help the public good. Someday I want to run for Congress."

Wow, you don't mess around, do you? But do you even meet the basic requirements?"

She laughed. "I shall not tell you how old I am, but I am not twenty-five yet, so do not fret."

"No kidding. Enjoy your youth while you can, kiddo, as we all get older. Nothing you can do about that."

"I have heard that before, but that will obviously be many years from now. How many, I cannot say."

"But suppose Americans don't want a superhero in Congress. What do you do then?"

"I guess I become a gracious loser and figure out why I lost, and re-group for the next time. The people will decide if I am suitable. If not, I need to find another job just like anyone else. That is what is great about America."

"So, one more thing: what party are you?"

"It is a little too early for me to declare that, Millie, so I will wait a decade or so before my announcement."

Chapter Forty-Four

Ronald Reagan Washington National Airport
2401 S. Smith Blvd.
Arlington, VA

Paige decided to keep her promise to Wendy to visit the White House—as herself, of course, not *Stella.* One of the M2 corporate jets had taken her from Sulphur Springs to Ronald Reagan National Airport, where Will and a Presidential limousine were waiting.

"Have a good trip, Paige?" he asked, guiding her down the steps.

"Sure. It's only about an hour. No TSA security or anything with a private aircraft." She stepped into the limousine as he closed the door.

Will entered from the other side and sat down. "So, what's the story, so we have everything straight?"

"I am a relative of Nick Stannous, it seems, which is technically true since my stepfather is his uncle. And I am your friend, we met in Alaska, as you recall. I am merely a high school dropout here for a visit."

"Sounds good to me."

"What's it like, living in Washington?"

"It's a fun place, very busy, but much to do. It's a hassle going out, especially if we go anywhere there are young girls. They drive me nuts."

She laughed. "What a tough life. Well, if you think it's bad now, wait a few more years. Then you'll have young women throwing themselves at you."

"They already do. Maybe I'll feel differently about it then. Right now, I just don't want the attention."

They went to a desk where she was handed a badge.

"What is this, Will? A visitor's badge?"

"Yeah. You get the highest level which allows you access to the residence and the West Wing, except for the classified areas. This way you can bypass security, as I didn't think you wanted to be scanned."

"That would not be useful, as MRI and x-rays cannot penetrate my body."

"Your alter ego will probably get a higher level clearance, I would imagine."

• • •

They walked through the building into what seemed to be a large room, from the acoustics. "Where are we now, Will?"

"Where do you think? The Oval Office. I only thought it appropriate."

"They let you come in whenever you want?"

"Pretty much, if she's not here meeting with people. Mom will be in a moment if you want to wait."

"Where are you going?"

"I thought you two might want some time alone together."

"Really? Is it okay?"

"Of course, we are alone in here, and she's expecting you. Walk around, do whatever you want; she and the staff won't care."

She walked around and felt the legendary Resolute Desk of John F. Kennedy, the desk of the most powerful person in the world—figuratively, at least. A few minutes later, she heard someone come in.

"Who's there?" She stood with a regal presence in the office of the most powerful woman on Earth. That fact, however, was surely in question right now. "Your steps are too heavy to be Bella's, and the shoes you wear cannot be Will's. You can only be she."

The soft sound of large women's pump shoes on the carpet stopped suddenly.

"Dear, I've been in this room with many kings, queens, Prime Ministers, famous athletes, and more Senators and Congressmen than y'all can shake a stick at. But I've sure never been in here with a deity before." The trembling low-pitched female drawl was unmistakable, she remembered from the cornfield in Indiana.

"Huh. Is there a third person here too? There is, reportedly, only one God. I assure you that I am not He, merely a humble servant of mankind, albeit one who talks too much."

"Maybe—I'm not usually at a loss for words, but I'm more nervous than I've ever been in my life," Wendy said. "I feel like a little schoolgirl."

"Hard to imagine you ever being 'little.' No offense."

Wendy laughed. "I suppose I never was, at that."

"But, about being nervous—are you kidding me? I am standing in the Oval Office. I grew up in Fairbanks North Star Borough, Alaska, yet I am standing a few feet from the President of the United States. How nervous do you think I am?"

"I suppose we're even there. Anyway, thank you for coming. I know this is weird for both of us." She could hear Wendy approach her and stroke her hair. "I was the first human being to ever touch you, but you probably don't know that."

"What do you mean?

Wendy laughed. "Exactly that. Despite their many talents, your parents weren't the best at time management, and your mom didn't quite make it to the delivery suite before I had to deliver you on a gurney in the emergency entrance of Bethesda Naval Hospital."

"Really? You did it yourself? No way."

"Yep. I was the first one to see that hard cranium of yours, with a full head of hair, I might add."

"Mom never told me that. I suppose she never told me many things. It would not have made sense. It hardly makes sense now."

"I was the first Surgeon General to deliver a baby in the line of duty. I signed your original birth certificate, which I still have, by the way, since you are, well—legally dead. Sorry to be so morbid."

"I guess if what you say is true, your description of this event clears up any doubts that I am adopted."

"Really? Was that a concern of yours?"

She nodded. "A long time ago, is that not logical? I do not seem to be much like my mom at all, except for the way we talk and our stubbornness. A few years ago, I realized she likely was my real mom. And, with my abilities—it was always a concern, like I had something else to learn."

"You are more like her than you know, and she has some 'special abilities' as well. And I am sure I can locate some witnesses to your live birth if you need further corroboration of my tall tale."

"That is good, I may need proof of my citizenship someday."

"For a passport?"

"I already have that, although it is obviously forged with my 'new' name of Cheryl Paige Marshall. No, I will likely need proof of my citizenship one day when I, well—apply for a certain job, the only one I know of that still requires I be a natural-born citizen."

"I see. It's good to know you've thought ahead. But you don't actually 'apply' for that job, by the way; it's a little more complicated than that. I can help you figure it out in a couple of decades."

"I suppose." She touched Wendy's hair. "But I did not know that about myself, the way I was born, I mean. Why is that not in the history books?"

"Lots of things in life aren't in books, honey. Only a handful of people even know about that."

"I guess we are even, then."

"Say again, dear?"

"In a way, we saved each other."

Wendy laughed. "I don't think anyone is keeping track, but you would've popped out one way or the other as there was no stopping you, then or now. You sure let out a mighty holler when you came out. What you did for me was a bit harder to accomplish. You do remind me a lot of myself at your age, minus the powers, of course."

"Huh? Beg pardon, Aunt Wendy, but you know virtually *nothing* about me."

"I don't? How's that again?"

"No. Being President should have taught you not to assume things you cannot possibly know. Life experiences have drastically changed me from the little girl you remember."

"Hmmm. Now *that* definitely reminds me of myself. Point well taken. So, I guess there's a lot we need to catch up on."

"My, that is an understatement."

"This is like a dream, like you don't really exist. But you do, and I'm still taking it all in." Wendy paused for a few seconds. "You're almost as tall as your mom." She imagined that Wendy was looking at her Titian hair and heterochromic eyes. "You have your father's complexion, and both your parents' eyes. Complete heterochromia iridum—one of each, I remember. The left is a deep blue, just like mine. Your dad's wasn't quite as deep blue as ours." Wendy paused for minute. "Oh, my gosh. I'm sorry, Paige. I certainly didn't mean to insult you—"

She shrugged. "It is okay. Do not worry about it, everyone always does that, then apologizes, as if complimenting me on my unusually attractive eyes is insulting, merely because I cannot see normally. One thing you will learn about me is that I do not offend easily. I have pretty tough skin, my newly found kin."

"I guess that's true, figuratively and literally."

She felt for the sofa and sat down. "I receive compliments on them all the time as well as on other parts of my body. Yet, I have found out many things—it is not as you think."

"I would never offend you. Is it all right to call you Paige? Or do you prefer Cheryl?"

She nodded. "Paige is okay, I go by my middle name, as you do, I guess that might have been planned by my folks. I have learned a lot these last few days. I am not ready to use the name Aurora yet; I may never be. The expectations of my famous name are beyond what I can deal with right now. I have not earned anything, I merely passively did what my mother knew was within my genetic potential."

She felt a tug on her ear. "I like your earrings."

"Thanks. Bella picked out all my clothes and accessories."

"I should've guessed. She has good taste *and* lots of money."

"The earrings are clip-ons, though."

"Clip-ons? Oh, yes, I can see now." She felt the hand brush by her left ear. "I didn't notice at first. The wires are very thin."

"Pierced ears are not possible, of course. I certainly tried."

"I never thought of that. I do remember you as a child. It would have been tough to pierce your ears, I always thought. You could use magnetic studs, though."

She shook her head. "Nope, been there, done that too, but any magnetic field cannot pass through my body, even an ear lobe."

"Huh. How about that?"

"But you knew at that time when I was a child?"

Wendy laughed. "I did, although I'm not sure your mom and dad knew I did, until one day—you were two when I was over at your house with Cassie and was boiling some water for spaghetti. You reached up to the stove, turned a pot of boiling water on yourself, and stood there laughing after you did it."

"I do not remember anything about that or anything about my childhood. At some point, I want to discuss my youth, you know."

"We surely will. Can I give you a hug? Your mother didn't like to be touched very much. I didn't know how you were. The plane landing in Indiana didn't seem like the proper time."

"It is not a problem for me. I touch a lot; it is how I find out about my environment." Wendy gave her a hug, which she returned eagerly. "I suppose, over the years, I realized I have many characteristics of my mother, like her characteristic speech and verbosity. I seem to lack her mathematical and scientific abilities, though."

"Being like your mom is a good thing, don't let anyone tell you it isn't, although I know she can be very annoying at times."

"That means a great deal, coming from you, but I thought you did not like each other."

"Untrue. We grew apart, became more distant, but it was never about not liking her, despite what she may claim. She was like a sister to me, Paige."

"When did that change?"

"It changed after you were born; she left the CIA to do research in Tennessee, she became extremely liberal, and she felt I was self-serving and wanting to take over the world."

"Do you?"

"What?"

"Want to take over the world?"

"I did the things I felt I had to do. Historians will debate decades from now whether or not they were the right ones."

"How long have you known? About the Alaskan me, I mean."

Wendy chuckled. "A while. For one thing, you wore my father's stolen Russian battle suit until it was damaged. She saved my life wearing that, you know."

"That is right, in that she had much might."

"But you are built rather differently than your mother, despite being of similar height. Wearing that must have been very uncomfortable."

"A tight fit in the chest area, to be sure, but I do not really feel or understand pain as you seem to know it, so, not uncomfortable, really, although it is definitely not frilly."

"Where are your mother and Jim now?"

"Who?"

"Jim Krakowski. He was your father's best friend in the world. *Tinman's* uncle."

"Oh, you mean Jack Marshall, who is my adoptive father. Sorry, I am just not used to the name Jim, although I know they are the same person. And, yes, Nick told me he was Jack's nephew. They are back at the homestead in North Pole, I am sure. I have not been back to see them since the incident. I am sure they wish you well."

"Really? That's rather hard to believe."

"Well, Jack probably does; my mom, however, likely would say things which are unrepeatable in this hallowed office. Sorry."

Wendy laughed. "I would expect as much. I'd like to see them as well, although I know that may be difficult, if it's even possible." She poured some coffee from the sterling silver pitcher; she could tell it was silver by the characteristic sound it made when Wendy sat it down. "Do you want some coffee, water, soda, or anything?"

"Coffee would be okay. I assume you must also have some Darkkin whiskey in your office as a sort of symbolic memorial or to help ignite the fireplace."

"Well, if you really want that, I can see what I can do. But we actually don't have it in here, as I don't drink, given our glorious family history of substance abuse, but I can get anything from the pantry, as many of our guests enjoy—"

She laughed. "It was a joke, my deadpan humor. It does not matter anyway. I appear to be immune to all toxins."

"I assume you know this from experience, not speculation."

She nodded. "Of course I do. Would you have expected anything different from me?"

"No."

"Apparently, only water is absorbed into my body, as I cannot create that, of course. My energy needs appear to be met by something unknown."

"I see. Your mom was unintentionally funny sometimes, with some of the weird things she used to say. How is she?"

"Mom? I guess she is as good as she can be. She teaches high school math and seems troubled much of the time."

"Not much has changed. She always seemed to be worried about things weighing heavily on her mind."

"I guess so. Her mind is pretty big compared to mine. Like the universe, it seems to be expanding."

"Not so sure about that. I'm also sorry about your blindness. I've known your mother since she was thirteen, so I know how hard it was for her to deal with a physical handicap."

They sat on the sofa. "Do not be, as I do not remember anything else. It is something that keeps me close to humanity. I have to think it is a trial I must overcome. And, I am quite used to it. It is not a problem; I can do virtually anything a sighted person can, albeit a little slower, sometimes. Occasionally, a little faster."

"Yet you have some sight, per my understanding? I was very familiar with my dad's suit. It had enhanced visual capacities which were transmitted directly into the brain."

She nodded. "Yes, that is correct. I seem to have a unique form of cortical blindness due to extreme sensitivity of my eyes to light, which is what happens when you stare into a thermonuclear blast detonating twenty feet away. Do not ever do that should the occasion arise, as it is unwise."

"Cortical blindness?"

"Yes, that is a condition when the eyes function fine, but the brain does not properly interpret the signals—"

Wendy laughed and patted her on the shoulder. "I know what it means, dear; I'm a physician. I was just curious that you knew that terminology, as it's not everyday language for high school seniors. I can see that you track and appear like you're actually looking at something. Most blind people have disconjugate ocular movements. You don't."

"I have learned much but still know little. But, about that suit, how would you have known of it?"

"Because your mom wore it well before you, and saved my life. When the satellite cameras saw you, I knew deep in my heart it was you. That suit had no propulsion, and no Earthly device could fly like that, anyway."

"There is much I do not know. I am aware of the aberration that was once your other brother. He has now been reborn as one who resembles Rad Darkkin. He calls himself *Orthoman*."

"Yes, I had heard that. The first guy was evil incarnate. That's what he called himself before; I don't know why he would be any different now, though."

"This person is a bit odd, as befits a relative of ours, but he is not evil in the least. We did not hit it off right away, as he seemed to lack a proper understanding of a sightless person's personal space, but we are pals now. He is the one who found me after my suit malfunctioned as a result of one of your weapons."

"That was a horrible mistake, I had nothing to do with that. I fired the guy who was responsible—the Secretary of Defense. Look what it got me—almost dying in a ball of flame over Aurora City."

"I figured as much. But it was Bella who rationalized my 'blindness' was simply the misinterpretation by my nervous system as overloading, that somehow the explosion on *Darkkday* overly sensitized my brain."

"Can it be fixed? I have access to the best medical specialists in the world."

She shook her head. "Thank you, but as far as we can tell, it is irreversible."

"Dr. Royce Garrison Bivereaux III is not the world's preeminent expert in neurology or ophthalmology, just so you know."

"Biv? Are you an authority on *Photraman?*"

"Yeah, you might say that. We went to medical school together. The B's and G's were close enough in the alphabet that we had lots of the same clinical rotations, as it's how they were assigned. He's a smart guy, but we can do better. He hasn't had the most illustrious career."

"No, you miss my point. Even if my vision could be restored to normal, do not assume I would even want it to be."

"What? Why in the world not?"

"You should know the answer—because it is part of who I am. I may not have your intellect, but I know I would not be the person I am today if not for that. Life is not meant to be easy."

"No—I suppose not. This happened after *Darkkday*. Not easy for any of us."

"Yes. Bella theorizes that when I touch someone, part of my invulnerability is transferred to that person. This would not be significant in most cases; however, the brightness of the blast seems to have irrevocably messed up my brain in that aspect."

"Which is how your mom survived, obviously."

"Yeah, but she must have had her eyes closed. Half my power must be enough to survive a small nuclear warhead, or we would be dead."

"If your eyes had been closed at that time, you wouldn't have the problem now."

She shook her head. "Apparently not, but things seem to happen for a reason. I have so much more richness in my life because of my sight problem."

"Run that one past me again."

"Without it I would surely not have the patience and humility I do now. The dark sapphire goggles allow me to have 'vision,' albeit with limited color perception, it seems, but fair penetration into the near infrared spectrum. It is a work in progress. If I take them off, my brain shuts off within a fraction of a second." She pulled the visor out of her cleavage and unfolded it. "It fits in here pretty well for when I need to see, whenever that may be."

"That's incredible, and so simple, and amazing it fits in there. So why don't you wear that all the time, then?"

"Come on. They are large, unattractive, make me feel 'distant' with others who cannot see my eyes, and I do not want to be *Stella* all the time anyway. Blindness is all I remember and I am comfortable with it. I do not view it as a disability. Sight is necessary for my other endeavors, but as a pediatrician specializing in children's rehabilitation and friend of my mother for many years, you surely can understand that one can live with a so-called 'deficit' and still have a full life, although, like most teenagers, I do have much emotional strife."

"Of course, I wasn't implying that you don't, but there has to be some way to create contact lenses or something that would work."

"Perhaps someday, but it is not a pressing priority now, as I have declared. In a way, it is sometimes good not to see some of the time. It is hard to fake blindness."

"I guess so. We sort of talked your mom into having cochlear implants when she was a teenager. I think they were as much for us as they were for her. In the end, they stopped working due to nerve degeneration. I think, in a way, that was a relief to her."

"She can hear fine now. Exceptionally well, in fact."

"Yeah, which makes no sense to me."

"Apparently, the combination of the blast and transference of some of my powers corrected that problem in her while leaving me in this altered state. Would you not want someone like me to have humility?"

"I suppose. But what do you want to do now? This is an awkward situation. If you make it public that you're Aurora Darkkin, it sets into motion all kinds of questions. But there's much you can do for the world in other ways."

"I have no intention of that, at least for now. Blindness grants me a sort of invisibility in that people basically ignore me. For now, I will remain merely a friend of Will's. Surely with facial recognition software and all, I should have been discovered by now."

"No." She heard Wendy sit her coffee cup down. "That should never happen. All biometric records of Aurora's existence have been removed, likely by Jim—er, Jack."

She frowned. "And by you."

"Wow. You're pretty bright for a kid."

"I am no genius, but I know the score and much more. I may talk like my mom, but I assure you I do not have her naïveté."

"Let's just say that we both played a role in your anonymity."

"I am sure it was easier for them to hide things from me because of my blindness, but I am smart enough to know that if you had wanted to find me, you would have. You probably knew exactly where I was."

"You are wise beyond your years. I stayed away out of respect because it's what Jack and your mom would have wanted. And, in the end, what was best for you."

• • •

After lunch with Wendy, Jay and Will, the two women went back to the Oval Office for more conversation.

"Are any relatives from the Gallinsworth family still around, Aunt Wendy? I have never heard of any."

"Not a lot. Mom has a brother, Charles, who's still living, but in somewhat poor health at eighty-five. She wasn't terribly close to him. He had a daughter, Anna, and a son, Terrence, whom I've met a couple of times."

"Why wasn't Marianne close to her brother's family?"

"Well, you could imagine why. She was from a well-to-do British family who sent her to Princeton, where she met and fell in love with someone the family disapproved of."

"Because he was from Tennessee?"

"Being Appalachian was the least of it. Dad was brilliant and came from money himself, from the zinc mines and whiskey business, of course. But he was a wild man who lived life on the edge and could be very engaging when he wanted to be. I suppose the odd combination of a genius intellect coupled with a hard-drinking mountain-man persona was appealing to one of such British upbringing who spoke posh English."

"And the family didn't approve."

"Oh, not one bit. He didn't fit into the Gallinsworth social hierarchy very well and didn't care about pleasing them. In retrospect, I wish I'd spent more time in England with my family there."

"So, tell me more about my biological father."

"Surely you've heard about him from Jack and your mom."

"Of course, but you knew him longer than anyone."

"Well, he was very handsome, had a way with the ladies, and was tall, about six-two. He got my mom's looks and I got my dad's build, go figure." Wendy laughed. "You got his looks, too. You were a gorgeous little girl, even more so now."

"That is what I am told. We come in all shapes and sizes, so it is okay," she said seriously. "But would we have wanted a President who was a skinny supermodel?"

"Come on. Is that a serious question?"

She nodded. "Of course."

"Let me tell you, I wouldn't mind for a minute, even though I wouldn't have an Olympic gold medal if that had been the case."

"You have the height of one, at least. You have pretty skin and freckles and nice hair to spare, ye of great flair."

"Gee, thanks a lot. My gray hair gets a lot of help from synthetic dyes. Otherwise, I'm not so great."

"Sorry. I may seem to resemble you in certain ways, but in another I think I am very different. Sometimes I get this funny feeling about it, but I am who I am. You probably will not like it." She moved her head around as if looking about. "Not in this room, surely, it would not be proper to make such a declaration in the office of the head of the nation."

Wendy sat down and put her arm around her niece. "It's okay. I understand, and you can talk to me in here. I know your mom isn't the most perceptive person. Neither was either of your fathers."

"You *do?* But I do not think you will enjoy what I have to say. It concerns a fundamental, er—orientation I have, which is far different than yours."

Wendy put her arm around her. "Hey, it's fine. It can be hard to discuss, and we all had some questions about our 'orientation' at your age. I did a little bit of experimentation, too."

"You did? You did not always know about yours? Surprising."

"No—many teens don't. Don't try to think through everything all at once. Give it time."

"Whew. That's good. However, it is hard for me to imagine you that way. And I am the way I am; time shall never change it."

"You'll get it all sorted out. It's nearly the year 2029, and there's nothing wrong with being a lesbian, Paige. I have many friends, including three members of Congress, who are—"

Huh? A *what?*" She jumped up two feet and hovered in the air, trying to process what the President had just said, then floated back to the carpet.

"Um . . . I guess something came out wrong? Just speculating."

"No offense, Aunt Wendy, but we must be talking about two different things."

Wendy stood up and gave her a hug. "I'm very sorry if I misunderstood you, Paige, but I thought you meant your sexual orientation."

"Hey, an indestructible flying blind girl from North Pole may not get many offers for dates, but I do sort of have a boyfriend, and I am not—"

"Ohmigod, I am so embarrassed."

She smiled. "I am sorry, as I know you surely meant well. Of course there is nothing wrong with being a lesbian, were that my preference, but I am not, as I think guys are hot."

"Well, Aurora, the Roman goddess, did have a strong desire for men, so I guess your parents named you right."

"Yes, your passionate championing for gay, lesbian, and transgender rights is well known, but we still have not discussed our dire conflict, which will surely impact our relationship."

"Hmmm—your mom often had trouble getting to the point. I kind of feel some *deja vu* going on here; I'm just not getting it, so please help this old lady understand."

"I have a different type of inclination, which you will certainly think is bad; it will make you sad. The worst that could possibly be; soon you will see, and there will be no glee."

"I'm sorry, but I really don't follow. And there's nothing you could do that I would think is bad."

She frowned. "Oh, just wait before you decide that, as we will surely have a spat; I am, and shall forever be—a Democrat."

"What? A *Democrat?* Is *that* what all this discussion is about? Are you sure?"

"Yes, I am certain I am a donkey and not an elephant like you, and you would probably have preferred anything else to me being *that*. I certainly can act like an ass, especially in class."

"I don't think of myself as elephantine."

"I meant the Republican mascot, not you personally."

Wendy laughed. "Now, that's not true—that I would prefer one over the other, and I figured as much. I was just a little surprised about all the drama surrounding it like you were a mass murderer or something. You had me really worried."

"I assumed you would consider a Democrat roughly equivalent to a mass murderer."

"Don't take everything I say so literally. I can be quite the comedian, you know."

"You are too kind. But I was eighteen in October. Know that I share my mother's penchant for perfect honesty."

Wendy thought for a moment and laughed again. "Yes, of course—October twenty-third is your real birthday. So, you're trying to say that—"

She nodded. "Yes, I was old enough to vote on November 7, and, as the dedicated Democrat I am, I did not vote for you. I did not know you were my aunt then, though. I guess my vote was legal since I was eighteen. In the end, even Paige Marshall was not enough to swing Alaska's three electoral votes."

"One question: would your knowing I'm your aunt have made any difference?"

"Seriously?"

"Yes. The answer is important to me."

She chewed on her lip. "Well, then, the answer is *no*. I liked what Senator Saleh, the other candidate, had to say and thought she had some new ideas. I like the underdog, and you will find that I am quite opinionated."

"Huh. I guess that makes perfect sense, given who your parents are."

"And you are any different?"

She laughed. "No, and I would certainly want nothing different from you. I've taken a few knocks in my life, and I accept that as I do you, so we're good. I respect your integrity."

"It is not anything personal. We can still be friends."

She felt strong hands grab her. "You listen here, little girl. I'm far more than your friend—I'm your family. As long as I'm alive, don't you ever forget that. I don't care if you agree with my political views or not. You may be way stronger than me, but you can say anything to me anytime you want. How you voted in the 2028 election has nothing to do with it."

She laughed. "That is good, because it certainly will happen. Probably more often than you would like."

"Those will be interesting discussions, and I will look forward to them. But I've been around the block a few more times than the folks up in North Pole, so be ready."

"I want to make a big difference in the world. I will go to college, then law school. I will run for U.S. Representative when I am twenty-five. When I am thirty-five, I will be eligible to be President."

"Wow. Those are lofty expectations. Yet, know that you can go to school wherever you want. Georgetown is one of the best law schools in the country. Harvard and Yale may also be good choices. Being in a top ten law school is important."

"I think maybe I should graduate from high school first, then obtain an undergraduate degree. For that, I would have to take the SAT and get into some unsuspecting college."

"You seem to have the gift of gab and for writing. Both are important attributes for a boisterous, budding barrister."

"Lofty expectations? Funny to say from someone in your position." She began counting on her fingers. "Physician, Surgeon General, Olympian, Governor, President—"

"Wait a minute. I didn't become President until I was forty-eight. I did some eccentric stuff with my time, and was darn lucky."

"I would not call being shot and what happened to our family being lucky, although you are surely quite plucky."

"Regarding luck, I surely didn't mean anything to do with the explosion. I have been fortunate in other ways. But I also meant that I don't have the immense natural writing gifts you do."

"What do you mean? How do you know anything about my literary abilities?"

"I have the letter you wrote to me a couple of months ago, as well as the others."

"Really? I did not think you would have time to read the millions of letters you probably get; most are likely ones to forget."

"Yes, but Miranda scans and reads the physical letters and emails for me. She insisted I personally read this one and several others. That is rather rare, as she is pretty picky."

"Why? They were not in Braille. I wrote them all in longhand."

"I know. Miranda selected them because of your peculiar use of words, specifically rhyming, alliteration, and the avoidance of contractions, somewhat like your mother. Your peculiar usage of language is rather unique."

"I have been told that, and I guess that is one way we are similar, in contrast to the far greater number of ways in which we are not."

"And, of course, because she selects it based on content. I read it because it was a darn good essay for a masters' degree student, let alone a high school senior."

She shook her head. "Who is this Miranda you speak of with such reverence? Your secretary? How can she read all those letters? No one person has time to do that."

"No, she is *far* more than that, dear. More than human in some ways, less in others."

She shook her head. "I am afraid I do not understand, some concepts are above my pay grade of zero dollars per year."

"Miranda is an advanced holographic artificial intelligence quantum computer created by your mother and father when you were a small child, and she resembles my mother, Marianne Gallinsworth, as a young woman; she also speaks in a strong Upper Received Pronunciation accent, like my mom did."

"Ah, the speech of Old Country in southern England: of money, power, and influence. Kind of different from the way you talk."

"Yeah. My mom and I didn't quite match, either in looks or personality, other than our complexions. But your dad was quite the computer expert, like your adoptive father. Newer computers may have marginally greater processing power but not the sophisticated algorithms that Miranda uses. She can provide profound advice and updates on a variety of topics that she selects based on intelligence feeds and my preferences. My reading glasses and earpiece provide instant information on hundreds of informational items. It's how I stay on top of things. She's sort of my Chief of Staff."

"One who does not argue with you."

"On the contrary. Your mom and dad programmed her, so she can be quite obnoxious and confrontational."

"Ironic that an artificial intelligence programmed by my mother and father would help lead you to me."

"I suppose. I sort of knew you were around, anyway."

"Not to change the subject, but I could use some advice, and I just know what I want to do. Right now."

"Give yourself some time to develop some other skills. While you have great abilities, you lack experience, and—"

"What I also have is some advice for *you.*"

She laughed. "I didn't doubt you would, so go ahead."

"In particular, regarding the Seven Deadly Sins, you exhibit many of them: Greed and Pride. We maybe can cut Gluttony out, as you have reformed somewhat in that regard."

"Why, of course, Paige, I'm one of the most flawed people you could ever know, and I've never tried to hide it. Every person has faults, a dark side, and you can't get anywhere without that. Learn to channel it into something productive. Yes, I can be quite arrogant at times. There's no way to do this job another way. And I also have the humility of losing two of my children and nearly dying in an assassination attempt on President Reardon."

"You are saying you possess both arrogance and humility. The two qualities seem mutually exclusive."

"I don't believe so, you have a simplistic view of leadership. It is possible, almost necessary, for a good leader to have both. And remember you have faults as well, Paige. Arrogance is *not* an appealing attribute. Your mom, once the humblest of the humble, somewhere along the way acquired a massive ego and got worse as she got older. I can't imagine what she's like by now."

"Oh, I know that! She can be intolerable sometimes, but I am sure she often feels the same way about me. I was not criticizing you but merely comparing our similarities. Somehow, I sense that there is something—sinister inside me. Maybe you can help."

"Hey, don't I know it? My dad, your grandfather—was one of the most flawed people ever. But he gave his life to save mine. He had his demons. We all do. Including me, of course."

She shook her head. "I have heard about my infamous Grandpa Rad. Yes, he had human flaws and did some things that were not so good. But I do not think you know what I am talking about. Sometimes I feel that I could do something terrible had I the notion. And who would stop me?"

"I don't think we need to worry about that, do we?"

"You do not? And the entourage of military personnel at your side? I am sure they are quite concerned."

"I can't worry about what I can't control, honey. I learned that hard lesson decades ago."

"Mom and Jack had worries and said we had to hide. That people would come and find me, experiment on me and such."

"You know now that's never going to happen. Why come out of the closet now? I guess you have been around for a while, but—"

"The answer should be obvious. You will see me as an ally. While this information will not be made public, I do not think you will allow people to experiment with me. And I have matured much in the last two years. I can do almost anything."

"One query: don't you think you might've done more good as a secret force? Was putting your life in danger in that stupid suit your mom's idea, or your dad's? Probably both."

"No, my decision. They let me decide when I turned eighteen."

"I'm not buying that completely. With your visual impairment, there's no way you could've known about that suit without Petra or Jack telling you it existed, so they played a huge role in it."

"She was doing some experimentation to see if my sight could be restored, which led to other things, and the rest is history."

"That included the rescue of Alan Thomasson. You saved his life shortly after that."

"Yes. That was easier than I thought."

"And, before that—the three golf balls. What the heck was up with that?"

"I suppose that was rather absurd, a grandstanding stunt which was rather blunt."

"Well, it's just like your parents, believe me. And it caught my attention, for sure, and the attention of a lot of other people, some of whom were scared silly. It drove my scientists crazy, wondering how and why any being could throw a golf ball at such a velocity."

She yawned. "I know not of such scientific concepts. That activity was lamentable, yet I can be a symbol of good; I cannot do that as some secret strike force. Not unlike you. I do not want people to fear me. And as far as being in 'danger,' I am indestructible, as far as I know."

"People always fear what they can't understand. And everyone has a weakness. It's just that no one has discovered yours yet. Always keep your friends close and your enemies closer."

Which was the President? She wondered. No one got to her

position without being able to take advantage of situations; hopefully, their association would be mutually beneficial. If not, she was prepared to deal with that also.

• • •

"What's your father like, Paige?" Wendy asked as they sat down in the kitchen after dinner. "I would like to hear more about him."

"Pastor Jack?" She opened her mouth in astonishment. "I do not understand the purpose of your question. You knew him from way before I was born, so why are you asking me? Do you not remember such a character?"

Wendy laughed. "Of course, but he's surely a bit different now than before. He had a sarcastic sense of humor, and we argued a lot when he wasn't laughing at me. We didn't see eye to eye on most things and probably still don't."

"Why was that, do you think?"

"He, like many people, never took me seriously, as he considered me a perpetual source of entertainment, which I was, just by being me—not always by intention."

"Really? I do not think of you as being especially funny—no offense, I am just expressing my initial perception of you, and I do not know you that well. You seem friendly but rather serious and matter-of-fact."

She laughed again. "I was kind of a late bloomer. The serious person you perceive now was not always this way. I hit six feet by age twelve, was always rather overweight, and have a rather unique voice. I can go this low, 'you stupid, superfluous, sniveling, snake-like snail,'" she said in the perfect Southern Appalachian baritone voice of Metabolismo J. Ubiquitoid, Ph.D., the weight-challenged anthropomorphic feline who was one of her more famous cartoon characters from her early twenties. "He was an alliterate, too, just like you."

She burst into laughter and choked on her coffee, spewing it everywhere. "I remember that voice from reruns. It is so weird."

"Or, I can go this high. People usually forget my range and associate me with a contralto voice, but I usually sing mezzo-soprano and can sing in limited fashion even as a soprano," she said in her highest-pitched voice, a robust soubrette with a mid-range tessitura.

"I could never do that, as I have absolutely no musical talent."

"Most good singers can go two and a half octaves, maybe three. I can do four and do all the notes well. Your mom has the gift of absolute musical pitch but only a 1.5-octave vocal register. I also did Kadmium K. Katt and a bunch of others, but it was worth it to finally get a laugh out of you. Do you need a Heimlich maneuver?"

She wiped the coffee from her mouth. "I think I am okay—but please warn me when you are going to do that again."

"I sang and did a few CDs which you've probably heard and invariably laughed at, from pop songs to Christmas music. I had a pop one-hit-wonder in 1993 with British band G4, and I've sung the National Anthem at pro football games and other events, including the Super Bowl where Jay's Las Vegas Conquerors won their one championship. I also sang it on their opening game when your mom was pregnant with you. I sang the opening credits for a spy movie. I did stand-up comedy to entertain kids and adults when I wasn't working at the hospital and didn't really start getting my act together until I was made fun of on national television about my weight when I was Surgeon General at age forty."

"Yes, Will earlier told me your wiener-eating championship trophy is displayed prominently on your desk, an award surely quite statuesque."

"He told you that?"

"Yes. While I cannot see it, I am sure it is quite impressive."

She heard her walk over to the desk and return. "Well, here you go, Paige. Decide for yourself."

She felt the cheap plastic award and laughed. "It is no fitting tribute to your gastronomical gifts, which surely deserve better."

"Yes, it's just a crummy piece of junk."

"Then why is it in the Oval Office, of all places?"

"Because it was a turning point in my existence, and I likely wouldn't be here if not for that."

"Huh? I do not follow, as your logic is often hard to swallow."

"I always had lots of energy and only slept maybe three hours a night—we all know now why that was. They laughed at me on The Evening Show and said there was no way I could make the Olympics unless there was a hot dog eating contest, which my future coach also agreed with later. Which at that time was clearly true, even though I blew up, threw a cup of coffee at the wall, and stormed off. Ten minutes later, I got a phone call that changed my life."

"From whom? The President?"

She laughed. "No, *that* call came the next day. Rest assured, he was not pleased—either by my foray into competitive eating or my behavior on television. But the first call was from your father, of all people. All he said was, 'meet me at your apartment tomorrow evening at seven. We're going to kick some ass.' Then he hung up."

"Meaning what? He was going to beat up the guys who laughed at you?"

"I had no idea, as he'd never been terribly interested in my athletic career or much of anything I was doing; but he also didn't like me being ridiculed unless he was the one doing it. He wasn't an expert in track and field. And, no, he wasn't going to use his fists; he could be a tough guy, but he basically was a lover, not a fighter."

"So was he there the next evening?"

"Yeah. He laid out his master plan—said he was going to help me train, to show them who the real fools were. He was on a big wellness kick, was in excellent shape, and was the only person who could push me to the limit without me getting mad. I was in such pathetic condition my old coaches wouldn't have wanted anything to do with me. Your mom was extremely busy at that time, and I wouldn't have listened to her anyway because she's very impatient. As great a natural athlete as she was, she would've been a terrible coach at anything, as you need to have an understanding of human behavior. It's ironic she's now a high school teacher."

"I had been told a little bit of this by Janaki when we met in Aurora City recently."

"I wasn't aware you had met Jan. You told her everything?"

"Well, she had figured most of it out already, as she is pretty shrewd. She told me to work on my body language, as blind people are apparently not very good at that. But, she did not tell me the details of your transformation. My biological dad helped you get into shape?"

"Yeah. By doing cardio, something I was always bad at. And he did it by teaching me how to box."

"I cannot imagine you being a very good boxer; you are far too slow, although you could likely take a good blow."

"That was the whole point. Besides being excellent at burning weight off, it helped my speed and coordination because that's what I needed at that time."

"That makes no sense, as shot put is a power sport."

"You might think that, but he was right. He worked my butt off ,and I lost about sixty pounds in two months."

"How did you manage that with your job and family?"

"The job was fairly understanding, as it promoted physical fitness and America. I still did all my work, and we trained in the early morning and in the evening. And if they didn't let me, they knew I'd quit and join Great Britain's team."

"You really would have done that?"

"Absolutely, although I probably would've never been elected President had I gone through with it. But my family wasn't so understanding; Stan viewed it as another Darkkin obsession, which it essentially was."

"But it was important."

"Was it? For whom? Paige, please listen to me: my life has been full of things that were so very 'important.' *Science Squad* action figures, vitamins, and lunchboxes were 'important,' but also a colossal waste of time and money. Then came all the magic shows I did with your mom. Maybe that entertained some people, but I see little lasting value from that. I'm sure becoming a minor celebrity helped accelerate her gambling addiction. Then, the Olympics.

"More stuff later, like being Governor and President, which I guess were somewhat valuable. Most of all, I think of all those hours I could have spent with Jake and Cassie, and I always thought I'd get the time back. I didn't. Our marriage didn't survive it, Paige. For all the accolades I've received, remember all things have a cost, and everything in life is a compromise. I can't get any of that time back now. I don't regret what I can't change, but always remember that you have to make choices in life."

"I am so sorry."

"I know you are, but I can't change it now. Those things have changed me, as I'm sure Jim's life has changed him. My perception of him, and his of me, is likely far different than yours."

"Jack does not speak of you much. He believes in God first and foremost. Me, I am not quite sure about that stuff; sometimes it seems like just a bunch of fluff."

"Okay, now *that's* far different from the person I knew then, so that's why I asked. He used to talk about how it was impossible for God to even exist in a world which we try to explain by science. I guess life changes a person. It certainly has changed mine."

"There is much I do not know about Jack."

"Your mother, however, was always a very spiritual person."

She laughed. "Sure, she claims to be, but you do not think it is just an act, or is that really an actual fact?"

"No way. You would expect her not to believe, given that she is a woman of science and all who demands proof of things in order for them to exist, but she always stated the natural state of the world was to be in a state of extremely high entropy and disorganization, and there is no way life could have evolved on Earth into such a magnificent form without God."

"What about you?"

"Me?"

"Do you believe in God?"

"I didn't believe at one point. My early life wasn't the greatest, and I used to think it was a bunch of bunk. My mom was a Christian, but my dad was probably an atheist. But I've been through some hard times lately, almost dying myself and seeing my family disappear, so I became very spiritual after that."

"Just like Jack, I guess. A guiding light who always tried to give me good advice." She took a sip of juice. "He is kind of the forgotten man in the history books, but one of the most important. How long ago did you know him?"

"He and your dad were best friends, and they were both two years older than me. He brought Jim home from college many times when I was still in high school, so I would've been sixteen when I first met him. Forty years ago. You also know, of course, that I was best friends with your mother."

"I know that from history class, but it's rather hard to believe. I *still* find it hard to grasp that she was really Bonnie Mendoza."

"You said 'was,' in the past tense. She's still alive, of course."

"Weird how we are talking about her and Jack, as they do not even exist, what a twist." She shook her head. "Bonnie does not; that person no longer exists. Mom seems quite intelligent on theoretical matters but unfocused and rather bizarre. She rants and raves about various trivial things which bore me to tears. Not befitting one of the most storied theoretical physicists in modern human history, whose brief career was cut short by, you know. And, you are right about the arrogance. She has that in spades and often goes into melodramatic tirades."

Wendy laughed. "I don't mean to burst your bubble or show disrespect to your mom, who is really a wonderful person under her obnoxious exterior, but she doesn't seem to have changed much at all."

"What? But the historical documents depict—"

"They are painting your dear mother in a most favorable light, as she deserved in 'death.' I suppose I had as big a hand in that as any. She was, among other things, an excellent magician—good at fooling people—that metaphor extended into her real life, as the 'superwoman' image we built up never reflected the truth: that she barely could master basic activities of daily living. She was a multi-millionaire by age twenty-two, at which time they threw her out of the casinos permanently after they figured her out; she was good at playing the sad deaf girl and gaining sympathy, because she could be very conniving, but you can't fool those people forever.

"And yet, she could barely shop for her own groceries without getting lost. She had no idea how much anything cost and was a disaster at managing money. We had to give her an 'allowance' while my husband Stan managed her accounts. What good would it have done to tell the world about her fallacies? We all have them, me probably most of all." She felt Wendy's hand touch her face. "I loved your mother like a sister from the time I met her in San Diego at eighteen—your age. When she married my brother at age thirty, she finally became one. I hope that I played some role in her successes, her desire to excel. But she always needed some guidance from others. Just like you will need."

She pulled her hand away. "I do not have the same problems, so why do I need that?"

"No, but you have others, such as a disability that impairs your functioning, obviously. It's hard to do the things you do without sight. You must surely agree."

"Maybe, but I do not plan on doing this forever. I want to go to college and law school and then make a difference in the world, as you do."

"Huh. Not much career counseling available for that, but it's kind of hard to be a superhero and retire in your teens or twenties. I hope you've thought this through because I won't be President then. Not that you need my help. You've done pretty well on your own, it appears."

"I guess I wanted to grow up so rapidly; that was a poor choice.

Life is more complex than I had envisioned. Life in North Pole does not make one terribly worldly."

"You shouldn't worry about making decisions, but the consequences of yours may have more impact on society than those of most teenagers."

"I guess so. Being a teen is hard enough. Being a teen like me, that is indescribable."

"Yep. But no one gets anywhere without the help of others. I certainly didn't. Just remember that pain can make you stronger. I wish every day *Darkkday* didn't happen, but it did, and all the wishing in the world won't make that go away. That, plus the assassination attempt on Reardon made me strong beyond comprehension. I wanted to kill myself after I lost Jake and Cassie, and I have to believe God kept me from doing so. Jay was a very unreliable person for most of his life, but after that day he was always there for me. So trust me when I say you need to rely on others, sighted or not, even those you thought would be gone forever."

"And if I don't want to do that?"

Wendy slurped her coffee. "Then you will have a very lonely existence, trust me on that one. Accept help from others, and return the favor when you can. because we all need each other."

She strummed her fingers on the table nervously. "Aunt Wendy, I need to discuss a rather delicate concept—"

"What? You sound like you're afraid to tell me something. Again. Don't ever feel that way."

"Well, the reason is because there is one other thing you should know. For some reason, my mom does not paint a very warm and fuzzy picture of you."

"She doesn't like me, eh?"

"Not so much, no; hopefully, that is not a blow to your ego."

"What a surprise."

"Me, I cannot see it at all. You seem to be a pretty normal, nice, albeit loud and intense, person. Softer than I expected, not the terrible subhuman primate she describes."

"Well, I'm far from normal. And many have described me 'terrible' on occasion." Wendy laughed. "But I wish I knew w•hy that was with her. We used to have some minor arguments in the early days like most friends do, but nothing big. She always did have a short fuse. I have to think part of it was an act, to throw you off, so you didn't suspect that we were related."

She shook her head. "You must know her better than that. Mom does not have that kind of flexibility in her social repertoire. Despite her intellect, she cannot think on her feet. She is who she is—very opinionated and a very poor liar, despite apparently being an exceptional magician and poker player. No, she genuinely shows disdain for you, I am sorry. One thing she is good at is telling the truth about what she thinks."

"I suppose you're right. But our philosophies digressed as we got older, and we grew further apart. I hope that some day we can come to terms with it and rectify the problem. I don't know if I'll ever see her again, but I hope so."

"Tell me more about my biological father."

"I was wondering when you would ask about him. Alex, or Dirk, as his family called him."

"Why did they call him that?"

"It was his middle name; he was named after our grandfather Dirk Thaddeus Darkkin, who started the distillery business. Later on, he didn't like to be reminded of that, given his alcohol problems."

"I did not know that."

"About his alcoholism? He finally overcame it, and I'm sure discovering your mom was part of how he stayed sober."

"Did you ever drink?"

"Nope. Two alcoholics in the immediate family was enough, and I didn't need a social lubricant as I was pretty chatty to begin with. I was addicted to other things like food. I don't think alcohol and I would have mixed very well."

"But I would like to know about him when he was younger."

"Well, he was two years older than me. He always looked out for me when we were kids and was intolerant of anyone picking on me, although from age ten to thirteen I was actually bigger than him, since I got my growth spurt early. And I was stronger, too, until he was about fifteen."

"Really?"

"Yeah. We also argued sometimes, as most siblings do, and one day I found him melting cerrobend alloy in a coffee can."

"Cerrobend alloy? What the heck is that?"

"It's a dense eutectic alloy made of bismuth, lead, tin, and cadmium, which melts at a low temperature."

"You sound like an Appalachian version of my mom."

"I don't know whether to take that as a compliment or not."

"It was, in a geeky way." She shook her head and laughed. "I told you I know very little about chemistry. What happened?"

"He melted that stuff, which my dad always had lying around, and dropped my dolls into it, which reduced them to molten plastic."

"I bet you were not happy."

"I wasn't. I found out what he was doing, and I knocked him around good."

"But he was two years older than you."

"Not a problem. As I said, by age ten, I could kick his butt good if I could catch him, that is; my main liability was that I wasn't very fast. Dad asked him where he got the black eye; he was too ashamed to say he got it from his little sister, so he made up some lame story about getting into a fight at school. Dad would never have let him live that down."

She laughed. "That's funny. I wish I had a brother. I feel badly for Bella, too, losing Jose."

"Well, you have Will. He looks up to you, you know. He's also pretty close to a brother."

"He is?"

"Of course, he's your double cousin, the same genetically as a half-brother."

"I guess I never thought much about it, mainly because I have not known about it for very long. Anyway, what was my dad like as a teenager?"

"Well, unlike me, he was very good-looking; he took after my mom in that aspect. He was quite popular with the girls and fancied himself as quite a swinger. He was a decent athlete, although he never worked very hard at it. He was very bright, a much better natural student than me."

"I do not believe that. You seem extremely intelligent, much more so than I had imagined."

"Really?"

"Yes. No offense, but my mom says you are a hillbilly dullard."

"Ha. The IQ tests say I'm pretty bright, but I have a relatively short attention span and tend to bounce around all over the place. You probably know why that is. I wasn't aware until I was in my mid-thirties, and I can focus much better now, but I still have my moments. Like fine wine, I get better with age, I guess."

"Yeah, I can sometimes see the genie almost coming out of the bottle, and I have not known you very long."

"Sometimes the genie definitely gets out, but Will, Jay, Jackie, and my other staff make sure people don't see that. It allows me incredible bursts of creative energy. Use the gifts you have to your advantage, Paige. No one has it all, not even you."

She sighed. "Yes, but, about my dad—"

"Sorry. Sometimes he didn't work all that hard. He graduated and went to Vanderbilt, which is in Nashville, not that far away from Oak Ridge. Vandy is where he met Jim—Jack—and I met him when he brought him home for some weekends. He was equally as irritating as your dad. After that, he went to Stanford for medical school, where he graduated very high in his class. So, we were both on the West Coast for several years, although he was in the Bay area and I in San Diego."

"What happened then? I know history pretty well, but I am sure the books left out some details."

"Rad the Dad and I didn't get along too well, as you can imagine. I won't go into that now, but after I won the state shot put championship, I won a full-ride scholarship to San Diego State, which was about as far away as I could get from Tennessee, my primary intent. I also changed my name from Darkkin to Gallinsworth—my mother's name—when I turned eighteen."

"I guess I know that, but why?"

"I was ashamed of my dad and didn't like him very much because of the way he treated my mom. I was mad at her too for taking it from him all those years, and later saying she was doing it for her kids, although I had no choice in the matter.

"Alex and I kind of drifted apart, as I rarely came back home to Tennessee because of the bad memories. I tried to build a life here. I wanted to be a physician, and I wanted to help kids, so I volunteered at a children's rehab center during my freshman year at San Diego State, which was where I met your mom when I was your age, eighteen."

"Yes. I understand you knew both American Sign Language and Spanish, so your skill set makes sense."

"Right. But your mom and dad met in San Diego many years later. He came to my hospital to do some temporary work for a colleague on sabbatical, and it was the unlikeliest romance I could have ever imagined. The two of them didn't really hit it off at first, and in fact argued a lot because they were both so obnoxious. I guess, in many ways, they were alike."

"It is conceptually challenging to imagine how two such intellectually gifted individuals could have produced me."

"What do you mean, dear? You're quite intelligent and very obnoxious. I would have predicted nothing different."

"Thanks a lot." She laughed. "I barely make it through my mom's math class. I do not know much about science."

"Intelligence comes in many forms. You are quite gifted with words and pretty good at making an argument, despite your inexperience. You have the capability of great creativity and abstract thought, which your mom has at times, but paradoxically lacks at others. It's not important that you necessarily understand the science behind your abilities. Maybe no one else does. But I can tell you that, right now at age eighteen, you possess a greater maturity and awareness of the world than I or your parents ever did. In case you didn't know, your future isn't in science or math. It's to change the world."

• • •

She heard the knock at her bedroom door around eight-thirty PM. "Come in."

"It's me," her uncle said. "May I enter?"

"Huh, of course, it is your house."

"Hmmm, technically not. Last I heard, it belonged to the people, I am a mere guest."

"Huh, no way. If historical memory serves, the wife of a knight is addressed as 'Lady.' Do you have a similar title of nobility?"

"Wow, I neither thought nor cared much about that, but I'm sure there's someone in this building who knows the answer."

She walked towards him and spread her arms wide. "Which room is this, anyway? I forgot to ask."

"It's the Lincoln Bedroom."

"President and Mrs. Lincoln slept here?"

"That's correct."

She laughed. "Wow. But I doubt this house is part mine, the way I voted in the last election."

"No problem. You are certainly an American, though, and I am decidedly non-partisan."

"Really?"

"Yeah. I don't care a lot about politics. And families can survive a lot, even this." She heard him sit on the edge of the bed. "I know you've been talking to Will and Wendy a lot, so I haven't had much time to be with you."

"Makes sense. I get it."

"I kind of function as the reactor control rod in this place when everyone else goes bonkers. That happens a lot in this family, although Will is the real adult around here. It's good to have his guidance and immense life experience to draw upon."

She laughed again. "I appreciate it, Uncle Jay. I knew we would have some time to talk later."

"Your mom and I were very close, despite our eight-year age difference. Closer than we were to our other brother."

"Bella's father—what was he like?"

"Miguel, or Mike, as we called him, was the All-American guy, was friends with everyone, worked hard; he wasn't nearly as smart as your mom, but got his bachelor's and master's degrees with honors. He was the one who followed our dad into law enforcement, of course, and made lieutenant in record time, and was a captain at the time of his death. He was the one who provided stabilization to me, Bonnie, and our mom, as the three of us had our heads in the clouds most of the time. He would have been almost exactly the same age as Wendy now; their birthdays were only a month apart."

"You do not seem to have much in common with my mom. I mean that as a compliment."

"You'd be very wrong as, besides our mom—Elisa—I was probably the person in our family most like her if you can believe that. We had a lot of fights."

"You did?"

"Yeah. When she was three, and I was eleven, we were at about the same mental age and maturity level. It was all downhill for me after that."

She shook her head. "You two do not seem very much alike at all. I cannot believe you had much in common except what typical siblings do. Maybe less so."

"Not much in common on the surface—but we both kind of see the world in a different way. Same with our mom. Not like Mike, who was a practical sort."

"So many memories—I wish she had spoken of them more."

"She was trying to protect you, Paige, you know that. But she's not dead, you know, and she can share those memories of you now. It's really weird, talking about her like that."

"I am sure she would want to see you, and vice versa. But I do not know how that would be possible right now."

"Yeah. When Will came up to see you in Alaska, I wanted so much to see and talk to you and your mom. I'm surprised she didn't detect my presence."

"Maybe she did and chose not to say anything. I think she has probably changed a bit since then."

"Of course, but I realize things can't be the same. What she did, she did for a reason. I still remember the day Jackie came in to tell me about *Darkkday*, when we thought you all had died."

She touched his arm. "I know. Wendy said perhaps I should not touch you because it might be uncomfortable for both of us."

"Yes. Your mom and I could communicate, almost telepathically, before she lost her hearing at age eleven. After *Darkkday* I began seeing her again, hearing her voice. And living through you. Believe it or not, it's a relief to know I wasn't going crazy, having all those nightmares about flying faster than sound and everything; now I know why—especially hearing the Russian. It was you speaking it, of course. As far as I know, Bonnie can't fly."

She laughed. "Yeah, the dumb thing only worked in that language. I get it now because a Russian guy invented it." She touched his face. "I do not feel anything different now than before I touched you, so whatever 'link' you had with my mom does not appear to exist with me, and such dreams must have been facilitated by you in some manner, if only unconsciously. Despite my other abilities, I feel I am just an average girl with regards to intellect and sensory perception. I do not have any unique skills there."

"Paige, Will told me you are a 'B+' student in calculus. I barely made it through basic high school math and science; I wouldn't have even done that if your mom hadn't helped me."

"Did you work hard at it?

"Huh? No, not so much. I was pretty lazy, if you must know, which made her, Mike, and my parents really mad. If I had put my mind to it, maybe it would've been different, but probably not a lot. I was the extravert in the family and had other ideas about my activities, most of which involved people with two X chromosomes."

"You did okay, I must say, Jay."

"I suppose, with some help, of course. But several of us have special abilities."

"*Abilities?* What do you mean?"

"Surely you know your mom is different. She has what's called an autism spectrum disorder, with primary manifestations of a high-level synesthete. She smells colors, hears sounds, etc. Surely you have noticed that."

"Of course, I am aware of that and her many eccentricities. She can be very irritating at times, but also profoundly wise on occasion while being a child at heart, but at times she does not seem very smart."

"You're a part of that, too, like me. Maybe not the math abilities, but you talk eerily like her, you know. Most of her life she talked with that lispy deaf speech, and you don't have that, of course, but otherwise, it's uncanny—the high-level vocabulary, the formal speech with avoidance of contractions, and so on, but she did use them some; you never seem to, from my brief experience with you today. The rhyming and alliteration seem to be unique to you, however."

"Yes. She does not talk with the lispy speech any longer but often talks with a Central Russian accent, but other times does not. I am familiar with how she used to talk from the historical records."

"And you never suspected for a moment? Surely the vocal pitch was the same."

"What, that my mom is Bonnie Mendoza? Not for one second could I have believed that. Mom acts almost crazy sometimes, gets obsessed about stupid things, and often doesn't have a lot of sense. That doesn't sound like the great Nobel Laureate of history."

"Yeah, well, let me tell you, it's exactly like Bonnie. What you know from the historical records is not, well, entirely accurate. She was far more flawed than what is depicted in the media."

"I have been told that before. Mom said once that Wendy lied by not depicting Bonnie in an entirely realistic light in the biography she wrote, although Bella's movie was a bit closer to the real truth. Why was that done?"

"I wouldn't call it lying, Paige, but more of telling the story in a kinder, gentler way. It wasn't just Wendy, but me too. Most thought she was dead and wanted her to be remembered in the best way possible. Aurora, too."

"I guess so. Maybe the world was not ready for the real Bonnie."

"Also, I have limited precognitive abilities and can almost sense things a split-second before they happen. My mom, Elisa—your grandmother—was also a talented mathematician. My grandmother Gabriela was a wonderful musician and singer; she could play instruments and sing music she'd never seen before. And you've spent some time with Bella, obviously, who most people grossly underestimate because of her beauty and smart-aleck attitude. They think someone who looks and acts like a shallow airhead can't be very bright."

"Sure, she must be intelligent, having a doctorate in engineering, and she is very colorful, to say the least—but what can *she* do?"

"Hers is one of the most unusual abilities, which is why no one ever thought anything about it. While her IQ isn't genius caliber, she has the uncanny power of parsimony."

"Parsimony? The concept of simplicity?" She laughed for about fifteen seconds and choked. "I am sorry, but Bella hardly seems to be a simple person with simple tastes. I have experienced her credit cards in action."

"Don't underestimate her. Most people do, and that's her advantage. There are very few people with the skill and tenacity to take on Wendy and survive, but she's one of them. She has the ability to see any problem in its simplest form and solve it in the shortest time possible." He tapped her on the head. "Your visor—who besides Bella could've figured out that you're on sensory overload all the time, with your eyes basically shutting down, and that your vision can be restored with a piece of sapphire? That's pretty simple, yet neither your mom, nor Jim, or the rest of the, ahem—*Science Squad*, had thought of it."

"I suppose so. I am grateful."

"Parsimony abilities are extraordinarily rare, but she built an empire with them. Without Bella, we might not even be in the White House. Maybe that would be a good thing."

"Money is important, but it cannot buy everything."

"No, but it buys a lot. I hear you want to accomplish great things. To do that, you need some money, don't think you don't."

She shook her head. "I suppose I should start figuring out what it is I do want to accomplish. I haven't worked out the details yet."

Chapter Forty-Five

The Talia Show
WBS Network Studios
New York City

It was inevitable that the topic of the world's most famous teenager would make headlines on national media, and Talia Johnson spoke up on the set of her New York City talk show.

"So, you have made your opinions on *Stella Scura* quite clear," five-ten brunette media personality Talia said snidely.

Mallory Turner, the famous former attorney and current liberal political consultant for American News Network, spoke up, as she was prone to doing rather spontaneously.

"Yes. I know everyone thinks she's the greatest thing since sliced bread. But I happen to disagree, which I am still allowed to do in America. First of all, why do we need someone like that?"

"I don't follow. She sort of just showed up, and no one could've anticipated her arrival. Why do we 'need' many pivotal figures in human history? I'm no philosopher, Mallory, just a reporter."

"Don't you think someone needs to be? Who is she? Where's she from? Does anyone care? Why did she show up now? Is she an alien? If so, is she harboring other aliens or pathogens that could kill us all? Would our pathogens harm her?"

The tall blonde talk show host shook her head. "No one knows all that for sure."

"Correct, Talia: all questions for which no one has answers, and no one seems to give a damn, which is even worse. We have, within a matter of weeks, converted the most powerful potential destructive force ever known to man into a teenage rock star. Those are the things that bother me, Talia, not the mere fact of her existence. In our society, it's not surprising we would hold someone like that up like she's the Second Coming or something."

"Listen, POTUS claims to have proof she is a natural-born American citizen."

Mallory laughed. "And you take Wendy Mendoza at her word? Just like that? What is this proof? And, even if it's true, so what? How does that fact mitigate the possibility that she could wipe us all off the face of the Earth?"

She nodded. "I have no reason not to trust her. You may not like her politics, Mallory, but she's always been a straight shooter."

"Yes, for things you actually know about, but she is also one of the biggest media manipulators of all time. What else is she going to say in the face of this? She stole the moon from the rest of the world so her famous niece could mine helium-3 on the far side and get filthy rich, when it was supposed to belong to all mankind. Where's the ethics in that? Am I the only one here who thinks this is a crappy idea?"

"You deny that mendozium energy technology hasn't helped this world? Come on. We were headed towards a global warming catastrophe, and M2 has also created technology to extract carbon dioxide from the atmosphere. Greenhouse gases are at 1980s levels, Mallory. Give those women some credit."

"Yes, it has reduced fossil fuel emissions and repaired most of the atmosphere, I must admit. That doesn't make how it was accomplished legit."

"It should, as no one else was figuring it out. Congress even approved Luna as a state."

"A Republican Congress, no less. What else would they do?"

"There are those who would disagree with you; nationalization of the Moon was the only logical way to mine its vast resources. Trillions of dollars went into that enterprise."

"And quadrillions came out of it. That's a bunch of bull crap, and you know it."

"I disagree. But let's put Luna and money aside; I think we should be very glad this young lady is on America's side."

"Really? What evidence is there to suggest that is truly the case? And since when does America need more power? This young woman clearly manipulates fundamental physical forces in a way no one really understands."

"You don't know that, Talia, and you're no scientist."

"No, I'm not, but I've seen science go awry. I would imagine the things she does require a lot of energy, but that's just me. Is it safe? What is her effect on other living beings?"

"Yes, those are valid concerns, but tests show—"

Mallory shook her head. "No, please don't start on how the President, *Photraman,* Bella, *Tinman,* and *Gravi-Golfer* all declare she's safe. Are these unbiased, credible sources? That's like cigarette ads in the 40s and 50s where doctors said smoking was healthy—pure propaganda. Wendy's freaking dad was Rad Darkkin, for God's sake, a prominent Cold War nuclear weapons creator. And suppose all of what you say is true—the President is being honest, *Stella* is a great person, born in the USA, all that, and life is great, for now. But what if she's also a Typhoid Mary, the carrier of some horrific infectious organism that could end mankind? Or she accidentally loses control of her powers and blows us all up like a thousand Tsar Bombas all going off at once?"

Talia shook her head and laughed as she took a sip of coffee.

"There's no evidence that could happen; you're embellishing, as usual."

"Really? Well, then, what happens someday if this person has enemies who are just like her and they come calling to settle a beef? Can you imagine several of those folks out there duking it out in one of our major cities with no way to stop them?"

"There is also no proof there are any other beings like this out there. Why would you think that?"

"That's an absurd statement, Talia, and you've been drinking the Wendy Kool-Aid of misinformation way too long. This girl looks to be eighteen or nineteen."

Talia nodded. "Possibly, but what's your point?"

"My point is that she's obviously been around for a while, and nobody knew about it, or nobody shared that info—so there could certainly be others out there." She shook her head. "Doesn't the mere existence of this person scare anyone? We don't need whatever problems she could be bringing our way. Soon, the novelty will wear off. People will look to her to solve their problems instead of doing it themselves. First, it'll be big things but will eventually become trivial tasks that they could take care of on their own, as laziness is human nature. Maybe there are some things only she can do, but again, I say: do we really need someone like that?"

"Neither of us are philosophers, but she exists, and there's nothing we can do about that. Maybe her best destiny is to serve as a symbol of sorts. What is it you want her to do, and where do you want her to go?"

"Like a lot of things, that's not my problem, and there are far bigger issues at play. But, hey, let's assume again she is a benevolent force and doesn't accidentally destroy us all. When we put faith in any one person, we become dependent on her; then what happens when she's gone one day? Teenagers have a short attention span, so suppose she gets bored with saving the world? Talia, we are setting ourselves up to fail. Look, I have nothing against this person, alien or not. I am sure she is nice and wholesome and all that. I just can't make a case that this world is better with the incredible *Stella Scura* than without her."

"What do you propose, then?"

"I would like answers to simple questions, such as: who is she? Why does she hide behind that visor? We know virtually nothing about this person, yet everyone thinks she's great. We all know who's behind that: one of the finest Chief Executives to ever manipulate the media, and The Great Dame has sure done it here."

"Would you rather the people be out in the streets panicking in fear because a being like this exists?"

"Maybe. At least then we might be prepared for what could be coming. I don't know when that will be—next year, ten years, a hundred years from now."

"Yes, that sure makes a lot of sense. You can't ever agree with the President who freed hundreds of millions of people from the oppression of dictatorship. Would you rather *Stella* be out there secretly doing things, Mallory? At least she's out there in the open."

"I just want the truth, Talia; is that too much to ask? Doing some good deeds entitles Wendy Mendoza to do whatever she wants? You can't deny there are things being hidden from us. We don't know who else is out there, either."

"What do you want this *Stella* to do, then? It's not really her fault she's here. Do you want her to just go live in some remote part of the world and leave us alone?"

"She did it for at least eighteen years. She can do it again and still have a worthwhile life. She could be doing all these things in secret or at least with a little less fanfare, as she seems like a typical attention-seeking teenager."

"Perhaps she can't do them in clandestine fashion. There seemed to be only one way of rescuing Air Force One in Aurora City. Maybe she also wants to raise money for charity. I, for one, don't see anything wrong with that."

"A lot of people raise money for charity who aren't superhumans, Talia."

"I guess we will have to disagree on many things here, Mallory. That's what makes America great."

"I just hope it's still around in a couple of years. It's time for a reality check of what's really going on." Mallory looked at the teleprompter. "Hey, it's time to take some questions from callers, Talia. The board's lighting up with questions."

Chapter Forty-Six

Paige sat down to breakfast in the White House dining room as she smelled that one of the servers placed bacon and scrambled eggs in front of her and poured coffee.

"Will you spend Thanksgiving with us, Paige?" Wendy asked. "Only a few more days to go."

"I had contemplated going back to Alaska. Yet, the degree to which I am still welcome there is largely unknown." She hadn't thought about that. "But perhaps I will, on one condition."

"Okay, shoot."

She laughed. "Be careful before you agree; you may not sing with glee, Aunt Wendy."

"Well, whatever it is should be fine."

"I will stay if we do an activity of my choosing. Are you okay with that?"

"Sure, we can do anything you want. If you even want a football game on the White House lawn, that's cool. I don't think the cold bothers you."

She shook her head. "While I enjoy fun, I desire nothing so trivial. I am certain that there will be a lavish meal prepared by the White House staff."

"But of course. The Presidential Thanksgiving dinner is truly something. If that's what you want, it's already done."

She shook her head. "I am certain that means much to you. I intend no offense to your traditions or those of the Presidency, but material things mean little to me. If you want to give something, give an item of true value. Something money cannot buy."

"I'm sorry, I'm not following you."

"Give the gift of your time to others less fortunate. Honor my request to travel to a homeless shelter; the funds that would have been spent on a holiday dinner can be used for those who have nothing. You, Jay, Will, Jackie, and I shall go there and spend the day serving food to those who have much less than we."

"Serve at a shelter? Why, sure, I have plenty of staff, and they would be happy to do something like that—"

"No, no, no." She grabbed Wendy's arm. "I did not say the 'staff,' I said you and me and the rest of us. This is not something you can delegate to your minions with a snap of your fingers."

"That's an interesting idea, Paige, but hardly practical. It takes weeks for the Secret Service to plan events like that out from a security standpoint. Jackie will have a fit."

"Then Jackie will have to get over it. Somehow, I think you'll survive." She laughed. "In case you don't remember, I doubt we shall be in any danger."

"But you want the First Family to spend Thanksgiving doing *that?*"

She sat up and puffed out her chest. "Why? Are you too good for something so humble? Not enough press coverage for you? Jay will miss the crummy football games? I know there was a time in your life you would have done so without hesitation or went on mission trips to Honduras or Guatemala."

"Huh, you're really serious, aren't you?"

"You should know the answer to that. If you want to spend time with me, this is who and what I am. Realize I am not easily persuaded otherwise; I will not put on a guise."

Wendy paused for a half minute. "You share one quality of your mom, that's for certain."

"What is that?"

"Her stubbornness."

She nodded. "Agreed. Most would also lump you into that category, too, from what I have observed."

"I guess you're right, as it takes one to know one. I could set a better example. And the publicity alone will be—"

She shook her head and frowned. "Stop it, remember that this is not about *you.* Or publicity. It is about helping others. No newspapers, no television, no Bipper, Digigram, Tekvids, or any other social media. If something gets out, which will probably happen, no one can help that, but do not make promoting this a priority. What would you have possibly to gain by that, and what else do you need to prove? Do you need more publicity?"

"I suppose not, dear. Point well taken."

• • •

They rode in a discreet vehicle to the selected food shelter, not in the usual electric-powered Cadillac One, although the Secret Service vehicles were still present in front and back, Will had said.

"I hope the press doesn't follow us," Wendy said.

"Probably not," Jay said. "We lead kind of a boring life. On the other hand, you're a pretty popular figure."

"You've done your share of charity, I know," Wendy said to her. "I really do admire that."

"How do you know those things?"

"I know lots of stuff about you and have for years."

"You mean you were spying on me?"

"Protecting you is more like it. You should be thanking me."

"Huh. I do not need any protection."

"Oh, yeah, you need it, trust me. Let's discuss one of your more famous capers: you were arrested for setting up a hot food station for homeless Anchorage people in a public park, you and two classmates, in defiance of multiple local ordinances. That was pretty bold. I was impressed that you were able to organize all that."

"You know all that?"

"Of course I do, don't be a dummy."

"Well," She sighed and pointed her finger at her aunt. "They said we needed a permit, and it was illegal to do that in a public place, what a disgrace. Busted for feeding a bunch of poor hungry people. We did not charge them or anything, so I did not see the big deal. We would have cleaned up afterward."

"Was it your idea?"

"Of course it was," she said proudly. "I am quite the mastermind and got trucks and stuff to drive us down there. I just needed the others' help to get set up. Kind of hard to do on my own."

"I figured so. It sounds like you."

"My dad was furious that I had been arrested; the judge was

very embarrassed the top cops had arrested a blind girl, and they dropped everything and let us go with just a warning, and there was no mourning."

"Did you give the police a hard time when they arrested you?" Wendy asked.

"Yeah, Paige, you should have kicked their butts," Will said loudly. "That's what I would have done. Those dudes would've sure been sorry they laid a hand on me, as they'd be flying all over the place."

She sneered at him. "No, I did not, William, how juvenile. That is why you are not me. I am no colorful combatant but rather your mother's niece of peace."

Will laughed hysterically. "*Niece of peace?* That's just too funny, your choice of words sometimes. They either rhyme or are alliterative. Weird."

"It is in my genes, sonny, it ain't funny. But I raised some public awareness that way, I must say."

"Did they take your mug shot?" he asked snidely.

She yawned. "Yes, of course they took my 'mug shot,' that is what happens when you get arrested, dummy: you get a booking photo taken. Not that I would know what it looks like."

"Trust me that it isn't terribly attractive," Wendy said.

"I wouldn't know about any of that, Paige," Will said. "I've never been inside a jail. Don't plan on it, either."

"Hey, your life is not over yet, boy, your mom you will invariably annoy. It is not as bad as you would think, I will not embellish on my experiences in the big house. Food choices are not great, you get your pick of a bologna or peanut butter sandwich."

"Did they fingerprint you after the mug shot?"

She snarled. "No, because they already had those on file from the last time I had been arrested—in Fairbanks." Will laughed again. "Then I had to sign some dumb form, and I sat around for six hours until my dad showed up, who was not amused, as you seem to be. They dropped the charges, and we drove the six hours back to Fairbanks, not saying a whole lot."

"You've been in some protests, too," Wendy said.

She raised her right hand. "Guilty as charged. I can attest that there were no fatalities or flag burnings. A few bruised egos."

Wendy laughed. "Now, I'm not your mom, but I've done some do-gooding in my life, too, and did some stuff like that back in the day—"

"You did? What did you get arrested for, Mom?" Will asked. "And they let you be President?"

"I never got arrested, but that's not the point. I am a bit less abrasive and have better people skills than your cousin. Given who your parents are, this can't be helped."

"Thanks a lot."

"You're welcome a lot. I would like this to be a learning exercise, so can you see it from both sides and understand *why* they arrested you for feeding the homeless in a public park. Okay?"

She nodded. "Public order, as I guess we were causing a disturbance by upsetting the order of the universe and setting a poor example, as defined by the establishment. Probably killed off a few blades of grass and made people walk around us. I thought all that stuff was off the records by now. I guess when you are President, you can find out a lot about a person."

"Never mind that, and no, you really don't get it. You don't know everything, you know."

"Yeah, she does. Paige knows everything," Will said.

"Hush, sonny. I do not? How profound your wisdom is; at a mere eleven years of age, you are quite the sage."

"Shut up, Paige. I'm almost twelve."

"I am twice as wise now as I was at twelve, into the details we should swiftly delve."

"Two times zero is still zero, hero. Math just isn't your thing."

"Now, children, don't argue. The disturbance is secondary to the underlying principle. More important is public health and the potential danger."

"Huh? Public health? Danger?" She scratched her head. "Three teenagers serving food risked the raucous ruination of mankind? Please elaborate and give it to me straight, Dame who is great."

"Look, I'm still a physician, and I was the Surgeon General, so I know what I'm talking about regarding epidemiology. Y'all meddling kids just can't go out and start serving perishable items to random people in a public place just because you feel like it. They could have gotten very sick if what you served hadn't been prepared or stored properly, even ended up in the hospital from *Salmonella, E. coli,* or *Bacillus cereus* poisoning."

She crossed her arms and yawned. "I am no microbiologist; I am not familiar with the last microorganism, it concerns me not, it will not make me rot."

"Of course it doesn't; there are many things to think of here that you children had no awareness of. And who would have been responsible? You. Who would be responsible for their medical costs if they got sick? The taxpayers."

She slapped herself in the face. "Ah, I see, this is now turning into a Republican vs. Democrat debate. Entitlement to healthcare, the tax system—"

"No, it's not, so let me finish, Paige. My guess is you and your accomplices didn't even wear gloves or adhere to even the most basic sanitary standards the law requires for food service workers."

She shook her head. "Unfortunately, the North Pole public school system did not provide such doctoral-level food service instruction, but my puny mind concluded that it seemingly was superior to them eating garbage from trash cans."

"You really believe that, don't you?"

She nodded. "Do you think what we prepared was inferior to week-old rotten food from the dumpster they would have otherwise consumed? Do you not think they could have ended up in the hospital that way? Which is the lesser of two evils?"

"I see your point and realize you meant well, but there would've been a way to do it safely and legally if you'd only had the patience to do so and bothered to go through proper channels to learn proper procedures. Did you even bother to talk to anyone at the city building or the health commissioner's office?"

She shook her head. "No. That seemed like too much trouble. Endless governmental red tape for such a simple action."

"Well, there you go, then. It's not all black and white—you against the oppression of the big bad 'man.' If you want to be a symbol of justice, you need to see the big picture. Laws exist for a reason, you know."

"Yes, to serve the bureaucrats and fat cats, present company not excluded." She heard Will snicker. She imagined that not many people used that kind of sarcasm with his mom, but she had surely met her match.

Or maybe not. "Okay, smarty, I see we have a debate on your hands, so get ready." She heard Wendy rub her hands together. "I didn't get here by being wimpy in the mouth department either, girly."

"That's for damn sure," Jay said, the first time he had spoken up during this discussion. "I'm staying out of this."

"Good."

"You're gonna get it now, Paige," Will said. "When my mom's mouth gets going—"

Wendy laughed. "Be quiet, Will; I need no help with this. Paige, you're not the first young person to disagree with the laws of the land. One option, which you have exercised multiple times and remains the choice of most young people throughout history, is simply to break them. Typical, yet not very mature and befitting one who wants my job someday."

"Your job? Paige? That's a laugh," Will said.

"Shut up, William, there is nothing funny about me wanting to be President. What is the other option, pray tell, Ma'am?"

"You have only one other choice. If you don't like the laws, then you need to learn how to change them. Legally. Pass around a petition, become an attorney, lobby your representatives, become a legislator yourself. Advocacy in action."

"An admirable choice, but that would take forever."

"Yeah, tell me about it, kiddo. How juvenile to take the easy way. Mine is very hard work and not a lot of fun sometimes. You have a lot of passion, but take big steps, not tiny random ones that won't make a difference in the end. It ain't simple, but it can be done with work and perseverance. Getting arrested in defiance may make you feel a sense of grand accomplishment at age eighteen, but it does little to help the ones you care about in the long run as far as permanency."

"I guess so. You sound kind of like my dad."

"Your father is a very smart man."

"Really? You truly think that?"

"I have a new-found respect for him. We'll talk about it later."

They arrived at the West Street food shelter in preparation to do a day's work, preparing and serving food for the less fortunate. She could lift the heavy objects. The President was carving turkey and cooking mashed potatoes. She had been the Surgeon General, after all, albeit one who was a pediatrician.

"Are you having fun, Aunt Wendy?" she asked several hours later as they were cleaning up.

"Yeah. It kind of takes me back, wearing only jeans and being a regular person. I'm not sure the patrons here even know who I am. It's kind of nice."

"That doesn't matter, does it? Does they having that information make their meal any more important?"

"No, it doesn't. You're right, Paige. In a way, it's liberating."

"In addition, it is probably fewer calories for you, too, than the White House meal. A win-win."

"What? Thanks a lot." Wendy punched her in the shoulder.

"You are welcome a lot. An honest day's work never hurt anyone."

• • •

The morning after Thanksgiving, Paige went with Will to the White House workout room. He took her around the room, letting her find where all the machines and free weights were. She went to do some heavy bench presses.

"This is a pretty nice gym," she said. "You work out here often, William?"

"Most every day. Mom makes me. Not that I enjoy it."

"Huh. I would like to see my mom make me do something."

"Do you need a spotter or help loading your bar?" he asked curiously.

She put two 45-lb plates on each end of the Olympic barbell. 135 pounds counting the 45-lb bar. "What do you think?"

"I guess you don't need any help."

"The plates are standard size, so, no. All such plates are engraved, and I know the weight of something I pick up within a few hundred grams, anyway."

"Is that weight really a challenge for you?"

"Yes, three sets of ten reps is a good workout for Paige."

"I don't understand. *Stella is* Paige. You flew Air Force One safely to the ground, but you're going to stress yourself with a mere 135-lb barbell? That makes no sense to me, so explain it."

"135 pounds is a pretty big stress for a girl." She did ten reps and put the barbell back. "But I am not as strong as you, relatively speaking, at least not as strong as the man you will become."

He laughed. "You're not nearly as strong as I am now, don't kid yourself. I can bench 250 for ten reps easy."

"Well, your mom could bench 315 pounds back in the day, I heard, without any special abilities, except some good genetics and hard work."

"Right." He laughed. "Never for ten reps, she didn't; five at most. She for sure can't do 315 or even 275 now; she's got degeneration of her left rotator cuff from shotputting in her forties, and she has some back and chest wall pain after she got shot. She just uses the Zybex machines now with high reps."

"For now, yet I am certain you will surpass her in a couple of years."

He laughed. "It won't take a couple of years. I'm there already. I let her think otherwise, though."

She did ten more reps. "See? I am sweating a little bit now. The heavy lifting and such is done by my dark energy powers, not by me. I need to maintain an attractive shape."

"Does it hurt?"

"Huh? Why would lifting weights hurt?"

"The burn. If you have to ask, then you obviously don't know."

She shook her head. "I guess not."

"How fast can you run?"

"I do not really know. At Sulphur Springs, I could run a little over a seven-minute mile, about like back home."

"Huh? That's not even eleven miles an hour, not very heroic."

"Well, I can leap very high, as you saw my vertical leap in the gym, but I cannot really run any faster than normal."

"I don't get it. I mean, I've heard of dark energy and stuff, but no one knows where it is."

"It's apparently an incredibly powerful force, as you have seen. I guess I am living proof that it is everywhere." She picked up the 135-lb barbell with one hand and twirled it over her head like a toy.

"Impressive. What happens if you drop that on yourself?"

"Watch and see." She lay down on the bench, still holding it, extended her arms, and dropped it onto her chest. "Nothing. The kinetic energy gets absorbed."

"That mass, at that height—it's about three hundred joules, like a defibrillator shock. Where does it go?"

"I do not know; where my dark energy is, I guess. My mom thinks that someday I may be able to control the energy and send it back as other forms of energy, but for now I can just absorb it."

"So you might be able to shoot force beams from your hands or something, to blow stuff up?"

"I would imagine I could do that by now if it was possible, so, no. And I do not need any more power, thanks. This is it."

"I've noticed something else."

"Yes? What have your impressive juvenile powers of observation revealed now?"

He pulled her right arm up over her head. "Your armpit is smooth."

She frowned and pulled her arm back. "Yeah, so? Do you like hirsute girls with hairy axillae? I guess if that is your thing—who am I to judge a prepubescent lad's fetishistic fantasy? Remember, I am still your cousin."

He laughed. "No, of course not, but do you have hair there?"

She scowled. "Of course I do, just like I do on my head and some other places that *you* shall never see, should you wish to remain among the living. I guess you have never seen a naked female, huh? We are not that much different, really."

"Not that different? Are you kidding me?"

"Physiologically, we are very similar."

"Whatever, Paige, that's an incredibly moronic statement; you make a lot of those."

"So I am told, I must be something to behold."

He sighed. "Just tell me how you get rid of the hair!"

She shook her head, this conversation reminiscent of one she had with *Photraman* recently, although he was forty years older and seemingly less mature than Will.

"Did your mom or dad or your health ed instructor not teach you anything? How do you think girls get rid of their unwanted hair, dummy? We shave our armpits and legs with razors, duh." She walked over, groped for his face, and felt the smooth skin. "But, as discussed in our first meeting, I guess you have yet to learn about razors, young lad who is barely a grammar school grad."

"No, no. I get all that, Paige, but *you're* not getting why that makes no sense to me. You can, apparently, survive a nuclear explosion. You just dropped a massive barbell on your chest and laughed about it. How can you shave with a mere razor from the drugstore?"

"Oh, I see what you mean. It is because the hairs are not living cells, so they are as vulnerable to cutting as yours. I can cut my hair or trim my nails just as easily as you can."

"So, if I took a blowtorch to you, it would burn off all your hair and outer skin but leave you unharmed?"

"I believe so. I have used a blowtorch as a depilatory, although it leaves me kind of red as it burns off the outer epidermal layer, so I have moved on to other methods of depilation. *Photraman* burned off one of my eyebrows. Burnt hair and skin smell bad, lad."

"Do you tan?"

"Well, there is not much natural sun in Alaska, but I do not believe so. I am half Mexican-American, like you, so I have some natural color, I am told."

"Huh. What about your teeth?"

"What? My dentition? These queries are becoming more personal than I like, sonny, it ain't funny."

"Yeah, do you brush your teeth or go to the dentist? Some portions of our tooth anatomy are alive, but others not."

"I never thought about that, having little interest in dentistry. I have tried chewing rocks and metal without any damage, so I do not believe so. Those items do not taste very good. I wanted to drink some mercury once but thought being a walking biohazard a rather bad idea. It might have excused me from school for a few weeks, though, which would have been a plus."

"Where would you have gotten enough mercury to drink, and why would you even think about doing that?" He laughed. "I've never met a girl like you with such male-brain traits."

"I decline to say on grounds it may incriminate me."

"Anyway, the inner tooth is alive, but the enamel isn't."

"Yes, but the enamel protects the tooth, so it must be deemed important enough to protect, as it shields the remainder of the tooth."

"I see. It doesn't protect hair because it can be regrown, but not enamel as it can't regrow. That energy field of yours must actually have intelligence. It can differentiate what is essential to you and what isn't."

"You are indeed a deep thinker, William Conrad, to contemplate such profound matters. All I care is that it works, not all the scientific quirks."

"What if you needed braces or something? What would you do then?"

"OMG, I do not know, let that titanic thought go. Who cares?"

She heard him load some plates on a barbell. "What about other things? Infections and such?"

"I guess I do not ever remember being sick. I suppose it filters out harmful junk, or maybe I just cannot be infected. I have tried various toxic things with no ill effects in my younger days."

"'Various toxic things in your younger days?' When would those great events have taken place?"

"When I was a mere child, long ago. Sixteen or seventeen, when I was very green and not very mean."

He howled with laughter. "What types of things?"

"The usual immature teenage ones: smoking, drinking, you know—those seem childish now, I have better things to do with my time."

"You think I would know about that?"

"I sure hope not, as it is dumb. Listen to your folks. I drank most of a bottle of Dirk T. Darkkin whiskey once with no ill effects, so it ain't all it is cracked up to be. You cannot do the same and survive." She pointed an authoritative finger at him. "So just remember that; being drunk is not where it is at."

"Hey, I don't need anyone else lecturing me. I get enough of that as it is. You have no idea."

She came up to him, smelling his perspiration, and looked up at him. "And I am weary of talking about my abilities like I am a freak or something. All I want to do is hang out, talk about stuff you do—bands you like to listen to, your friends, how your classes are going, etc."

"I really don't want to talk about school. Music, that's another story. What groups do you like, Paige?"

"I like the old stuff, like from the seventies. Led Zeppelin, Aerosmith, Bachman-Turner Overdrive, Edgar Winter Group, The Osmonds, those guys were awesome."

"That was a long time ago, about the time my mom was born. I never met any girl before who liked those things."

"Well, you have met one now. There is more to me than meets the eye, not just because I can fly."

"What about, you know—"

She shook her head. "No, I do not know. I cannot read minds."

"Yeesh, come on. Sex."

She put her hands on her hips. "Are you not a little young to be talking about that?"

"Come on, Paige, get real. What I mean is, can you have it?"

"Uh, sure."

"Have you?"

"What kind of a question is that? Have you?"

"I'm almost twelve, of course not."

"I certainly hope that that is the case. Well, yes, I have, not that it is any of your business. Those kinds of things are private."

"Can you get pregnant, or does this energy field prevent you, from, you know—"

"I guess I never thought about that. Might be good to know for future reference."

"Well, don't you think you'd better find out soon? Yeesh. Even I know about that stuff."

"I suppose so, but it is not really a problem right now, do not have a cow."

"So, what else you have going on?"

"A lot, tot. Jackie is shipping me off to southeast Georgia for a couple of weeks."

"What in the world for?"

"I get to learn how to shoot a gun and have other fun in the cold November sun."

"What? They're sending you to Special Agent school? Is that such a great idea?"

"I will tell you all about it when I get back. I might be back sooner if they kick me out prematurely."

Chapter Forty-Seven

Federal Law Enforcement Training Center
1131 Chapel Crossing Road
Glynco, GA

Stella went for her first day at the "special" federal police training academy Jackie Levickis had set up for her. There was no way this administration was going to sanction a vigilante going around fighting crimes or doing anything else official without some training—especially one as strong as *Stella Scura*. To that end, she'd have to learn the law—and proper police procedure. She didn't have a problem with that, although she wondered how well she would actually be accepted by them—not just as a novelty.

The physical fitness tests were waived, of course, as there was little purpose in doing those and attracting a crowd. She had to read many books to learn basic law and pass a number of examinations. She wasn't the best at taking multiple-choice examinations, but the subject matter seemed easy because it was so logical.

It had never occurred to her until she was well into her studies that she was now reading 'regular' books with the visor; how could she do that? She hadn't anticipated this, but realized that she must've read before *Darkkday;* otherwise the written words would have no meaning to her. What was she, six, when that happened? Maybe she did inherit some of her mom's language skills, after all, but reading at a high level at six was unusual. She certainly didn't get the mathematical skills. But it gave her hope that some of her early childhood memories would return later.

She then realized that maybe some things were better left in the past, as not everything in life is pleasant.

The law, however, was something that had long fascinated her. Maybe it was genetic, as few remembered that her mom actually had been a very skilled forensic scientist before achieving fame as a theoretical physicist and discoverer of mendozium; her deceased maternal grandfather and uncle had been police officers. Everyone had forgotten about that now. Arrest. Search. Seizure. Federal vs. state laws. Two weeks of intense tutoring and grilling by some tough Secret Service and FBI agents.

At first, the instructors seemed a bit in awe, but then they were the ones giving her a hard time. She didn't care. They stopped making her do pushups by the second day, however, as, after she did fifty of them in two minutes, they realized it was not much of a punishment.

There was one other minor thing to attend to. A police officer needed a document almost all other eighteen-year-olds had, but blind girls didn't: a drivers' license; another bit of stupid schooling she had to go through. They thought it a bit strange she didn't have one, but she passed the driving tests with flying colors.

• • •

"How did she do the first week, Jackie?" Wendy asked as she sipped a glass of stevioside-sweetened lemonade in the Oval Office and plopped onto the sofa, joining her security chief.

Jackie sneered. "What did you ask? How did Princess Paige do with the watered-down training you suggested?"

"Yes, although I would prefer a little less sarcasm."

"Sorry, ain't gonna happen. Do you *really* want to know? I don't approve of this, mind you."

"I know that, and that's why I value your opinion. I'm trying to bring her some legitimacy. This is one way."

"Really? *Legitimacy?* A better way is to have her earn it and pay her dues like the other officers and I did, but you didn't select that path. That's the only way a real cop will respect her."

She shook her head. "Uh-uh. Don't let your pride get in the way. You know this is a special person, and we have limited time to get her up and going, so we can't send her to the regular academy.

Most of the regular officer issues don't apply here."

"With all due respect, what the hell do you know about it?"

"Excuse me?"

"Ma'am, how would you feel if someone attended a several-week mini-med school to become a physician instead of going through the twelve or so years of seventy-hour weeks you had to? Would you think that was okay? Amateur hour in the hospital and clinic, taking care of patients? Let's do that next, starting with brain surgery. The normal length of the Academy is twenty weeks, not two. We'll cut down the training by a factor of ten for an individual with unbelievable physical power and see how that works out for everyone. Sounds good."

"Don't be absurd. I hardly think it's the same thing."

"No? You sure don't seem to have much respect for the scope of law enforcement and the vast responsibility it entails."

"Now, that's not true at all."

"And *you* also have no comprehension as to what it takes to be a sworn peace officer. If you want her on the street, Ma'am, she needs to be as accountable as anyone else."

"Fine, whatever, I'm just trying to solve a problem here in the most effective way possible. You and the instructors then decide how she did, as you have the final say."

"At least we agree on *that*." Jackie scowled. "Well, to be fair, she isn't regular material, as you say, and that's part of the issue. Most of the instructors were all googly-eyed, and it was pretty much impossible to give her a good physical test, of course, which for the most part, we decided to forego, as it seemed unnecessary. Even in a 'de-powered' state she is a remarkable athlete, with hand-eye coordination beyond anything I've ever seen. Her reaction speed and reflexes are off the charts."

"The physical tests shouldn't even be considerations."

Jackie pointed her finger at her. "Hey, you say that, but no one knows how these crazy abilities of hers even work. What if her powers crap out her suddenly, or she faints or something? As I understand it, she's completely blind without that sapphire visor, which isn't indestructible like her."

She pointed at Jackie. "That's highly classified information, and you had better make *damn* sure no one else knows that."

"And just because she has no physical limitations doesn't mean she's stable emotionally."

"She seems perfectly fine to me."

"Oh, are you a psychologist now?"

Wendy stood and put her large hands on her wide hips. "No, but I have many years of medical experience dealing with difficult children and adolescents. I know when someone is stable and when they aren't, Jackie."

"Wrong, you have *no* experience dealing with someone like this because no one does. You just think you know her because she's your niece, but you haven't seen her for twelve years; she's a completely different person now, both from aging and life experiences. And you know *nothing* about law enforcement, Ma'am. Just because you hung around the Mendoza police family in your youth and played amateur detective with your brother and Bonnie doesn't make you an expert on the police."

She looked out the window and shook her head. "I know her. She's my flesh and blood. We all suspect there's a part of her not of Earthly origin, but I can neither verify nor do anything about it."

Jackie laughed. "You have it totally backward, Ma'am. The part that *is* related to you is what I'm terrified of."

She puffed out her ample chest. "Excuse me, Jackie? Please explain your acerb assertation."

"You know what I mean; it requires no explanation."

"I don't, so please enlighten me."

"Okay, it's pretty obvious. Do you deny that emotional instability and substance abuse run rampant in your family?"

"Not all of them, what an exaggeration."

"Yeah, right. Let's postpone discussing *your* complex behavioral health issues for the moment. Your brother was an alcoholic and her mom a compulsive gambler who went into rehab. Your dad, of course, defies psychiatric description, as he took every type of recreational drug known to man. I've met the shining star of the family, Cousin Smiley, a musical prodigy who went from an IQ of 135 to 25 after his incident where he vaped a mixture of erectile dysfunction drugs dissolved in benzene, reportedly after Rad dared him to do it. Uncle Dusty, what a piece of work. They weren't the most emotionally stable folks. Paige might have a meltdown the first time she sees blood, some dude having a seizure and foaming at the mouth, a guy with his arm blown off, etc."

She shook her head. "That won't bother her. I've seen all those grisly things more times than I can count, working the graveyard shift in the ER."

"So have I, Wendy, but just because you're a physician and that stuff doesn't bother you doesn't mean it's the same for her. This could be a great thing we're doing or incredibly haphazard if it goes wrong. In the end, it's all on you if it goes south."

She shook her head and threw her hands down. "Okay, okay, I get it. I'm making this up as I go along and doing the best I can. *Stella Scura* didn't come with an instruction manual. Would you rather I just let her go out and do whatever she wants without at least some rudimentary training in law and order? She's going to do it anyway, and there's not much I can do to stop her."

"I guess not, but it's still unorthodox."

"Let's avoid speculation on things we can't control. Just skip further unwelcome commentary and tell me how it went today."

Jackie sighed. "To her credit, she has well above average intelligence, but not to the point she can't relate to people like Bonnie. She's very quick at grasping concepts, has exceptional common sense, and doesn't seem to have any of the strange positional or directional disabilities Bonnie has. She's an auditory learner, as you might expect from a blind person; you tell her something once, and she's got it, no repeating, mistakes, or backtalk. With the visor, she has remarkable visual acuity, but limited color perception, but can see in the near-infrared range, which may be useful; that, combined with her amazing reflexes, make her a singular cadet. She can be very talkative or very quiet and is getting better at being the latter, as her speech is very irritating, like her mom. Very serious, but with a somewhat self-deprecating sense of humor.

"The other cadets were kind of in awe at first, but she broke the ice and volunteered herself to be a 'tackling dummy' and let the others run her down, do taser and handcuffing practice on her, you know, although we can't use a live taser, it would burn out. No one worries about hurting her or getting hurt by her. She is, for all practical purposes, one of them, and they accept her. And she has one other unusual thing I've never seen in a cadet before, or any other person, for that matter."

"What?"

"She's entirely unflappable: impossible to make angry or feel bad, no matter what you say or do to her. Two of the instructors got really nasty with her because they were told to do so, and she just smiled and took it all in stride. Sgt. Roger Bennett asked her if she was 'wet behind the ears,' and she said 'no, sir.' He then threw a bucket of water in her face and said, 'You are now, rookie. What do you think of that?' The other cadets were cringing, but she just smiled, wiped it off, and said 'Yes, sir, I certainly am now, and I have much to learn. Please tell me how I can improve to prevent a future occurrence.' Amazing control of temperament."

"Yes, yes, I know all that stuff. Blindness teaches you humility, Jackie; she knows things we couldn't possibly understand. And she has to be that way. I assumed all this already."

"But, I have to give you this one: even standing there soaking wet, this kiddo has a certain, well, regal stature, an elegance. Not a movie star quality, like Bella; I really can't explain it, but she carries herself like royalty. It's not really arrogance or anything like that. We've all seen it: the person in college, in the police academy, whatever, who is destined to be the leader. That's her."

"She is a freaking *goddess*, Jackie, likely the future occupant of this house in twenty years. She could be the ruler of us all, but she's out there getting water thrown in her face like a plebe. How could she be like that and people not be in awe of her?"

"I wasn't in awe of you twenty years ago, and, while I respect you, I'm not in awe of you now, Ma'am, sorry. Paige, I am, although she is a pain in the butt sometimes."

She laughed. "No comparison. But what I really need to know is—is she someone we can competently condone being out there by herself?"

Jackie nodded. "I believe so, aside from the reservations I mentioned earlier about things we may not have anticipated. This teenager acts far more mature than a lot of guys in their thirties or forties. She isn't someone who can be physically threatened, of course. But the next challenge will be the greatest."

"What's that?"

"Putting her on the streets for some on-the-job training. I'm going to find the toughest SOB I know to run her through the wringer in a gritty, real-world setting."

Wendy nodded. "Good. I assume you have the fortunate preceptor picked out."

"Huh. Where else? The rugged streets of Baltimore PD. It's finally payback time for this one individual."

"You, Jacqueline Levickis, are one mean individual."

"That's right. I helped make Ed who he is today."

• • •

Baltimore Police Department
Northeastern District
1900 Argonne Drive
Baltimore, MD

The police lieutenant hung up the phone in Baltimore Police District 7 and addressed the heavily-built man in front of him.

"Sarge, do you know who that was?"

"Don't know, I was never much good at guessing, sir."

"It was the Commissioner," Lt. Robert Kistler said sharply. "You've got a new rookie partner."

"What the hell?" Sergeant Edward J. Levickis growled. "They don't spring something like this on me; I got a lot of seniority, *and* a partner."

"Officer Graffis has just been reassigned for a couple of weeks to another division, Ed. You'll get him back after that."

The large Black man pointed at his boss. "Hey, waitaminnit, that stinks, Bob. Tommy is the best partner ever."

"You'll get Tom back, eventually, but today you don't have a choice. The request comes from a rather, uh, high source."

"High source? Sir, I don't care if it was the Commissioner, the fricking mayor, or even a Congressman; it's my way or the highway. I'm just old-school that way."

Lt. Kistler pointed to the ceiling. "Yeah, well, you're not even close, as you need to go up a few levels of magnitude beyond a measly Congressman. This is something fraught with potential excellent publicity or unemployment for you if you don't do it, so you *will* comply, Sergeant Levickis. Got it? Otherwise, you'll be the one hitting the highway, straight out of town."

The muscular, slightly heavyset, five-eleven sergeant shook his head and laughed. "Naw, you're bluffing, Lieutenant. The union won't let me be fired over this crap."

"Well, maybe not, but we can find some pretty unrewarding clerical work for you to do otherwise. Your choice."

"Is that an order, sir?" he asked sarcastically.

"Absolutely. You're the only one who can deal with it. You were hand-picked for this job, so be grateful for once."

"Up a few levels?" Sgt. Levickis looked at his boss nervously.

"Is that what you said, sir?"

Kistler nodded. "Yeah. Get the concept yet, Einstein?"

"How far up are we going?"

Kistler pointed to the ceiling. "As far as you can go. Top floor, penthouse suite. It's not rocket science, Ed."

He thought for a minute and then stomped his black size twelve boot on the floor. "*The White House?* Are you kidding me? Did my loudmouth bossy little sister have something to do with it?"

"Don't know, it's just orders; you're a smart guy who can figure things out, so put two and two together."

"Thanks a heap."

"And you don't need to concern yourself with the mundane details of how lucky you are for your selection. Just do your job and don't treat this officer differently than anyone else."

Levickis threw his hands down. "Well, who the hell is this fancy-pants, then? The suspense is killing me, sir."

"Not a regular officer, but some very special federal person, who they want to have some field experience."

He stomped his foot on the ground. "Goddamn it, just because Jackie's the Presidential detail chief doesn't give her the right to run my life. This better not be some celebrity cop thing for the media."

Kistler shook his head. "I guess it does, Ed. Yours and mine, 'cause we're public servants, which means shut the heck up and do it. You were picked because you're the toughest training officer around. And you can decide for yourself if this person is a celebrity or not. Ten thousand other cops would line up for miles to do this, yet you're complaining before you even start. You're unbelievable. But, typical for you, I expected nothing less. In a way, that confirms you're the best guy for this."

He pointed his right thumb towards his chest. "No, I'm a tough bastard, so I bet that's why I was picked."

"Probably so. That doesn't make you any easier to work with."

"Yeah—well, where is this 'special person,' Lieutenant?" He looked at his black Casio G-Shock. "He's late already, and it's time to roll. I can't stand being late, 'cause I'm an old-style cop. No room for running behind on my watch. These damn entitled kids today drive me nuts."

"*She's* coming down the hall right now, Ed, as there was some special paperwork to complete. It's rather complicated and somewhat beyond your sergeant's pay grade. Beyond mine. Beyond the Commissioner's and the mayor's, too."

"What? A *woman?* Awww, no, that's even worse, man: playing nursemaid to some celebrity girly-girl chick who can't even fire a gun and is worried about her makeup and nails. This really sucks, sir, if you want my opinion."

"I don't, and settle yourself down. I'm sure she can fire her weapon, Ed—likely better than you or anyone on this planet."

"Huh? No way. What does that mean?"

"Just chill out. I also doubt if this 'girly-girl' is concerned about her makeup or nails, either. Trust me."

"Are you kidding me? This some kind of joke? That's it, it all makes sense now."

"Why don't you decide for yourself? Here she comes now."

Ed Levickis watched as the gorgeous five-eight uniformed black-haired young woman walked down the corridor, with a dozen other officers following her, almost stumbling over themselves.

He sized her up as she stopped three feet from him and saw her black name tag, which read "SCURA." He slapped his face in disbelief as he saw his reflection in the visor.

"You have to be kidding me. It's not April 1, or Halloween, or my birthday, and I don't like practical jokes, Lieutenant. Whose kid is this?" He pulled on her black hair. "This must be Rick Taylor's girl in a wig and sunglasses, come on. That you, Brittany? It's not funny at all. And take those shades off in here! It ain't California."

She sighed. "Excuse me, I am not Brittany, whoever that human being is. I also am not laughing, so let go of my hair, please, do not tease." She pulled his hand away gently as she pulled out a compact. "Look, you have now mussed it, on my first day, too. Luckily, my photo has already been taken for the files."

"What did you say to me? I mussed your hair? Why, you bratty little juvenile cop wannabe—"

"Listen up, it's not a joke, so pay attention. Sergeant Ed Levickis, meet DSD Special Agent *Stella Scura.*"

He snarled as he stared at her black hair and shiny visor. "No way. What the hell am I supposed to do with her?"

"She needs some routine field work to meet the requirements for a sworn officer. Like I just said, figure it out, Ed."

"I don't need this kind of circus stuff, and I don't want to get killed, either. This seems like a good ticket for both."

"Well, I trust your fine judgment, Sarge. She's all yours."
He sighed. "Thanks a lot, Lieutenant. I'll get you all for this."

• • •

Ed Levickis stared at her and sighed as they walked out towards the patrol cars. "Come on—you're really her? The real deal?"

She picked up a basketball-sized rock from the parking lot and crushed it into gravel. "I suppose. As real as anyone can be, as you can see. I do not think I am a hallucination. although others may disagree."

He snarled. "You smarting off to me, rookie? I don't need any philosophy lesson from a teenager."

She shook her head in all seriousness. "No, sir. I am always to the point and factual. What you see is what you get, do not fret. I am honest, I pull no punches and do not act on mere hunches, I say it like it is, I am full of hubris, I also can—"

"Lord Almighty, I've got a headache already. Right now, I just want to see if you can shut up."

She nodded. "Yes, sir. I concur, as I do not wish to create a stir."

"I don't hear much shutting up."

"Huh? If I was shutting up, you would *not* hear anything, so your argument is flawed."

"I don't need a rookie arguing with me, Scura."

"Sorry, experienced Sergeant, whose hair is argent."

"Let's get one thing straight, Scura. I don't want this job, and you probably don't wanna be here either, but we're stuck with each other. Nothing personal. I'm sure you're a nice enough gal, but I'm a career cop and not meant for this kinda crap."

"Yes, sir, I am grateful for the opportunity. I will try to defuse any reservations or predetermined stereotypes you have about me. Especially about me resembling fecal material. That is not the positive image I wish to convey my first day on the job, as I aspire to be much more than a mere slobby blob."

"That'll be the day. So, you've been certified on the range with your weapon? I ain't going out with some idiot."

She nodded rapidly. "Yes, sir. I am quite competent. Perfect score at the firing range with all weapons categories, equally proficient with either hand."

"You shouldn't shoot with one hand, showboat."

"I have no problem with strength or coordination, sir. It is unlikely I will need to discharge my weapon, however."

"Yeah? Why's that, rookie? You got no idea what you'll have to do on the street, and Baltimore's a tough customer."

"I am good at dealing with conflict, and I have many other nonlethal abilities at my disposal. I can go where others cannot safely go. I am a rather 'tough customer,' too, and superbly speedy, in order to nurture the needy and grab the greedy."

"Oh, I bet. You have your other equipment?"

She nodded and patted her equipment belt. "I really do not need a baton, sir, as I am quite capable of handling myself. If I need to break a window or something, I can just use my finger. I have my handcuffs also, although they are seemingly unnecessary. I will use them, however, if I need to detain a suspect."

"Yeah, you wait until some druggie is busting down the partition in your car trying to kill you and see if you don't need him cuffed."

She nodded. "I agree. I will do so for the safety of everyone concerned. I am a humble public servant."

He poked her in the sternum. "Hey, you don't have your Kevlar vest on, young lady. Regulations."

She shook her head. "No, sir, I do not require that either, and the Commissioner has waived that requirement. It would be a waste of departmental funds and might even be more hazardous."

"Huh? How is wearing body armor dangerous?"

"The bullets could be deflected from the Kevlar and cause injury to others or damage it, while if they hit my skin, they will merely drop to the ground when I absorb their kinetic energy. Bullets would destroy the uniform either way."

"So, you really can take a bullet?"

She nodded. "Yes. I cannot be harmed by any known means."

"They don't bounce off, like in the movies?"

"No. My skin is no harder than yours; it's just that I absorb all the energy." She patted her sidearm with her right hand. "Would you like a demonstration?"

"Are you nuts? There'd be a dozen forms to fill out for discharging a weapon without cause, and I ain't got any idea how to write that one up. But I don't need any grandstanding or any nonsense about kinetic energy crap. This is a police department, not kiddie science class. You do what I say and only what I say, is that clear?"

"Absolutely, sir." She smiled.

"Otherwise, I'll bounce your famous butt outta here, 'cause I don't care how tough you are or who you know."

"Yes, sir. I would surely want it no other way, once more into the fray."

"I don't care what you want, Scura. Why do you talk like that? Are you trying to annoy me?"

She shrugged. "I cannot seem to help talking that way, it is in my DNA." They reached his squad car as she raised her right hand. "I have a question if that is permitted."

He sighed. "Yeah? What now?"

"Do you drive or do you want me to, sir?"

He stared down into her visor. "Are you some dummy?"

She shook her head. "No comment, I will defer that to your proper judgment. It still does not answer my query."

He scowled. "Get in the passenger side, Scura. No rookie drives *my* car! What's wrong with you?"

"Yessir. I shall remember that."

He looked to the sky as he opened the drivers' door. "Lordy, what did I do to deserve this? This may be a dumb question, but do you even have a drivers' license, young lady?"

She smiled excitedly and proudly pulled it out of her chest pocket with her left hand. "I just got it two weeks ago, Sergeant!"

"Fantastic. You got less driving experience than almost all the kids in school." They got in the car and fastened their seat belts.

"I obtained my FAA pilot's certificate with instrument rating well before my driver's license, actually. Would you like to see that, too?"

"Hell, no. Why does a kid like you need a pilot's license?"

"Huh? Is that a trick question, Sergeant? I do far more flying than driving."

"I don't get it."

"Because I am the only person who is also an aircraft."

"Never mind, sorry I asked." He slapped himself on the forehead as he slowly pulled it out of the lot. "Can you answer me one final question before we go on our first adventure together?"

"Yes, Sergeant Levickis?"

He stared at her face as they sat in the front seats. "How old are you, anyway? You look younger than my daughter, who's in high school and has been driving for two years."

She shook her head. "I am sorry, sir, but that is classified information known only to the President of the United States and a handful of other individuals. However, I am a legal adult."

"The *President?* You know her, do you?"

She smiled. "Yes, sir. We have met privately on many occasions at her residence."

"Her residence? You mean the White House?"

She nodded. "Yessir, that is where she lives, all right, a house of might; to our enemies it will provoke fright."

"Well, ain't that special. Understand that don't cut no mustard with me; I don't care who you know. I'll tell that to her face, too."

She put her head down sadly. "Of course, I should receive no special treatment, as I am the lowest of the low. Ants and termites are higher on the food chain than me, it is therefore clear I am not your cup of tea. Such is how it is meant to be."

"You finally got something right, although you have a rather wordy way to state your opinion." He smiled condescendingly. "Are you even old enough to go grab a beer after our shift? I always buy the rookies a beer."

"Huh. I am sorry to break the custom, but I will just have coffee and a doughnut, as I do not wish to get an FWI citation, sir."

"FWI? You mean OWI, get it right, if you're going to be a cop."

She shook her head. "No, FWI, flying while intoxicated. There *is* such a law on the books." There was just a hint of sarcasm in her voice as the inner Paige couldn't be suppressed completely.

"You're serious, aren't you?"

"Yessir. The FAA is not to be trifled with. Fines galore and more would be in store."

He smirked at her. "You trying to get smart with me?"

She stared at him with a straight face. "Oh, no, sir, I again am merely being factual." Passive-aggressiveness at its finest.

"Huh. You're probably not old enough to have a beer or even go in a damn bar. You'd have to give yourself a citation for minor in possession."

She frowned and crossed her arms. "Well, it would not matter. Alcohol has no effect on me anyway; I cannot become intoxicated."

"No kidding? How do you know that?"

"Huh. How do you think? I have consumed alcohol before in my immature days, as many irresponsible teenagers have."

He thought for a minute and pointed to the run-down bar across the street as he pulled out of the parking lot. "So, you could go to Thirsty Turtle Tavern over there, drink a fifth of cheap whiskey, and not be smashed?"

She shook her head. "Correct, sir; however, I might physically have alcohol in my blood, which could still be illegal. I really do not know, as those things have never been tested, as drawing my blood is not an easy feat. Nevertheless, there is no point."

He grimaced. "Damn, that would really stink."

"Yes, sir. Sometimes being me is not all it is cracked up to be. I can never experience the simple joy of being drunk as a skunk, passed out in my bunk."

"When you put it that way, it doesn't sound so good, Scura."

"Agreed."

"So, since you frequent the White House, I assume you've met my sister?"

"Jacqueline?" She nodded rapidly. "Oh, of course, sir, your sibling is rather hard to forget."

"Huh, no kidding. What does she think of you, Scura?"

"She was not terribly fond of me initially, but is beginning to come around now that she has fully experienced my ebullient personality."

"Not sure what that means, but it doesn't sound so good."

"It means she is a hard ass, kind of like you, Sarge, but she has a kind heart."

"Don't call me Sarge, Scura."

• • •

"Driver was going forty-five in a damn school zone, get out and give him or her a citation. I'm not in a forgiving mood today. Run the plates, Scura."

"Already on it. Registered to Maria A. Tobley, no outstanding warrants. Prior speeding citation 67/55 in Arlington, Virginia in 2027, two points."

"Whatever. Hop to it, Scura! We ain't got all day."

"Yes, Sarge."

She approached the car as the woman rolled her window down.

"Hello, Ma'am. Are you doing okay today?"

"I would be better if I hadn't been pulled over. Not the best day for me."

"I hope your day gets better. Do you know why we stopped you?"

The woman nodded and frowned. "Sorry, I know I was going too fast. Was late to work. This sure won't help any."

"Yes, Ma'am. We will get you going as soon as we can, and I am sorry for your bad day. May I have your license, registration, and proof of insurance, please?"

The overweight fortyish woman fumbled through her purse and glove box as she stared at the teen. "Here you go, Officer."

She looked at the information. "License and registration are fine, but your insurance is out of date."

"Oh, I'm sorry, I just don't have the new card in there yet. It's at home."

She smiled. "No problem, but you will need to submit that information within thirty days; your insurance carrier can do that online to the Maryland Department of Motor Vehicles. But do you know how fast you were driving?"

"A little over the limit, Officer."

She shook her head. "No, twenty-five over. That is substantial, and you are in a school zone. Very congested with children, who often do not have the best judgment when it comes to crossing the street, and they are often not very fleet."

"Oh, come on. You're really going to give me a ticket? You said you were sorry for my bad day."

"Yes, Ma'am, I am. Me feeling sorry for your substandard day has nothing to do with enforcing the law. You had another speeding ticket a year ago, so you should know better than to drive forty-five in a school zone." She wrote out the citation. "Please sign this, Ma'am. It is not an admission of guilt, just a notice to appear in court if you choose not to pay the fine. You may contest it if you wish."

The woman looked at the officer's name and then craned her neck around, looking for something. "Scura: is this some type of joke? World's Funniest Videos or something?"

She frowned and shook her head. "Oh, no, Ma'am. Speeding in Baltimore is certainly no joke. This area has some of the worst congestion around, as I have mentioned."

The lady kept staring, sizing her up. "You're really her, aren't you? It's not a stunt of some kind?"

"I am *Stella Scura,* yes, if that is what you mean. There is nothing funny about this, but if humor helps you deal with it, that is your choice, but you will likely not rejoice when you see your next car insurance bill."

Maria laughed. "But what are you doing, going out giving speeding tickets? Don't you have anything more important to do, young lady? Saving falling planes or stopping natural disasters?"

"I am a duly sworn police officer and no masked vigilante. The enforcement of all laws is important, you know. What I do is not yours to decide."

The woman laughed. "You *have* to be kidding me. But I thought you lived in Aurora City or Washington."

"I am on loan here for a while."

Mrs. Tobley looked at her citation proudly and pointed to the officer's signature. "I just realized something."

"What's that?"

"I now have your autograph. Can I sell this on E-Auction?"

"It is your copy, so you may do with it what you wish after this matter is resolved. Just make sure you mail in the copy with your payment or use the online option, or you or your attorney may bring it to court to contest it, at your discretion."

"So, if I contest it, I will see you in court?"

She nodded. "Yes, Ma'am. You have that right, always. Rest assured, though, I will show up. Do not ignore it, however; that could end in more trouble."

"Wouldn't that be a sight. *Stella Scura* in traffic court over a speeding ticket."

She shrugged. "There is no matter too small for the law."

• • •

"Motorist with a flat tire. Get out and help that old dude change it, *Scura,* pronto, hurry your sorry butt up. You took about three times too long for that speeding ticket, so don't dilly-dally."

"Yes, sir. I exist to serve; it is what I deserve." She got out of the vehicle, popped open the man's trunk, removed the jack and four-point wrench, and walked towards the elderly motorist.

"Are you really that lady *Stella Scura?*" the older man said.

She nodded. "Yes, sir."

"Then why are you using that?" He pointed to the jack and

wrench. "It's all a hoax, isn't it? All fake? I knew it."

She sighed. "No, sir, it is not, I can lift a lot."

"Then why don't you just lift it up?"

She kneeled down and knocked the hubcap off the old sedan with her right hand. "Firstly, because it is what is required under regulations. Secondly, there is no purpose in unduly attracting attention by grandstanding when a simple maneuver will suffice. Thirdly, I cannot remove the tire and hold the car up simultaneously without damaging the vehicle. Finally, I must instruct you how to do it so you do not need my help next time since I will likely not be here for that."

"Huh. I'll be darned."

She jacked up the wheel, removed the lug nuts with the wrench (not her hands) and replaced it with the spare.

• • •

"You handled that just like a regular cop would've, *Scura*. Why didn't you just lift the car up?"

She shrugged. "He wanted me to, but, as I told him, he needed instruction on how to do it so he can do it himself the next time it happens. I will likely not be present then. Also, there was no need to attract attention."

"You could've lifted that car up, though, right?"

She nodded. "Yes, of course, what a ridiculous question."

"And you could've just removed the lug nuts with your hands?"

She sighed. "Naturally, I am no weakling."

"Yet, you did it with the wrench."

"He would not have known how to do it otherwise. I doubt he has my level of strength."

"How much can you lift? Several hundred pounds?" He felt her biceps. "You're fairly solid for a girl, but you don't look all that strong. Maybe you can't lift it."

She shook her head. "I do not know my limits, Sergeant; there is no way I am aware of to test that with certainty. I lifted Air Force One, which weighs two million pounds; it was a little tiring, mostly because I did not want to crash it into anything. The more expansive a heavy object is, the harder it is to control, as even a weightless object has inertia. So I do not know, but my limit is far more than a mere automobile."

"Two million pounds? I don't believe you can really do it. I want some proof." He pulled over in an alley. "Get out, *Scura*."

"Huh? What are we doing?"

"I want you to lift the car up. If I'm going to work with you, I need to see. No one will see us back here."

"This is irrelevant to my current assignment. Plus, you said I was not to do that, and there could be cameras out here."

"Well, guess what, I'm giving you permission."

"I do not think that is a good idea, Sarge—"

"There's a part of me that thinks it's an exaggeration. I still don't believe all the hoopla."

She frowned and crossed her arms. "This is absurd and juvenile. I do not have to prove anything to you."

"What did you say?"

"I said—I think it is childish for me to give you a demonstration of my strength when we are supposed to be working. We are wasting taxpayer dollars just to satisfy your curiosity!"

"Okay, look, I need to understand who I'm working with, and this helps with that. The sooner you do it, the sooner we can get back to protecting the taxpayers, Scura."

"You cannot order me to do that, Sarge."

"Ha. You scared of doing it, rookie?"

She uncrossed her arms and pointed at him with her left hand. "I am scared of nothing. I just do not enjoy drawing attention to myself, Sarge."

"That's hard to believe."

"Oh, okay, if you insist." She crawled under the car.

"I thought you were going to lift it, not change the oil."

The supine female peeked out from under the side. "Sergeant, I do not want to damage your very special car, and I am quite adept at determining the best way of lifting things. This is the best way to lift the car, like a service station lift, if you get my drift."

"Okay, fine, just do it, then."

"Hold on." He watched in amazement as she gradually stood up under it, hoisting the car over her head like a toy barbell.

"Holy shit," he said. "That cruiser weighs forty-five hundred pounds. Is it hard for you to hold that?"

She sighed. "No, of course not, are you daft?"

"Can you fly with it?"

She rose ten feet off the ground, car over her head. "Yes." She sat it back down and crawled back out from under the car. "Do you have any further questions?"

He shook his head. "Crap, I guess not."

"Good. We had best get back to work, sir. The taxpayers would not be fond of us fooling around like this."

• • •

One hour later, they received an emergency call and raced towards the dilapidated neighborhood on the east side of downtown. This wasn't a traffic stop, changing a flat, or fooling around lifting cars up; someone was attempting suicide, and they were the closest vehicle in the vicinity.

They pulled up, exited the vehicle, and raced towards the commotion as multiple onlookers gaped at her.

"What's the plan, Sarge?"

"Scura, that pregnant lady on the ledge has a gun and is threatening to jump. You'd better stay back while I take charge, at least till the rescue team gets here."

"How long for that to occur?"

"A few minutes. May be too late by then."

She looked up and saw the woman on the twelfth-story ledge as a large crowd had formed in the street. "Sergeant, I can take care of it, do not have a fit."

"We need to go get her down; I'm not messing with this."

"Just let me talk to her, okay? There is no harm in that. You are the one who said there was to be no grandstanding. I am very persuasive, and not always abrasive."

"What if she jumps?"

"I am fast enough to grab her before she hits the ground."

"At the speed she'd be falling, she'd break every bone in her body when you catch her."

She shook her head and removed her gloves. "No, her kinetic energy will be instantly absorbed by me once my hands touch her, just like when a bullet hits me."

"Okay, but you've got five minutes until the backup and fire department arrives, Scura. Don't do anything dumb or make me regret this."

"Not to worry, Scura must scurry."

She climbed up the fire escape twelve stories to where the

young gravid woman was on the twelve-inch ledge. There was no purpose in attracting any further attention by flying. To most of the bystanders, she likely appeared no different than any other officer. She walked onto the narrow ledge and stopped about ten feet from the woman.

"I'll jump, lady, don't come any closer," the twentyish brunette woman said harshly, waving a revolver with her right hand.

"I am not coming closer, I just want to talk to you."

"Why would I want to talk to you, kiddie cop?"

"I am sure you would like to talk to someone. Can you tell me why you want to do this?"

"How can I start? I'm broke, I'm on drugs, my boyfriend cheated on me, and I'm pregnant. How about them apples? Like I've got a lot to live for."

"Despite your misfortune, you really do not want to do this."

"I do, and what do you know about it? I got nobody. You don't understand my goddamn life."

"What is your name?"

The woman shook her head. "Doesn't matter."

"It does to me."

"Okay, fine, lady: Debbie. Like anyone gives a shit. You happy now that you know a druggie's name? Make you feel all warm and fuzzy inside, hero?"

"I know what it is like to be rejected, to be different, Debbie. You say you have nobody, no friends. Surely there is at least one person who must care about you, someone you can reach out to. Someone whose life would be worse if you died."

"You don't know a damn thing about my life. And there ain't no one who would care."

"Yes, there is one—inside of you. You will be that child's mother, and that person will need you for many, many years. But if you take your life, your baby will have no chance. Think of what a child will be able to do for you."

"I don't want any of that. I didn't want this baby, lady, and they'll take it away from me, anyway, with the life I've led."

"Maybe not, but only if I can help you."

"Yeah? What if I don't want a baby?"

"Then you can give him or her up for adoption. There are many childless people who would gladly love and raise your child for you and love him or her as much as you would."

"How do you know I'd love it at all?"

"I know better. But you must give him or her a chance at life. It is not up to you to make that choice."

"How do you think you can help?"

"It may not be easy, but we can get you a job, the help you need to have a healthy pregnancy."

"Yeah, well, I have a gun. I'll shoot you and everyone else."

"I know you could, but you don't really want to do that. Give me the gun, Debbie. You are better than this."

Debbie waved the gun, not very menacingly. "I'll do it; I'll blow you away. Why shouldn't I? I bet you're not as tough as they say."

"Why? Because you will never forgive yourself if you shoot me. This is not what you want to do, you are just scared."

"So what, lady? I've made shitty decisions all my crummy life, so why should I change now?"

"Then make the right one this time. Can I come to help you? I promise you'll be safe." She sat her gun on the ledge. "See, I put mine down, so why don't you do the same?"

"I'll feel lots better if I shoot someone, starting with you."

She shook her head. "No, you will not. You will regret it for the rest of your life. This is a turning point, so make the right choice."

"It's so hard, though."

"I know it is, but just take your time. Think it through."

A long, three-minute pause. "Okay."

She walked across the three-inch ledge briskly and grabbed her. "Give me the gun; I shall not hurt you." She took the nickel-plated revolver away, put it in her left pocket, and pinned her against the outer wall, then moved her towards the window and put her back inside as officers grabbed her and closed the window. After she was safely inside, she walked down the fire escape again, as that would attract less attention than going down the "other" way.

• • •

"I don't get you, Scura. If I were you, I would've just taken that gun away from that chick and let her jump. You say you could've safely caught her, correct?"

She nodded. "Of course I could have done it that way, but that was not my play. I would have absorbed her kinetic energy the moment we made contact, so it would not have injured her. But she was pregnant, so why take that risk? Even if that would not have caused physical injury to her or the fetus, it could have caused emotional distress, yes?"

"I dunno. Then why did you do things the hard way yet again?"

"Sergeant Levickis, I will loudly opine with no attempt to be offensive: just because that took more time and patience did not make it the 'hard way.' Certainly, we did not need the commotion, but mostly because she needed to make the decision herself, sir, or she would have gone down the dark path of destruction."

"What? 'Dark path of destruction?' What a dramatic statement, and I don't need a philosophy lesson, holy cow. I didn't know you had a degree in psychology too." He slapped himself in the face with his right hand.

"No, but she might never have emerged from that. Her life may not be perfect, but she can have the self-respect that she made a correct decision for once in her life. Sometimes less is more."

"She's a drugged-out pregnant lady, not some heroic person on the brink of a grand decision to save mankind. Get some perspective here. The sooner you stop trying to save lost souls, the better."

She shook her head angrily. "And she is also a human being deserving of our respect, which many seem to have forgotten. There is heroism in even the smallest of tasks. What Debbie did was a small step on a long journey of building her self-esteem. And when I stop trying to do that, it will be time to hang it up."

He laughed. "Oh, my, Scura. Don't think you're the first rookie cop who saw the world this way his first day with rose-colored glasses. Wait until you're on the streets for twenty or thirty years, *then* see how you feel about seeing drugged-out Debbies every day. This job changes you, and not for the better. I know you're moving on to bigger and better things this old cop can't even comprehend, but this is my world and how I see it."

She shook her head. "It would be the same way. She is one who can be more than she believes is possible. It may not mean much to you, but for this tiny fraction of her life, she can know that someone cared."

"What did you tell her up there, anyway?"

"I told her that she would never forgive herself if she shot me."

"Why? To spare her the guilt of trying to kill someone? What good was that dumb remark? It wouldn't have hurt you."

She shook her head. "No, of course not, but the mere act of

discharging that revolver might have caused irreparable psychological damage, despite the fact it would not have harmed me. She needed to come to that decision herself, not by the use of force."

"Ah, so you are a shrink now. What if she had started pointing it at others?"

"Well, then, I would have had to take it away, and I could have easily reacted quickly enough to do that. She would not have gotten a shot off, trust me." She tapped on her service weapon. "Besides, she didn't even have the safety off, so she didn't even know how to use it."

Sgt. Levickis shook his head. "You know, Scura, you're kind of okay for a gal."

She patted him on the back. "Thanks, Levickis."

"Hey! What happened to 'Sir' or 'Sergeant'?"

"I figured I earned the right to call you Levickis like the other guys."

"They don't call me that, but I'm sure they call me some words I can't say in front of a lady."

"You know what? You remind me a lot of your sister."

He laughed. "Hell, you got that right. And I'll take that as a compliment. Jackie is one tough customer."

"Let us go buy you that beer. I will, of course, abstain."

• • •

Two hours later, a Baltimore TV station broke the news about the rescue event on the noon news as a blonde woman's face appeared on screen.

"*Stella Scura* walked up a fire escape—didn't fly—and talked down a young pregnant woman with a gun who was going to jump," the eyewitness reporter said. "She didn't threaten her, or use any force or any display of super-powers—she merely talked to her for a while and the lady gave her the gun. No one was hurt. I swear to God I never saw anything like that. She could've easily flown up there and taken it away, but there you have it, folks: the incredible *Stella Scura,* for some reason working as a police officer in Baltimore, saved a pregnant woman by talking her out of it rather than by using force. To this reporter, she's a real hero. Anyone who says she's a grandstander, call me, because I was there. Holly Young reporting for Channel 5 Eyewitness News."

Chapter Forty-Eight

United States Penitentiary, Lee
Hickory Flat Road
Pennington Gap, Virginia

After a thirty-minute flight on Marine One and a brief drive from an airfield in southwest Virginia, an armored Presidential vehicle entered the gate of the maximum-security federal prison and drove through the heavily guarded area.

"What on Earth is this place?" *Stella* asked, sitting across from the President. "It looks like a penitentiary of some sort. Hideous."

"You would be very perceptive," the President replied. "Hey, you wanted to come here, so figure it out, genius—where did you think he'd be? I have far better things to do with my time, but it's your school field trip. Not my favorite place."

"You will see. And I do not believe you will find it to be a waste of time."

They exited as Wendy brought *Stella* through a series of corridors to a dimly lit room as a guard opened the door, and led her inside, Jackie following.

"I'm not in favor of this activity, young lady," Jackie stated sternly. "What do you possibly hope to accomplish by visiting Private Last Class Brant Gallagher?"

"Not that I answer to you, Jackie, but I want to see the true evil in the world. This is it. Make sure all the recording devices are turned off."

"They are, but you are way out of line here." Jackie turned to her boss. "And *you* brought her here, Ma'am."

"I did, as she needs closure on this particular issue."

"Huh. I am tired of you bossing me around, Jackie; your voice makes a very irritating sound, like your brother. For now—"

"Then I'm outta here. I'll be outside if you need anything. I don't want to know what happens in this place."

"Let us stop the bickering." She put her hand on Wendy's shoulder. "Where are we, Wendy?"

"We're where *you* wanted to go. The man across from that two-way mirror in this interrogation room is the one who killed your father, Cassie and Jake, their father, my mom, your cousin Jose and uncle Mike, and a dozen other people. He also helped kill President Graham."

"This mere man?" She looked at the man through the one-way mirror. "He did all those horrific things?"

"He and Sung Shoi-Ming, the former 'President' of Tosia."

"Former President?"

"Well, dictator is more like it. Yes, when you die, you become the 'former' President, duh."

"You always had maintained the North Koreans did it."

"That was for the media. I'm smart enough to know what really happened, dear."

"Well, what happened to this Ming? Did we assassinate him?"

"Did 'we' assassinate him? Hardly. Someone sure did, though. He was found decapitated in his palace a few months later with the number 119 burned in his chest by a hot implement. What a creative signature from a big thinker."

"Decapitated? With a saw or axe?"

"Nope. His head was just ripped off his body."

She shook her head. "No single person has the strength to do that, except for Juriann."

"We're pretty sure it wasn't him. Think again; it'll come to you."

"119 is an odd number. Does it have significance?"

Wendy snickered. "Yeah, I'm sure it does to one person."

"To whom?"

"We never proved it for sure, but we have our suspicions. You really don't want to know."

"I do not?"

Wendy shook her head. "No, trust me on that one. Go to the

periodic table of elements and figure it out. Anyway, Gallagher is also the one who took your sight away."

"My sight is not gone; my brain just perceives things wrong."

"You know what I mean."

"This does not look to be a very nice place, so he must be 'paying' for his crime already." She walked up to him as they went through the door. "Is this true? Are you the one who did these terrible things to us?"

Brant Gallagher stood up and looked at Wendy. "Well, well, look who's here. With a new friend. Who the hell is this idiot in a Halloween costume? You really are off your rocker, Mendoza."

"The President says that you are the man who helped cause *Darkkday*. Is that correct?"

He stared down at her. "Little girl, I would do it all over again. There is nothing you can do to me that hasn't been done already. I'm just amazed the President had the guts to come down here herself."

"You think this to be so? Should I have my revenge?"

"What is this dumb teenager going to do to me that hasn't already been done?" He laughed. "I get sick of this. Just kill me already, if that's what you want to do."

"A death with honor, eh? You do not even begin to deserve that. And I forget you do not get very good TV reception down here, so you have missed out on some things."

Wendy pointed at him. "She's what you wanted, you evil miscreant. You remember, don't you?"

"Remember w1hat?"

"Our first meeting, when you killed President Graham, and how you wanted to get rid of the 'genetically defectives.' Like Hitler, to build your Aryan prince or princess. Well, here she is, Gallagher. Rejoice."

"This girl? She can't be more than seventeen or eighteen years old. Doesn't look so tough to me." He laughed.

"You dare laugh at me? I can reduce you to dust."

"Yeah? Who are you?" he yelled.

"I am *Stella Scura*, the Dark Star. I could crush you with the force of a hundred Gs."

"Really? Then do it, and put me out of my misery."

"Is that really what you want?" Wendy asked.

"He killed my family and many other Americans."

"I brought you here to face your past, not to do this. You are a hero, not a person of revenge."

"What? Do you not want me to do it? He would have done the same to you."

"Yes, I feared you would say that. An eye for an eye? Is that what you want to do?"

"I am not a violent person, but in this case, hell yes."

"It's a dichotomous choice. You can't be both." Wendy stared down into her niece's visor. "Matthew 5:38: *'You have heard that it was said, 'Eye for eye, and tooth for tooth. But I tell you, do not resist an evil person. If anyone slaps you on the right cheek, turn to them the other cheek also.'"*

"You sound like someone else I used to live with."

"That's good. While I can't ever forgive this SOB for what he's done to innocent people, neither can I destroy him."

"No . . . but *I* can." She floated ten inches off the ground and stared down at him. "It would be so easy."

"Who the hell are you? How are you doing that?"

"I am *Stella Scura,* the Dark Star. I have the strength of a million men. You may soon find out."

"Seems like a rather unfair fight."

Wendy stared at her as she slowly returned to the ground, ripped a metal stook from the concrete, and crushed it into a spheroid. "I could do this to your head." She then turned away. "But I will not right now. Maybe later."

"What?" Gallagher said, astonished. "You're not going to take my head off? That's insane. You have no hatred for me? What kind of an idiot are you?"

"I would not expect you to understand, lowly cretin. You never will." She hurled the crushed stool into the concrete wall.

"You're an imbecile, just like these other people."

"Yeah? I surely am, a fact no one can retract." She looked back at him, then at Wendy. "Thanks for showing me the light, Madam President; it was truly an epiphany. I now shall leave this place." She walked out the room door.

"You wanted to come here. Do whatever the hell you want."

"I will." She pushed Wendy aside gently. "I said I am leaving. You do not give orders to me; no one does. I will do as I wish."

"Come back." She walked down the dimly lit corridor to another area as they went into another conference room.

"I am the one the powers were given to. Not by God, but by someone. Not to you, Wendy, or my mother. It is not so purely by chance. If that is a harsh realization for you, then so be it."

"Trust me, I'm over it, honey."

"I need to realize my destiny, as I have the power of a god. Since you are quoting scripture, try this one on for size—Judges 16:28: *Then Samson prayed to the Lord, "O Sovereign Lord, remember me. O God, please strengthen me just once more, and let me with one blow get revenge on the Philistines for my two eyes."*

Wendy laughed. "How prophetic. But, as you have likely determined, I am not you." Wendy pushed her aside. "You're not Samson, either, nor are you the 'sovereign lord' you envision yourself to be. I desire no revenge for the loss of my family, as going down that path lies madness. It has, rather, made me into something I wouldn't otherwise have been."

"Your choice, not mine. But what about our family?"

"Killing him won't bring them back. Ask your mom if she's any happier after having ripped Ming's head off with her bare hands."

She stopped in her tracks. "What . . . what did you say?"

"You heard me. Element 119, mendozium. Put two and two together, Einstein."

"My mother did that? How? You're lying."

"I wish I was, dear, but ask her yourself when you see her next; she's pretty much incapable of lying outright. Her mind has grown to be so powerful that she is apparently capable of almost anything. Go on, are you going to follow in her footsteps or not? First Malachi Argon, then Shoi-Ming, now Gallagher. There were also a couple of additional lackeys I forgot to mention. Go for it."

"What? You cannot possibly excuse what he has done."

Wendy shook her head. "I don't; I'm not Christ, who can turn the other cheek, but neither can I just kill him. And, like Detail Chief Levickis, I don't like your little stunt." She poked her finger into her aunt's chest. "I also don't like to be manipulated, and I thought you would just talk to him, stupid me. Don't *ever* order me around or pull this kind of thing again, you read me? You need me about a hundred times more than I need you right now."

"That is not what I was trying to do."

"*Bullshit*, Aurora. You're not talking to your mom, with an IQ of 300 coupled with the interpersonal skills of and less common sense than a chimpanzee. Gallagher may be destined to live the rest of his natural life in a cave like this, but I can't stoop to your level." She faced her niece angrily. "I don't take orders from you or anyone else. Like I said, You didn't vote for me, so it appears that was the right decision. You are also as stubborn as your mom and quite possibly as violent, maybe more. And way out of line."

"Shut up. You are used to bullying people, are you not?"

"I have immense responsibilities that you can't possibly comprehend. I give orders; I don't take them. If you perceive that as 'bullying,' then I'm sorry. Do you want to be me in twenty years? Well, welcome to my world, missy. It ain't easy. Everything in Washington is done the hard way, navigating a bureaucracy beyond your comprehension. I wasn't given a smorgasbord of superpowers like you were. Yet, I seem to get by somehow."

"And do you have any comprehension as to the responsibility having *my* power is? Every action I take—every touch, every handshake—could potentially injure or even kill someone." She stuck a finger into her aunt's right breast. "So you just think about that. I just want justice."

"I have some anger too, as I am certainly not devoid of emotion, but does killing Gallagher bring any of those people back? Do two wrongs make a right?"

"Honestly? It sure as hell will make me feel better, Wendy."

"Then go back and do it! You're big enough to take him, I imagine, the guards and I can't stop you. You've known about this for less than two months; I've known about it for twelve years and have dealt with it. But, hey, go beat the crap out of him, for all I care, if it will satisfy your primal needs. Just don't ask me to participate. Your mom would be so proud."

"But I need resolution."

Wendy shook her head. "Maybe initially that would help, but it's something you'll surely regret later. This isn't who you are, reducing yourself to a mere thug. I'm so ashamed of you."

"Wait—"

"No, *you* wait. You think long and hard about this. I assume you can provide your own transportation back to the White House, as I would rather fly back alone right now."

• • •

After returning to the White House (having traveled the 400

miles from USP Lee in twenty minutes), she removed her action costume, took a quick shower, put on a sweatshirt and some shorts, and took a brief nap. An hour later, she sleepily heard the inevitable knock on the door.

"Can I come in?" Wendy asked.

"Sure, it's your house, whatever. It sure took you guys long enough to get back." She munched on some peanuts she had left on the bedside stand. "What do you need?"

"I feel the way I feel, Paige. It was wrong for me to take you out to USP Lee."

"Huh? I am the one who wanted to go out there, so why are you apologizing? If you have any lingering thoughts I am the daughter of God, then that trip should have cleared that up mighty fast."

"Believe me—I never thought that. But I could've refused to take you there, so I own part of it."

"I could have made it out there myself. You have something else to tell me? Nothing excuses my behavior."

"I suppose it could have been worse. Yes, will you go with me to my room? I want to show you something."

She sighed. "I suppose. What of value would be there?"

"Let's go and find out." She and Wendy walked down the hall to the master bedroom, as she felt the bed and sat down.

"Why are we here? I know you are still mad about what I did."

"Yes, I am definitely mad, but I also want you to learn something from this. I would like you to feel two things that are very important. This is the first." She felt a small box thrust into her right hand and opened it. It was pointed on several surfaces, made of dense metal, hanging from cloth.

"It feels like an award or medal of some kind. Texture and weight—brass. It is not nearly large enough to be your Olympic gold medal, which sits on your desk. It is also clearly not your fabled hot dog eating contest trophy. The shape, a pentagonal star, is also not the same. I assume it is to have some significance," she said sarcastically. "Physical possessions mean little to me if you did not know that already."

"This one is far more than a possession, and I went through living hell to get it, and I hoped it would mean something to you. I'd rather not have it, but I can't go back in time; I don't show it to many people or display it prominently in my office. But it's my Medal of Honor. President Reardon gave that to me in 2014 for almost giving my life to save his. We were at a conference discussing health care reform when some crazy idiot pulls out a ceramic pistol and starts screaming fifteen feet from us. I was standing right next to Reardon and Prime Minister Truesdale, pushed them both down, and took four bullets in the chest after I knocked down the assassin. I almost died. They cracked my chest open, removed most of my right lung, patched up my right atrium while I was on open heart bypass, and I was in the intensive care unit for three weeks and rehab for three months. Had I not been in good shape from the Olympics, I probably would have died."

She patted Wendy on the left shoulder. "Every American school student knows about that, and I am grateful for your sacrifice, do not get me wrong; I know the pain you must have suffered, but I still do not see the connection or relevance to what I did today."

She felt Wendy touch her face. "Do you understand, now? *Really?* You know the pain I've suffered? You have *no* possible idea what physical suffering is like, do you? I'm not criticizing you for something you don't comprehend, but I'm trying to enlighten you. If you want to be me in twenty years, then you'd better learn to understand the people you want to represent. You can't afford to have missteps like I did."

"How do you know what I understand?"

"You don't. You think you perceive human behavior better than your mom, but for all her many shortcomings, she's one up on you there, as she understands real pain and suffering."

"Hey, I was bullied when I was younger. Being blind is not easy, lady."

"Yes, but you knew you could retaliate and chose not to. Your mom wasn't that way. She was so weak after her bout of meningitis at age eleven that she couldn't walk for months. Unless you can be one of the people, you'll never be more than a novelty to them."

"I do not experience physical pain, but I have had emotional suffering. Not of the magnitude you have endured, but I can sympathize nonetheless."

"To some small extent, perhaps. But I have more to tell you."

"Great. But I still do not understand what you are trying to tell me, Aunt Wendy. What does it have to do with me? I cannot possibly understand that perspective."

"That's exactly my point. I'm *not* trying to impress you or want you to think I'm great or anything, and you seem to have a relatively low opinion of me, which I may deserve."

She shook her head. "You misunderstand, and I am quite sorry if I gave that impression. I have immense respect for you and the things you have done. I also think you are a good, albeit occasionally flawed, person. Yet, that does not mean I will fall at your feet and agree with everything, though. It is not all or nothing."

"Understood. You seem to have your own opinions, and I respect them. But realize that there are many persons who put themselves selflessly in danger every day, knowing full well they may never see tomorrow. Your mom almost died after she was stabbed in the chest, chasing after some criminal."

"What? My mom did that too?"

"Yes, she has led a rather bold life. Only my brother's—your father's—makeshift surgery saved her life. You can't possibly know what that's like."

She sighed. "Mom likes riddles, but I certainly do not care for them. What is your point?"

"What I'm trying to ask is—have you ever feared for your life?"

She thought for a few seconds and shook her head. "No, not even when that missile blew up my armor in Alaska because I knew I would not die. Sorry, I do not know what I can do about it."

"You can try and understand it and that there are many real heroes out there, all beside you and Juriann, all without special abilities."

She shrugged. "I have much to learn, it seems. I am not being facetious; I really mean that."

"Then please try to understand where I'm coming from. We all can be a little bit better each day. I know I can, and I've already learned much from you. Did you learn something today?"

"I suppose so, and I am just not used to people standing up to me like that."

"I know. I wish Gallagher was dead, too. But don't preach as if you're this all-knowing soothsayer because I've yet to find anyone who knew everything. Fame can go to your head, and you can learn a little bit, too. Your uncle Mike—Bella's father—and grandfather Carlos were police officers who put their lives on the line every day, knowing they could be seriously injured or killed. That's one thing you don't know: the fear of mortal injury."

"So, are we done admiring your medals of precious metals?"

"We are. But that's not the main reason I brought you in here."

She felt Wendy put something else into her left hand. "Finally, I have something else for you."

"What's this? I am to be impressed by yet another medal you have been awarded?" She yawned. "You said we were done."

Wendy laughed. "No, not hardly. It's a very simple thing, but something of great significance to me and the world. You tell me what it is. You should know as it's now being returned to its rightful owner after many years."

"Huh?" She felt the smooth metal object; it had a thin twisted chain; it seemed to be a bracelet of some sort. Too small for her wrist; it must have belonged to a child. The solid plate was engraved with cursive letters that spelled a name. She went over it with her fingers and smiled in excitement. "It spells my name—*Aurora*. Did this bracelet belong to me when I was a child?"

"Yes, it is indeed the lost bracelet of legend, but it represents much more than that. It was discovered by a farmer in northeastern Virginia six weeks after *Darkkday*. It must've fallen from the sky and is the only known completely intact personal effect of anyone on the doomed plane. There were small fragments of the aircraft found and a piece of a sapphire watch crystal which we think was from your mom's Rolex, but nothing else."

"The bracelet contains a small gem of some kind, above the 'o.' What is it?"

"Your birthstone—tourmaline. This stone is the pink variety, made deeper in color, my scientists say, only by intense gamma ray exposure, which converts the manganese from the divalent to the trivalent form. You can probably imagine how that happened."

She shook her head. "But how could that have been possible? While I understand now how Mom and I survived, how could this have endured?"

"You must've removed it and had it in your closed hand at the time of the blast, then dropped it as you both plummeted to Earth, but it clearly absorbed some gamma radiation along the way. You couldn't fly at that time, so you and your mom hit Earth at terminal velocity. I wasn't there, of course, just speculating."

She thought for a moment. "Correct. For as long as I have remembered, I have been invulnerable, but I did not gain the full power of flight until sixteen, and then it was slow, until I learned how to handle it."

"As your closest living relatives, it was returned to Jay and me.

It represents hope, honey. There are millions of people who think Aurora Darkkin somehow saved Washington. They were right."

"So can you."

"I can what?"

She sighed. "Save Washington."

"I don't understand, dear. Save it from what?"

"From you and what you have created—the military might to destroy the planet, an unbalanced government the likes the world has never seen. You were once not this way, Wendy Gallinsworth Darkkin. I know better."

"Well, this job wears on a person. But how would you know anything about me or what I've endured? I didn't think I was one of your favorite historical figures."

"I know much no one else does. Mom killed Malachi Argon in revenge. You tried to stop her, in a scene reminiscent of the one we played out earlier today, with Gallagher—just as I am squabbling with you now. Yet, she carried out her threat and killed Shoi-Ming in grisly fashion as well, you claim. I have no reason to doubt you after thinking about it further."

"Have you then reflected on your actions today?"

"Yes. I believe crossing that line has affected her in a way from which she can never recover. Knowing this now, how could I have been so stupid?"

"You aren't stupid, but you're still an adolescent, prone to impulsivity. But you believe me now about your mom?"

She nodded. "I do, for reasons that will make you even more ashamed of me, because I have seen it."

"You've seen what?"

"Mom killing Malachi Argon."

"What does that mean? How?"

"The morbid incident was recorded by the original Vladimirov armor almost twenty years ago. *Admiral Ampere* was able to retrieve the old video from the damaged helmet and was finally able to decrypt it, so I saw it all. You were in the background, pregnant with Cassie." She put her hand on her aunt's shoulder and embraced her. "And, yet, I almost did the same thing."

"But you didn't . . . you stopped yourself."

"Barely. You do not know how close I was."

"But the Argon incident was over twenty years ago, and I thought the armor was destroyed after you went down near the

Bering Strait."

"The helmet was damaged, but Todd was able to recover some of the data. I am rather sorry he did, as some things are better left alone."

"Paige, I can't take the pain away from either of us or change what your mom has become. If I had one wish, it would be for her to be normal, or as normal as Bonnie can be."

"But my dad—your brother—your Jake and Cassie, and many others—are gone forever, and that man is responsible."

Wendy nodded. "Yes, they're gone, and no amount of hoping will ever bring them back. Therefore, we can only remember them for the wonderful people they were and not for the time they lost on Earth because the past can't be changed, Paige. But remember that without that event, Will would've never been born. A part of my brother lives within you. And within Juriann lives part of Cassie and Rad and Travis Argon. From the death of others come new lives. You have to take the good with the bad."

"How foolish I have been. I thought I knew everything, but my wisdom pales compared to yours."

Wendy put her hand on her shoulder. "Not really. We're all just human, most of all me, but it's not too late for you to be better than who you are now. Most kids at eighteen feel they are omniscient. It takes a while to realize you don't know everything."

"Agreed. And *you* have four more years of greatness." She took Wendy's large hand. "Come, let us go on a brief field trip to a place more enlightening than the last one."

"Where? I wasn't too fond of our last adventure."

"It is not far but I doubt you go there much. Time to change my hair color again. I need some more shampoo."

• • •

The Secret Service presidential detail cleared out the area surrounding the Franklin Delano Roosevelt Memorial as *Stella* and Wendy walked through the simple pavilion, honoring the only President elected to four terms. Wendy looked around curiously and smiled.

"Okay, I give up: why did you want to come here? Because FDR was a Democrat, or because he was President as long as I will have been by 2032?"

"Neither; those would be rather shallow reasons. No, for two purposes." They walked briskly to the bronze statue of FDR in his wheelchair. "This, the first reason."

"FDR had poliomyelitis, or possibly Guillain-Barré syndrome, everyone knows that. Salk's vaccine wasn't available until 1955, although that wouldn't have helped with GBS."

"Yes, but in the thirties and forties, it was shameful to have a disability. Television was in its infancy. He made sure he was never seen in his wheelchair, as he would have been seen as weak and not deserving to lead a nation. He spent much time at Warm Springs, Georgia, to try and get his legs back. But it never happened."

Wendy rolled her eyes and shook her head annoyingly, looking at the massive crowd that had gathered around the perimeter. "I know all that, *Stella*, I'm a well-educated physician who specialized in pediatric physical medicine and rehabilitation, for Heaven's sake, so I know about those diseases. What is your point?"

"That he was flawed, yet he had much to contribute. Now, let us go over here, to the Great Depression monument." They walked over to the depiction of a number of unemployed men waiting for a handout before the New Deal. "Read the plaque out loud."

Wendy looked at it and sighed. "The test of our progress is not whether we add more to the abundance of those who have much; it is whether we provide enough for those who have too little."

"What do you think?"

"I'm embarrassed to say I've never seen this before. Amazing what you don't see in your own town."

"But do you not believe it to be true?"

"I suppose it contains some truth, yes. But life is more complicated today than it was almost a hundred years ago, as I have many problems to deal with Roosevelt didn't."

"Not so much, Madam President. You only have to believe in what's right. The Middle East. The Russians. South America. All could benefit from fusion energy. They have many people like those depicted in this display."

"What? We're not talking about money, but technology they aren't ready for and could use for something else. You can't possibly be suggesting that we give that to them for *free?*"

"What is your alternative? Surely you can't expect the poorest countries in the world to pay for such technology or develop it on their own."

"Huh? Why the heck not? Who gave it to us?"

"My mom and cousin did, and not to be used this way. You say you want to be the benevolent person you once were? Prove it now. Give them what they need to rebuild their countries. It's what FDR would have done."

"They could pervert those technologies into weapons and probably blow themselves up in the process. It's wonderful you admire this great man, but your reality is a bit distorted. Roosevelt himself *created* the Manhattan Project, the objective of which you clearly know. He was clearly no pacifist, lest you think otherwise. Don't be so damn naïve. It's not what he would've done at all."

"You always think that, don't you?"

"What, that an eighteen-year-old girl from North Pole is naïve? Another inane question."

"Well, do we not have sufficient missiles and weapons? Why would they want that?"

"That should be obvious." She pointed to herself with her thumb. "Hey, I have to worry about that stuff. I don't have the luxury of thinking about whatever I want like you do."

Paige paused. "Well, remember that you will always have me to back you up."

"Or you to stop me, is that what you really mean?"

"That, too."

"Good luck with that and public opinion. North Korea was a horrible communist regime. I cleaned it up, and their tyranny is gone. Same with Iran, Iraq, and Cuba. Many others talked a good line, but I stand by my actions."

"I agree that those regimes were less than ideal. But there are many poor people in the world. You know there is a better way. Show us the path to enlightenment."

Wendy frowned. "Who do you think you are, *Stella*—the Ghost of Christmas Past? Showing old Scrooge the error in her ways?"

"Of course not, but maybe we can rethink things. Are you so surrounded by yes-men and yes-women that you cannot tolerate constructive criticism?"

Wendy paused for a moment. "No. No, I'm not. Maybe you believe otherwise, but in the end, I do what I think is right, and I value hearing diverse opinions. Yet, perhaps you are correct in that I should value them more."

"But Juriann thought I was Santa Claus, remember? All I need now is a red and white suit."

"I've got one around here somewhere. I *am* the White House Santa Claus, you know, I'm sure the right size."

"I did not know that. Do *not* expect me to sit in your lap."

"Don't worry."

"The clothing will be too large for me, though. A flying Santa will be quite a sight."

"Thanks a lot for the comment."

She shook her head. "I meant the height."

"Sure you did." Wendy punched her in the shoulder. "That feels really weird; it's like hitting a marshmallow." Wendy punched her again, harder. "Cool."

"Ha. I assure you that if I punched you back it would not feel like a marshmallow."

"You wouldn't hit me, though, would you?"

"I would not strike my Commander-in-Chief. That would get me in much worse trouble than protesting and serving food to the homeless without a permit."

"Likely so. What's next on your agenda?"

She stood up. "Taking a little trip."

"Good. With whom?"

"Flying solo. I am going to New Persia to visit an old friend of Nick's who offered me an invitation."

"Well, say hi to Fahnaz for me. She's a pretty sharp gal."

"You really think so? Your opponent?"

"Just because we were opponents doesn't mean I don't like and respect her, *Stella*. You have a lot to learn about politics, and life."

Chapter Forty-Nine

Falton Strategic Air Command
New Persia

The Air Force staff sergeant saw the report on the screen and opened her eyes wide as she woke up from what was usually a pretty boring job. Today was destined to be different, he knew.

"Major, there was an optical sighting of a tiny object traveling at Mach 5.9 across the Mediterranean Sea towards the border. There is a non-directional beacon broadcasting. Non-hostility verified."

"Call sign, Staff Sergeant?"

"Sir, there's only one possibility, given its estimated size and mass." She pointed at the LCD monitor, which spelled out "*STELLASCURA*" on the readout. "There it is. *Stella Scura* is now entering American air space."

"Wow. Are you kidding me? Wonder what's up?"

"Don't know, Major. I'd better let Becker at Graham Army Base know."

"She's headed into town, not the Army base, but I suppose that's the courteous thing to do."

• • •

She landed on U.S. soil outside the airport downtown as a tall brown-haired man was waiting to greet her at the private VIP gate she was instructed to go to as dozens of onlookers gaped. She had stopped in the restroom briefly to take off her aviation helmet and comb her hair.

"Ms. Scura, I am Shalid Ahmad, the Senator's chief aide. Welcome to the great State of New Persia."

She nodded and removed her helmet. "Thank you, Mr. Ahmad, please call me *Stella*. I appreciate your hospitality, and I look forward to my visit."

"I will take you to a guest area so you can, er, freshen up. The clothing and other personal items you have requested are there as well."

"Thank you. My hair is a mess, it will need some repair work, and I did not bring clothes."

"Our hairdresser is ready for you, and we have a complete wardrobe, per your request. But no luggage?" he asked curiously.

She shook her head. "No, I travel light for a flight. What you see is what you get."

"We have someone to help with that, as well."

She showered in the large airport VIP lounge set aside for her and put on the white blouse, navy slacks, and matching navy jacket that the female attendant provided. While New Persia was part of the United States, it was still culturally Middle Eastern, and it was considered appropriate for women to dress conservatively. This generally meant that arms and legs were covered and hair covered with a *hijab*, or head covering. This was not enforced on any official level, as this was still American soil and subject to American laws, but she wanted to be respectful of the customs of a new land. She walked out towards where Ahmad was positioned and smiled, carrying her action costume in a small satchel that she had requested.

"You blend in pretty well," he said.

"I try," she said dryly. "Most of the time, I succeed. Not always. Lots of people wearing sunglasses here, it seems."

She got in the door of the limousine that a male attendant opened for her as they drove off towards the Senator's residence.

"So, why are you in our fair state for the first time?" Ahmad asked as they pulled away.

She smiled and took a sip of coffee he had poured for her. "It is really not my first time in New Persia, but it *is* my first visit to Freedom City." Her first visit was flying California Senator Doug Thomasson's brother Alan back to America from Taraq and she didn't want to talk about that. "I've only been across the border once."

"Oh, I'm sorry, I didn't know."

"I am also an ardent admirer of Senator Saleh's and have been for some time. I wanted to meet her, and this seemed like a good opportunity."

"Yes, but that was a long flight for you to come here. She isn't even here that much, as she spends most of her time in Washington like the other members of Congress. It would've been easier just to meet up with her there in a few weeks."

Well, she was a bit tired of Washington and wanted to go somewhere more scenic. "I know, but I had never been to the state capital and wanted to come. I have never been to the Middle East except for one short trip, as I said, when I had no time for sightseeing. There is so much to see and learn. And the flight is not that long."

He opened his mouth wide. "*Not that long?* It's a thirteen-hour flight from O'Hare, JFK, or Dulles after you get your connecting flight from Aurora City or Indianapolis."

"Maybe for you, but it's only about two and a half hours for me. Plus, I don't have to deal with airport security and such."

"I see. You must have chartered a private flight, Ms. Scura. But you must have the time wrong, confusing time zones." He laughed. "You can't fly ten thousand kilometers in two and a half hours."

She shook her head. "That is one way of putting it. My way makes it a lot easier, especially since I cannot pass through an airport scanner. And it is about a hundred fifty-minute flight."

"You can't go through the scanner? Why?"

"X-rays, ultrasound, and such cannot pass through my body, and it probably would freak the TSA folks out. I also do not care much for a hand search."

"I didn't know that, but given your status you wouldn't be subject to any TSA search, I'm certain of that. So, you flew here in a private plane? Two and a half hours?"

She nodded. "From an FAA standpoint, that statement is factually correct."

Shalid looked at her and opened his mouth wide. "I'm not sure I comprehend. Indiana to Freedom City in two and a half hours? Am I to understand that you flew here under your own power?"

She nodded. "Yes. It would have taken much longer to do otherwise and would have wasted valuable fuel. I am fully compliant with all FAA regulations; I have advanced onboard avionics in my helmet and broadcast my call sign with my beacon, unless I am doing something in secret, naturally. And, of course, I am a fully licensed pilot with instrument rating."

"That's unbelievable. Will wonders never cease."

• • •

The limousine pulled up to the entrance of the Senator's house. A male attendant opened her door as she was greeted by the Senator, wearing a black pantsuit, who held her arms out at the front door.

"*Stella,* welcome to Freedom City. I'm Fahnaz."

She shook the shorter woman's hand. "Yes, I know. It is certainly an honor. Sorry, my Farsi is a little rough."

She smiled. "That's okay, I get by, but English is my first language, too. I wish you could meet my husband, Ali. He is a financial attorney and works in New York frequently. He's out of town currently. I have to catch myself to avoid saying 'out of the country,' but that's not technically correct any longer."

"It would have been nice to meet him. Perhaps on my next visit, we can do so."

A young boy came running up. "This is our son, Tarik."

"Are you really *Stella Scura?*" The boy, perhaps six, said. "You are awesome."

"Yes, Tarik, I am she, yet I do not know how 'awesome' I am, though I will try to meet your high expectations. I am merely a young woman. Your mother is a United States Senator, so she is the one who is awesome, young man. I am a big fan."

"Aww, she's just my mom." The boy peered up at her. "Can you show me some cool stuff?"

Fahnaz put her arm around him gently. "That's very rude, honey. *Stella* is here to visit, not to do tricks."

She patted him on the head. "That is all right; maybe later we can do some things, okay?"

"That would be great!"

"Now go and do your lessons," his mother said.

"Yes, Mom. See you, *Stella.*"

They walked into the living room and sat down. "Would you like some coffee and dates?"

She nodded and broke a smile. "Both *Coffea arabica* and male companionship! Two of my favorite things, preferably enjoyed in unison. Your Arabian hospitality is unparalleled."

Fahnaz burst into laughter. "I'm afraid the only 'dates' we have available for you are the sweet kind. The other type, you're on your own, although I am sure you would find many handsome takers here." She held out the plate of the edible sweet fruit.

She bit into one and savored its potent flavor. "*Phoenix dactylifera.* One of the Middle East's greatest gastronomical gifts. A fitting fruit, given your burg of birth. Thank you so much."

"You're welcome. I can't offer you an alcoholic drink, though, as New Persia is entirely a dry state."

"Dry state?" She looked at the Senator curiously as she chomped on another *P. dactylifera* fruit. "It is rather arid here, but what does that have to do with alcohol? That it might spontaneously combust, with everything reduced to dust?"

She laughed and shook her head. "No. You've heard of 'dry counties,' correct, like in many Southern states? Well, the vast majority of the population, like me, is Islamic, and the populace voted to keep this a dry state in the initial statehood documents."

She smiled as she recalled Tennessee had several 'dry' counties, although the old D.T. Darkkin & Sons distillery wasn't in one of them. "Oh, I get it now. I just had not heard that term applied to an entire state before, but that makes sense. No problem, I do not drink either, mostly because I am not old enough." She watched Fahnaz smile. "Hey, I know what you are going to say, Senator—"

"It's bad form to drink and fly."

"I know, I know. That is *my* cheesy old punch line. I have to get a new one."

Fahnaz laughed. "I want to thank you for flying all this way to see me. I'm flattered."

She sipped the rich coffee. "As I said before, I am a big admirer of yours, both personally and politically."

Fahnaz looked at her curiously. "That's what you said when we spoke on cyberchat. That's surprising, as your, er, political leanings would seem to be diametrically opposed to mine."

"Do not believe everything you see or hear in the media." She shook her head and laughed. "Just because I frequent the White House and hang out with President Mendoza does *not* mean I am a Republican or agree with all of her views, you know. I prefer to remain nonpartisan and would befriend any President in office."

She didn't need to mention that Paige had voted for her, too.

"We don't need to talk about such things. You also know my old friend, Nick Stannous, also known as the *Tinman*. We go way back, you know."

"Yes, I had heard that. He has mentioned you on numerous occasions. You, he, and Johnny Kepler's daughter were playing golf that one day when I flew overhead at Miracle Park."

"Yes, that's true, although he and Hanna are the ones who actually play golf—what I do is more akin to 'weed whacking' than sport. I suppose I should take some lessons when I get some free time. *That* won't come for a while."

"I am sure there are more pressing matters that require your attention than learning the links." She laughed. "You knew Nick from school, right?"

Fahnaz nodded. "Sure did. My dad was a banker in Phoenix, and my brothers and I were born there, as you already mentioned. We started in the same middle school. He was always interested in things he shouldn't have been involved in, such as playing with dangerous things and being an amateur detective. It looks like he hasn't changed much."

"I concur." She took another sip of the strong coffee. "So, you would have known his first wife. He does not talk about her."

Fahnaz nodded. "Yes. I knew both of them, though, since Bella went to our school for part of our junior year, and she's rather hard to forget."

She nodded. "Now *that* I did not know. I can only imagine what she was like as a teenager."

"Over the top, then and now. Thirty percent girly girl, seventy percent tomboy. And *way* smarter than one thinks. But he and Marcy knew each other since they were eight or nine. It was so horrible what happened on that day. I still have dreams about it."

"I know. What was Marcella like?"

"She was soft-spoken, the nicest person you'd ever want to meet. Tall and rangy—about six-two—and athletic, she was all-State in basketball. They didn't start dating until they were juniors, go figure, even though they hung out all those years. I guess we have to be thankful for the people we do have left."

She bit into another date. "Why was Nick not on the plane that day? I know about the others, but not him."

Fahnaz leaned back. "Well, Marcy was already in Washington.

He and Molly—his mom—were in Indiana visiting some relatives—that was well before Aurora City even existed, of course—and they were going to join them when she fell down on some ice and broke her arm. Stavros was at a conference in Denver, so he had to take her to the emergency room and obviously missed his flight to Washington; otherwise he would've been on board, too, but he scheduled a commercial flight for later, which he never took, of course. A medical emergency saved his life, as well as the President's. How ironic."

"They hadn't been married long, as I understand it."

Fahnaz shook her head. "No, they hadn't. About six months, and her death almost killed him. He'd found the love of his life literally in his own backyard, and it was taken away from him in an instant by an act of terrorism. The stark realization he would never see his unborn child almost killed him."

She paused in mid-sip of her coffee. "Excuse me, Fahnaz? *What* did you say?"

"Nick never being able to see his unborn child was a devastating blow to him. I can only imagine."

She shook her head. "Wait, Fahnaz, are you saying that—"

"Marcy was pregnant with their first child when she died on *Darkkday*. About twelve weeks. We had been good friends since elementary school, so I knew."

Tears came to her eyes. "I—I did not know that. Neither he nor Bella has said anything, and I have been with them a lot."

Fahnaz stroked her thick hair. "Hey, I didn't mean to upset you, I thought you knew. I'm sorry, I shouldn't have said anything."

She wiped the tears away with her left hand. "It is okay, as nothing can be done about it now."

"But I imagine they don't want to burden anyone with that; it doesn't do any good to dwell on it, *Stella.* It's their private problem."

"I understand, but I still feel a lump in my stomach about it. Life is *so* fragile. I can do all these things and am, to my knowledge, completely indestructible and impervious to disease, yet people experience immense personal losses and still go on. I am still trying to come to terms with why the world is the way it is."

"I am sure they would appreciate how much you care. I can see that you are mature beyond your years, asking such existential questions."

She wanted to change the subject. "I try. I do have an unrelated question if it is not too personal."

"Of course."

"Being of Persian descent, do you approve of what has become of your mother country?"

"In what aspect?"

"Becoming a state, of all things. The concept would have been unthinkable in the past, but here we are."

Fahnaz looked at her for about thirty seconds. "Honestly? It's a complex subject that I've thought much about, and I'm a bit ambivalent."

"It is okay if you do not want to go there."

"No, it's just that it's odd—everyone else thinks it's great, and no one has asked me that before, so you are quite perceptive."

"Not sure about that last comment, but thanks."

"Ironically, had I been born here, I couldn't have run for President at all, as you know, because you still have to be a natural-born citizen—and I had never been here at all until after it was made a state. My mom and dad taught me Farsi and Arabic at home, plus we learned it at the Persian school in Phoenix, which I attended in addition to San Marco Laboratory School, where Nick, Marcy, Bella, and I went. I don't mean to speak for everyone, but my observation is that we of foreign ancestry who were born in the States often romanticize our homelands as something perhaps they were not when I know the government was totally dysfunctional and getting worse by the day. I don't think the old regime was a big military threat to the United States of today, so I question the decision to make it a state, but seeing what happened with Iraq in the 2000's it may have made sense."

"Yet, it is ironic that you are now here as a Senator and even became the Democratic Presidential nominee."

Fahnaz laughed. "You think being the Democratic opponent of Wendy Mendoza was a coveted opportunity? No one wanted to do it, but I stepped up. Look how badly I got creamed."

She patted Fahnaz on the arm. "It took great courage and honor to do what you did, and I admire you deeply. You need to run again in the next election. You won the electoral votes in your state as well as your birth state of Arizona and prevented a sweep, so way to go. Next time will be better."

"Thank you. I did give it my all. I don't know about a 'next time,' though, and I'll have to think about it."

"You'll win next time. Wendy will have run out of terms."

"Ha. We'll see about that. But, to answer your question: I know our citizens have a better life now than before. There is almost no poverty, good schools, clean streets, ample food and water. Housing and employment are far more plentiful. There is some crime, of course, but less than in other large American cities, and far less than before."

"In New Persia, perhaps, but what about the rest of the Middle East? Look at Taraq. A country in disarray with no leadership."

"I agree. These were once countries with a good economy due to oil. Now hardly any technology uses fossil fuels, except for small vehicles and a few old appliances like lawnmowers and other gardening tools, those folks with classic cars, etc. Big deal."

"Unintended consequences of the great element mendozium."

"Correct. We have the reactors now, and our cars run on hydrogen fuel—a byproduct of the fusion industry—and most planes use fusion engines or hydrogen. But the great industrial economy of the United States and its allies—Canada, Great Britain, France, Germany, Japan, South Korea—doesn't necessarily translate well into others that time forgot. China is doing okay, as is the rest of Asia, due to their computer and electronics superiority, as America has put most of its resources into the military and the energy industry. Despite our wealth, South Korea and Japan can still make cars better than the USA and at lower cost, which is fine—but the rest of the world is no different. Like they don't exist."

"I know what you're saying—as if they are invisible." As a blind person, she knew the hurt of being the person no one noticed. "But few care about that."

"Agreed." Fahnaz nodded. "Another thing—I don't like to speak badly of the President, as she has vast responsibility, has accomplished much, and can't be on top of everything, but the American military can be bullies, and rumors are it's getting worse. You can't take over entire countries in months without being that—a ruthless, efficient fighting machine."

"What do you mean by that, Fahnaz?"

The senator shook her head. "I have no tangible proof yet, but there are reported practices which take place on this very soil that are against all we stand for as Americans."

She tilted her head and opened her mouth wide. "I am afraid I do not follow."

"Graham Army Base, near the Eastern border. There are reports of the detaining and interrogation of prisoners that would seem to parallel anything this country did in its heyday."

"Are you sure? You are saying that American soldiers are torturing and mistreating prisoners?"

Fahnaz nodded. "Pretty much, yes. Governor Mahmoodi has some information he shared with me that he procured from reliable sources. I haven't shared it with anyone else."

"Well, why has nothing been done about it? You are a Senator of this state, a Presidential candidate."

Fahnaz put up two fingers with her left hand. "First, as I said, because there's only anecdotal evidence; what Mahmoodi has likely won't stand up in court. They keep things pretty covered up there, and going up against the U.S. military is no piece of cake. Second, it's out of the state's jurisdiction, so not much I can do, even as a Senator. For now, at least."

She sat her coffee down and looked out the window, her face bathed in warm sunlight, a realization of destiny dawning upon her.

"Perhaps *you* cannot, Senator, but there is someone who can go where others would never dare and achieve what others are unable to, one who cannot be harmed or threatened."

Fahnaz stared at her and leaned inward. "Are you serious? That could be horrifically dangerous."

"For most, yes, but not dangerous for me, so maybe I should pay them a little visit. Have your staff notify me of the exact location. If there is any funny business going on there, I shall surely find out and deal with it immediately."

"You're going in there secretly to find out?"

She shook her head. "No. I am no sneak, so I will go there in plain view."

"Is that wise?"

"I will not opine on whether or not this action is wise, but there will not be anything they can do about it one way or the other."

"You sure you'll be okay with that?"

She patted the junior Senator on the shoulder. "Positive. I am not an impulsive individual prone to emotional outbursts."

"But will the President be okay with it?"

She shook her head and laughed. "Perhaps not, but that does

not matter to me because I am not intimidated by her, even if I create a mighty stir."

"Really? No?"

She shook her head. "No. She needs my goodwill far more than I need hers. If what you say is true, the press will be all over it, and your problem will be solved, evil will be dissolved."

"Listen, you need her a lot more than you think, and maybe you should talk to her about it before you go busting heads. Take my advice on that."

"Why?"

"She's still our Commander-in-Chief, and let me assure you she's not intimidated by you, either."

"That statement makes no sense. Are you serious?"

Fahnaz nodded. "Yes, listen to me—she's been through too much to be scared of you, despite your immense strength. She is the ultimate badass President, so don't push her too far. Wendy is way smarter than most people believe and can hold a grudge. You need her on your side to accomplish your goals, too."

She shook her head. "No heads shall be busted, I assure you the situation will take care of itself, should these atrocities exist. But many egos will be bruised, definitely."

"It's one of the biggest military bases in this part of the world, so be careful."

"Huh. Worry not, I am not scared of them. But unless they are very stupid, they should be very scared of *me*."

"*Stella,* please don't do anything foolish. I didn't tell you this for you to fly over there and ransack the place, I was just venting my frustration."

She laughed. "I will not do anything except bring to light what they have done; if it is true, then they will be blue. No one can fault you for wanting to expose the truth. But if that is so, there will be hell to pay, to their dismay." She got up and gave her a hug.

"Are you leaving soon?"

"I promised to show Tarik a few tricks, then I will go on my little 'unexpected visit' to my military friends. It sounds like that is a pressing priority."

"After dinner, of course. We are serving lamb."

She smiled. "Agreed. I don't like to fly on an empty stomach. I have not had lamb before." They didn't get much of that up in North Pole.

• • •

Graham Army Base
New Persia

After meeting with. Sen. Saleh, a fine dinner, and playing with Tarik for a half-hour, she decided to fly around to look for the interesting happenings Fahnaz had told her about. She had some extra time before going back home, anyway.

She began her descent to the military base and interrogation complex, where she had heard that U.S. soldiers were mistreating suspected terrorists. The new sensors *Tinman* and *Photraman* had put into the enhanced helmet visor allowed for radar, infrared, and ultraviolet-enhanced vision; it wasn't as good as the Vladimirov helmet, of course, but that was history. She left the beacon on, so they probably had seen her call sign as she flew overhead. Good. She had nothing to hide, and there wasn't anything they were going to be able to do about it.

She hit the ground hard, kicking up an enormous cloud of sand. She walked around for a few minutes and heard a man screaming inside and tore through the metal doors of the concrete building like they were made of paper. She gasped as she saw them waterboarding what appeared to be an Arab man.

"What the hell?" one of the men asked. "Get back!"

"No, it's that *Stella Scura* girl," another of the men exclaimed, smiling as if he'd seen a rock star. "I don't believe it. Heard of you but never dreamed I'd see you in person."

She pointed at him. "What a treat for you, then. Wipe that stupid grin off your face, mister, because I assure you this is not a pleasure trip, so get a grip, drip."

"Yeah, what a laugh, the President's right-hand girl."

"The President is left-handed, Sergeant," she said.

"Whatever."

"Rest assured, I neither belong to nor take orders from anyone, not even the President, so do not throw names around with me. It is not impressive in the least, as you are no threatening beast."

"You come to wail on this guy too? Here, have at it." Army First Sergeant Ellison handed her the steel bar.

She shook her head in puzzlement as she looked at the soaking-wet man who was gasping for air. "You want me to beat up this unarmed man? With a steel bar?" She shook her head. "*Why* would anyone do such a ghastly thing? Has someone invented biotechnology sufficient to reincarnate Adolf Hitler in the form of a U.S. Army soldier? That is very sad and does not make me glad."

"Hey, don't you dare say that name," the sergeant said, shoving her in the chest. "And this bro's a terrorist; he has it coming to him. He has information we need, sister."

She snarled. "I do not take orders from you. I will say what I please. And, by the way, Sergeant, do not *ever* shove me again or call me 'sister.'" She shook her head in disgust, pointed angrily at him, and stepped away and walked around the room.

"Yeah? Or what?"

"Are you an idiot? Do you have *any* comprehension what I could do to you were I of a different temperament? Your belief that this man is a terrorist is sufficient reason for you, it seems. Judge, jury, and executioner, all rolled into one." They watched with awe as she grabbed the one-inch-diameter steel bar, molded it into a three-inch diameter spheroid, and tossed it aside. "But not nearly good enough for me."

"Shit, Sarge, chill out—" one of the men gasped.

"Hey, what the hell you doin', girl?" the sergeant asked as he shoved the private back. "Get back, or I'll tase you." He pointed a handheld taser device at her. "Seventy-five thousand volts. The guys outside may have been scared of you, but I'm not. Put your hands up."

"A taser, are you joking?" She laughed. "Please, go ahead and try it and see how well it works."

"Don't think I won't."

"Huh. I think you are bluffing, dolt, threatening me with a mere volt. But, go ahead if you are that ignorant." She began walking towards him.

"I warned you, missy." He fired the taser pistol from fifteen feet, as two claws embedded in her action costume under the left breast, held by thin wires. She smiled, then took the barbs out and held them in her hands. The men watched as the gun became too hot for him to handle and burst into flames.

"I am no electrical expert, but I think your seventy-five thousand volts just met a very high resistance and shorted out. 'Ohm's law,' I think it is called." *Admiral Ampere* would know for sure."

"Girl, you're in big trouble now."

"I am? How is that? Because I broke your toy, little boy?" She stared up at him angrily. "You have called me 'girl' multiple times now. Do not *ever* do it again. Has this man been convicted of a crime? Even so, his sentence cannot merit such harsh mistreatment, it is against all known laws, domestic and international. And you are no judge."

"Hell, no, we have our own laws and carve out our own justice here, and you ain't no lawyer. You know how it is."

She shook her head. "Pardon me, but I do not 'know how it is.' You are a power upon yourself; is that your crude meaning?"

He nodded. "Yep, pretty much. I am the law here."

"Understood." She went to the man, broke off the handcuffs restraining his hands behind his back, and gave him a drink of water, then molded the carbon steel into another uniform steel sphere, which she tossed to the sergeant. "I do not think you will be using these again. You are in a *huge* heap of trouble."

"Thank you, Miss," the detainee said.

"You are welcome. Not all Americans are like them." She helped him sit down as she went back towards the sergeant, who backed up warily. "*You* are the law here?" She looked around, picked up a steel trash can, and crushed it into another nearly perfect sphere four inches in diameter as two of the other men opened their mouths wide. "Well, in case you giant intellects have not figured it out already, there is a new sheriff in town. I have full federal police powers, and we happen to be on American soil."

The sergeant drew his weapon. "You don't have shit here. Stand down and get on the floor before I shoot your ass, kiddo. I don't care about your little toy badge; this is a military base. You ain't got no jurisdiction."

She yawned and patted her mouth. "That is a minor legal issue that does not concern me at this time. You also should put down that weapon before I ram it where the sun does not shine, or else you will quickly not be very fine."

A short, stocky corporal stepped forward and stood next to Ellison. "Sarge, you need to back off—we're way outclassed here in terms of power, in case you haven't noticed. This isn't the battle to fight, and it's gonna end badly for everyone, especially you. Kick it upstairs and be done."

"Shut up, Tanner! Don't give me orders; I don't care who she is. I back down for no one who threatens our base, and I don't wuss out by sendin' it to the Colonel, you fucking pussy."

Tanner shook his head. "Just saying—it's your funeral, pal, and I want no part of this shit anymore. I didn't in the first place, because it's wrong." Tanner looked around the room. "Who else has the guts to be with me?"

The five other men in the room voiced their agreement loudly.

"What the hell? You and you other scumbags disobeying me, Tanner? I'll court-martial your asses. All of you."

The shorter Tanner stared up at his superior non-commissioned officer. "Yeah? Well, bring it on, Sarge. Better for me to have a 'live ass' to court-martial than a dead one that obeyed your stupid order. I'm not messing with the President's top brass either. So go screw yourself, asshole." Tanner poked him in the chest and walked away angrily.

She walked up to the six-four sergeant and stared up angrily at him. "You are not content merely to bully a prisoner, so you now threaten your fellow soldier, who looks up to you as his leader, with your amusing façade of authority? At least he has the guts to stand up to you, despite threats of military discipline. Tell you what, I shall make you a deal—why not pick on someone your own size? Like me? You big enough to take on this piece of pussy?"

Sgt. Ellison howled in laughter. "My size? You're three-fourths of a foot shorter than me."

"So I am." They gasped as they saw her rise forty inches in the air, floating, her hair waving in weightlessness. "How about now? Physical power seems to impress you, so is this better? You are a truly reprehensible man, no doubt led by a base commander of equally enfeebled ethics. Well, it stops now." She floated down and stepped towards Sgt. Ellison. "You want to shoot me? Let me help. However, there will be no funerals here."

She grabbed the pistol from him in less than a tenth of a second, stepped five feet back, and pointed it at herself, discharging the entire clip into her neck, leaving only a few reddish marks. The group watched in amazement as the bullets dropped to the ground without ricochet, their energy absorbed. She then handed the empty weapon back to him.

"You—you shot that whole clip at yourself," Ellison said, gaping in disbelief.

She nodded. "That is right, you should get a promotion to General for your astute observation, but the bar seems to be very low, Jim Crow. Sorry to squander Government property. But you should have listened to Corporal Tanner because you are the one who will be incarcerated soon, lowly goon."

"Holy shit—"

"*'Holy shit?'* That is the best retort the military's finest can concoct? Do you really want to take me on? I can take out you, your whole battalion, and a squadron of fighter jets in about thirty seconds. But, because I am not a bully like you who abuses his power, I will not do that. I will, rather, let the military courts mete out your well-deserved justice." She rose up to his eye level, then hovered over him. "Tell me, *now,* before I *do* get upset, Sgt. Ellison—who the *hell* is in charge of this God-awful place? I am weary of dealing with mere underlings."

Ellison looked at his shoes, breaking eye contact. "That would be Col. Becker."

"Well, let us go see him, then."

"Col. Becker's a *she*. And she's busy."

"Huh. She will make time to see *me,* or I will simply tear this place up until I find her. It shall not take long."

"Go to hell."

She looked around and laughed. "I do not have to travel far to get there, as it appears we have already arrived. It is as dreary a place as I imagined."

Cpl. Tanner stepped forward. "I'll take you to see her, Ma'am. I'm not goin' down with this dumb ass."

Ellison pointed at him. "You just wait till I get a hold of you, Tanner, without your tough buddy there."

"Good, we'll go a couple of rounds, which is all I'll need. You're goin' to jail, Sarge. Maybe I will be, too. But it stops now. You come towards me and I *swear* I'll kick your goddamned ass."

"Back off, Sarge," a tall, blond private said, approaching them. "Tanner's right, you know. Shut the fuck up."

Ellison swung at Tanner with a right hook; the shorter but more mobile Tanner dodged the punch, then swung and struck Ellison with his right fist, knocking him back, as the rest of the group cheered.

"I was middleweight boxing champ back at my prior company, Sarge. Your sorry ass had better stay down there, or I'll really teach you and your big mouth a lesson you'll never forget."

Ellison rubbed the blood from his chin as he lay on the ground.

"I've got witnesses, Tanner. You're gettin' drummed out of the Army for striking a superior non-commissioned officer."

"Is that right? Anybody here see anything?" Tanner asked the other five men, who all shook their heads.

A tall private stepped forward. "Man, I *swear* I saw Sarge trip on that electrical cord and cut his chin open. No, sure didn't see a fight. Clumsy asshole should watch where he's going."

"I agree," she said. "He is very clumsy. Physically as well as mentally."

She and Tanner walked out the broken doors to the commander's office, leaving the laughing battalion behind them.

"Thank you, Corporal. That took guts."

He shook his head sadly. "No, Ma'am, it didn't, because I should be ashamed of what's happened, and I should've done that a long time ago. I only hope I can make amends now. We treated many detainees badly."

"Doing the right thing and admitting mistakes is difficult."

"Yeah, but if you think Sarge Ellison was bad, just wait." Cpl. Tanner knocked nervously on the commanding officer's door and opened it cautiously.

"What the hell do you want?" the woman at the desk yelled.

"Col. Becker, there's someone here 'demanding' to see you."

The fortyish, short-haired brunette looked up angrily from her desk as she put the phone on the table. "Corporal, I'm busy. Don't you *ever* interrupt me again like that. Who do you think you are?"

"But, Ma'am—you need to see this person now."

"Get out of here, Tanner, unless I request your sorry presence!" she yelled as she pointed to the door.

Stella gently pushed the man out of the way and stared at the taller woman, who was about twice her age. "Do not blame him; I insisted on seeing you urgently, Colonel. I insist pretty well."

"I'll call you back, Major. Thanks for the update." The mid-fortyish, five-eleven brunette angrily slammed down the phone and looked down at the five-eight female figure wearing her dark blue action uniform. "What the hell is this carnival shit in my barracks?"

"This 'shit' wants some answers. And I would prefer being addressed with a little more respect than as fecal material. Since my unannounced arrival, I have been threatened with guns, yelled at, shoved, and tased, and I do not like it one bit. And, by my first impression, I do not like *you*."

"Aww, that's just too bad. I don't really care if you don't like me, And, yes, Air Command said you were in the area, in Freedom City, so I knew I would see you sooner or later. I've seen you now, so what? Not impressed."

"I decided to do some sightseeing on my way back. It was not what I wanted to find on my New Persian vacation."

"You smart-ass little girl—you barge in here like this, joke around, and you want *respect?* You aren't my superior or anything to me unless you have stars on your shoulders I don't know about." Col. Amanda Becker pointed to the door. "Get the hell out while you still can."

"I assure you, Ma'am, this is no joke." She extended her hand, which Becker refused. She scowled, realizing she had encountered the first people who hadn't just fallen at her feet.

Good. Finally, someone to argue with other than a relative or a member of the President's staff.

"*Get out while I still can?* So, sadly, this is how it shall be, not at all pleasing to me." She nodded. "Understood clearly. I hear that you are in charge of this battalion. Ample accolades on your august achievement."

"Got that right, girlie."

She shook her head. "No, that is not something to be proud of, trust me. You are the base commander—you, therefore, are the one who will ultimately answer for what has happened here."

"Yeah?" Becker made a gesturing motion with her hands. "Bring it. I give as good as I get."

She stared up at the senior officer and cracked a smile. "Do not worry, I will, but not in the violent manner you are accustomed to. I am not here for petty matters such as debating who reports to whom. While these things are apparently the essence of your empty existence, such banal trivialities are beneath me. The fact is undeniably this: these men were torturing a prisoner to extract information here in the United States. Undoubtedly this has occurred on multiple other occasions. It is unacceptable to me."

"Well, now, isn't that too bad, but you have no idea what we do here. While all this may seem violent and unnecessary to you, in fact—"

"I do not wish to hear it, as I desire no education from you. Your actions speak to outrageous acts of violence, which I have witnessed firsthand."

"For the last time, get out of here the way you came. Washington will hear about this."

"Yeah?" She laughed. "Or *what?* You will make me?"

Becker nodded. "If you don't comply, yes."

"Sorry, I do not mean to insult your vast intelligence, but have you figured out exactly *how* you are going to do that?" She crossed her arms, scowled angrily, and stared at her for two minutes, knowing that Becker couldn't see her eyes. She then picked up the portable phone and tossed it to her. "Aww, go ahead, Colonel, call Washington on your little phone, then. Call the President, for that matter. I will dial her private number for you if that is what you want to do."

"I don't take orders from some alien freak."

"No? How *dare* you insult me? I was born in the USA, too, just like you. Then you will watch while I dismantle this place."

That hurt. Was she really an alien? Even if Dr. Wendy did deliver her on a hospital gurney in Bethesda, that didn't exclude the possibility of her somehow possessing extraterrestrial genes. What things had her mom not shared with her? But the pain of rejection was there again. This was the first time anyone had said that to her. And this was a high-ranking military officer.

Like all the other times, it took her about twenty seconds to get over it.

"Awww. Am I making you upset?" Becker asked angrily.

She scowled. "Yes, finally. It takes an enormous amount to make me angry, but you seem to have achieved what few have accomplished. That is not a good thing, just so you know."

"Wow, that is just too bad. So, what now? We have a Mexican standoff, it seems."

She smiled, given her lineage. "Hardly, you of such high rank show much ignorance."

"How so?"

"A 'Mexican standoff' is when two adversaries are so closely matched that neither has an advantage, leading to a stalemate. That is clearly not the case here. *Now* you will take me on an inspection of where you are holding your detainees. It is your business why they are there, not mine. But if I discover that they are not being treated well, it shall be addressed."

Becker crossed her arms. "And if I don't?"

"Then I will find them myself without your help; rest assured of that. I am in no hurry, I have all week, and have no problem tearing this entire base up with my bare hands. Your time, as well as your military career, on the other hand, has surely run out. This is your best chance to salvage something of value of what is left."

"Go to hell, asshole."

She laughed. "Sgt. Ellison said something similar, so that must be the company motto; therefore, I see I am dealing with immense intellects here." She got in Becker's face. "You think you stand for America, but you are nothing more than a bully. You should be ashamed, because you are a disgrace to your uniform. I am going to bring you all down, and if you think you can stop me, then take your best shot. Otherwise, *get the hell out of my way* before I reduce this place to rubble."

She was unhappy to find four additional human rights violations in her "tour" of the Army base, with Cpl. Tanner leading the way, as Col. Becker refused to participate. At least one person seemed to be on the right wavelength—Tanner and the privates in the interrogation room. She would put that in her unofficial "report" to the President.

Had she crossed the line this time, though? Probably. She knew she was doing the right thing. But convincing others of that might be challenging.

Chapter Fifty

Oval Office
The White House
Washington, DC

Gen. Larry Kriger burst into the Oval Office as the President was reading papers at her desk between meetings.

"Yes, Larry? I was told you needed to see me. What is it?" she said softly, not taking her eyes off her desk.

"There are tons of reporters outside, Ma'am. I guess they heard about it first."

"Reporters?" She took off her reading glasses, looked up at him, and sighed. "Heard about what? I hear about hundreds of things per hour. The illustrious newshounds are always getting riled up about something, it goes with the territory, and I'm sorry one of our greatest military minds and my chief of staff can't handle it. A statement about whatever it is will be issued to the media within the hour."

"Well, this is too much, even for me. Your little adolescent friend decided to fly to Freedom City to visit Senator Saleh."

She crossed her arms, staring at him. "Yes, I know she went there, she told me she was going; so what? It's a free country. Why would I care about that? Fahnaz is a very competent young Senator and it's good they're getting together. She could learn something."

Kriger frowned, shook his head, and pounded his right fist on her desk. "It's not good at all because *Stella* took a side trip on the way back—to Graham Army Base."

She looked up from her papers, surprised, and stood. "Really? Why would she have gone there? She is decidedly anti-military and certainly possesses no musical, comedic, or other entertainment talents which could amuse the troops, other than doing physical stunts, which is not her style."

"You got it, this certainly wasn't a pleasure trip. That obnoxious girl pretty much shut the whole base down after apparently hearing rumors from Saleh about 'illegal' interrogations and such, and she took matters into her own hands."

She stared at him and smiled. "Well? Did she find any?"

"What? She shouldn't have been there in the first place, Madam President. She's a civilian without proper clearance."

"Wrong. She's now a DSD Special Agent, so her jurisdiction is pretty much anywhere I say it is," she said as she stood up and pointed at him with her large left index finger. "But that isn't what I asked, Larry. Answer me."

He nodded. "Apparently so. At least one soldier has come forward, spilling the beans. A Corporal John Tanner, with tangible evidence of numerous accounts of human rights violations regarding foreign prisoners. It's pretty bad, Ma'am."

She sneered angrily. "Were there any casualties or injuries, other than the mistreated prisoners?"

"No, of course not. There was some minor structural damage, but mostly she was just threatening people with that big mouth of hers. I guess one of the guys tried to tase her, that didn't work out real well, as you can imagine. He then tried to shoot her, but she grabbed the gun from him and decided to fire the whole clip into her own head, which raised some eyebrows."

"Not too smart." She put her reading glasses back on, sat down, and returned to her paperwork.

"Well?" Kriger put his hands on his hips, obviously expecting a different response.

"Well, what? Did you need something else?"

"What are we going to do about it?"

"Me? Nothing. *You* are going to deal with it; that's why you have this job, Larry. I'm sure it wasn't all that bad. Burned out a taser and wasted a few dozen bullets, big deal."

"Not that bad? This is terrible, Ma'am!"

She pointed a large red manicured index fingernail at him. "Don't embellish, General. She could've destroyed the whole base with minimal effort, and there's nothing we could've done about it. *That* would've been bad; it's all relative." She looked back at the papers on her desk. "Nevertheless, I can't do much about it now, as I have other work to do for our taxpayers."

"I thought that's what you might say."

"If you knew my response, then why are you here? I'm sure Miss *Stella* will be showing up soon, anyway. Rest assured that we shall have a talk about the proper protocols. Then we'll have a profound discussion about what's been going on over there."

"You'd better, Ma'am. You know, this isn't like anything else the Presidency has ever dealt with. This person has the power to do almost anything, they say. From my understanding, she could take on our entire military."

She shook her head in disbelief at such a stupid comment. "Yes, and we would surely lose—very badly. What's your point, Larry?"

"Doesn't that worry you?"

She leaned back in her chair and pointed the ornate 14K gold nib of her Montblanc 149 Meisterstück fountain pen at him. She sometimes wished it was like one of her dad's Cold War Montblanc 149s that supposedly could shoot acid or poison gas, as she'd like to shoot both at Kriger right now. Ah, those were the days.

"You know what your problem is, Larry? You aren't a people person, but that's typical of military leaders. You want to give orders all the time, yet you have no interpersonal finesse and don't understand how people think, so you dump it on me when you can't solve a problem which requires delicacy and tact."

"A teenager with unchecked, unlimited potential destructive power threatens not only the base commander but to destroy the whole place, and you're talking 'delicacy' and 'tact?' Are you kidding me, Ma'am? And when were you ever known for those two qualities?"

She laughed. "I use them all the time; you don't want to see the alternative. Did this teenager of immense 'destructive power' actually destroy anything except for some overinflated egos?"

"She broke down a wooden door in the CO's office. I told you it was just minor damage."

"How terrible, it will ruin the federal budget. Anything else?"

"Well, no, but that's not the point—"

"You're a four-star general, so go read some fancy leadership digi-books or something. If she'd really wanted to cause damage, that base would be totally destroyed. What is it you want me to do about it, anyway?"

"We *want* you to do clean-up."

She looked down at her papers and sighed. "I always have to clean up messes, don't I?"

"It would be nice if you could this time, Ma'am. She's in the conference room. You seem to have more influence than any of us."

"All right. I'll be in there in a few minutes. I can't get any work done around here, because it's always something in this place."

• • •

Stella waited in the Presidential conference room, dressed in blue slacks and a light blue blouse, as Gen. Kriger walked back in, as she and Secretary of State Sam Redding were engaged in a rather intense conversation.

"You don't interfere with our operations like that, *Stella*. You've caused a media nightmare," Redding said, pointing his finger at her. "I've got reporters at the White House gate about ready to break it down. I don't even know what to say at the press conference."

"Well, do they not teach you those things in Secretary school, or did you cut class that day? Let me in that nonsense press conference, as I will have plenty to say on this day."

"Don't you talk to me that way, young lady."

"But they were torturing this man with no just cause. They cannot do those things in the United States. What the hell is wrong with you and General Kriger? Tell the truth at the press conference, for God's sake!"

Kriger shook his head. "Things like that are necessary and are more complex than I have time to explain to someone like you."

"Huh? No time to explain to *someone like me?* You had better find it, sir, or you will get an earful of complaints. And perhaps some other things you do not like, go take a hike, Ike."

Redding got in her face. "Yeah? You have no authority here, and I don't expect someone of your maturity level to—"

"Maturity level? Excuse me, Secretary Redding?"

"You heard me." Redding shook his head. "You're just a child and couldn't possibly understand. I can't believe we're even in here talking to you."

"*Whaaat?* I am incapable of understanding violence and illegal tactics? My relatively young age somehow makes me insensitive to such awful actions? Must I be forty or fifty years old to get that? As that famous book says, all I needed to know, I learned in kindergarten, and no one promised me a rose garden—"

"Besides, the damage you've caused Col. Becker's and the others' careers are irreparable. They'll be dishonorably discharged, most likely, after their court-martial. Becker could be facing prison time."

She nodded briskly. "Good. Do you not think that is what they deserved? They threatened me with guns and bodily harm. One of them tried to tase me, which did not end well for him. Then he tried to shoot me. And explain to me why any of that is my fault. I was not the one who did it. I was in New Persia on business."

Redding got in her face. "Wrong—you had no legal right to be at that base because it's treated as different property than the other parts of the state, as any military installation would be. You flew in there without warning, so what did you expect would happen?"

"My beacon was on, and I landed in plain view, and I am a sworn federal agent. They knew I was coming, as my intent was not to be cunning."

"And the whole court-martial will be screwed up because of what you did, due to the media outrage. While what they did was wrong, they were defending their base, as any good soldiers should've."

She laughed. "A base that was on American soil, violating basic human rights. Do not dare debate right or wrong with me. You are sorely out of your league, and you will get a real blitzkrieg. Had I not gone in there, it would still be going on, do not patronize me."

Wendy walked in, sighed, and slammed the door. "What's going on here? As if I don't know already. I'm not sure where there's more noise—in here or outside."

"Madam President: *Stella* threatened to destroy an internment camp in New Persia. Got the CO all riled up, as you can imagine," Redding said.

She nodded annoyingly, rolled her eyes, and sighed. "Yes, I know all about it, as Gen. Kriger and I have discussed it at length already. Stop bickering like children, as this isn't accomplishing anything constructive."

She turned to Wendy. "President Mendoza, did you know

about this before the news got involved?"

"I know there's a base there and they have some detainees, but do you think I know about all these little details?" Wendy shook her head. "I didn't know they were doing that stuff; come on, you know better than that."

"Do I? Sometimes I wonder. Do not lie to me."

Redding got in her face. "You don't talk to the President of the United States that way, young lady."

"Huh, I will say what I please when I please. Now get out of my face, Redding, go do some shredding."

"Now wait a minute—"

She smiled. "It's all right, Sam. I can handle this." Wendy turned towards *Stella* and pushed Redding back gently. "Listen. I have a responsibility you cannot fathom. For me to have minute knowledge of all the goings-on of the military—"

"Well, you should, since you are ultimately responsible for it all. Do not make excuses!"

Wendy dropped her head sadly. "I know, and I'm ashamed. I take full responsibility for this debacle, despite having no personal knowledge." Wendy shook her head. "But I never authorized anything like that."

"May I speak freely, Ma'am?" Kriger asked.

"Of course, Larry, you're never at a loss for words."

Kriger turned to *Stella* and started moving his arms. "She's a child with the power of a star, for Christ's sake. What have you done, bringing her in here? This is a media disaster, Madam President, so I hope you're happy with all this because I'm not."

"And with more wisdom than you will ever have, General Kriger," she said, getting in his face.

Wendy scowled. "I believe you can see from my expression I'm not happy. But would you rather she be in the office of some other head of state, Larry? I don't think so. You can debate my wisdom, but she exists, and this is the best potential solution to a difficult problem without exact answers."

"I'm out of here, Ma'am. Your problem to deal with now. It's beyond my comprehension." Kriger left hastily, slamming the door behind him.

"Wow. Some people just get buzzed up," she said.

Wendy pointed at her harshly. "*You* will be quiet, Miss, and shall not speak again until spoken to. I will surely address *you* in a moment."

"Hey, wait a minute, you do not tell me—"

"This is the highest office in the land, and, yes, I do." Wendy separated her from Redding again and got in his face. "I didn't 'bring her 'in' here, Sam; she saved us all from crashing into the Aurora City skyline like 9/11 because of what Ashburn and *Santaman* did, so have a little damn gratitude. Or have you forgotten that otherwise, we would've both been plastered all over downtown? All because you didn't do your jobs?"

"I am grateful, Ma'am, but her presence here is unprecedented, and that event has nothing to do with this debacle. Gen. Kriger is furious. I'm not sure how to handle these types of things."

She snarled. "Let me at General Kriger or anyone else, I will handle them just fine; they need not whine."

"*Stella,* please. Have a bit of patience. Listen, that's what I'm here for, and I can handle Larry." Wendy pointed at her again. "What do you think you deserve for what you've done, a medal?"

"I desire no medal, Ma'am, I was more disruptive than heroic, and I was in no danger."

"Good, as you aren't getting one anytime soon."

"I did what I believed was right, although others seem to disagree." She looked towards Redding. "No offense, sir, but you are far too tense."

Wendy gestured towards Redding. "I'll take care of this, Sam. Count your blessings. Better this way than another. We can spin it into something positive, we always do—"

"You'd better, Ma'am. Or you can start looking for another Secretary of State. I don't like passive-aggressive games. Not even from you."

"Shut up, Sam. I may be a lot of things, but 'passive-aggressive' I'm assuredly *not*. There's nothing 'passive' about me. I'm just trying to be collaborative with a messy situation."

"Yes, Ma'am. Whatever you say." He exited the side door quickly.

"Young lady, let's retreat to my office where we can have more privacy. We have a few matters to discuss."

"I cannot wait for you to set me straight; it will not be great."

• • •

She and the President went back to the Oval Office as Wendy poured coffee from the ornate coffee set.

"Coffee?" She asked.

She rolled her eyes behind the visor, realizing Wendy couldn't see them. "Sure, whatever. I hope it is strong, as the forthcoming lecture will surely be long."

Wendy poured her a cup. "*Stella,* the world is complicated. It's not as simple as you make it out to be. I wish it was, but it's not, so we need to discuss some things."

"Huh." She stirred some cream and sugar into the aromatic black liquid. "You sound like Redding. Because I am chronologically an adolescent without advanced degrees like you, you think me to be a simpleton who cannot understand complex concepts?"

"Hey, I'm not Redding, and I wasn't implying that—"

"You were. I may not have very good mathematical abilities, but I assure you I have far greater common sense and reasoning skills on things that matter than my mother."

Wendy shook her head. "Well, that's not saying much. What a pitiful example for comparison. I expected far better from you, one advertised as an ace arbiter. How sad."

"I guess not. Sorry."

Wendy sighed. "Look, I didn't say you were simple, and I'm not deriding you for your youth, but you must understand the big picture, because it takes experience. I wasn't always the most responsible person when I was younger."

She took a slurp of coffee. "Your statement implies you fully understand me. I do not think you do at all."

"Really? I understand far more than you think. Before I was a politician, I was a doctor of medicine, a pediatrician. I know an awful lot about psychology and how to get along with people, especially difficult adolescents."

"Huh. By the acerb tone of your voice, I assume you place me in that pejorative category then, Aunt Gwen?"

Wendy sipped her coffee and looked up, frowning. "Again, how disappointing. That dim-witted question doesn't even deserve an answer. You, my dear, are rapidly sinking in quicksand."

"Huh. You sound like my mom and dad."

"Maybe that's good. But there's a huge difference between you and me."

She slurped her coffee. "What is that? We are *so* much alike."

"Cut the sarcasm. I wasn't the President then. What I have now, I earned gradually over the last thirty-five years; I wasn't born with it."

"What do you know about me? If you think my life has been easy just because of my abilities, then you are as naïve as my mother. I have worked tirelessly to have the control that I have, and I possess patience beyond your comprehension. While I may have become Miss Mighty Mouth at Graham Army Base, I damaged little except some over-inflated egos."

"I am many things, dear, but *never* naïve. We both have a lot of power and responsibility. You may not have physically damaged anything, but you've caused quite a media stir."

"Oh, and the 'big picture' includes torturing Middle Eastern soldiers in New Persia. How am I not 'responsible?' And you? I saw laws being broken, and I did something about it. We were in an American state, ye of substantial weight."

"I don't mean to seem callous, but—if they have information that is dangerous to this country and to the world, then, yes, we must deal with it. Compromises must sometimes be made, as we cannot tolerate terrorism against the United States. We, of all people, should know that. Life is about compromises, and this is one I must make. I'll clean it up, I promise, but stuff like this inevitably goes on. Some of it, unfortunately, is necessary. Maybe not this, but wise up. This isn't North Pole or Fairbanks."

"No, it is definitely not. Sometimes I wish it was."

"Well, you wanted to be here in the big leagues, so get used to it. However, if you can't deal with that, then fly home to Mommy and Daddy and come back in about ten or twenty years. Or, stay home and let the grownups run things."

She opened her mouth wide in disgust and stared up at Wendy angrily. "What would they possibly have that could threaten us? What could anybody have?"

"Your memory is short, *Stella*. Taraq and Thomasson, that was two months ago. *Darkkday*, twelve years ago, which killed our family. Air Force One plummeting to its doom a month ago. Something like that or worse will eventually happen again. Maybe you can stop the next disaster, but you can't do everything. Just because you showed up now doesn't change those facts. History has proven this to be so, time and time again. I thought history was one of the few things you respected."

"They at least had wealth in their oil at one time, but now no one wants petroleum products, except maybe to run the occasional lawn mower."

"Which is a good thing. We have significantly reduced carbon emissions and now possess the technology to extract carbon dioxide from the atmosphere."

"Wonderful, yet I have told you this, and I shall tell you again: I do not take orders from you or anyone else. And I do not need accolades. What I do, I do because it is right, not because I have unparalleled might."

"Talk's cheap, dear. You are skilled at high school debates, per my understanding, although I have yet to see that talent emerge. Now I'm going to take you to the advanced class since you know everything, junior league."

She smirked. "Go ahead, take your best shot."

Wendy smiled and shook her head. "It's good to have principles, but now you're contradicting yourself. That's suicide in any debate, the media would eat you alive. You'd be done."

"Huh?"

"We've had this discussion already. You can't have it both ways—on the one hand, say you're upholding the law and then *not* obey it on the other, which is exactly what you did when you threatened to tear up that base. You're now a sworn federal officer, and you can't decide which laws to enforce and which not to, or else you've become a vigilante. I can't do that myself. I took an oath to uphold the Constitution and the laws of America. You may not like some of them, but that's the way it is."

"Wait a minute, now. That seems to be what the soldiers were doing."

Wendy nodded. "You miss the point. I agree that what they were doing was wrong, but you went about correcting it illegally, and two wrongs don't make a right, do they?"

"I—I guess not."

"There needed to be an investigation and due process, not the media circus you've unintentionally created via your immature meddling."

"You could have done better at my age?"

"Are you kidding? What kind of an idiotic question is that?" Wendy shook her head. "I would have done far worse. I wasn't very mature at eighteen, twenty-eight, or even thirty-eight. But

I finally grew up and learned from my mistakes. What you did wasn't due process, and no credible attorney would condone that. You could've stopped the interrogation, then called me, and left. My maturity at eighteen is irrelevant. Just a little bit of apples to oranges there. Unlike me, you are a force of Nature. Act like it."

She sighed. "I guess I have caused quite a stir. Senator Saleh sure got me all buzzed up, and I should have shut up."

Wendy frowned and raised her left hand, holding up two fingers. "You've just made fatal mistake number two—blaming it on others and not taking ownership of your mistakes. Don't blame it all on Fahnaz. One more, and you're down for the count."

"But she is the one who told me about it— "

"Come on, you'll have people trying to goad you into doing incredibly stupid things your whole life, you can't act impulsively. But if you screw up—and you will, believe me—you'd better own it, *Stella*. People won't cut you much slack."

"Sorry. I did try and think this through, give me my due."

"Sorry doesn't cut it in our business. There must be order and laws in any successful civilization, or chaos ensues. You like history, I understand, so am I not right? If you don't follow the laws, then you're no better than the people you're criticizing, despite your powers. People must know that you respect process and the law, or they will fear you, because no one should be without balances and checks."

"Why? You are."

Wendy shook her head. "I have nowhere near the power you think I do, and the comparison is laughable. I have more personal flaws than almost any other President in history. I have to pick and choose what I want to go forward. Yes, I have a favorable Congressional makeup, and yes, I did my best to help make it that way, as any astute politician would. But that doesn't mean everything. The judicial branch tells me what to do all the time."

"Perhaps. Perhaps not."

"That being as it may, you have many valid points, but you must follow process to be worthy of that federal agent shield you have. A Middle Eastern rebel group kidnapped Alan Thomasson a while back and you rescued him. There is much evil still out there."

"And there is evil here, in this very country and city. Your men violated a number of laws."

"Yes, they did, and we have a process to deal with those things, which does not include a metahuman flying in there and puffing up her chest. However, I said I didn't know anything about it. I'm the President. I can't possibly keep track of all those details."

"But you allow such an environment to exist, which is almost as bad. Maybe worse."

"Look, now, young lady, no one is happier than me that you're around, but —"

"But *what?* You wish I was gone?" She crossed her arms in defiance. "Sorry. That is not likely to happen anytime soon, although you think me to be a goon, in your presence I shall never swoon."

"I was *going* to say, if you'd stop interrupting, that we need to set some house rules."

"Huh. Well, one day, you may not be happy I am here, Madam President. When the inevitable day comes that we have a disagreement far worse than this one, it may not be pretty."

Wendy stared her down, obviously not knowing if she was staring back through the opaque sapphire visor, then smiled.

"Sure, I'll be ready, so bring it on. I don't go looking for a fight, but I assure you I won't run from one, either. I can provide many character references who will vouch for that particular aspect of my behavior. And there isn't a single thing in this world I'm frightened of, not even you; so if you want to play showdown with me, you'd better bring all your cards to the table and get ready for battle the likes of which you've never seen before. You're right about one thing, though: it ain't gonna be pretty. Maybe you win in the end, but you'll sure know you've been in one helluva fight."

"Am I to understand you fear nothing? Not even death?"

Wendy shook her head. "Nope, not even that. I've been to Hell and back, Paige, and I'm still around. Maybe not everyone is happy about that, but it's too damn bad. If you think you understand what I've been through: losing my children, getting my chest blown open, and coming back to run for President, and dealing with the horseshit I do every day—I'm afraid of *nothing*. If you think you intimidate me in the least, trust me, you don't. The worst you or anyone else can do is kill me, and I don't fear that."

"Huh. That is exactly what Fahnaz said."

"What?"

"That you are not the least bit intimidated by me."

"You talked about me?"

"Yes. She has immense respect for you, but also warned me."

"Smart lady. Wish some of it had rubbed off on you. The only tougher character than me would be your mother."

"Really?"

"Yes, really, how can you even ask that? She is one badass lady. Don't mess with her. Or Jackie. She's pretty formidable as well."

"I am also very sorry. I did not mean for you to bring that up, about your kids."

Wendy shook her head. "Don't be sorry; it is what it is and nothing can change the past. Those events are part of me, and I can't separate them from who I am. You wanted me to know who you are as a person as you claim I don't know you—I just want you to realize the same about me." Wendy paused for a few seconds. "But promise in the future that you'll run these things past me. Not with Redding, Kriger, Jackie, or any of my staff, but with me directly, no matter what they say to you."

She shrugged. "Okay, that seems fair. But that doesn't mean I'll agree with you, understand that."

"Understood. And you can't be everywhere, all the time. What happens when something comes up you started, and you aren't around to fix it? Huh?"

"I am not perfect. I have to suspect that in some way, you will want to spin this the right way."

"You *have* to be perfect, sorry. This was a bad mistake, and I'll see that it doesn't happen again, but it could've been handled differently. And, yes, part of what I do is masterfully manipulate the media minions' mentality. How's that for alliteration?"

"Not bad, I guess, for a beginner."

"Thanks, but I can't accomplish the things I do without having the majority of the people on my side. Maybe you should've tried a little diplomacy when you went to New Persia by not being such a badass."

"That is an absurd statement coming from you, the ultimate Presidential 'badass.' Sorry to give you such sass."

Wendy laughed. "You may think of me as a threatening, violent badass, but the things I have done have been relatively peaceful in nature. Unlike you at times."

She smirked. "I hardly think so."

"No, you think about it carefully before you answer: have we actually had an armed conflict with another country since I have been in office?"

"Well—I guess not, but look at all the threats, especially with North Korea. You were going to blow them out of existence."

"I see—you think I was going to take over North Korea, Cuba, and Iran by nuking the hell out of them and threatening them with force, just because that's what I said would happen if they didn't stand down."

"That would be the logical conclusion, that you would have given them a real bruisin'."

Wendy laughed. "Get real, that would have killed millions on both sides. The undeniable facts are this: there have been far fewer military casualties in my administration on either side than any since well before World War I."

"Well, let me think about that—"

"Nothing to think about, dear. Walk down the street and go into the office of any of the plentiful Democratic political consultants, and they'll tell you the same thing. We brought those governments and military down with carefully planned cyber-attacks which corrupted pretty much everything, leaving their whole operation a shambles." Wendy laughed. "You believe your mother to be such a liberal and opposed to my supposed jingoistic beliefs, yet she provided much of the help, you know."

"Huh? What do you mean, Mary, Mary, quite contrary?"

"She was a master at hacking and cracking passwords because of her cipher abilities; she invented 'little black boxes' that could cut through any encryption, despite how the media may have portrayed her as a saint devoid of political opinions. So your mom knows better than stating I am going to blow the Earth to smithereens. Just so you know, she can be quite prone to theatrics as well."

"So you are saying those were merely threats, not something you would have actually done."

Wendy nodded. "Exactly. Unless there was absolutely no other choice."

"And people are fearful of your unpredictability."

Wendy laughed. "That's a polite way of putting it."

"But you said I could have used more diplomacy. How so?"

"By telling me about this whole thing first, then we could've made an investigation and shut it down through the proper channels. You could've been an ambassador of goodwill instead of a kick-butt superhero."

"Well, by that time, that poor man might have been dead, come on. And I thought my being a superhero was desired."

She stuck her finger in her chest. "Hey, I respect our political differences, and I won't try and convince you otherwise. You're obviously an intelligent young woman with a mind of her own, and I guess I can't stop you."

She nodded. "That is correct."

"Understand this, though: just because I can't stop you doesn't mean I won't tell you off. Remember that I am the one who was elected President for the third time by four hundred fifty million Americans, not you. That may happen to you someday, but that day is not today. So I told you once, and I'll do it again until you finally get it: if you want to be the world-changing person you aspire to be, you'd better listen to me and become *more* than the energy-manipulating curiosity known as *Stella Scura,* because that ain't gonna cut it for long around this town."

"Huh?"

"If you don't like the laws, then you have to change them. Paige Marshall, not *Stella,* needs to become an attorney or a judge or lobbyist or someone who can make a difference."

She sighed. "We have been over that. Maybe that is true, but it also takes a long time. Too long for me."

"Is that right? The impatience of youth. I know better than anyone what that means." Wendy threw her hands up. "You're damn right it takes a long time. Look at me and the route I took to get here. I will be sixty-two by the time I finish my Presidency. I have to decide what to try and push through and what not to, and it's a royal pain in my big ass 24/7. Some things you have to get done, others you can't, but that's politics for you. You're either in or you're out—if you go around threatening people with your power and dismantling military bases, then you're no better than the people you criticize. I don't mean this to be insulting, but—I am a full-fledged human being. You are not."

She looked down humbly. "I know in a way that you are right. Thomas Jefferson said that the less one uses his power, the more powerful he becomes."

"Jefferson was a pretty smart person. You are, too."

"Huh. Not sure about that. But it is hard to be me, you know. I can do all these amazing things and do anything I want."

"Then earn respect by not doing it the easy way, but the hard way—the right way. If you want people to trust you as one of them, you have to play by the same rules, you know. We can work through all this together. This is the main reason I wanted to be President again. To help you."

She looked at Wendy curiously. "What?"

"I knew you would show up someday. I had no idea your powers were of this magnitude, but I knew you would need a mentor."

"A mentor for *what?*"

"To decide how to best plan on becoming President yourself someday, given your career aspirations."

"Maybe I do, maybe not, but you have a son. Why not mentor him? He seems far less high-maintenance than me."

"He's only eleven, and I doubt he has any interest in politics or anything else I do."

"Sounds familiar. How do you know I do?"

"You're different than him. You have passion, but you must learn to direct it. Will's path likely lies elsewhere. If he changes his mind, I'll be there to help him, though. And he will always be there to help you."

She wasn't so sure about that; it seemed too much, too soon. Washington was certainly a more complicated place than North Pole, Alaska.

Speaking of North Pole, maybe it was time for a visit, as she had some choice words for a couple of its finest residents. But first she wanted to do something important to her by finally visiting the country's largest state by area, but with the smallest population.

• • •

Capitol Building
Armstrong City, Luna

The fourteen-hour trip took less time than she had anticipated on the shuttle John F. Kennedy, one of four moonbase shuttles in use besides NASA One (for official Government business only).

The state capital on the lunar south pole featured a region with crater rims exposed to near-constant solar illumination, yet the interior of the craters was permanently shaded from sunlight. It also contained substantial portions of water ice, an obvious necessity for a small human settlement.

This was in one of the few lunar areas which appeared to have protected water for billions of years: the permanently shadowed craters at the Moon's south poles. At the lunar poles, some craters experienced complete and continuous darkness, while a few peaks and ridges received sunlight over 80% of the time. This was caused by the Moon's axial tilt of only 1.54 degrees away from the ecliptic (compared to the 23.44 degrees of Earth's axial tilt). In contrast to the majority of Luna, which had wide temperature fluctuations, the lunar south pole had a relatively benign temperature of eight degrees Fahrenheit.

The underground Capitol Building was utilitarian, and people bounced around in one-sixth Earth gravity. She found, to her delight, that her abilities worked just as well in space and on Luna as on Earth, and that, after a few minutes on the surface, she had adapted and could walk normally. She could also do that stunt in space, as she entertained her fellow military and M2 passengers by walking "normally" in the corridor and on the ceiling. It did require a bit of concentration to drink soda from a bottle by creating a small gravitational field around her.

It was still unknown if she could survive on Luna or in space without a protective suit; aside from the oxygen issue (she could survive without oxygen for at least several days, maybe longer), the need for a pressurized suit was uncertain, although the Sulphur Springs experiments seemed to indicate it wasn't needed.

She didn't require protection against radiation for obvious reasons, but her advanced avionics helmet might. And her skin would be quite a sight after being out in the elements with no protection; with no atmosphere or magnetic field, Luna was constantly bombarded with the full force of the solar wind during the lunar day.

That didn't stop her from going out on her own for "unofficial" NASA experiments in a standard excursion suit. She easily rose up to low Lunar orbit (about sixty miles) and propelled herself with delight.

She did find she was far more aerodynamic there, given the lack of atmosphere. She was easily able to complete a lunar orbit in about fifty minutes (compared to the Apollo command module time of about two hours). Seeing the Earth rise was quite the experience, even with limited color vision.

She had a special pressurized helmet created with the aviation electronics inside because she spent half the orbit on the dark side of the moon. Even with the visor, she would, of course, be unable to see there.

As she passed over the far side (which was not necessarily the same as the "dark side," depending on Luna's phase), she saw the small settlement Aldrinville, the site of most lunar helium-3 mining. She also saw the multiple nuclear-powered radio and optical telescopes on the far side, free from the radio and atmospheric interference of Earth.

She hadn't planned on visiting Aldrinville on this trip, as it was mostly an outpost to manage the army of robotic mining rovers that collected the regolith and returned it to the main processing plant for extraction of helium-3. Bella had explained the basic process, but she didn't understand chemistry and really didn't care anyway.

After she returned to Earth tomorrow, she planned another trip back to our forty-ninth state to visit a couple of people. There would probably be some fireworks, and she secretly wished it was the fourth of July instead.

Continued in:
Book Five
Now I am become Death

www.ingramcontent.com/pod-product-compliance
Lightning Source LLC
Chambersburg PA
CBHW070643310726
48982CB00001B/392
* 9 7 8 1 7 3 4 9 3 7 2 1 3 *